The

RIVER

TWICE

The
RIVER
TWICE

a novel

JOHN BEMROSE

**Thistledown
Press**

Thistledown Press Ltd.
P.O. Box 30105 Westview
Saskatoon, SK S7L 7M6
www.thistledownpress.com

Library and Archives Canada Cataloguing in Publication

Title: The river twice / John Bemrose.
Names: Bemrose, John, 1947- author.
Identifiers: Canadiana 20220141517 | ISBN 9781771872201 (softcover)
Classification: LCC PS8553.E47 R58 2022 | DDC C813/.54—dc23

Cover and book design by Tania Craan
Cover images
    Soldier detail: Canadian Infantry, April 1916, Alamy Stock
    River photo: Unsplash / Nathan Anderson

Thistledown Press gratefully acknowledges the financial assistance of
The Canada Council for the Arts, SK Arts, and the government of Canada
for its publishing program.

For my grandsons, Jacob and Owen

May their generation see an end
to the folly of war.

I walk the secret way
With anger in my brain.
O music through my clay,
When will you sound again?
—SIEGFRIED SASSOON

You could not step twice in the same
rivers, for other and yet other
waters are ever flowing on.
—HERACLITUS

1.

The flag was a mistake, Miriam announced to her mother, though she was hard put to say why it bothered her so much. What, after all, did she know? Ted's recent letters had told her little, raising fears they'd done nothing to assuage. "I just feel he won't want it," she managed finally, brazening it out. She had long found it difficult to confront Ada McCrae. Never mind that she was twenty-five and married. Never mind that she'd left her mother's house years ago. Now she was back, and here again was Ada's raised eyebrow, the glint of a teasing skepticism. It was as if Miriam had never left home.

Earlier that week she and Ada had clashed over the number of guests for Ada's "little welcome party." They had argued over whether it should be held at all. Miriam hadn't thought so, not after what Ted had been through. But in the end, she'd given in—their families had their claims, after all; and Brockwood *was* her mother's house; and perhaps Ted *would* be pleased, because what did she know?

Early that morning a trestle table had appeared on the terrace. By noon, it had been surrounded with chairs from the dining room and covered with rose-coloured cloths. And now the flag, like an uninvited guest. Behind the chair where Ted would sit, it stirred languidly in the warm May breeze.

To Miriam's surprise, Ada threw up her hands: "Do what you like with it, my dear. He's your husband, *Mrs. Whitfield.*"

Furling the flag as she went, Miriam returned it to its place
in the hall closet, a slash of red behind their coats awaiting its
usual resurrection on Dominion Day.

FOR THREE YEARS all they'd had was letters: the long letters she
wrote over the course of a week and posted each Friday, and
his stampless letters that arrived in envelopes marked *Field Post
Office*, their pages spotted with mud or tea—letters that broke
off in midsentence and were resumed in some village or camp
behind the Line. Twice every day but Sunday, Miriam walked
downtown to the post office. Often the place was crowded with
women on similar missions, but none detained her with more
than a greeting as she made her way to her family's box—it was
understood that nothing must come between a soldier's wife and
her hopes. The insertion of the tiny key. The opening of the
little glass door, its number stencilled in orange paint. The rapid
shuffling through letters and bills. Most days there was nothing from him, but on the rare day when she found one of his, a
rush of anticipation bore her into the street. In good weather she
would read it on a bench by the bowling greens. Otherwise she
carried it up the hill to Brockwood, her parents' home to which
she'd returned after Ted had left, for economy's sake.

Usually, they were four at Brockwood: Miriam, her mother
and father, and her nine-year-old brother, Will, sharing the
large old house built by Ada's parents in the days of their
prosperity. During holidays, Miriam's younger sister, Grace,
was with them as well, home from teaching at a private girls
school in Toronto. Brockwood had room enough for all, but a
claustrophobic curiosity prevailed in the matter of Ted's letters. *Did you get one?* The question would catch her halfway up
the stairs. Answering *"Not today,"* which was the usual case,

spared her further enquiries. But if they knew she had one, expectant faces met her at the supper table. She would tell them what she could, but if she had not had time to digest his words, the intimacy they summoned felt broken into.

Each letter as it arrived seemed proof that he was safe. She knew this was not credible. Anything might have happened in the weeks since he'd sent it off; yet his voice, rising from the page, spoke to her out of a present they seemed to share.

At first, he'd described his progress through the training grounds of Valcartier and southern England. But suddenly, in the late spring of '16, he was *there*, in that place of destruction she feared on his behalf. The dun, lifeless ground stretching in every direction, the ruined bits of equipment and buildings— he described it all in a spirit of intense interest, a thing that unsettled her, for it left the impression he was unconscious of the danger. The surviving bits of greenery fascinated him: the way a shell had unearthed part of a former meadow, so that within days it was sprouting poppies; a line of poplars, ruffling like feathers along a distant ridge, glowing in morning sun.

If there was comfort for her in such letters, it was in the strange fact of the seeming desertion of the battlefield. "Since I've been here, I haven't seen a single German, though we know they're out there. They shout to us at times. Now and then the odd pot-shot comes over. But it's as if they're living underground. Well, we do live underground here, after a fashion. Earth walls wherever you go, and the pure sky above—how far away it seems." There was no mention of actual fighting, just occasional references to "Jerry," who at times was "up to something" like some disreputable uncle shuffling about on an upper floor.

He had gone away a private and been made a lieutenant shortly after reaching England. "Somehow the men found out

I'd been to university. They call me 'the professor' behind my back. This officer business takes some getting used to—telling the other fellow what to do. I've always been more of a live-and-let-live sort of chap, as you well know. But the littlest things count here. It matters that a soldier takes care of his feet and keeps his rifle clean. I'm afraid I've become a nag on such subjects. The men are sterling, most of them. My sergeant, McElroy, is a fisherman from Parry Sound. He has his reservations about me, I can tell: I'm too inexperienced, maybe too strict about rules that don't matter. He may well be right."

Later letters, arriving that summer, struck a new note. "I took a few men out on patrol last night, just to have a look around. Jerry was out fixing his wire—we gave him quite a scare. A royal drubbing in fact. We got off pretty lightly ourselves." Sitting in the window seat of her room, she paused a long time over that. He was making light of something terrible, she realized. He might easily have been killed. Yet he wrote as if he'd won at football or gotten mixed up in a schoolyard scrap. She had heard this tone of hail-fellow jauntiness before, when he'd described one of his boyhood exploits to her. He had played hockey and lacrosse, relishing the punishment in a way she had never understood. He'd been in fights. Yet his energy and good humour had always buoyed her. Where she was cautious, he seemed carefree: scandalous in his comments in a way she secretly enjoyed. Now she sensed the tension of things withheld. Perhaps it was his way of protecting her, and perhaps he needed the pretence himself, but they had used to talk so candidly—those Saturday mornings lying late in the little cottage on Barks Lane! She had never revealed herself as much to anyone; he had said the same. As similar letters came, his evasiveness—for so it seemed to her—began to wear thin.

Didn't he realize she would have her own experience of the war? It was nothing like his, of course, but telling enough. Letters from the Front had been printed in the *Star-Transcript*. One in particular had stuck with her: "Oh Mother!" the young soldier had written, "What a few were left when the roll was called. It seems a miracle to me how our little company was not swept out of existence in that hail of shrapnel, shells and bullets pouring at us like rain." Of course Ted was facing the same. *What a few were left.* The publication of such letters had caused a furor, and no end of trouble for her friends, Horace and Nan Williams, who owned the paper. People had accused them of undermining morale on the home front. And while others were supportive, a rock had shattered the front window of the *Star* office.

She tried to console herself with the thought that Ted was not with the local battalion. For reasons he had never made clear, he had signed up with another outfit in Toronto, where he had gone to university. But the dodge provided little comfort as reminders of the war continued to multiply. It was a small-ish town, scarcely more than four thousand people, its houses and mills scattered along the forking valleys of its two rivers. Standing on the heights that bordered the town's eastern edge, she could easily see, past spires and rooftops, the hilly pastures and woods on the other side. Yet along with the surrounding farms, it had sent hundreds to war. By the summer of 1916 the number of fatalities listed in the *Star-Transcript* had passed fifty. There were houses, known to all, where shades and curtains remained drawn. Around the memorial to the South African war, wounded veterans began to appear, men too badly hurt to be sent back to the Front. All day and well into the night they loitered in the little park with their bandages and crutches, their smell of defeat. The excitement of August '14 had long passed.

She plunged into work for the Patriotic League, canvassing donations and taking cheques to soldiers' wives—those with large families who needed extra support beyond the government money they received. In the League's rooms above Fisher's store, she wrapped packages for the troops—all this while continuing to sing in the church choir, long a joy to her, and doing the lion's share of the work it took to run Brockwood. She had always been cheerful at her work; now she sensed her labours were driven by muted panic, subtle but persistent, as if she were rushing to quell an emergency that was never clearly defined but that flooded her rare idle moments with a sense of helplessness.

In her room, on the ledge above her window seat, she had made a kind of shrine. Their framed wedding picture was there, as well as dried flowers from their first dance, her New Testament, a pink marbled pebble from Georgian Bay that Ted had given her, a photo of them at Beamer Falls, the two of them balancing on stepping stones, looking so very young. As she prayed for him, the makings of a private ritual accumulated. She must touch the little stone. She must let her fingers rest on the Testament. She must pray with her eyes closed, but when she opened them her gaze must be fixed on a gap in the trees that showed the fields to the east of town: the east, where *he* was. If she did not do these things, in the right order, she had to start over. She knew she was flirting with superstition. Not my will but Thine, she had been taught. Yet in her heart she cared nothing for God's will if it did not keep Ted safe.

He loved hearing her stories, he wrote; he meant the humorous stories she collected in the week, mainly anecdotes of her family, often using her mother or little brother as foil. She was no Leacock, but she gave him the goat that had invaded the council chambers, drolly reported in the *Star*. She told him how her father, driving to visit a patient, had escaped a stand-off with a runaway bull. Meanwhile, he filled his own letters with the anomalies of trench life, the stray dog adopted by his platoon, the framed picture hung satirically on the trench wall; he recalled a chaotic meal with a French family whose paterfamilias had been too fond of his Calvados. But of the war itself he said almost nothing. Increasingly she felt they were creating a false world—two false worlds. Even her joys, transferred to the page, seemed false, lacking any reference to the sorrows they had relieved.

One day, determined to write a more honest letter, she described a walk out the east river road. She had taken it in despair after hearing about the death of a young man she had grown up with, a neighbour's son. An old farmer had stopped his team to talk. He invited her into his farmhouse to meet his wife. Both their sons were with the army. "Their tinted photographs were on the wall," she wrote. "Handsome lads and clearly the loves of their lives. The poor woman looked like she hadn't slept in weeks." She also told him how, walking home, she had plunged into a woodlot where she blundered among the trees in her grief, seized by a catastrophic awareness that the lives of so many young men had been suspended over an abyss. And for what?

The moment she posted the letter she knew it was a mistake. He needed her support, not wisdom in hindsight. He was *there*; it was too late for philosophizing, especially about what must be obvious to him. She wrote again, apologizing for her "glooms" and offering a few of her usual "entertainments."

For three weeks she heard nothing, while sending off four letters of her own. Such gaps had occurred before, but this one seemed ominous.

Finally, a letter came. He did not mention her walk. But again he emphasized how much he enjoyed her "jolly news" of the town, singling out her description of a picnic with the Williamses: "Horace lecturing the cows—I can see him with his finger up, one eyebrow up too—I split the old sides laughing!" She felt he had given her a clear signal. Writing back, she described the afternoon her father had driven her and Ted's mother, Rose, into the Reid Hills north of town, where he left them for a few hours of berry picking: the bushes stooped with elderberries, their pails and bowls littering the embankment, and later, Rose's kitchen redolent with simmering fruit. She omitted their tears.

One day, yielding to a heavy wave of nostalgia, she walked to their old cottage on Barks Lane at the south end of town, perched high on a wooded hillside. A storey and a half, two small bedrooms. A single apple tree casting shadows across whitewashed walls. They had lived here for eighteen months after their marriage. Her mother had been scandalized by their choice—such a poor little place, situated in the "wrong" part of town. But Miriam had been as happy as she ever had been, the two of them alone together, setting out on the grand adventure of life. And those Saturday mornings! She sitting up in bed, the sheets a rumple of sunlight around her, while Ted brought her tea up the stairs . . .

HE HAD STOPPED referring to his life in the trenches. No more jokes about lice or references to his adventures in no man's land. Now he wrote only of events behind the Line—times when his battalion marched into the countryside for a few days' rest. "Rest!" he joked. "A funny name for laying track all day." In his complaint she sensed relief. Once he escaped entirely for a few days of walking with a fellow officer. He had taken an interest in country churches. He described the "beautiful prospect" of such a church on a hill, the "golden slabs" of its floor, worn into hollows by generations of feet. In another church, the pew posts had been deeply grooved, the sexton told him, by the chains restraining the parishioners' mastiffs five hundred years before. The depths of time moved him. "Even our war—just a hiccup in the centuries. You feel this land has seen it all before. In a strange way, it's a comfort. Those people lived through wars themselves, so we can too. It's only life, after all." Another time, he went to Paris. When you walked down the aisles of Notre-Dame, he told her, the pillars in the galleries moved overhead, revealing and hiding each other like the branching limbs of a forest.

She read these letters again and again; he seemed so wholly alive in them, and while she could not forget what he must return to, she knew he had not forgotten it either. In their way, they lived in sympathetic parallel.

After the crisis of her "country walk" letter, they had achieved a kind of balance. She worried some slip might upset it. Worse than having him killed would be to have him killed while they were estranged. She hardly dared acknowledge this thought. But she was getting used to the arrival of thoughts she had never had before.

OVER THE SPRING of 1917, his letters came less frequently, and those that did come were much shorter than she was used to, often just an assembly of scraps written at different times and in different places. His once-neat handwriting had become a hurried scrawl. Sentences broke off in mid-thought; some words were indecipherable or omitted altogether. She told herself he was simply busier than usual, but "busy" was a thin dodge that could not staunch her fears. Often, she could not tell if he was writing from the Line or from some safe place behind it. The confusion haunted her. His broken sentences might be explained by conditions on the Line—reason enough to worry—but if he wrote from a safer area, what could they portend? Again, her own experience instructed her. She had seen the men hobbling up Brockwood's walk to her father's surgery, looking to have their wounds abraded, or for something to help them sleep: men with trembling hands, or with eyes fixed in the endless moment of their terror. Sometimes it was the wives or mothers who came, gaunt with exhaustion, seeking advice or pills for themselves.

Lacking definite information, she scoured the Toronto paper her father subscribed to, but the reports had an anodyne sameness. It seemed "our boys" were always giving better than they got, the Germans forever being driven back—and yet, they remained, the Line across France and Belgium scarcely shifting. She read of a Canadian victory at a place called Vimy. Ted's battalion belonged to a division that had taken part. Yet the victory meant nothing to her because she had no news of him. Then a letter came—another tangle of incomplete sentences and broken-off thoughts, concluding with apologies for his haste. He did not mention Vimy, but the envelope was postmarked with a date after the battle: did it mean he had survived? At the bottom of the last page he had written, "I love you dear Mim, oh how I love you!" It was the most plainly written, coherent sentence of the lot. More determined than ever to give him what he needed, she wrote soothing words back, as well as her usual descriptions of her daily activities and news of the town—a reminder of normal life in the midst of what he was enduring. "It can't be much longer," she added, grasping at the latest rumour. "They say the Germans are running out of men and with the Americans coming in, it's sure to be over soon. Keep safe, darling. Remember what we have!" Just as she believed her own encouragement was needed to help him stay alive, so he too needed to be as keen as knives. Yet her sense of helplessness had become overwhelming. What was she accomplishing by wrapping bandages or singing some pretty tune by Handel, when all she wanted was to be *there*, hauling him out of it? But all she could give him was words, words that might mean nothing to him, words that might be misunderstood, words that reflected nothing of the full tide of her life—its sunlit surfaces, yes, but not its shadows.

A letter came, more coherent than the last. She had enquired after his health, but he admitted to nothing more than fatigue. He described yet another church. He told her of a walk along a towpath, a young woman ducking out of the low cabin door of her canal boat with a fat, naked baby in her arms—the sketch broken off in mid-sentence. Then came a longer letter, more coherent still. He and a fellow officer—not the same chap as before, apparently—were in Normandy, trout fishing at some little *auberge*. Some mornings he just sat in a chair, reading and "letting in the sun." He sounded better.

Another letter, much shorter, followed. He was back at the Front, he said. But he wrote only of remembered sights from a more peaceful France. Then came a long spell, over a month, when no letters came. She sent off half a dozen of her own without response. It was the autumn of 1917, and there had been large battles in Flanders. She scoured the newspapers for information and sent off enquiries to his battalion in Toronto, receiving little satisfaction in return.

Moving through the streets of the town, she seemed to be leading an automaton's existence, smiling because someone else had smiled, nodding at conversations she had not heard. She conceived a superstitious fear of the telegraph boy. It was he, in his peaked leather cap, on his heavy bicycle, a man-boy people called simple, who brought the messages so widely dreaded. From a cousin whose neighbour had been killed, she knew how the wording went, typed on an ordinary piece of telegraph paper: *DEEPLY REGRET INFORM YOU PRIVATE PETER SYLVANUS JONES . . .* Once, seeing the messenger approach with his tortured smile, she had turned away in panic.

SHE SOUGHT OUT her father. A double thickness of doors separated his surgery from the dining room. She knocked and found him at his desk in his shirtsleeves, sharpening a scalpel on a stone with a slow, polishing motion. The air smelled of fresh plaster.

"Mim," he said, brightening as he looked up.

As she told him of her worries for Ted, something in his listening—his small, keen eyes holding her steadily—troubled her. "I know there's nothing you can do," she hastily concluded. "But it would help to know what you think. You really are a closed book sometimes." Smiling regretfully, he shrugged: it was who he was.

She had long felt closer to him than to her mother. She had tried to help him with the extra workload from the war but found she didn't have the stomach for it—that poor veteran's leg, or what was left of it, and her struggling not to faint when the bandage came off! Her father had to hire a retired nurse.

She knew he hated the war as much as she did. He had served as a medic in the South African war, and the experience had apparently inoculated him to the excitement that swept the town in the late summer of 1914. She sensed her own opposition to the war had come, at least in part, from him—a low-key antimilitarism he had carried through the years: a dissenting comment delivered here, a questioning glance there. These things had built an attitude in her that she was largely unaware of until war broke out; then her opposition had been immediate and fierce, half surprising her.

"Most armies are too big for their own good," he said at last. "The left hand scarcely knows what the right is doing. It's a miracle when anything goes as planned. Ted's letters—they could have gone off to the wrong place—Halifax, Timbuctoo . . ."

She had thought of this herself; did he have nothing better for her?

"How are you sleeping?" he said abruptly.

"Not very well. I suppose you've heard me in the hall."

"I don't think you're eating enough."

She was silent.

"If you carried a little more weight it would help with the tension."

Already she regretted coming. What did she imagine he could do? She wasn't ten any more. Yet she clung stubbornly to her intent, held by a shred of hope she knew belonged to her girlhood: a sense of comfort he had long given her. Around the familiar room, nothing seemed to have changed for years: His diploma with its scarlet seal, next to the little painting of two horses in a field corner. His old medical texts behind glass.

And over there in the corner, the metal examining table with its cushioning of beige leather, a fresh sheet folded neatly at one end. "Why do men have to fight?" she asked suddenly.

He gave a derisive snort.

"Is it in the blood or what? Did you ever have to fight in South Africa?" The British were worse than the Boers, he'd said once, with their prison camps for women and children. But he'd told her almost nothing about it.

"My brother and I—I'm talking about Clarence—we used to fight like wildcats. It upset my mother—she was forever having to break us up—but Dad, he just let us go at it. I suppose it seemed normal to him—he'd had five brothers. The thing was, with Clarence and me, we enjoyed it. On occasion Clarrie'd get pretty mad, more so than me; it was more a game to me—I suppose because I was older, stronger. But he'd want to try again the next day. Determined to beat me, you know."

"Did he ever?"

"It would seem fighting interests you," her father said, eyes laughing.

She felt heat invade her face. "But what's happening in France—*it's* no game."

"It will be for some," he said soberly.

She did not know what he meant and did not ask. There was a dull knock at the window. A bird had blundered into the glass. "Do you think he'll be all right, Dad?" The question broke unexpectedly from her, on a girlish note. Almost immediately she spoke again: "Well, you can't know that, can you? It's unfair of me to ask. No one can know except the Almighty Father."

Her father said nothing in response, his usual reaction when God was mentioned. She was a little angry with him, her earthly father. She appreciated his straightforwardness, his refusal to offer false hope, but still...

They talked a while longer. In the end she came away dissatisfied.

IN JANUARY OF 1918, Grace came back unexpectedly from Toronto. Miriam's sister had just been with them for Christmas and was not expected again until Easter. Yet here she was, snow melting on the shoulders of her coat, confronting Miriam in the front hall. In answer to Miriam's questions, she tore off her hat. Her hair, a deep coppery red, worn for years in a tight chignon, had been cropped like a boy's. "Do you think it suits?" she demanded angrily.

"What's happened, Gracie?"

"I've cut off my hair!" she cried. "Isn't it obvious?"

She jerked her head to the side as if inviting admiration. But there was self-satire in the movement, and a muted violence. Here and there, unruly tufts stuck out. But more than the hair, it was her eyes that struck Miriam. Their gaze seemed brighter, unnaturally so, and somehow fixed. When Miriam moved to hug her, she pushed her off. "I don't want coddling. I'm perfectly all right."

"But you're here."

"Where else would I be?"

"Are you ill, Gracie?"

Grace lugged her suitcase past her to the stairs.

Her arrival shook the household. Her job teaching English and physical education to the girls of Watson College had marked, in the family's eyes, a welcome improvement in her fortunes; her return seemed to indicate their collapse. Grace took to prowling the house at all hours and sleeping till noon, emerging from her room in a state of prickly dishevelment, at times looking feverish.

In a way, her return fit a familiar mould. From girlhood, the family had called her their "original"—a kindly summary of her eccentricities: the impulsiveness that once led her to invite a beggar to Sunday dinner; her sudden fits of brilliance at school, followed by weeks of careless indifference; her preference, to her mother's chagrin, for playing with boys, at times outshining them in their games. But this was different. She was suffering—that was clear. Anxious conversations sprang up out of her hearing. Catching wind of them, Grace accused her family of "muttering" behind her back. They lived, worrying, on tenterhooks.

Like Miriam and her mother, Grace had been a student at Watson College. Her junior years had been the rough march everyone feared. There had been "incidents," including the night she slipped out a bathroom window to meet a boy. Cigarettes and wine had been discovered in her room. The unflappable headmistress, Evelyn Fonger—who had taught both Miriam and their mother in her day—had not been deterred. In response to a desperate letter from Ada, she had written that she sensed something "grave and responsive" in the girl. Her patient nurturing had paid off. In her final two years at Watson, Grace had transformed into a winner of scholarships, the writer of a prize-winning essay. In her final year, she was given a trial as a residence donna; a year after graduation she was hired as a teacher of English and an assistant instructor of physical education.

She had apparently blossomed in both roles, the family exulting in her success. But when the beloved Miss Fonger retired, it wasn't long before Grace expressed a dislike of her replacement, Berenice Banks. "She's so nervous you want to hug her," she wrote home. "Though she'd probably faint if you did. She talks like an actress in a bad play—hardly speaks a sincere word, as far as I can tell." After such a judgment, Miriam held her breath, but the fall term passed without incident.

And now this. When Grace continued to refuse all questions about what had happened, Ada wrote to Headmistress Banks. Hearing nothing, she wrote to her old ally, Evelyn Fonger, but the letter came back stamped *Not at This Address*. Later she learned from an alumna pal that Evelyn had gotten married. Married and vanished, evidently. By this time, Grace seemed to be improving; her ready anger had cooled somewhat, and she was a little more sociable. But the questions remained.

Sitting at the kitchen table with her sister and mother, Miriam heard Ada demand, out of the blue, "Now Grace, you've left us rather in the dark here. Tell us what happened in Toronto."

Bowed over her teacup, Grace fell still. It was a sign long familiar to the family: the calm before the storm.

"Mum, I don't think this is the time," Miriam said.

"Well, when is the time?" Ada said, drawing herself up. Unlike Miriam, she rarely shied away from confrontation.

"It's all right," Grace told Miriam. "I've left my job, Mother, but it was necessary—you need to trust me about that." She flushed as she said it, but she lifted her face a little, defiantly.

"Oh my Lord," Ada said, heaving back in her chair. "Were you let go then?"

"Mother," Miriam warned.

"Sorry to disappoint you," Grace said, sarcastically.

"You've left your job? Or were you let go?" Ada demanded.

Grace sent a furious sidelong glance to Miriam.

Ada softened her tone. "But Miss Fonger couldn't say enough about—"

"Miss Fonger's gone," Grace said acidly. "I don't want to say any more."

All three sat in silence, Ada's fierce poise demanding more, Grace stubbornly resisting.

"Would anyone like tea?" Miriam said too brightly.

Her mother and sister seemed not to hear. All at once, gathering her indignation, Ada shoved back her chair and left the room.

Often, after one of these contretemps with their mother, the sisters would say to each other what they could not say to Ada's face. Miriam hoped this would happen now. But when, after a protracted silence, she prompted Grace with a remark, her sister looked at her with blazing eyes, as if demanding to know what right Miriam had to speak at all.

AS THE WINTER wore on, Miriam struggled to hold her panic in check. Twice a day, she trekked to the post office. Finding nothing but letters and bills, she would slog up the hill to Brockwood where, out of consideration for her, there were no more cries of "Did you get one?" Yet the whole family was waiting anxiously for a letter.

One day, Grace took Miriam's hands into her own. "Dear Mim, I don't know how you stand it. You must think me terrible, so mixed up with my own craziness that I . . . I've been so selfish! What can I do?" Tears glassed her sister's eyes but did not fall; her hands were cold, as they so often were. When they embraced, it was Miriam who wept.

Often, nothing was said between them. Passing in the hall, they might exchange a touch; or Grace would appear in the doorway of Miriam's room with a tray of biscuits and hot tea.

They would chat as they drank and ate, often lapsing into separate silences. Miriam had a queer sense that they shared griefs, different but balanced: impossible, surely, as she had Ted's life to worry over, while Grace had only lost her job. At least this is what she thought in her less charitable moments. At other times, her sister's suffering pierced her, and for some moments she forgot even Ted. Her sister was not the person she had been. The vibrant prankster and rebel had been captured by some profound melancholy that drained her energy and vitiated her spirit. She was no longer in love with life.

One morning they were alone in the kitchen when the bells on their cord over the front door jangled. It was Miriam who went. Through a small window in the storm door, she saw the rumpled face of the telegraph boy, his wide mouth breathing clouds of mist. In his mitt he held the striped envelope of the telegraph company. The next thing she was conscious of was the light fixture hanging from the ceiling—that mass of metal and ice. And there was dread, a cold, scaly thing she struggled to push away even as she tried to understand it. And why was Grace lying with her mouth open beside her, apparently asleep? And where was the sound of weeping coming from— weeping mixed with laughter?

As the sisters understood later, it was Ada who had discovered them, who had managed not to faint herself but plucked the unopened telegram from Miriam's grip. It proved to be from Ada's sister-in-law, the girls' aunt Peg, who was coming to town on Thursday and was proposing lunch.

THE NEXT DAY, opening the family's post office box, Miriam found a letter from Ted. Oblivious to the women around her, she tore it open on the spot and read its broken sentences.

"Dearest Mim, so terribly sorry it's been so long. I'v been wounded but am much better now—mustnt fret. In England in good hands they took some impressive chunks metal out of me—shuffling about now with help of these kind nurses. Expect I'll be running graces when I get home. I *am* coming home talk runs—So much has changed, been badly shaken— out cold for some time they tell me, weeks, not exactly the fellow you knew, afraid. A pile of yours arrived the other day—been chasing me for a while by the looks of it. Not sure when they'll let me go. I love you—oh God I do that love Ted."

She strode homewards up the River Street hill, stopping near the top to read it again. *Not exactly the fellow you knew.* Across the street, by the wrought-iron fence of the Bannerman estate, a group of boys were shouting as they pelted each other with snowballs. Lost in the whirl of her thoughts, she scarcely noticed them.

2.

After a final shock travelled through the cars, the train stood motionless in the glare of spring sunshine. Somewhere metal clanked, water trickled; up the track, the engine hissed impatiently. For some seconds it was as if the long line of cars with their dust-skimmed windows were sealed against the movement of time. Waiting on the platform, Miriam and her family—Ted's parents were there as well—hovered suspended, not sure where he would appear.

"Where is he?" Will demanded, and at once, twenty yards away, a door banged open and the conductor swung down with his stool. Family in tow, Miriam hurried towards him, stopping to watch as a few passengers descended from the vestibule of the car and hurried off. Was there no one else then? The vestibule was empty. Glancing up at a window, she saw the tall white wings of a newspaper open and close. Nose pressed to the glass, a child peered down at her.

When she looked back to the vestibule, a man was there, leaning on a cane. Something in her recognized him before *she* did, her heart's leap coming before understanding. She had often imagined their reunion, but she had never imagined this: the conductor reaching up for his bag, while Ted, with a grin that seemed half pain, slowly descended the steps. Upon reaching the platform, he looked, not at her, but around for his bag.

"Ah, there it is," he said in a strained voice. The conductor had passed it to his father.

He did turn to her then. Their embrace came awkwardly, her face pressing into an unfamiliar suit coat. In a moment he had turned away to their families. They offered their greetings, spoke his name, but softly, conscious of the change in him. Only Rose, his mother, let herself go, sobbing against his chest until pulled away by her husband.

"Edward," Ada said in an undertone when her turn came. She had extended a gloved hand. "We've planned a little lunch for you at Brockwood. I hope you don't mind."

He said that would be very nice. When Ted took Will's hand, the boy glanced wildly at Miriam.

As the train chuffed off behind them, the little party proceeded along the platform, leaving Ted and Miriam to follow. Her arm in his. His cane pecking at the concrete. In a letter she had written, "We're going to talk whole days and nights when you get back," but she could think of nothing to say. "Sorry about all this," she managed finally, indicating the group ahead. "I tried to tell Mum you didn't need a party. But you know how she is when she takes the bit." Her voice sounded too loud to her, not quite hers.

She wondered if he had heard. His face, scowling into some deep space in front of him, indicated absence. At the top of the stairs to River Street, he asked if he might smoke. She watched as he took out a pack of Old Chums and tapped out a cigarette, while trapping the cane under his arm. His hands trembled a little as they cupped the flame, but when she reached out to help him, he turned his shoulder against her. He had not been a smoker when he left.

Across Banfield, the gardens around the Martin property were a mass of early flowers spilling over limestone boulders. They assaulted her with their whites and yellows, shocking in their intensity, and for a moment she felt she was seeing as he was seeing: everything strange, and somehow too much. "Dad wanted to be here, but he was called away to a birth last night," she heard herself say. Four in the morning, the telephone shrilling from the downstairs hall, she had hastened in her robe to answer it. "We were planning to bring you home in style, in the Buick."

"He has a Buick now, does he?" He met her with a sidelong glance, eyes slitted against the smoke.

"Didn't I tell you?" She knew she had; he had responded to the news with a joke about the luxury they were living in.

"Perhaps you did," he said. "Yes, you must have."

"It doesn't matter," she said, squeezing his arm. "All that matters is that you're here." It was what she believed, but again her own voice seemed to carry meaning away from them. As they neared Brockwood, Will ran ahead to open the gate, staring up at Ted as they passed through, flushing with pleasure at his brisk "Good man." The boy walked solemnly beside them for a few steps, then hurried on at a call from his mother. As the others filed past the side of the house, on their way to the terrace, Miriam drew Ted to a halt. They were alone in the sloping yard.

"Darling," she said, looking up at him. The voices of their families had faded.

"They've been painted," he said. His was looking past her to the house.

"Oh yes, the shutters," she said, turning. "We had quite the debate about the colour. Ted—"

"I always thought of them as dark green—almost to black."

How ill-fitting his suit was, hanging loosely from his shoulders, his belt-end flopping. And his face, so gaunt, the eyes in their deepened sockets almost furtive; and yet it was him, she could see, as if he were trapped inside, peering out.

"Darling," she said, her voice dropping as she drew closer.

"Who's that," he said suddenly, pointing with his cane. In a second-floor window, a figure in white waved before retreating into shadow.

"Only Grace," Miriam said, frustration rising. "Sick to her stomach last night. Dad ordered her to stay in her room until we know it isn't catching."

At a shout of laughter, reaching them from behind Brockwood, his gaze darted to the opening between hedge and house where the others had disappeared. "We don't have to stay long," she told him. "We can go off by ourselves, whenever you like. I'm sure they'd understand."

"S—sorry it's like this," he said, flicking away the butt of his cigarette. "I'm actually better than I was, if you can believe it." It was a bit of a joke, evidently, his grin revealing the gap where a tooth had been.

"You're *fine*, darling."

"Are *you* all right then?"

Saying of course she was, she had everything she wanted now, she embraced him. His free arm came up and for a few seconds, his hand gripped the back of her neck, but stiffly, as if he had forgotten what else to do.

UP AND DOWN the long table, in the flickering light dropped by the elm, their families fell silent when they appeared. Nan and Horace Williams had joined the party, Miriam avoiding

32

Nan's searching, worried gaze as her friend rushed into her arms. Turning to Ted, Nan broke the ice with a remark about his losing weight. "I see we ladies will have to fatten you up again," she said, raising eager laughter from the others. As Ted hooked his cane over the back of his chair, his father George's voice came, thick with the Nottingham of his youth. "I was just telling the assembled about the time you brought the stray dog home."

"Oh yes, the start of my life of crime," Ted said, to more laughter. It was something they recognized, his joking. They watched as he held out Miriam's chair for her and took his own. When he touched at the edge of his plate with his fingertips, it seemed a prelude, but he said nothing more.

"You were a *good* boy," Rose insisted stoutly, patting her son's arm.

"A mother's love," George said wryly.

"Never mock a mother's love," Ada said with authority, her eyes on the brimming cup she was about to pass on. George sent a wink to Miriam, who let out an abrupt, barking laugh that drew everyone's attention and made her blush—she had no idea where that had come from. Beside her, Ted unfolded his napkin. She kept glancing at him—at his knobbed, raw cheekbones, at the way his gaze flicked continuously over the table. After a swift blessing, muttered by Ted's father, Julia Clarke, the cook's niece, rolled in a trolley and began to offer platters of food.

Ada's "little lunch" was rather lavish: sandwiches, cold meats, four kinds of salad, a large platter of cheeses, while two pies, a cake, and other sweets waited in the kitchen. They'd been saving up sugar for weeks, Ada informed them. Everyone appreciated this lapse from the usual wartime restrictions. But their pleasure in the food could not banish their awareness of the young man at the end of the table. From time to time, Ted answered a question or volunteered a comment, but he said less as the meal wore on. He moved bits of food around his plate, and despite his mother's urging, put little in his mouth. He made a show of listening to the others, but Miriam could see how his attention kept drifting. When someone spoke to him, she more than once had to give him a nudge.

After a while, they left him alone, talking to each other with a show of cheerfulness that kept failing. Forks clicked on porcelain. Cups were lifted and set down as Julia Clarke ferried dishes to and from the table. When Will's voice sang out, everyone looked up, glad of something new.

"George? What happened to the dog?"

"And just what doggie would that be?" George said with a wink to Nan. *Not our kind,* Miriam's mother had said of the Whitfields when Ted had first begun to pay attention to her. Years before, Rose and George had worked in the local mills, George in the knitting department, Rose counting stitches— work she later said had driven her "half mad." After a couple of years, she had begun to give piano lessons. She was currently the organist and choir mistress at the Methodist church. George had worked his way up to foreman. In the end, Ada had come around to the Whitfields because she had little choice. She and George had a sparring relationship that Miriam suspected her mother secretly enjoyed.

"You know, the dog that Ted brought home."

"Ah yes, *that* doggie. Well, as I was saying, we didn't know he'd done it at first. He'd hidden the little fellow in his room."

The story was soon over. They watched as Ada filled more cups from the urn. The silences that kept wrapping them in the deepening heat of the day exhausted them. They did not really want to speak, not in the tone of ready cheer they felt was required. They had had hints from Miriam of the state Ted was in; to be with him was another thing altogether. But perhaps he needed their banter, their good cheer? They could not be sure, so gamely they kept trying. When George rose to make an awkward toast, they backed him with a show of enthusiasm. And when Ted stood to respond, telling a disjointed anecdote about the boat trip back, they laughed encouragingly at any hint of his old wit, falling into a heavy silence when the performance was over.

"Ted?" Will again, leaning out from his place to regard Ted. "Were there animals in the fighting?"

A stir of discomfort went around the table. No one until now had mentioned the war.

"I don't think we need to talk about that," Ada scolded. "Another cup, George?"

Chastened, the boy sat back in his chair.

"Quite a few," Ted said, looking down the table. At once, Will leaned forward, attentive again. "There were horses—lots of horses actually. They weren't in the fighting very much, not after the beginning. They kept them behind the lines mostly, the cavalry horses. But the workhorses and mules—they used them to pull wagons, and limbers—what the guns were on— they came rather more forward."

"Did any of them get killed?"

"*Will,*" Ada warned.

Ted nodded. "Sometimes they were unlucky."

Everyone was listening intently. Despite his letters, for three years they had not known his experience. It was if he had taken a cautious step towards them.

"Birds?" Will said. He was an odd, solitary boy, small for his nine years, but wiry and strong, keen on books, an habitué of the woods that fell behind the Bannerman estate to the river. He had once picked up a skunk by the tail because he had read somewhere that you safely could.

"Lots of birds," Ted said. "The larks, in spring, the whole sky—full of them—sometimes so far up you could har—hardly see them. The twittering, you know. We used to stop and look up." When Ted smiled, a flush of gratitude went around the table; beside him, Rose's face was wet with tears. "Once, some cranes went over—big fellows, you know. Geese as well—we'd hear them in the night."

They were all intent, held by the frail strand of connection between man and boy.

"Weren't they afraid of the guns?"

"Well, the guns weren't going off all the time. There were peaceful times. That's when they came."

"Birds are very smart."

"You think so?"

"A racing pigeon can find his way home over hundreds of miles."

"We had those too—used them for sending, ah . . . ah . . ."

"Messages," Miriam said.

"That's it. The Germans used them too."

"Do you think the Germans like animals?"

"I don't know why they wouldn't. Just about everyone does, don't you think?"

"Not everyone," the boy said, a bit mysteriously. No one spoke. With a whir of wings, a flock of sparrows hastened from a bush.

"Uncle Ted?" It was the boy again. He had always called Ted uncle, while in fact they were brothers-in-law.

Ted did not respond. He was staring at the opening of the path from the front yard. The Reverend John Scott was there, his big, open face beaming with anticipation as he strode towards them. "John!" Ada cried in pleasure and relief. "I was afraid you wouldn't make it."

"So sorry, Ada. No rest for the wicked."

A ripple of laughter met his remark. He was the most popular minister in the town, even among non-Presbyterians, with a common touch that could set the town's old fellows chortling on their bench outside the firehall. He had married Ted and Miriam, and was often at Brockwood, as much friend as guest. Ted stood up abruptly, Miriam rising slowly beside him. She sensed a gathering tension in her husband as the minister moved past the others, greeting them generally, his eyes behind their spectacles watering as he approached Ted. "Ted, Ted my boy," he crooned as he took Ted's hands in both of his. "Well, boy no longer. You're all right then?" he said, lowering his voice.

"As rain," Ted said. "Now that we—" His glance to Miriam was beseeching.

"Yes, yes, you're a lucky man to be coming back to *her*. You two have much to talk about, I'm sure." Before the war, a strong friendship had developed between the two; yet now Ted remained stiffly aloof. It was the strangeness of the situation, Miriam decided; it was *whatever had happened to him*. Already, she was making allowances for it.

A gentler note began to inform the minister's questions. Clearly, he sensed the change in Ted. How was the voyage back? How was the leg doing? Ted answered abruptly, minimally, while Miriam squeezed his arm and tried to fill his lapses. John Scott stayed for over an hour. He said his wife, who was something of a recluse, sent her warmest greetings, and he bantered humorously with Ada as she tried to get him to sample everything. His arrival had injected a new energy into the gathering. Out of the blue, George told them about missing his train in Nottingham station. No one knew why George had launched into this story, which had no connection to anything that had been said. Perhaps he was simply offering the best he had to stave off the silences that kept descending. Everyone laughed a trifle too strenuously; even Will, pulling a face, laughed in exaggerated imitation of the adults. Since they were now on the subject of travel, the minister told the story of a vexed crossing on the Belfast ferry one storm-tossed day before the war. The cook's niece poured more tea; portions of dessert descended on patterned china; Ted fidgeted while Miriam worked to draw him into conversation with his mother.

The sun had made its way under the elm, throwing glare into people's eyes, when the minister announced he must be going. *Would he offer a prayer?* Ada asked. All bowed their heads as John Scott stood a long moment in silence, his hands spread, palms upturned. "Almighty Father," he began, and at once Miriam began to quietly weep. It was as if chaos had retreated and some other possibility was glimpsed. The minister thanked the Lord for Ted's return. He prayed for peace and for our men in France. He prayed for healing and for acceptance.

Distracted by a rattling sound, as if a can with a stone in it was being furiously shaken, Miriam glanced to her left and saw her father in the open-topped Buick, passing down the street that ran past their back garden. He was steering with one hand as he leaned back in the seat, his goggles pushed up on his fore-head. He looked exhausted, Miriam thought. Seconds later she heard the Buick stop, then back into the former stable where it was kept. The engine of the car fell silent as John Scott's rich baritone continued to beseech, to remind, to console. She glanced at Ted. He was sitting perfectly erect, alert, his gaze travelling over the low bowl of floating tulip heads, over abandoned napkins and fragments of pie as if he were searching for something he had mislaid among the ruins of their feast.

3.

A patch of sun quivered on the wallpaper's patterning of leaves and vines. In the hollow between him and his sleeping wife, tiny phosphorescent numbers glowed on his wrist. Five thirty-two. When they took away his uniform, he had managed to hang on to his watch. He had told them it was lost.

Mim had her fist tucked under her jaw as if she pondered some matter in her sleep—another thing he had forgotten! His first glimpse of her from the vestibule of the train had stunned him—all his memories of her, all the times he had stared at her photograph, suddenly nothing, compared to *this*. When she looked up at him, he had averted his eyes in shame.

Wrapped in her father's spare robe, he reached the yard. Overhead, the crests of trees burned in the sun; but where he stood, touching a trembling flame to his cigarette, it was still dim, night-cool. A garden bed lay flecked with the butts he had scattered in the night. He took in his first draught with relief. Nearby, his men were busy at their tasks. They were always there—if he turned he would see them, one cleaning a rifle, another bent over a letter or chatting with a mate. And overhead, the bright, clear air that was death to enter.

At a sound from above, he whirled.

"Sorry!" his wife's voice said. A movement behind the screen. "Didn't mean to surprise you—"

"That's all right," he said, trying for nonchalance. He drew fiercely on his fag, thought of tossing it aside—he'd seen her eyes when he'd smoked the first one.

"I've been watching you."

"Hope I pass muster."

"*Loving you,*" she whispered. Her parents' windows were nearby.

"Just having a smoke." He held up the cigarette as if she might not believe him. He kept having this impulse to justify himself to her.

"Were you able to sleep?"

"Off and on."

"When I woke—I don't know what time it was—you weren't there."

"Just stretching the old leg," he said. "I'm used to getting up in the night in any case. It'll take a while to break the habit."

"How is it now?"

"What?"

"Your leg—"

"Right—well stretched."

"Good."

He found the pause that followed excruciating, filled with a sense of expectation he did not know how to meet. He tapped ash into the flowerbed. "What's that?" he said.

"I asked if you'd like breakfast."

"Not just yet—later. Thanks though!"

"When you're ready, we could eat in the gazebo. *More private,*" she whispered down to him. In the night they had tried to make love. He knew before they started it wasn't going to work. He had tried anyway; now, in the touch of her voice, he heard a reminder that he would have to try again.

"That would be great." He sucked again on his cigarette. Behind shrubs, a black shadow slinked. "That's not Bailey, is it?" "What, a cat? I can't see from here. Bailey died, didn't I tell you? He ran under a car. It might be Gracie's—what does it look like?" "Its face—black and brown, like a mask." "Yes, Kiki. Gracie's devoted to it." Another pause. On the train, he'd chatted more comfortably with a stranger than with her. She was speaking again. All he caught was: "You don't have to if you don't want to." "Want to what?" "Go to church." "It's all right," he said. He examined the butt of his cigarette. "Really, if you don't want—" "If I don't want to do something I'll let you know," he snapped, hearing too late his harshness. "Of course," she murmured. He turned brusquely away from her. It seemed to him that her gaze laid a pressure across his back as he limped down the yard to the fence overlooking River Street. He lit another cigarette, and as he went on smoking, a buggy clipped past behind a spirited bay, a white fetlock flashing amid a blur of hooves. Whatever moved was free. In the officers' hospital at Lewes, walking had done as much for him as any doctor. He in his dressing gown, with his trusty bamboo cane, tramping up and down the driveway between the yews. As the weeks passed, he went farther, one day as far as Dunstable moor. In the distance a wedge of blue sea.

Postponing his return to the house, he followed the bricked path beside the south wall and emerged onto the terrace. All the chairs had been removed, the plates and linens put away; only the trestles stood exposed, crude board platforms where sparrows had shat. Shame at what he had become. As she was in the beginning, so she still was. As for him, he had failed the pact their bodies had made. He no longer matched her, life for healthy life.

THE CURVING BANISTER handed him into the dimness of the second-floor hall. At its far end the door to the WC opened and a figure in a white nightdress briefly appeared before hurrying out of sight. Miriam was waiting for him in bed. "I think I just saw Gracie," he said, sliding in beside her.

"Well, you could hardly mistake her."

"What's happened to her hair?"

Not responding, she wriggled under the sheet towards him, fitting her body to his.

"This is what I've missed," she said.

"She looks like a nun—"

"What would you know about nuns?" Miriam said, giving him a gentle punch. He had one arm around her, the other behind his head, faking his ease. "I wrote you about it," she told him. "I guess you haven't had time to read that one yet." He'd told her, the night before, he'd read all the letters that had caught up to him in the hospital, but that was only partly true; reading was a struggle. She told him about Grace coming home shorn. "She's let me trim it since—she still prefers it bobbed. Mother wasn't pleased, of course. She didn't want her leaving the house looking like *that*."

"Why would she do that to herself?"

"She hasn't told us. You know her temper—it's worse than ever. If you push her too hard, she takes your head off. Consider yourself warned."

He was with Grace now, listening for some sound of her in the hall. They had been close before the war, in a teasing, sibling-like way.

"What would you like to do today? Do you fancy a walk? Can you go far?"

"Leagues and leagues," he said, coming and going from her stream of words. Ten minutes by his watch and already restless. Distantly the Catholic bells tolled, a sound he pricked to—a place not here.

"Sure," he said jovially to her interrogative note, not quite sure what he was agreeing to.

"The Abutments, then. After church."

"That would be fine."

"It's not too much for you?"

"No, no. I'm champion."

She toyed with a button on his pajama top.

"I can't wait till we have our own place again."

"Right," he said.

"When I knew you were coming, I walked up to Barks Lane, just to have a look. The people who have it now—they've let your garden run to seed."

"It was never much of a garden," he said.

"I should say it was—those carrots!"

"Yes, those were good carrots," he acknowledged. His best crop in the little garden too much in the shade. It hadn't been much of a house, either: crumbling plaster and lath, as leaky as a sieve. Winter nights, they'd had to pile overcoats on their blankets.

She reared up, a sudden tumult of nightgown and hair, resettling with her back to him.

"Rub my neck," she commanded. It was something he used to do.

He lifted and parted the heavy fall of her hair. Her neck so pale, as if never touched by sun. He set to work with his thumbs, working the groove under her skull.

"Harder," she demanded.

He pressed harder.

"Ted, what's wrong!"

He had burst from the bed. In three strides he reached the armoire, where he swivelled to face her, grinning gamely. "My leg," he told her. "I get these shooting pains sometimes." And to lend credence to his lie, he bent to rub his leg.

"Do you want me to do that?"

"No."

"I could get Dad—"

"I said no, dammit!"

She stared at him in shocked silence.

"Sorry," he managed. These days I— Take time, as you said."

HALF AN HOUR later, calmer, dressed, he stood smoking at the front yard fence. Behind him, the door latch rattled and a young woman with bobbed hair moved swiftly across the porch. Shoes flicking at the hem of her narrow skirt, she hurried down the bricked path. As she reached him, she stretched up, her blazing glance slipping past his own. Swiftly, her cheek brushed his. "What are you gawking at?" she demanded as she stood back. But she was blushing, as if she knew. She had changed.

"Gracie," he said, moved.

"You don't look well, Ted," she scolded. She was clearing tears with her fingertips. "You've gotten awfully skinny."

"That's what your mother tells me. I'm sure she'll put it right."

"She says you have shell shock."

"Not so bad as that," he managed, throat constricting. "Once I've been home a couple of weeks—"

"That's what Mim says."

"Yes, well, your sister is quite right." He imagined them talking about him. Hushed voices behind closed doors. He was their problem now. He rebelled at being anyone's problem. "I'm sorry," he said. "I missed what you—"

"You've got a lot on your mind," she repeated, more gently.

"Not really. All safe and sound now."

"Not very likely," she said, adding that she'd read the papers. "What you had to do over there—I don't imagine you've forgotten it."

"Well, no, of course," he stammered.

"Something like that—it doesn't just go away."

He looked at her curiously.

"Here. I'm pressing you too hard." She touched his arm, and for a moment he seemed to see her through a sheet of flame, watching him steadily with those bright, fixed eyes. "Inappropriate, as usual."

"You were always the most honest McCrae."

She smirked at his compliment.

When Miriam sang down to them, Grace preceded him up the walk. She was silent as she passed her sister, who was waiting on the porch. Calling for her cat, Grace disappeared around the corner of the house.

"How did she seem to you?" Miriam said, dropping her voice as he climbed the steps.

"She's grown up."

"You didn't find her rather—I scarcely know how to put it. She's been very good to me, I mean with you away and us not knowing—but she's distracted somehow, not *playful* like she used to be, and quite violent at times—I mean in her speech. I keep having this feeling she's furious with the lot of us."

"I found her very direct, if that's what you mean." Direct, yes, and something else. He thought of the officers' hospital at Lewes. Those rows of beds, the curtains flung back to let light into that long white room with its air of fragile recovery.

Steaming tureens and chafing dishes waited for them on the sideboard. All the family were there except Grace. No one seemed to find her absence remarkable. When Ada asked Alec to offer thanks, he lowered his head a little, and with a wink to Will, launched into the Selkirk grace, immediately drawing a sigh from Ada.

> *Some hae meat and canna eat,*
> *And some wad eat that want it,*
> *But we hae meat and we can eat,*
> *And sae let the Lord be thanket!*

"He only gives that grace when he wants to provoke me," Ada said.

"Provocation becomes you, my dear," the doctor offered gallantly. Ada blew through pursed lips but was clearly pleased.

"I like it," Will said. "It's funny."

"Yes, and not just funny, it has wit. Ted, help me out here—"

"Wit's the right word," Ted said. Taken off guard, he struggled at first, the boy's eyes on him, but eventually got out his anecdote of the Scottish minister who'd pronounced the Selkirk grace at a mess behind the lines. The men had roared their approval afterwards—something direct and honest in the rough Scottish dialect that proper English could not match. "It sounded true to them—even if they didn't entirely understand it. Truth was often in short s-supply there."

"What do you mean?" Ada said, sounding offended.

"Rumours," he said. "We were never sure what was happening." He kept flushing as he spoke; it was hard to believe his own words sometimes. He was sorry he'd said so much, opening an avenue to discussion—his flank exposed. The whole table was silent, the boy waiting with the others, the trusting openness of his face a torment; but the doctor gave an assenting rumble. Under the table, Miriam squeezed his thigh and kept her hand there. He wished she wouldn't.

Scolding him for not eating enough, Ada served him seconds from the sideboard—more egg spilling in scrambled confusion onto his plate, more pocked faces of pancakes pooled with syrup. Jovial in her tyranny, she wielded tongs and lectured him on the necessity of fattening up, her fatted calf. For her sake, he got some down. He could scarcely smell food these days, let alone taste it. "Delicious," he told her.

The doctor launched into a story from his medical school days—drawing their attention to himself, Ted realized gratefully. That blunt, square, almost handsome face, like a sculpture not quite freed from the rock; the glint of small eyes conscious of some irony that escaped others. He supposed the doctor had his own secrets. Well, men did, didn't they? Chewing some bitter memory, while pretending it wasn't so. Miriam had worried her father drank too much. Did she still? A faintly crimson cast to the doctor's wide face, the nose a little redder.

Grace entered amidst their merriment at Alec's story. Gliding from his right, she smiled faintly at their laughter and turned away to peruse the sideboard. "There's still scrambled

egg," he heard Ada say. Aware he was staring, he lowered his
eyes while remaining supremely conscious of her.

TO THE TOUCH-TAPPING of his cane, the family descended the
River Street hill to church. Ahead, behind, on the opposite side
of the street, others poured with them, a din on the board-
walks. Grace and Will led the way, Alec and Ada next, while he
and Miriam brought up the rear. "You should feel honoured,"
Miriam had joked earlier. "Ada hasn't been able to get Grace
to church since she's come home." Ahead, the pyramiding
roof of the Presbyterian church levitated above houses, disappeared behind leaves, was replaced by a vision of walls in dull
red brick. The church had a fortress look, its hunched ascent
pierced with pockets of stained glass—a hulking, defiant thing.

In the shadow of the church, Miriam left to join the choir.
He was instantly off balance. With the family, he climbed oiled
steps into the blinding dimness of the vestibule. Ghostly faces
swam up. His damp hand was grasped by the gloved hands of
women. The calloused hands of farmers. "Yes, yes, so kind.
Yes, it's wonderful to be back. Mrs. Laing, of course. How
could I have forgotten? How's Matt? Mac, yes! So sorry! How
could I ever—" Knotblades in the brain.

A relief to slip into the family pew, under the low overhang of the balcony. The organ played its grainy tones. Pews
creaked under the weight of settling bodies. Covertly, he consulted the dial under his lifted cuff, the rotating second hand
screwing time into the bones of his wrist. Ten fifty-eight and
eleven seconds. Another countdown—to what? Space seemed
to be shrinking as the church filled. The ceiling too low, under
the weight of the packed balcony. And ahead, the wide bulwark
of flags fronting the loft and the pulpit, their silken stillness a

wall of red, blue, and white, like the drapery of an immense catafalque, exactly as Scott had placed them four years before. He had asked Miriam to write to him news of the town; it was important that it had not changed. Now, finding the flags unchanged, he felt their presence as an assault.

A blast of the organ and the Reverend John Scott was there. He had always been striding there—so it seemed to Ted— striding towards his pulpit, black robes astorm, his broad face lifted and shining in the joy of the Sabbath. In his distraction, Ted had missed the choir. They were already in the loft, Miriam tall among her sister sopranos. Across the spiked summits of the flags, their gazes met. His hills, his still waters.

Scott was on the steps of the pulpit now, seemingly borne upwards by the triumphant organ. Opening the great Bible, he threw off the ribbon that marked his place. His rich baritone enfolded them. *The Lord will command his loving-kindness in the day-time. And in the night his song shall be with me, and my prayer unto the God of my life.*

"Let us pray," he said. As he lifted his arms, the sleeves of his gown fell back, revealing the black arms of his tunic. Scarcely conscious of the heads going down around him, Ted stared, transfixed by the radiant face of the man who had been his friend and mentor.

HYMN, DOXOLOGY, OFFERING, hymn, announcements, prayer —the service's slow progress filled him with a deepening pressure. He kept checking his watch. He was a boy again, like the boy two places to his right, crammed with impatience, a bare-kneed boy attuned to the airplane or submarine he had made of the folded pocket knife he moved about until Ada's hand quietly suppressed it. Again, Ted rose with the others.

Again, Grace offered the open hymn book. Their hands held the book together, their thumbs clamped on either side. What queer things thumbs were. Animal digits. In their nakedness he saw the bodies of dead men.

While her alto rose beside him, he remained silent. At last the final stanza limped to a halt. One body going down with the rest, he sank into his pew. Wood creaked, throats were cleared as John Scott stepped forward to deliver his sermon, its theme taken from Psalm 42. *As the hart panteth after the water brooks, so panteth my soul after thee, O God.* Gesturing, strolling in his pulpit, mantled gown swaying like a living thing, he turned with sudden effect to face the massed faces staring up at him. He spoke of the soul's natural hunger for God. We are born to want God, John Scott said. It is our soul's need to join itself to Him—to avail ourselves of the succour and yes, the joy only He could offer. In times of direst need, times of loss and hopelessness, that yearning is not quenched, though it might seem that it is; and God's loving response is not withheld, though that too might seem to be what is happening; and again he quoted from the psalm: *In the night his song shall be with me, and my prayer unto the God of my life.*

Ted wanted to believe those words in their antique beauty. Yet he knew they were not true. What God gave, if there was a God, was a poisoned fruit. There were many who no longer stood within the circle of human life. God, if there was a God, had abandoned them. In the trenches, in the hospital at Lewes, in mirrors he'had learned to avoid, he had looked into their eyes.

AT LAST it was over. As the congregation rose, he joined the shuffling mass filling the aisles. Ahead, just visible in the vestibule, a tight mass of dark curls touched with silver nodded as the minister greeted the members of his flock. In the afterglow of his eloquence, many wanted to linger, to have a few words, to touch the hem. Awaiting his turn, Ted inched forward behind the McCraes. The fringe of Grace's hair cutting her pale neck. Ada's great hat, aslope like an abandoned wheel. Sunday school had taken the boy. *Ah yes, we must talk,* he heard Scott say to some eager parishioner. Abruptly turning away, Ted pushed through the crowd and escaped by another door.

He was soon back at Brockwood. On the porch, keeping an eye out for the family, he smoked, thinking of the man he had once loved.

THE AUTUMN OF 1914. After an initial period of reticence, John Scott had preached war. Sunday after Sunday, he patrolled behind his pulpit, speaking of the challenge the Lord had laid before them. *Poor innocent Belgium, rent by the conqueror's sword. Christian civilization, threatened as never before. You young people, especially you young men—what a privilege this is—to take up the banner of Christ. Onward my friends, onward Christian soldiers.* His phrases like the summons of a horn. A fife in the blood. Ted had felt it too, and the thrill of the crowds that wound through the town that fall, young people following the pulse of Charlie Hadley's bass drum, a relic of the South African war. And the bonfires on the heights, shadowy figures circling in tribal ecstasies. He was teaching at the high school at the time, walking each day to the stark red brick building on the north edge of town, returning late in the afternoon to the Barks Lane house. Evenings, hand in hand, he and Miriam walked the streets of the town. She disapproved of the war, he knew, and he did not mention it in her company; in any case, in those early days, the novelty of the general excitement could not compete with what they had together, entranced by a private future that seemed a sure conveyance out of the turmoil of the present. He would teach for a couple of years, then they would move to Toronto, where he would do graduate work. They liked to follow a dyke-top path overlooking the Shade River, the backs of the downtown stores. Water gleamed above the dam, the air softened by its hushing fall. Why couldn't the world learn what he and Mim had learned? Who needed war when you had each other? So they thought. But when cries rose from distant streets, he hearkened.

On Saturdays, he played cricket and lacrosse on the athletic grounds by the Shade. Under willows, tilting their bottles of ginger beer, his friends talked obsessively of the war. Two of their group had already gone. Three were on the cusp. He envied their excitement and, when they asked when he was going, spoke vaguely of having to finish his contract, leaving the impression he would go then. But—another secret from Miriam—he did not know. He wondered if he was afraid. He had read *The Iliad* and been much affected by Homer's descriptions. The spears through throats, the skulls crushed by rocks. *He fell with a clatter of armour and Hades took him.* Perhaps the poem had inoculated him a little. He tried to puncture his friends' enthusiasm, suggesting it wasn't going to be all *Boy's Own Annual*. He was met with blank stares. "Are you afraid then?" Matt Henley challenged. Ted said anyone who wasn't afraid was a fool.

They distanced him after that. He sensed their disdain.

But it wasn't fear that kept him out, not mainly. It was his own stubborn resistance to John Scott's volte-face. Early in the war, the minister had preached peace, moderation, understanding. It did not seem too late for such virtues, in the volatile early weeks. Ted admired the older man tremendously, as he bore up with patient good cheer under the storm of anger his position roused. Encouraged by Miriam, Ted was struggling to take his own Christianity more seriously. Christ's way was the only way, he had tried to believe—the way of the other cheek. He had found in John Scott the father he had longed for. Scott was learned and kindly, with a touch of worldliness, and a faith that suggested primordial strength—so Ted imagined. The minister's moral courage, his quiet loyalty to the message of the New Testament, had won his heart.

When Scott preached the first of what people would later call his War Sermons, Ted had had no warning. Sitting in the McCrae's family pew, he listened in disbelief.

Scott's appeals reaped a fair harvest. Every week, new spaces opened in the crowded church as more young men went off. And still Ted kept his place.

One Sunday, he confronted the minister about his reversal. They had come out to Brockwood's garden after a late lunch. Before Ted's angry accusations, Scott was evasive; he went red in the face, then all of a sudden began to speak with angry certainty. He had grown up in the north of Ireland and had absorbed the absolutes that haunted its religious tensions. He spoke to Ted of Christ's blasting of the fig tree and of holy war. He invoked the Christ of Revelations, who would come like a vengeful warrior to divide sinners and believers and send them to their rewards for all eternity.

To Ted, it seemed a different man stood before him, almost a stranger. He was as much devastated as shocked. Sunday after Sunday he sat in a state of mourning through Scott's sermons, feeling at his back the criticism of many eyes, the disapproval of many judgments. And before him, those motionless flags, like an army waiting.

Their friendship did not entirely end. At Brockwood, where he and Miriam were invited every Sunday, and where he had so many times talked with Scott of books and ideas, they talked still. The minister did not pressure Ted to sign up; the whole issue was left silent between them. But the pressure was there nonetheless—Scott's unspoken appeal to their friendship, a challenge laid down before his manhood. A thinness entered their conversation.

Miriam had several times to rescue them. He and Miriam talked little of the war themselves, but he knew she did not want him to go. She spoke scathingly of the parades and refused to watch them—the influence of her father, he thought. He murmured agreement with her disapproval. Yet something else was happening inside him. Was Scott the reason? He didn't like to think so. That fateful afternoon in Toronto, in the winter of '15, came back to him now, a mirage in the smoke of his cigarette. He'd taken the train to the city to talk to a favourite professor. He'd finished his bachelor's degree with the help of scholarships, and contributions from anonymous donors in the town. Now his plans for graduate work depended on finding an overseer for his thesis, a study of regional tensions during Confederation. His meeting with Dr. Horsefall had gone well, the man offering to back him for a master's. Later, killing time before his train, he wandered in the Ward, that dishevelled district of small factories and houses stretching south of the university, feeling free for the first time in months—free of Scott's harangues, free of his students and the monotonies of cramming them with "Horatius at the Bridge" and the kings of England, free of Miriam's anxieties.

Little houses crammed between warehouses and work-shops. Lanes filled with trash. Men pushing carts. Kids kicking a half-inflated ball. An old Jew in his kippah. And the young woman in the kerchief, struggling to wind up her shop's awning—he could see her yet. For his help, she'd given him a pear, rubbed it on her sweater then offered it with gleaming eyes. This was life, then, the adventure he'd sensed since child-hood. Eating the fruit, he found himself back on University Avenue. Across the road was a crenellated tower—the University Armouries. Under an arching window, a painted banner called for recruits. By the main door, a boy was selling newspapers. Sun had pierced a little way into the open door-way, picking out a wall of black and white tiles.

Three hours later, as he came through the back door, he found Miriam bent over the whir of her egg beater. She stopped, slowly straightened. "You've joined haven't you?"

Guilty, triumphant, afraid, he held her, aware of something remote in him that her tears could not touch. He was a soldier now.

THAT MAN IN the kitchen, holding his sobbing wife. That man, taking the d'Anjou pear from the woman in the kerchief—who was he? Where was he now? The trees around Brockwood's lawn lofted clouds of spring leaves. It would take time, as Miriam had said. Time to win back a little of himself each day. Time to give his devils their due, until they grew tired and went elsewhere. Was that a plan? He was on his feet. Up and down the porch he paced. Onto the walk and across the lawn. Circling the house, he smoked with a vengeance, waiting for the others to return.

4.

Will marched with the Junior Cadets. Around King's Park they went, wooden rifles sloped, tramping through the shade of maples, out into sun, past the bandstand, over the bare spot where the old French cannon had stood on its concrete base. One night it had disappeared: taken away for scrap, his father said. To make new weapons for the war.

The war was everywhere. It was behind the trees. It was in his bowl of porridge. It was in the songs the birds sang. People talked of it constantly. *How's the war going? Damn this war. Do you think the war'll be over soon, Mr. Goose?*

In the centre of the park, the Colonel shouted orders from under his pith helmet. *Left, right, Featherstone. Have you rocks for brains, Featherstone? How many left feet do you have, Featherstone?* The Colonel had been in the South African war—that's what people said, though with his round belly and wrinkled hands, it was hard to imagine him chasing the Boers. Between the Capitol Theatre and the flour mill stood a memorial to that war, pale stone carved with strange, unpronounceable names with war in them. Now there was a new war, with new names: The Somme. Ypres. Vimy. Daydreaming, he stumbled in the hollow where the cannon had been. The word war. Not wore but war. They wore the war—ha!

He would turn ten that summer. One night his father had sat on the edge of his bed, talking to him in the dark. He would never have to go, he'd said—it would be over long before he was old enough. The next morning, coming downstairs, he overheard his father tell his mother that the Colonel should be tied up until the war was over.

When the boys come home. That was another thing people said. The war was being fought by men who were also boys. It made him wonder if his father was right.

He stared at the back of Charlie Featherstone's head. Charlie's father was in the war. Will's Uncle Ted had been in the war, but he'd been wounded and sent home. Ted wasn't really his uncle, but his mother had said it was simpler calling him that. His Uncle Ted had asked him to call him Ted, which he did when they were alone. Ted was usually gone when Will woke up. "He's off *walking again*," his mother would say with a sigh. But he was usually at home in the evenings. He was a little afraid of Ted, the way his face could change in an instant, the way his eyes could empty. That was the war too—the nothing in his uncle's eyes.

THEY STOOD FIDGETING in their ranks while the Colonel spoke from the cave of shade below his visor. He had a surprise for them, he said. They knew what it was because he had told them the previous week—had he forgotten? In their marching they had passed the long canvas case, propped against the bandstand.

Now the Colonel held the case in his pink hands, undoing the snaps at one end before pausing to say, "But you don't want to see this, do you—"

He chuckled at their roar of protest and slowly drew off the case, revealing in turn the polished stock, the bolt, the dully shining barrel. Silent, mesmerized, they watched as he pointed the gun at the ground and worked the bolt. "Always make sure your rifle's not loaded," he told them. "You don't want to go blowing each other's heads off."

They laughed merrily at the very idea.

"On the other hand, if there are any Boche around, get them before they can get you." Suddenly he swung the rifle up, aiming it at the sky.

Now the Colonel held the weapon tenderly across his chest. He flicked an invisible mote from its barrel. "This is the newest version of the Lee-Enfield," he told them. "This is the rifle our men have now in France." As he continued to look it over, admiringly, it *did* seem to Will that the rifle he held was the same rifle the men from town were using *over there*. How could that be? How could this one rifle be in all their hands at once? And yet for a moment, it was so. Huge deeds were being done *over there*, where brothers and cousins, neighbours and fathers were fighting beyond the sight and hearing of everyone at home. There was a mystery about it—those men had simply disappeared.

"All right, boys, lay down your weapons."

Thirty wooden rifles tumbled to the grass.

"Not like that! Pick them up and do it again!"

They obeyed, laying the light pine weapons down carefully. With a few words, the Colonel straightened their ranks. Scowling, he surveyed his cadets. Finally, he solemnly approached them, bearing the upright Lee-Enfield like a flag.

"All right now, I'm going to give each of you a chance to hold it," the Colonel told them. "McCrae, you first." Will gripped the forestock, but when the Colonel let go, the unexpected weight tore through his hands. The butt hit the ground and the Colonel had to move fast to keep the gun from falling over.

Bloodshot eyes regarded him from on high.

"Have you noodles for arms, McCrae?"

"No sir."

"Quiet, you others. Louder, McCrae! I can't hear you!"

"No sir."

"Still can't hear you, McCrae!" the Colonel roared, cupping an ear. Will looked at the Colonel—looked up at the watery eyes in their cave of shade, at the pitted nose and the lower lip drawn down to reveal a palisade of crooked teeth, and he said nothing.

"*Well*, McCrae?"

Past the Colonel's shoulder, some yards away by the bandstand, a few sparrows were bathing in the dust. They hopped in the air and dragged their wings through the dust. For some reason this struck him as comical.

"What are you grinning about, McCrae?" He watched as the little flock took flight, pulsing over the Methodist church before vanishing.

"Nothing, sir.

"Nothing!" the Colonel roared. "The Boche are about to cut your throat and you're smiling at nothing! Ten push-ups, McCrae!"

He did his push-ups as the rifle was passed down the line. When its rounds were finished, the Colonel offered it to Will a second time. This time his arms held. "You can look at it, McCrae. It won't bite you." His gaze travelled up the barrel of the gun, a thin windowless tower against the sky.

MARCHING AGAIN, THEY crossed the street to the school, entering by the Boys' Door, plunging down a steep stairwell into the low-ceilinged basement. On benches around its perimeter, they stripped off their khaki jerseys, shouting and laughing as they flung them about, wild with merriment after the discipline of marching. Strutting before them, Geordie Squance imitated the Colonel's birdish cocking of his head. Stretching out the waist of his pants, he peered inside. "Bloody 'ell! What did I do with my balls!"

Will was laughing with the others when pain exploded through his arm.

On the bench beside him, Stink Henderson was looking at him with gleeful contempt. Stink with his wide cat's face and tiny eyes.

"What did you do that for!"

"Because I felt like it, asshole."

"Well don't," Will said. When he started stuffing his jersey in his satchel, Stink punched him again. "I said don't!"

"You're going to make a piss-poor soldier, McCrae." He grabbed Will's wrist. "He's a bloody coward," he said to his pal Jackie Herrendorff, who had turned to look. "Just like his old man."

Will struggled to free himself, but Stink was too strong; Will's arm was forced to his side and held there; in the general chaos no one noticed.

"Cowards run in families, McCrae," Stink said in an undertone, his face close now. Chipped yellow teeth. A smell of old sweat. "Your old man got sent home because he ran away." Stink glanced at Jackie: "His old man got kicked out of the army. They took away his uniform—my mum saw it. Got off the train without his uniform. You're a coward, McCrae, just like your old man. Can't even hold a fucking gun."

"My father?" Will said. "That's stupid!"

"You calling me stupid?" Stink said. He had Will's wrist in both hands now.

"Not you. What you said was stupid. Let me go!"

"Same difference, McCrae. You call me stupid, I'll punch your fucking face in." His tongue appearing between his teeth like a worm, Stink started to give his wrist a burn. Will tried to pull away and it was then the voice spoke, though apparently Stink didn't hear its sharp *Let him go* because he went on twisting Will's wrist. *I said let him go, Stink.* Stink looked up. Across the room, Beggar Creeden was watching them: Beggar Creeden, a captain in the Cadets, with his long face and smooth white chest, looking at Stink with eyes the colour of the sky.

Letting go of Will's wrist, Stink assumed a look of offended innocence. He hadn't done a thing.

THAT SATURDAY, MIRIAM asked him to take a loaf of bread, freshly baked, to Rose and George. "Don't dawdle. Get it up to them while it's still warm." Rose and George lived in what people called the Upper Town—the original village, his father had once told him, from which the town had spread, old houses circling the little green in front of the Anglican church. On the way, he stopped outside Smitty's forge. Smitty had the hind leg of a Clydesdale clamped between his knees while he tacked on a shoe with the nails he took from between his lips. Deep in the forge, a boy about Will's age was working the long pole that controlled the bellows.

When Will shifted nearer the Clydesdale's head, the horse's big eye looked down on him. He felt the horse knew him. It was there in the dark eye, with its touch of brown—a knowing that felt different from being looked at by a person. Were you someone else when a horse looked at you? A blueness behind that huge eye, a feeling he was sinking into it. With a dismissive snort, the great head swung away.

Later, he took the Station Hill route home. With the tiled roof of the station in sight, he noticed a cluster of boys coming down a side street: Stink, Jackie, and a boy he didn't know, shambling along in the torpor of the afternoon. When Stink shouted for him to stop, fear made his body light. He forced himself to keep walking, pretending he hadn't heard, but when Stink said *Get him*, he ran.

They caught him in the station parking lot. He had bent over to catch his breath when Jackie Herrendorff put him in a headlock. Then Stink was there too, puffing as he took Jackie's place, his big sticky arm circling Will's neck, mashing his head against his side as he walked Will around the parking lot, the two of them making a beast with four legs and one head, stumbling as it went. Then Stink threw him on the ground and sat on him.

Twisting and bucking, he fought until Stink got hold of his wrists and pinned him. Stink was above him now, his eyes avoiding Will's. They scanned the ground beyond Will's head, they blazed at Will's chest, but as for *him*, he was just this thing Stink had sat on. He was closer to Stink now—to the sagging front of his T-shirt and his pale, thick neck ringed with dirt.

"Stay still or I'll smash your face in."

Between Stink's heavy knees, he kept still.

"Say you're a coward," Stink demanded.

Furious, he fought some more, but it was no good. Again he lay still. Past Stink's head, the sky was a deep blue, the same blue it had been when he set off that morning. The ground shook; a train was passing, a pulsing din of boxcars behind his head. Jackie Herrendorff knelt beside them, watching Will with placid curiosity. Some boys said Jackie Herrendorff was a traitor because he had a German name. So why wasn't Stink beating up Jackie? And the other boy, the boy in the torn shirt, the boy he didn't know—where was he? Past Jackie, he saw the roof and back yard of a house, a pair of pants on a line. Farther away, a man was walking down the hill. He glanced at the boys and went on.

"Say it, coward."

Turning his head, he saw the boy in the torn shirt kicking at the cinders. In a tree, leaves moved in a breeze, flipping their pale undersides, and all at once he knew this place was true: Stink on top of him and the grinding of cinders in his back. It was how things were—like the bedrock his father said was under everything. Under soft words, under the kindness of his family and his father's promise he would never go to war, was this place that didn't care about anybody.

He knew it had to end; at some point it would end. Only he wouldn't cry and he wouldn't say he was a coward even though he felt like one sometimes, like that time he'd run away from the Meltons' dog. Not saying it seemed the only thing he had left.

"C'mon, Stink, let's go," Jackie said.

"No one's coming to help you, shit-face," Stink said. "Just say it."

"Yeah, say it," Jackie said, almost kindly. "Just say it and then we can go."

Stink's face changed now, his lips curling off his teeth as he took Will's hand and bent back his finger until he screamed.

"Say it!" Again Stink bent back his finger, farther this time. In a rage of tears and pain he said it. "Louder!" Stink cried. "I can't hear you." Again he said it. He said it three times before they let him go. He better not tell anybody what had happened, they warned, or he'd get it worse. They'd smash his fingers with a hammer. They'd kill his family—Stink's brother had a gun.

He walked away, not bothering to look behind him, not caring about anything any more, plodding dully across the tracks and up the weed-fringed path that climbed the embankment. When he reached the street, he ran.

They looked up when he came in, two women with blank, enquiring faces, Mim with an egg timer in her hand, Mother sitting at the kitchen table in her apron. When she asked what had happened to him, he said he'd been running.

"You know you're not to exert yourself. It's bad for your lungs."

He went on down the hall that was so dim after the sunlight he had trouble seeing. His body was heavy, a sorrowful weight he dragged up the stairs. He closed the door of the room behind him. His books were there, making a many-coloured wall of his bookcase. On a table, painted a deep blue, was the aquarium where he kept Riley, his red-eared turtle. But he was aware of none of this now as he flung himself on the bed and pounded the mattress in a fury of helplessness.

AT DINNER THAT evening, Mother remarked he was not looking well. "You really mustn't run," she told him, while he looked down, coldly seething, at his plate. "He ran home from George and Rose's," she explained to his father.

"All the way?" his father said, a spark of amusement in his eyes.

"No," he said, relieved he could tell the truth about this at least.

"You know when you're close to your limit, I think?"

"Yes."

"That's the time to stop, when you feel your limit coming on."

He could sense his mother's disapproval of this answer. His mother was stricter than his father. She liked the rules to be clear, and when you broke one, you quickly heard about it. He overheard them arguing sometimes and it seemed to him, whatever the subject was, it was always the same argument, the argument of the different people they were.

The conversation encircled him with the sound of familiar voices. Under the table, Kiki, Gracie's cat, twined about his legs, and on the wall the sun made a quivering red patch. He looked at the framed picture, hung over the buffet, of his family at a party on Blue Lake, years before. Mim and Gracie were little girls then, and his mother and father looked younger, and Grandmother Dunne was there too, the women in white summer dresses, the men in their shirtsleeves and straw hats, outside the old cabin on Blue Lake, a patch of dark water visible in one corner. He had not been born yet, and in the past this had been a comforting thought, to know that all these people were waiting for him when he got there, but when he looked at the picture now, it seemed they knew nothing about him at all. They did not know that he was on his way towards them. They had not prepared a safe place for him, and a gust of loneliness swept him, as if he were invisible among them still.

5.

As far as Miriam could tell, all her husband wanted to do was walk—not as one walks to the post office, but striding along, cane whipping at his side, long legs carrying him down roads, through woods, along river paths—she didn't know where all. She had tried to go with him but found she couldn't keep up. In any case, he seemed happier alone.

It was the war, of course; yet to say *the war* was to say nothing. *The war* was a phrase for all that had happened to him, about which he was resolutely silent. She sensed this war constantly: an atmosphere he'd brought home with him, a pressure behind his face, spaces between his words, nightmares he refused to describe to her. Early most mornings he would leave with a sandwich in his pocket, not returning till suppertime, exhausted but a little calmer; even, for a day or two, more like his old self. Her hopes would rise. But the change never lasted.

On his arms and sides were scars like pale little fish hooks, quarter moons. "Shrapnel," he said, guiding her hand to a bluish spot. "Probably pop out one day." He spoke jauntily, with an underlying bitterness.

On the outside of his calf was an opening, like a small, moist mouth. His surgeons had left that bit unstitched, so the wound could drain. It needed to be kept clean, wrapped daily with fresh gauze. That was Miriam's job. He sat by their bed, leg propped on a stool, while she daubed iodine. His curse came simultaneously with the jerking away of the leg.

"Oh Ted, I'm sorry, did I—"

"Yes, you did, goddammit! Look out—you're spilling it on the floor!"

In a fluster, she blotted up the mess while he fumed above her. He had not been an angry man when he left. "It's quite inflamed, darling," she said tentatively. "Maybe take today off?"

"It'll be all right," he told her curtly.

"I know Dad doesn't have anyone till ten o'clock. He could easily—"

"Tomorrow."

"He's chock full tomorrow—he was complaining about it last night at dinner. If there's infection—"

"Just put the damned bandage on."

Suppressing her hurt, she placed the pad and wound the gauze. Later she walked with him to the street. "See you at supper," she said lightly. She had learned to hold her hurt, telling herself he couldn't help these outbursts.

He grunted a goodbye and was off. Almost at once, he turned back.

His voice rasping, he said he was no good. He said he didn't deserve her care. He said he was sorry. He said he would not be alive without her. "I-I. . ." he stuttered, while her tears welled. At once, with a violent twist, he was off, striding away from her up River Street. He did not turn and wave. He never *had* waved, but his words held her fast to the sight of his retreating figure. Past the last houses it went, past the high school, a stick man with a flashing cane, dissolving finally in the haze of the fields.

Unable to settle, she drifted through Brockwood's high-ceilinged rooms, dusting in a desultory way. Since he'd come home, she'd had this idea that there would be a critical moment when he needed her. Of course he needed her at other times as well, but the sense of a moment of crisis haunted her. It was as if he were confined in a locked cell or an enchanted thicket, and when the time came for him to escape, she must be there to help him out. She sensed this notion was unreasonable, even desperate. After his parting words, it bound her. She had made plans to go out; now she was loath to leave the house.

The house, with its dark walnut furniture dating from her grandparents' time, oppressed her. That oriental vase stuffed with peacock feathers; that loveseat in grey damask, its stains hidden by an afghan her grandmother had crocheted: pieces of a dead world she longed to put behind her. Continuing to drift, she tidied papers and magazines, did up the breakfast dishes, stared out the window. Taking herself in hand, she entered her father's surgery. From a drawer of his desk, she slid out the metal box where he kept cash and IOUs; from a shelf, a heavy ledger. She had taken over the job of managing Alec's accounts soon after moving back to Brockwood. Ada had complained that Alec wasn't keeping track of his billings. Too few bills went out, too little payment came in, while the records that should have detailed these transactions were a shambles. As for the payments "in kind" her father accepted, Ada refused to countenance most of them. A bag of decent potatoes was one thing, she'd said, but what were they to do with a rusty shotgun or a horse collar fit for a Clydesdale? How were they supposed to live?

It was a cry Miriam had been hearing since her grandfather's death. Untangling Archie Dunne's estate, her parents had uncovered a mass of debt. They had managed to keep the house and the cabin at Blue Lake, but the farm adjacent to it had had to be sold, as had the carpet factory on the Flats. The dressmaker visited only once a year now; the cook came in only for special occasions. The shopping trips to Buffalo, once a spring high-light, had ended. And still some debt remained, to be chipped away at by whatever Ada could spare from her few remaining investments.

As Alec had pointed out, selling Brockwood would go a long way towards solving their problems. But Ada remained firm— she had an almost sacred devotion to the house she'd grown up in, not to mention the status it conferred. After a few attempts to mediate their argument, Miriam gave it up. The house was a symbol of something unspoken in her parents' lives, she sus-pected, a fundamental struggle for authority as old as their marriage. Ada's personality was strong, outgoing. Despite the family's reduced means, she still managed to play a lead role amongst the town's matriarchs. Alec was more reserved, but stubborn. Ada had married him against her parents' wishes. But there was some fundamental qualification in her mother's commitment to him, Miriam suspected, for she still thought of herself as a Dunne; *we Dunne girls*, Ada would say, speaking of herself and her daughters. She quoted her father so frequently that he still seemed an authority in the house. Miriam wondered how her own father stood it. Privately, she admired his willing-ness to tend poor people in return for little, while the decline in their living standards hardly bothered her, being modest in her needs. But their situation galled Ada. "Alec's main problem is he's too soft. We have to live, after all," she confided to Miriam. "Speak to him about it, will you? He won't listen to me on the subject. Tell him he has to insist on cash, cash on the barrelhead. He has to see more people of means. He has to decide what kind of doctor he is, a poor people's doctor or someone of quality."

Miriam had spread her work on the dining room table and was composing a letter to one of their patients in arrears when Ada swept in. Casting a sardonic eye over her daughter's papers, she pulled out a chair and sat—an erect, handsome woman of fifty with a bouffant forever escaping its pins. "Do you have a minute, dear?"

"Of course, Mother."

"I'm concerned about you."

"That's kind of you, but I'm fine, really."

"I know it's an awful stress, with Ted and all."

"We're doing just fine," Miriam said testily.

"Of course you are, dear—you're both very brave. I admire you, I really do. Now I've had a thought."

Miriam looked down at her work; when her mother said she'd had a thought it usually meant she had decided what someone else must do. Yet she did look concerned. "I was talking to Ted last night," her mother went on. "He said he's going back to teaching."

"That's right."

Miriam gazed at her mother without expression, as if to say, *So?* At once, Ada smiled a propitiatory smile. They had been at loggerheads so often that she was alert to any sign of opposition. "I just want to say, you're welcome to stay here as long as you like."

Miriam was used to her mother's strategic shifts. When one way was blocked, Ada quickly retreated, then found another. "We're very grateful, Mum. You've been so good. But sooner or later, we want to have a place of our own again. I know you understand that. We can't have our own place unless we can find the money—of course we still have a little from Ted's pay, and Ted will have a pension one day, but it's not going to cover everything. We'll need an income. Something ongoing. I know you can't help," she said, glancing meaningfully at her papers. "And in any case, we want to do it on our own."

"Of course you do, dear—that's the Dunne spirit in you. But while Ted is—before he's back to himself, you know, and can earn an income, you must consider this place yours. I have to admit I'm a bit worried—he seems to think he's ready to start now."

Miriam was taken aback. She and Ted had spoken about his teaching but he'd said nothing about starting soon. She wondered if her mother had got that part right or if she was bending the truth a little. In any case, she would not let any daylight show between herself and her husband. "I think he's the best judge of when he's ready."

"Of course he is, dear. But in his enthusiasm . . . I mean, I understand why he would want to get back to work as soon as possible—he wants to support his wife again—wholly admirable."

"I'm thinking of getting a job myself," Miriam said, looking directly at her mother. In Ada's view, women of their station did not work for pay. They did volunteer work, and they might work very hard at that: no one had done more for the new hospital project than Ada, one of her friends had told Miriam. For Grace, single and as yet unsupported, Ada had made an exception.

Miriam was surprised by her own announcement. It was true, she had been turning over the idea of job, but it was far from a definite plan. Now the contretemps with her mother had thrown it up, and she had seized on it, as a weapon. Her mother looked at her blankly, then continued as if Miriam had not spoken. "But do you really think he's ready?"

Miriam felt her face heat. She did not think Ted was ready; she had assumed he would not teach, even if a position were available, for another year at least.

"I don't know, Mum. He may be ready, he may not. As I said, it's up to him."

She could not meet Ada's eyes.

"You haven't talked about it?"

"Of course we have." Now it was Miriam's turn to offer a false smile. The truth was, they hadn't talked about his teaching plans in any detail because Ted was not talkative. "We just can't come to anything definite now. He hasn't spoken to Mr. Adams yet."

"I haven't heard he's in any need of teachers."

"He did say, before Ted left, that there'd always be a place for him."

"I'm sure he did. That's what he *would* say—I mean to a man going off to risk his life."

"I'm sure he said it in perfect sincerity," Miriam said icily.

"Of course. Of course." Ada paused. "But there would have to be an opening."

"What are you getting at?"

They were at a standoff. Miriam passed a hand over the letter she'd been writing: a hint she would like to get back to work. Inwardly, she was furious.

"The thing is," Ada went on, "this town can be very unforgiving."

"Whatever are you getting at?" Miriam said, unable to hide her irritation. Ada's remark had raised one of her oldest criticisms of her mother: that she cared too much for appearances.

"Don't be harsh with me, dear. I'm only thinking of you. The thing is, Ted's reputation is so high just now. He was a wonderful teacher, and now, with the war, his wound and all, it's never been higher. If he should go back to his teaching too soon—I mean if it doesn't work out—you know how tense he is these days, his temper and all—and he can scarcely sit still a minute. Think of him, trying to deal with a classroom of rowdy boys—"

"He's been dealing with rowdy men," Miriam said in exasperation. "I wouldn't think boys would be a problem."

Ignoring Miriam's defiant gaze, Ada went on. "If it doesn't work out—I mean if he goes back too soon and fails, dear, it could do no end of damage to his reputation. People in this town—as I've said more than once—vicious at times, some of them. It could be very hard for him to find a second chance."

When Ada left, Miriam found it impossible to work. Leaving the house, she stalked across the terrace and into the garden, pacing the brick paths between the beds. Ted's expression of gratitude—the hope and feeling of it—was gone. She went for a brisk walk and when she got back, returned to her accounts. Then Grace was there, still in her dressing gown as she so often was in the mornings. She trailed around the table, touching the backs of chairs, finally stopping at the window, where she gazed into the straggling branches of a spruce. "What were you and Mère talking about?" she said idly. "It sounded a bit *fraught*."

"Not so bad as that," Miriam said. "How was your sleep?"

"So-so." In the silence that fell, Miriam tried to keep working. Then Grace's voice came again. "Mim, can I say something?"

"Of course," Miriam said a little impatiently.

"About you and Ted."

"Why not," Miriam said, reluctantly putting her pen aside. "Everyone else has."

"You mean Mother."

"Yes, I mean Mother."

"I think you hover too much. Ted isn't going to break, you know, if you're not there." She turned to Miriam, who had paused in an icy stillness. "I mean, I don't imagine he likes it."

"How would you know what he likes, little sister? You scarcely know anything about us." Miriam tried to put some lightness into her remark, to dull its edge.

"Don't be mad, Mim."

"I'm not mad."

Grace gave her a sidelong glance.

"All right, I'm mad. I've just listened to Mother telling us how to run our lives, and now—I know you mean well, but what happens between a husband and wife—it's complicated, not to mention private. There are subtleties you can't appreciate. You have no way of knowing what Ted has asked of me. What he needs."

"So he's asked you to hover?"

"I don't hover, Grace—"

Grace looked thoughtful. Miriam sensed her sister was not convinced, which only added to her anger, as did the suspicion, which she immediately suppressed, that Grace might not be entirely wrong. She made a show of getting back to work, and after a while Grace left. Her concentration gone, Miriam shoved aside the ledger and went out to the garden. In another minute, she stood gripping the pickets of the fence overlooking Baird, overwhelmed by a sickening sense of exhaustion. For three years she had kept herself to the mark. By now, she had expected to rest, or at least to be resuming her old life. It seemed she had been sadly mistaken.

SHE HAD PROMISED to join a League wrapping party that afternoon. Afterwards, she and Nan planned to have tea—the two friends had not had "a proper jaw," as Nan put it, since Ted's return. Now both commitments seemed onerous. At one o'clock, not bothering to change, she splashed water on her face and left the house. The League's rooms were downtown, over Fisher's Stationery and China. Halfway down the River Street hill, the sight of the Presbyterian church drew her towards it. She let herself in the side door and went to the sanctuary, where she sat not in her family's pew but in one nearer the front. Between her and the carved wood of the choir loft stood the bright, still wall of flags. There was nothing Christian about them, she had often thought: nothing of the forgiving Jesus of the Gospels, of the New Testament's soft grey olive afternoons, nothing of Jesus scourged and heaved aloft by men bearing flags like these. And whether it was the flags that made prayer impossible or her exhaustion, for some minutes she sat grimly wordless until the knocking of the caretaker's broom drove her out.

Downtown, the air smelled of rain. The merchants were winding out their awnings. Climbing the stairs to the League's rooms, she was stopped on a landing by a burst of women's laughter from above. For three years she had come here glad of their company; today she felt almost a revulsion. Out a filthy window, she saw rain beating past a ledge where pigeons crowded in a dismal, pullulating mass.

She was about to retreat when she heard the street door open below. Willing herself onward, she climbed to the third-floor corridor with its smell of floor wax and stale smoke. Turning the last corner, she met the faces of a dozen women. Their mouths were open—singing, she realized, singing to *her. For she's a jolly good fellow.* She, who was the first of their number to have her man home.

In its white glove, her mother's hand, prancing, kept time.

Bright with welcome, they pressed around her, touched her, spoke kind words. Behind her smile, like the bad witch at a christening, came the bitter thought: *You have no idea who I am.* The package Nan Williams presented felt as light as if it were empty. They had to urge her to open it. Nested inside was a locket on a fine chain, the little pendant opening to reveal Ted's head and hers, facing each other in profile. As Nan fastened it around her neck, she heard her mother explain to the others how hard it had been to find just the right photographs. "We couldn't have Miriam staring at the back of his head!" Of course she would be here, Miriam thought: she was everywhere. Ada's voice came more loudly than the other women's. She chuckled heartily at her own jokes. But she could not stay. She simply had to rush off, she announced. There was a committee meeting for the new hospital. Pausing in the doorway, she offered a few final remarks, saying that although their celebration was for Miriam, she was so *entirely* proud of them all. Then she was gone.

The silence that followed her departure reigned for some time between Miriam and Nan as they cut and wrapped chocolate. Miriam had complained often enough of Ada to her friend that they had no need of words to acknowledge what had just happened. "Give me strength," Miriam murmured finally, drawing a chuckle from Nan. They had been friends since public school.

"It could have been worse," Nan said. "She could have stayed." She was a small woman, full of energy, compulsively talkative, with a quick, associative intelligence. She soon abandoned the subject of Ada McCrae and launched into a description of a wedding she and Horace had attended in the next town. Miriam kept losing the thread.

When Hazel Benson appeared before their table, she stared at the woman's gaunt, simian face. A week before, Hazel had learned that her husband had been killed. Two days later, she turned up for a League meeting. She didn't want them to make a fuss, she told the women; in fact, she would ask them not to mention Cecil. They honoured her request, though privately many disapproved—there was something aggressive in the woman's refusal of mourning, something *not quite right*. She had denied them the consolation of tending the wound they feared receiving themselves. As Hazel walked away, her tray piled high with wrapped chocolate, the very straightness of her back seemed a reproach. Miriam had what Hazel would never have; what right did she have to be melancholy?

Yet it was not melancholy she felt so much as weariness. Why had she ever committed to tea with Nan? Nan would want to know everything. Already, she could feel the pressure of her friend's curiosity. As they worked away, Nan doing most of the talking, opportunities to back out came and went. Out the window, rain pelted the surface of the river. The Shade had flooded that spring, covering a portion of the Flats; it was still high, a brown, racing torrent foaming over a ledge, dragging at the branches of a willow. She thought of Ted, huddled under a tree or holed up in some shed by the road, and it seemed for a moment they shared a common misery.

THE RAIN HAD stopped when she and Nan stepped into the street. Skirting puddles, they crossed to the *Star-Transcript* office, where Nan needed to make some final changes to her "Around the Town" column. Waiting, Miriam watched the great arm of the press as it lifted sheets for the rollers. The mechanical repetitions entranced her, while the deeper course of her daydream bore her away; again she saw her husband turning back to her, the pain of love in his eyes, and when Nan finally emerged it was a struggle not to beg off and hurry back to Brockwood.

They walked to the Williams's old plaster-and-lath house overlooking King's Park. On the veranda, they sat with tea and biscuits. Across the road, in the drenched grass, a robin cocked its head, stabbed for a worm.

Miriam scarcely noticed when Nan's voice ceased its chatter. But she heard when her friend spoke again, on a lower note. "You're not having an easy time of it, are you?"

"No easier than you," she said quickly, sending a bland smile at her friend.

"We can get to my problems another time. I want to know about you and Ted. How are you managing?"

"Well—" Miriam said, stalling. She was reluctant to confide in her best friend; there had always been things she'd kept from Nan, not entirely trusting her to understand. It was nearly always Nan who talked about *her* problems, while Miriam patiently listened.

"Horace saw Ted pacing along at midnight."

"And what was Horace doing up at midnight?" She smiled again, but it was no good. Fighting back tears, she turned her face away. Nan's hand was on her arm now. "I don't know where we are." Her tears were flooding now, an embarrassment. Yet it was true, wasn't it? She was as lost as he. "I can't get hold of it—whatever it is that drives him. All he does is walk. He hardly says two words to me." She shook her head. "That's not quite true. When he comes home from one of his tramps— Sometimes there are good days; he might tell me where he's been, something he's seen. He even made a joke the other day!" She gave Nan a grin, half false. "Dad keeps telling me I have to be patient. He's only been home a few weeks. I don't know what's the matter with me. It's like all my strength's gone. Of course, I didn't sleep well last night—"

Embarrassment had become shame. Shame at failing him, at not being able to bear up, at not appreciating the blessing of his return, shame that Nan knew her failure. Before Nan's steady, sympathetic gaze, she wept some more. She spoke to the green haze of the park. "I keep thinking, if there were just something I could do—if he'd tell me what he needs—I mean really needs. Nothing I do seems to help. Half the time I feel I'm in his way."

"He might not know himself."

"He just pushes me away. Not literally, of course," she said flushing. "I feel so shut out."

"Does he talk about the war?"

Miriam shook her head. "I've asked him about it. He started to tell me about the hospital he was in, but then he just clammed up. I feel like it's me—like I don't know how to listen. Whatever I'm doing, it just makes him angry."

"You need to get over that," Nan said, suddenly very certain. "You need to tell him you won't put up with it."

"This morning he was wonderful. He told me he wouldn't be alive without—" She shook her head.

"Well, I wouldn't put up with it."

"You might well," Miriam said, daubing at her face. "If you knew him, you might very well." *If you loved him,* she thought. She felt her experience, or a part of it, lay beyond Nan's understanding. It was their old problem.

They were silent for a time. Miriam decided it was time to go. The rain might have driven him home early.

"Apparently, it helps if they *can* talk about it," Nan said.

"Talk about—?"

"What's happened to them. What they've seen. When Horace was in Toronto, visiting his brother, he got talking to a chap at the sanitorium—a doctor. He told him about some experiments they're running in Britain. Treating men with shell shock."

"Oh, that's not Ted," Miriam said, indignant.

Nan stared at her for a moment. "In any case, it helps soldiers who've been through a lot—if they can get it out. You know, get it off their chests. I could ask Horace the name of the doctor. Maybe they do this kind of thing in Toronto."

"I'll keep that in mind," Miriam said, but her heart had closed. Their talk became desultory. A few drops fell, became a torrent. All she could think of now was Ted. In a few minutes, the rain stopped—her chance to go. She had gotten up to leave when Nan cried, "Listen!" From across the park came the chanting of young voices from the open windows of the public school, reciting a poem in unison: *Ten thousand saw I at a glance, Tossing their heads in sprightly dance.*

BROCKWOOD'S OCHRE FAÇADE swam into view behind dripping trees. The flagstones of the walk glistened. She passed over them with rising excitement. It was often like this when she came home, feeling herself on the brink of the change in him she craved. Today, after her visit with Nan, she experienced an upsurge of energy. She was not just rushing towards Ted; she was bringing him the gift of herself, newly minted. In stocking feet, she padded down the hall into the empty kitchen, where she stopped at the sound of voices. To her right, the green-house door stood open. The voices, she determined, were coming from there—a low subterranean murmur. "That's a long way to go and not—" she heard her sister's voice say. Now a masculine voice came—Ted. She stood listening as their dialogue continued, low note answering high note, man answering woman and back again, a few phrases coming clear, the rest a murmur, like voices heard from the shallows of sleep.

When Grace's laughter came—a loud, exultant burst—it startled Miriam into action. She entered the greenhouse. The air was oppressively warm, the corridor between plants narrowed by the overflowing leaves she brushed past. Neither Ted nor Grace was visible. She had to walk the length of the green-house before she found them in an alcove, among the delicate satyr faces of her mother's orchids. She saw Ted's back first, the shoulders of his jacket dark with rain. From behind this wall, her sister's face appeared. "Oh Mim!" she cried.

Ted turned to Miriam then. "Ah, there you are," he said matter-of-factly. As if he had been looking for her all along.

AFTER SUPPER, she and Ted went for the evening walk that had become a ritual—along with the wrapping of his bandages, the most treasured part of her day. He was more talkative than usual, swinging his cane at a bush to send raindrops pattering, tapping it on the rail of the John Street bridge. They stopped to take in the view. Below, the main line of the CPR curved gleaming towards the Junction, where the horizon burned red. "Beautiful," she said, ritually. He did not respond. He was taking out his cigarettes. Had he heard? As so often, she tried to tell herself it did not matter because they were together. But she was left wanting; and his smoking irritated her. "So what were you and Grace talking about?" she asked casually, as if she scarcely cared.

"What's that?"

"Gracie," she said forcefully. "The two of you were having quite a tête-à-tête in the greenhouse. What was she on about?"

"On about?"

"You know how she can have some axe to grind. This morning she was after me—"

"And what was she *after* you about?"

"It's not important. Come on, what were the two of you talking about?" She smiled at him, falsely. She was angry now and *had* to know.

He exhaled a stream of smoke skyward.

"She wanted to know about Paris," he said finally. "Apparently the fact I've been there is almost t-too much for her." His stuttering was a sign she should ease back, but she couldn't.

"What do you mean?"

"She wants to go herself." He shrugged.

"She's always been like that—always somewhere else that's better," Miriam said. "What made her laugh?"

"What?"

"In the greenhouse, she laughed at something you said."

"My Lord, I don't know!" He spoke roughly, flicking his half-finished cigarette over the rail. They walked into the depths of the town. Dusk had come early here as usual, the houses sinking behind blue transparencies, while on the lip of the valley the sun still blazed. When she asked him to slow, he complied, but rapped a telephone pole with his cane. A letterbox. The thing made an angry clang.

He had made her sister laugh—when was the last time he had made *her* laugh? What bothered her most was the intimacy of the conversation she had half overheard. The flowing give-and-take of it. Had she and Ted talked like that *once* since he'd come home?

OVER THE FOLLOWING days, she tried to take a lesson from the greenhouse incident: perhaps she was not as alert to his needs as she might be. Undoubtedly, she had missed signs, opportunities, warnings. But that he had turned to Grace! It galled her. She resolved to observe him more closely, listen more intently. His silences were as taut with meaning as anything he said—but what meaning?

Despite her efforts, the sense he lived a second life, closed to her, deepened. More than anything she wanted to be admitted to it—to share that other life and its burdens—hadn't he been sharing it with Grace? Wasn't Paris part of that life? He had been to Paris! And now she wanted Paris too, desperately. In the end, he spoke of his other life himself. They were in their room, getting ready for bed.

"I miss my men," he said. She could see him in her mirror, where she sat brushing her hair. He was looking out the window. At once, her brush stopped.

"Your men," she coaxed.

"I never expected it—what I came to feel for them." A long pause. Carefully, she put down her brush.

"Well. That's over now," he said abruptly.

Through the screen came the shivering cries of robins—they sang so late these nights. She turned on her bench to face him.

"What do you miss about them, Ted?"

He seemed not to hear.

"Did you have special friends—what about that fellow you went to Normandy with?"

"Who?" he demanded.

"That fellow you went to Normandy with—what was his name? You wrote about fishing. A chalk river—I thought that a lovely expression, a *chalk* river, though I had no idea what it was."

He shook his head. Had she pressed him too far? Later, in bed, she curled against him. "It must have been so hard for you, darling. Harder than any of us can imagine." He patted her hand, laid on his stomach—was it encouragement or a warning? "And darling, you know, it might help if you talked about it." Immediately she felt him tense. "Only if you feel like it," she hurriedly added. "Even the tiniest thing. They say it can help— you know, if you can get it out—it might relieve the pressure." As she sent her words into the unanswering dark, she sensed their frailty compared to what lay beside her—that silence, that furious thinking. It was like sending moths into a hurricane.

6.

From the gazebo where he sat with his unopened book, he watched Miriam at work in the garden. The changing planes of her skirt. The paleness of her hands as they appeared, were eclipsed, and rose again over the staked tomatoes. He felt he had died to life. Yet when she tugged out a weed, or stood to stretch, life was *there*, with her. His surrogate.

His love came more easily at a distance, in the stillness of the evening. His devils had fallen quiet, as they sometimes did.

"Oh, you're there! I didn't see you!"

"I've been watching you," he said. When she started towards him, he was a little disappointed. There would be talk, and the demands of talk. He shifted to make room for her on the narrow bench. She sat in a bustle of good will, and for a few seconds they gazed over the yard. High on Brockwood's rear wall, a few bricks burned in the late sun.

At a noise, he tensed. Someone was shuffling across Baird Street. The gate rattled and Sandy Robinson appeared, a stooping figure with a pannier. Before the garden's dim jumble, the old man paused, oblivious to the watchers. A few more steps and he knelt with difficulty among the lettuces. With the McCraes' blessing, their former gardener came and went from the garden, taking what he needed.

Miriam was talking now; subliminally, he heard her voice going on. For all he knew it might have been a wagon going by, or birds at their vespers, until, at her touch, he came back with a sense of violent rupture from the quavering glare of a spotlight on white shoulders. She had been making calls for the League, Mim's voice was telling him. A soldier's wife, Henny Gill, had reported a troubling letter from her husband. "Apparently he went out on a raid. He said he'd taken a club and knife. Henny thought that meant there weren't enough guns to go round. She was really quite anxious about it. I told her I doubted that was true, but really, I had no idea. Would that be the case?"

"Would what?" he said.

"That some are fighting without guns."

He shook his head. His throat was constricting. "On raids some men prefer them—clubs or knives," he heard himself say. "It's not always allowed, but—"

When he broke off, pressure built through her silence. "I've read about raids in the papers," she said, coaxing. "I suppose I know what that means generally, but what actually happens on them?"

He shifted on the bench.

"They're supposed to keep the Germans on their toes," he managed. "A few men go over." He paused and swallowed. "At night, they go over and get into the other fellows' trench. Do their job, get home again."

"Did you ever go on one, Ted?"

A tremor in her voice. She knew she was pushing him, he realized. If so, why did she persist? Over the past few days, she'd kept trying to draw him out on subjects he least wanted to talk about. *It might help*, she kept saying.

"Go on what?" he said, stalling.

"On a raid."

"One or two."

A bat jagged through the gloom.

She was waiting for more.

"We got caught out there once, by a German raid."

"Oh, how terrible!" she said.

"I can't do this!" he shouted, lunging to his feet. He slammed his fist into the post of the gazebo. In the garden, Sandy Robinson struggled to get up and fell onto his back.

LATER, SITTING ON the edge of their bed, he heard her voice behind him asking if she could do anything. Christ, he thought. She was too good. Her goodness would kill him. The tremulous touch of her goodness was smothering him. Struggling to control his impatience, he explained that questions about the war didn't help. He begged her to forgo them. He spoke straight ahead, into the dark, sensing her pain. When he said she would be better off without him, she hushed him as a mother might and rubbed his back while he bowed his head, defeated. He wanted to put his fist through the wall.

He had three bad days in a row. No feeling, then wild surges of panic that sent him stalking down the concessions. When he saw someone else coming—a boy with his cows, a farm wife in her cart—he would veer off into the woods.

Recovering a little, he redoubled his efforts to be good to her, in atonement. He tried to amuse her, the Ted of old—an earnest against the day when he was himself again—the day *she* believed in. To his relief, she said no more about the war. But his tensions continued. The nightmares he'd endured in the hospital came back. The stumps and splintered trees, and him on his knees, trying with his hands to staunch the blood welling from the ground. And silence, save for the rasp of quick breathing, knowing it couldn't be his breathing because he was already dead.

One morning, changing his bandage, Miriam suggested he see John Scott. "I'm sure he's hurt, the way you're avoiding him."

"Have you been talking to him?" he said, querulous.

Flushing, she allowed that she had. "Of course he's wondering what's happened. You were such good friends, Ted."

"No," he said.

"Surely, Ted, you *were*."

"The man had no idea what he was doing. What he was sending us to."

"But no one knew, surely." When he did not respond, she went on with her work, placing the pad, wrapping gauze. She had become quite expert. "There," she said, finishing. He reached for his trousers.

"I thought you were against him," he said, remembering how she had chided the minister for his war sermons. For his flags. They had considered joining another church. And now she was talking with Scott, about *him*? It seemed a betrayal.

"He's changed," she said. "I know he doubts his part in it— sending so many off."

"Too damned late," he said bitterly.

"He's not a bad man, Ted. I confess I feel for him. The way he preached that day you went—that's how he preaches now. It's about the Lord's succour, not war. And forgiveness, Ted—"

You have no fucking idea, he thought, bending for his shoes.

ONE DAY, RETURNING from a walk, he saw Scott in the distance. The minister was walking towards him along River Street, his head down. With a violence that was involuntary, Ted veered down a side street. Even in his panic, he knew he was acting unjustly. Scott had not invented the war; Scott had not made him go. He had chosen to go, if to act on an impulse was to choose. An impulse had chosen him.

Two days later, alone in the kitchen, he heard the back gate unlatch. The minister was coming up the walk. Ted went out to meet him.

As they shook hands, Ted could barely speak. "I'd like to talk," he managed. "Somewhere we won't be disturbed. Not here." He had no idea what he wanted to say. Talk had been their bond before the war; his request was an appeal to what no longer existed. They were meeting among ruins.

"We could go to the manse. There's only Abby there. We'd be alone in my study."

Ted saw the minister's wife prowling bleak, underfurnished rooms. He suggested Scott's office at the church.

"I can be there at ten Thursday." The minister had brought a book for Grace. He asked Ted to give it to her and went off.

HER EYE AT the cracked door regarded him. She invited him in, and for the first time since coming home, he saw her room. Before the war, its chaotic state had been notorious in the family: her things strewn everywhere, the bed unmade, teacups and plates drawing warnings about mice. Now her library was snugly confined to its bookcase, the top of her desk cleared; between window and bed, a simple rush mat absorbed the sun. Yet all around, the wallpaper's frantic tangling of flowers and vines made her tidying seem beleaguered, like a clearing in the jungle.

He handed her Scott's book and took the armchair she offered, while she sat on the edge of the bed. On the mat was a little gathering of red silky stuff. She snatched it up and stuffed it under the bolster.

"So John's sent you the Beatitudes," he said. He had leafed through it on the stairs. She fanned its pages, tossed it aside.

"I suppose he's trying to make an honest woman of me. I saw him the other day in the manse."

"You went to see him?"

"I did it for Mother—she wouldn't let it alone otherwise."

"And?" Since coming home, he'd felt drawn to her. She treated him with less self-consciousness than anyone in the family; it had always been so, but he had never appreciated her candour so much. She was abrupt with him, almost crude in her humour at times, chafed him when he acted rudely, ignored him when she felt like it, and behind it all was this reserve, the sense she was in hiding. He had seen her behind her flames.

"He talked about what a rogue he'd been when he was younger—drinking under a hedge and all that. He stole a horse once."

"I heard that one," he said, smiling. "The gallop on the moor."

"The thing is," she said, "I like John. Behind all that bonhomie, there's something half-destroyed in him. It's why he's honest sometimes, in spite of himself."

He wondered at that.

"He had to ask his minister's questions. But his heart wasn't in it. I felt he was running through a list."

"What sort of questions?"

"Oh, you know, how often do I pray? Have I read the Bible lately? What do I read? Then all at once out pops something else: he asked what I'm afraid of."

"And what *are* you afraid of?"

"Don't *you* start!" she warned, but then forged ahead. "Too many questions," she said soberly, looking towards the window. "And things that aren't—what they appear to be. And judgments, people's judgments. They're nearly always wrong. And—surprises. I can't abide surprises. What are *you* afraid of, Lieutenant?"

The question stopped him. He gazed into the deep space before him, where the little mat glowed in sun. "Just about everything," he said quietly.

He expected some wry riposte, something like, *That doesn't sound very soldierly.* But she looked at him directly, unexpressive. He hated being looked at like this: he felt she saw everything, knew everything. He looked away, and for some time they didn't speak. Lieutenant, she had called him; it had thrown him back into his other life. *Lieutenant, they're attacking on the left. Will we get leave, Lieutenant?* For a moment, he felt himself in uniform and had to glance at his knee to ascertain it was not so.

A sound yanked him from his reverie. Will was standing in the doorway.

"Brother mine, come in!" Grace sang. She had changed in an instant, something frantic in her cry. *Can't abide surprises.*

"I was wondering," Will said, "if we're still going to see the turtle."

"Of course we are!" she announced. "An expedition! You have to come too, Ted. He's found a giant turtle—monstrous, isn't that right, Will?"

"A snapping turtle," Will explained to Ted. "He's not really that big."

"You don't mind if I come?" he asked the boy.

"No," Will said skeptically, glancing at his sister. The family was worried about the boy: Shadows under his eyes. Nightmares.

"It's decided," Grace said. "We'll go right away." Saying she'd be back in a minute, she brushed past Will and went off down the hall.

Ted could think of nothing to say. Drawn to the boy, he was wary around him.

"The birds," the clear voice came. "I keep thinking about them, how they lived in the war. Why didn't they go somewhere else?"

Ted struggled through a fog. Then remembered the welcome lunch. "I suppose it was where they'd always gone—the birds," he began tentatively. The boy's innocence frightened him; he felt himself a threat to it, he who lugged around the bucket of filth that was the war. "Sometimes you'd find them nesting—right out where the shells would land. I-I was out there once—there was a nest, some young ones in it. Skylarks. They were raising their young in the middle of—all that. Owls, there were owls too, not on the Line, but in the places behind it. In the ruins, the ruined buildings."

"Why were they there?"

"Lots of rats and mice for them to catch. More than there had been, I suspect."

"Why were there more?"

Trapped, he stared at the boy. "Really, kid," he said roughly, turning away. "You don't want to know these things."

THE STEEP TRAIL spilled them through trees towards the river. At times they had to grasp at saplings, or abandon themselves to a sudden uncontrolled rush before fetching up behind some larger tree. Will was soon far below them, a shadowy figure dancing against the glitter of the Shade. Following Grace, Ted marvelled at how efficiently she managed the descent in her skirt. Her shoulders flexing in her light blouse, she moved with a fencer's poise.

They walked in single file upstream, away from the town, following a narrow trail that wound through grasses and weeds. The boy was going more cautiously now, stooping a little, signalling them to be quiet. Soon an inlet of brown water came into view. "That's where he sits," Will whispered, pointing to a large, flat rock near its far bank. "He's not there now, but sometimes if you wait ..." They waited, stooped with him in the heat of the June morning. Insects skimmed the little bay's surface, while bulrushes stirred dryly—a dank, saurian place, charged with intimations of nonhuman life. They waited in the spell of the boy's excitement, children themselves for a moment, Ted's shoulder brushing hers.

The snapping turtle did not appear that day. As they walked back, Grace drew their attention to a circling bird, a dot against a tower of cloud. Ted watched it longer than the others—a hawk, he was sure, probably a red-tail, its remote life turning in the blue—something far away, pure, not him.

7.

Letting himself into the church, Ted found the vestry unlit. The white collars of choir gowns, bunched on their rack, glowed in the dimness. Shards of yellow light flickered on worn hardwood. The door to Scott's office stood open. He peered into the little room with its walls of books. In a corner hung the dark chrysalis of the minister's gown. Ted sat, shifted, got up, returned to the vestry. Hearing a voice, he noticed the door to the sanctuary was ajar. Again the voice came, and in a moment, a small, solitary cry, like a child might utter in sleep. Peering in, he saw a sweep of empty pews, then Scott in a pew near the front. The minister was bent over and was gripping the back of the next pew. His forehead touching its wood.

Seeing Scott pray took him aback. It was like seeing one's own doctor in his sickbed—a breach of privacy that was somehow shameful. When Scott sat back with a sigh, Ted withdrew to his office. In a few moments, the minister swept in with his usual energy. Ted stood up immediately, the other man's presence galvanizing him as it had at the welcome lunch— something alive there, pent, unfinished. And fear. Why fear? He took Scott's proffered hand, but meeting the minister's teary eyes, turned quickly back to his chair. Scott too sat, not in his own chair behind the desk but on a wooden chair which he unfolded and placed facing Ted's.

"So," Scott said, his way of beginning their talks in the past. A bit of snot clung to a nostril—Ted experienced a flash of anger, seeing it. "I'm very glad you spoke to me. I've missed our talks."

Ted had trouble meeting the minister's gaze. There was too much desperate searching there. *Too much touch.* He moved his hand awkwardly to indicate . . . he did not know what.

"Yes, well," Scott said in a lowered voice. "It can't be easy coming back."

"Not entirely convinced I *am* back," Ted heard himself say. It seemed his voice, half-stuck in his throat, was going to betray him. "You've got marigolds," he managed finally. The pot was on Scott's desk, the little yellow flowers vivid in their stillness. He had not noticed them before.

The minister looked at them.

"Yes, marsh marigolds. Abbie McQueen brought me those. Lill's daughter. Picked marigolds don't last, but she brought the soil too."

Ted said nothing. He did not know why he was here but felt no impulse to leave. Again came the sense, common these days, that he had always been just here, trapped in a moment he could not escape.

"Ted, would you prefer to walk rather than sitting here?"

"This is fine," he said, stilling his jigging foot. And suddenly the words were there, delivered with a flash of accusation: "I'm not exactly that new man you prophesied, John. Didn't see any of them over there, either. All I saw was—" He broke off as a hostile grin distorted his face. What was the point? From the pulpit one morning in October of '14, Scott had forecast the birth of "a new man in the crucible of war." Fighting for a cause ordained by God, young men would be tempered to a whole new kind of courage and morality. That was the gist. "I've done terrible things, John. Things it would make you sick to hear—nothing to do with Christ. We're no better than the Germans." He spoke bitterly to the base of Scott's bookcase, then raised his eyes to the minister. There was a mass of poison in him—what he had said scarcely touched it.

"Yes," Scott said.

"Yes what?" Ted spat the words out. "You know nothing."

"No," Scott said.

Ted fidgeted, twisting in his chair; he threw his good leg over his bad and then shifted again, planting both on the floor. Why didn't he just get up and go?

"I've talked with some of the men who've come back," Scott offered.

"And you think you know? You'll never know, John. I could talk for a week and it wouldn't make any difference."

Again they were silent.

"We were naive," Scott said, his voice hoarse. "I was naive. We knew nothing of war. At least I didn't."

"That's a great help now," Ted said with scathing sarcasm. "You can't take it back, John."

"I don't take it back, Ted."

Ted looked away. So everything they'd been through, everything they'd done, was supposed to be assuaged by this admission of ignorance—by *words*?

"Belgium, Ted—were we to do nothing? Innocent people—"

"Lies, most of it," Ted said. "I have to get going."

"Would you pray with me?"

"I gave all that up—clearly not doing any good." He spoke savagely, trying to hurt the other man. Scott had once encouraged him to go into the ministry. He had been flattered but knew even then that his faith was a frailer thing than Scott imagined. He had cared more about studying history than the ministry; cared more, he suspected, about the Wars of the Roses than he did about God. Had he only been pretending then, to please the older man? Had he gone to war for him? He still did not know. That woman in the market. Some crazy impulse—

It was true that over there, *in extremis*, he had prayed. But he would not admit this to John Scott because he believed those prayers meant nothing—short, desperate prayers when the shells were screaming in. He had believed in God then—who hadn't? He would have prayed to the Devil if he'd thought it would help.

"We were carried away, Ted—but by what? God's will? I struggle to accept that, but I have to think that some good will come of it. We preachers like to say that God moves in mysterious ways, but then we get rather above ourselves and think we know what those ways are. It seemed true when I preached war, Ted. If I fooled anybody, I fooled myself first—the Devil's work, some might say. But maybe one day we'll see the good of it. A better world might come of it yet. After this, after what you've seen, isn't it reasonable to expect a change in people's attitudes? A war so terrible we never have another?"

"That's what the *newspapers* say," Ted said with contempt.

"Ted, the way you are now—the way I am, to tell the truth—that's the true business of Christ: not preaching war, making war. We've made a terrible mess. But He still offers His succour—I believe that, Ted. It's still here, to be taken up. It's not too late."

"I watched you praying, a few minutes ago. You looked like a man who was hoping to believe, not one who did."

Scott bowed his head. When he looked up, his eyes were watering. "Perhaps they're the same thing, Ted."

"What are?"

"Hoping to believe and believing."

"Sounds like sophistry to me."

His foot was going again.

"Pray with me, Ted."

"I told you I was finished with that."

"It isn't just for you, Ted. It's for me. Just be with me. Just listen."

Maybe it was inertia that held him in his chair, a kind of hopelessness. He did not want to look at the other man, not any more; but he stayed as the familiar voice wove its pleas, begged for forgiveness, promised humility. There was no God— the realization had come to him over there, not as a road to Damascus moment but through the slow attrition of his days.

As Scott's voice went on, his gaze strayed to the desk, where the marsh marigolds went on lifting their little flowers. For a few seconds, they became his thought: serene, mysterious, unchanging. The wreckage had claimed all of them, Ted thought—not just those who had gone away, but those who had stayed. Everyone was implicated. He had wanted to blame Scott, and the generals, and the Germans, and the animal in his own heart; he wanted to blame the men who'd grown rich from the carnage, and the women with their white feathers; but they were all implicated, himself no less than they, from birth implicated. They had broken a covenant—he felt this deeply. But what covenant? Again he looked at the marigolds. He had known those flowers as a boy when he plunged, carefree, through woods that led him to the river.

8.

Stink Henderson might be anywhere. Any alley might disclose him. A cloud might wear his face. Will took to going to school by the front hill—down River Street and up Charlotte—a detour that took him as far as possible from the territory ruled by Stink and his gang, although he still had to pass by King's Park, where they liked to loiter around the bandstand.

Once he tried to avoid the park by cutting through the Girls' Yard to the Boys'. But the girls jeered at him and evidently told stories, because the next day he was having a leak when Stink took the next urinal.

"So you're with the girls now, eh, McCrae? I think you *are* a girl, eh?" Stink crowed. He was in the relaxed mood of someone who knows he can have his way with the other guy, a cat with a wounded mouse. "McCrae's a girl!" he announced to Len Stott in the next urinal. Len craned to have a look. "Girly, girly," Stink sang, his eyes growing so small they nearly disappeared. "No wonder he's a coward!" Will's stream hadn't stopped when he stuffed his penis back in his pants. In class, he could not forget the cold, raw wetness or the odour he was sure made Carrie Manchester turn in her desk and stare at him.

In the yard, he kept close to Beggar Creeden—as close as he dared without appearing to follow. Beggar had saved him once; he might again. When Beggar moved, Will moved, imitating at a distance the measured, solitary drift of the older boy. Beggar Creeden's dad had been killed in the war. This fact, known to all, had conferred on Beggar a kind of sad glamour. With Beggar, the war was here, within the confines of the yard. It was in Beggar's deeply set eyes and long face, and in the way he took out his pocket knife and touched its blade as if to test its readiness, and in the blue gaze that seemed to conjure a space in front of him where events only he could see were happening.

As he kept track of Beggar, so he never lost sight of Stink, talking loudly amidst his friends. Beggar and Stink were the two poles between which Will turned, caught between hope and ruin. Stink's gang had claimed the spot where the Boys' Yard fence jogged off its line, making a sort of alcove where they hung about, shoving at each other or kicking at a deflated ball. Occasionally, one of them would look over at Will.

Beggar never stayed in one place for long. He would pause to talk to an acquaintance, then moved on to survey a game of flip-the-card. He took an interest in the garden of the house next door. He watched the passage in the street of a farmer's wagon before moving on, perpetually restless, as if searching for a chance, a sign, an opportunity—who knew for what? Others had lost fathers, uncles, brothers, but none of them seemed as alone as Beggar Creeden.

One day, Beggar spoke to him. "So is Stink giving you any more trouble, Will?"

"No."

"If he does—kick him where it hurts."

"Okay."

"You know what I mean—"

"Yup."

"He's all hot air you know. He'll go down like a horse."

"I know."

He didn't know; he didn't know anything as far as Stink Henderson was concerned. Stink Henderson wiped his mind of thought.

After that incident he felt hopeful and more frightened by turns—hopeful because Beggar had acknowledged him, but afraid because Beggar seemed to have abandoned him to his own resources. Kick Stink Henderson in the balls?

One day Miss Roberts kept him after school to discuss his geography project. On her desk lay his cardboard sheet pasted with pictures of Niagara Falls and the four short essays he had printed out, struggling to make his handwriting as good as he could for her: he loved Miss Roberts. It was not up to his usual standards, she told him. The wide, clear face, usually lit with merry good humour—her eyes were like a dolphin's eyes, he had often thought, recalling the sly, thin-lipped smiling of the creatures in *Animals of the World*—fixed him with concern. "You don't seem like yourself these days. Are you worried about something?"

He shook his head and wondered *Who is myself?* For an instant he felt there were two of him.

"Will, dear, can you look at me?"

His glance touched a place beside her eyes.

When he emerged from the school, the wide space of the Boys' Yard lay empty between its fences—everyone had gone home. Across the road, their backs to King's Park, Stink and two of his pals were sitting on the curb. He knew at once they were waiting for him. From behind him came the metallic clunk of the janitor locking the doors.

Light with fear, he walked towards the gate of the Boys' Yard. He passed through the gate and pivoted up Baird Street.

"Come over and talk to us," a voice called. "We just wanta talk!"

"We're not gonna hurt you. Just talk," Stink called.

When he heard the scuffle and slap of their shoes behind him, he did not run. He felt incapable of running. What good would running do? Ahead, the street sloped up Station Hill into a cloud of leaves. His home was there, in the leaves.

They surrounded him at the corner of Charlotte. "We just wanta talk," Stink said, panting.

He looked at Stink's crotch.

"Your family's rich, right?" Stink said.

Will said nothing.

"You live in a big house, up there on Snob Hill, right?" In Stink's sweating face was an eagerness Will had never noticed before—an eager, desperate wanting. "You got lots of money, right?"

"I haven't got any money," he said. He thought of the jar where he'd saved seven dollars for a microscope.

"Your mom and dad—they got money," Johnny Wilson said.

"Yeah, *them*," Stink echoed. "You can get us some."

"I thought you didn't want me to tell them," he said.

Stink looked baffled.

"He means what you did to him," Jackie Herrendorff said.

"*I* didn't do anything!" Stink protested.

"You bent back his finger."

"Oh yeah!" A grin of triumphant remembrance. "That's right," Stink said. "You get us some money or I'll break your fingers." His tongue between his teeth, Stink bent back his own finger a little to show what he would do.

"And if he tells—" Johnny prompted.

"Yeah, if you tell, you get it again."

They were almost friendly after that. Pounded him on the back and said they could all be pals. They might even let him keep some of the money. They wanted ten dollars. "Ten dollars!" Stink shouted as they walked away. "Bring it next Wednesday!"

"Wednesday!" Jackie called.

At home that evening, he listened to his mother's story about a buggy ride she'd taken as a girl. The horses had shied at a threshing machine and galloped down the road. He laughed when everyone else laughed—he was home with his family; he was safe, except that he wasn't. Out the window the branches of the spruce tossed crazily.

That night he dreamed he was trapped in a threshing machine, sliding ever closer to the teeth. Through a series of small openings, he could see his family outside. "Come out!" his mother cried cheerfully. She had huge wooden teeth. His father swung a rifle, aiming it here and there, the small dark eye of its muzzle coming to rest on him. "Don't kill me!" Will cried as his family went on smiling and waving at him.

Then Mim was in the room, hugging him, and soon Grace and his mother were there too. "A bad dream," Mother pronounced as he studied her teeth. Gracie coaxed him to tell the dream, but his mother said, "Don't make him live it twice. It's all nonsense anyway."

The next day, alone in his room, he took down the mason jar and spilled its contents on the bed: a few fifty-cent pieces, lots of nickels and dimes, a pile of shinplasters, a slew of pennies, the silver dollar his father had given him for his birthday, all of it reserved for the microscope he'd seen in a Toronto store. In its wooden carrying case lined with green felt, the microscope with its brass barrel was so beautiful, so promising of discovery, the very thought of it could cheer him. He had nearly seven dollars. He needed thirteen more.

Mim was in the gazebo. Through the sock stretched over her hand, her darning needle wove its way, dragging a strand of yarn. "How's my favourite brother doing?"

"Good," he said.

"That would be *well*," she said. "An adverb modifying 'doing'."

"Well," he repeated dully. The needle continued to work.

"Are you sure?" she said. "We're concerned about you."

"Are we rich?" he said.

The needle plunged twice before stopping. "What makes you want to know that?"

"Just wondering."

"In Grandpa Archie's time we were well off. But not any more."

"Why? Why aren't we rich any more?" His heart sank. He had imagined a plenty so great that a few dollars would not be missed.

"It's a complicated story. Your grandfather was in business, and at first he was very successful—he built this house," she said, gesturing to Brockwood's wall of pale ochre brick. "But then he made some decisions that didn't work out, so he—he had to go into debt—that means borrow a lot of money. And he wasn't able to climb out—"

He saw his grandfather, who he could not remember, struggling to climb out of a deep pit, and for a moment he felt close to him and to his whole family—something had happened to them, something he had not known about, and it seemed to him that a crack had grown out of his grandfather's action, like a crack spreading through ice towards the place where he stood. It wasn't just Stink. The crack had been coming for them for years. "So are we poor now?"

"Hardly poor. We're still better off than most. We've a lot to be thankful for."

When he started towards the house, she called him back.

"You know, if you're having trouble, you can always talk to us. Doesn't matter what it is. Or you can tell God—He's always listening, you know. Do you want me to pray with you?"

"Nope. I can do it."

But he couldn't. He lay in the dark in his bed with a lump in his throat trying to talk to God, but all he could come up with was the Lord's Prayer, and after that the Twenty-third Psalm, which he lost somewhere in the middle, its cadences passing him into sleep.

BEYOND WHAT HE had saved, he needed three dollars and twenty-five cents to make up the ten they wanted. His mother kept a bowl of change in a kitchen cupboard, from which she paid delivery men or the telegraph boy. He would borrow what he needed. He thought of it as borrowing because he knew stealing was among the gravest sins and he had every intention of paying it back. God had not said, *Thou shalt not borrow.* Yet hadn't his grandfather gotten in trouble because he had borrowed a lot of money, so there was a hole he couldn't climb out of? Was his grandfather in Hell?

And God was watching. God, who knew how many hairs were on his head and the names of all the sparrows who had died. One night, in the corner of his dim bedroom, he saw a cloaked figure pass through the wall.

The bowl where Mother kept her change was white with blue figures painted on it. People in dressing gowns met on an arching bridge. All around, little islands of trees and rocks floated in space. Lifting it down from the cupboard, he was surprised by its weight. He had planned to take only what he needed but ended by taking the whole ten dollars. Then, guiltily, he put the money back. So his microscope came and went. First it was saved, then lost again. Finally, it was saved. He was balancing on a chair, reaching to put back the bowl, when Mr. Sheaffer came in with a box of groceries. The old man said nothing; as usual he had a pencil tucked over his ear, and as usual his eyes glinted shrewdly behind his spectacles as if he guarded a secret that gave him an advantage over everybody else. Feeling his legs go weak, Will nearly lost his balance.

"What, no tip for me today?" the thin, mocking voice said. A peep of strangled laughter escaped Will as he glanced at the old man; and it was there in his eyes, lit now with gleeful triumph: *he knew everything*. Conscious of the weight in his pocket, Will left the room in misery.

HE SAW THEM in the bandstand—balancing on the railing, firing stones into the park. Noticing him, Jackie Herrendorff said something to Stink. They stared as he climbed the steps.

"You got the money?" Stink said with his eager smile, and for an instant he knew he had power over Stink. Stink needed what he had, and it seemed he might use this power to save himself. But Stink was here, waiting; his gang was here, and their power was here—the power to inflict pain, a thing he could not see but which seemed to hover in the air between them, brightening and sharpening the posts of the bandstand, their eager, half-smiling faces, the painted grey floorboards. He opened the little bag that had held his marbles, and with a sickening sense of loss loosened its string and tipped it over. Most of the coins stayed where they had hit the floor with a noise like falling chains, but several rolled away. The boys were on them in a second, crawling around his feet, scrambling under benches, stuffing coins in their pockets while Stink yelled that they had to share. Will watched them with contempt, but as he walked away, he knew he had joined them. There was a line he hadn't known existed, but now that he had crossed it he knew, with an ache in his throat, that he had left his old life for a life of theft and secret shame.

9.

The sisters were alone at the kitchen table. Miriam was writing up minutes for the League while Grace struggled to sketch her. "Keep still, Mim!" Grace cried, taking up her eraser. "Your nose is impossible."

"The story of my life," Miriam murmured.

"I'm no blasted good anyway. I don't know why I try."

Miriam looked up to see her scrubbing at her drawing. Grace was at perpetual war with herself—this was Miriam's long-held view. The furious way she brushed her thick hair or denigrated some hard-earned success—it had been going on for years, though Miriam felt it had grown worse since Toronto. "Here, let me see."

Grace shoved her pad across the table.

"You've certainly caught my eyes—and they're supposed to be the hardest, aren't they—the eyes?"

"The left one's too large and the brows are a mess."

"Well, *I* like it," Miriam said, flushing. She had only meant to be encouraging. When Grace scowled and took back her work, Miriam watched as she made a few more brusque strokes. It seemed to her that her sister was alone, alone with her drawing, alone in the unending fight with herself, alone with some invisible, immoveable object, fighting with all her strength to remove it, without avail.

"Gracie," Miriam said softly.

She had to speak twice before the startled, angry eyes looked at her.

"What happened in Toronto?"

Her sister's gaze flicked off into abstraction.

"You've changed—I imagine you know that better than I. Something's weighing on you, isn't it?" Grace made a couple of passes at her drawing before falling still. "Talking might help, you know."

"Talk," Grace scoffed. "I've told you before, I don't want it."

"Have you prayed about—whatever it is?"

Her sister blew out between compressed lips, dismissive.

"When you told us you weren't going to church any more, you did say you still prayed. You hadn't stopped believing—"

"I was lying. To get Mother off my back."

Miriam did not know whether to believe her. From childhood, her sister would sometimes say the opposite of what she thought, from sheer perversity. From a desire to shock. Restless, Grace kept looking around—anywhere but at Miriam. It seemed she wanted to leave, yet she kept to her chair like some errant pupil awaiting punishment.

Sunlight broke into the kitchen. Grace's face, backlit now, grew dim. "God has infinite understanding, Gracie. He knows our hearts. He's waiting for us to turn to Him—He won't force us. We have to turn to Him, but when we do—just that, the turning, that can help."

"Why do you always say *us* and *we* when you talk about God? I mean really, Mim, how do you know what anybody else's experience is? Why can't you just say what yours is? It sounds pompous, talking like that!"

Those dark eyes again, under the slightly lowered forehead, like a cornered animal.

"I'm sorry, Gracie, I didn't mean—"

In a single violent motion, Grace pushed back her chair, got up, and went swiftly to the back door, where she peered into the yard as if the source of her disturbance was there. Almost at once, she turned back.

"I don't believe any of it. What is this *God* we keep talking about—a bully who sends you to Hell forever if you don't tell him he's wonderful? And they say he has a loving heart! We've made him up, Mim. He's not there—nobody's there." Suddenly both her hands came up and slashed at the air in front of her while her face contorted. The spasm passed in a moment; her arms dropped to her sides, and she went on talking as if unaware of what had just happened. Miriam scarcely dared move. "I tell you I'm tired of it all—sick to death of it! I don't want to hear about *Him* any more!"

Grace stalked off, then turned back. "You're wasting your time on me—you can't help, Mim. There's nothing that can help. What's done is done. Can you understand that? *Done.* I'm sorry, but I can't—undo it. You know what I believe in? I believe in Time. Time cures all, they say. I don't believe that for a minute, but maybe it cures some things, and if it doesn't cure me then at least in the end it will get rid of me."

Miriam twisted in her chair as Grace swept past her, out of the room. Presently she heard the screen door bang shut, followed by the quick drumming of her sister's feet on the porch steps.

TWO DAYS LATER, the sight of the Presbyterian manse brought Miriam to a halt. In her hesitation came a hint of some other possibility, one not involving the visit she had planned. But the thought escaped her. With a sense of unease, she followed the walk to the grey door. In half a minute, her knock brought Abby Scott's anxious face. "Sorry, so sorry," Abby said, letting her in. "I was at the back. So sorry, Miriam."

"It's quite all right, Abby," Miriam said gently. "I was hoping to have a word with John."

"Yes, yes, certainly. I'll just check. So sorry." Like a convent nun, Abby hurried off on quick, silent feet, leaving Miriam in the entrance hall. Inevitably, her eyes were drawn into the parlour, to the framed photo of a small boy in a sailor suit, grinning from his place over the mantle. Little Paul, a presence in the house still. It had been three years since his drowning. To all appearances, John had moved on. Poor Abby in her black dress, murmuring her endless *sorries*, had remained trapped in her loss. The Scotts' tragedy had roused a world of sympathy for them both, but as Abby's mourning had extended, much of it had swung to her husband. Abby no longer appeared at church events to pour tea or support her husband. She rarely attended services. "She's hardly the first to lose a child," people whispered critically. Miriam sympathized with John but knew that Abby helped him in ways many were unaware of, researching his sermons and acting as his secretary, a godsend to John, who was on the executive of an international organization of presbyteries and needed her help managing his communications with them. She spoke three languages, including Korean, having grown up in that country as the child of missionaries.

Over the mantle, Paul continued to squint into the sun that would forever throw his shadow against the wall of the manse. He had crawled through a gap in a mill race fence to retrieve a ball. Reaching for it, he had fallen in. John, visiting a parishioner nearby, had had charge of the boy.

Before the war, Miriam and Ted had talked of having a family; they had played at names. But in John and Abby Scott's house, the prospect made her shrink.

"He said to come in, Miriam. In truth, I hadn't expected—his sermon, you know—well, I'm sure you know."

Entering the study, Miriam found the minister standing behind his desk. His welcoming smile cooled as he looked past her to his wife. Abby had followed her in. "Miriam, so sorry," Abby crooned. "I was just wondering—I've put on tea."

"Thank you, Abby. But I've had two cups already."

"Biscuits?"

"No thank you."

Abby seemed at a loss. She looked around as if granted only seconds to retrieve something crucial before the chance closed.

"You can leave us, Abby. We're fine for now," the minister said.

"Yes, yes of course! So good to see you, Miriam."

"You too, Abby. We must have a proper visit soon." When Abby left the door open, the minister strode to close it. On his way back, he passed behind Miriam's chair and at once his hands were on her shoulders. "Lovely to see you, my dear," his voice purred at her ear while his hands squeezed. She stared blankly as he took his seat behind his desk.

"I gather you're working on your sermon," she managed, feeling the heat in her face. "I could come another time."

He was smiling at her in his familiar, avuncular way. "No, no. Please stay, Miriam. It will do me good to talk with you. How are you?"

"Well, *I'm* quite well. It's not so much me, it's—" The great slab of his Bible, bristling with place markers, sat on his desk, while behind it he waited, the friend and comforter of old. She

was overreacting, she told herself. It was just the surprise of
the thing—

"Are you all right, Miriam?"

"Yes, yes," she said. "It's Grace," she said finally. "I'm terribly worried about her."

"Yes?" he coaxed.

Again she hesitated. "We were talking the other day in the
kitchen."

"Yes?"

"She's been troubled, as you know. Since she's come home.
We've been awfully worried about her." She was telling him
what he already knew; she was marking time, she suspected—
wasting *his* time. "She told me she doesn't believe in God,"
she said suddenly. Unable to look at the minister, she spoke of
Grace's anger against herself, and of the violence of her con-
tradictoriness. "I sometimes think there's something perverse in
her—I don't know if she really thinks these things or is pulling
the roof down for spite. I *know* she likes to shock people. She's
always done it. When we were children—" She broke off, aware
of hiding what had troubled her most: that uncanny spasming of
her sister's arms, and the contorting of her face in fear or rage.
For a second, she had been unrecognizable. *That* was the heart
of the matter; avoiding it, she felt she was being dishonest, but
the thing had been so strange, so utterly chilling, she felt she had
no words for it. Across the desk, his gaze had gone absent.

"Yes?" he said, coming back.

"I don't know—" Had he even been listening?

"It must be hard," he said.

Queerly, she thought of a snake she had seen as a girl—it
had reared half its body and looked around. A common garter
snake, but the movement had sickened her.

"As you know, she's stopped going to church, but I thought that at least—at least she still had *Him*. But she—she spoke positively ill of—" She had to break off.

"Yes, well," he said. "She's said the same to me."

She looked at him in surprise.

"Sitting in that very chair," he said, nodding at her. "About a week ago." There was a glint in his eyes, almost merry. How could there be? Was he mocking her? "It isn't final, Miriam—what she says or even thinks. It might only be a stop on the way to some understanding we can't imagine."

She considered this. "But there's only one understanding, isn't there—one answer?"

"In the end, yes. But there are many ways to it." His voice had grown thin, as if stifled in his throat.

"Ways that look like—"

"Like hers, yes."

"I don't know, John. It seemed so final. The violence in her—it frightened me."

"The very fact that she came here—asking—that means something, Miriam. It means she's searching—can you see that?"

"What was she asking?"

He chuckled. "She asked me to prove that God existed."

She looked at him, wondering.

"And did you?"

He laughed outright. "No, no, I'm no Jesuit." He looked at her with a sudden, grave directness. "I told her no one can prove the existence of God—that's all papist sophistry. You can only know Him, Miriam. Through faith."

"How can you know Him?" she said in a small voice.

"I don't think there's only one way. Some people, it seems

they're born knowing. Others—others have to go on a long journey, and even then they might not get all the way there."

He had taken up a glass of water and now drank from it, his Adam's apple working above the clerical collar.

"We're all searching," he said, and broke off to clear his throat. "When I was a young man—I actually was young once—young and full of myself. I felt I'd found the answer—"

"You mean our Saviour?"

He shook his head. "I hadn't really found Him. I was just swelled up with a sense of my own power." He looked at her meaningfully. The glint in his eye was back, but it no longer seemed merry. "I was burning with certainty—I felt I'd found the secret of life, and in a way I had, but I didn't know how to hold it, what to do with it—so I really didn't have it at all."

"I don't understand—"

"Finding Christ, feeling His power, what I *thought* was His power—I felt it gave me rights. That it allowed me to do what I—love, you know, there are so many kinds, and it's so easy to confuse them." He broke off, his face red. "Anyway, you haven't come here for this. I'm sorry."

"It's all right," she said quietly.

"I'm only a man, Miriam." His face filled with helpless candour as he stared at her, as if showing her his face—the sour, turned-down mouth, the eyes peering from their animal hollows. As if he had dropped a mask.

She did not know what to say. He took off his spectacles and rubbed at them with a handkerchief. She felt she had never seen his eyes before: they were small, like a bear's, and half-blind. He was blinking at his papers as if trying to make them out.

As she watched, he restored himself to his role. He cleared the few tears that had escaped; he put on his glasses. He was himself again, yet haggard and only half-convincing. "Don't worry too much about Grace," he told her in a dry voice. "I don't think she's lost—at least no more than the rest of us. Pray for her, Miriam, be on hand to listen, to comfort if she asks for it. And—I think it's best you don't tell her about her visit here. I shouldn't have spoken of it—she spoke in confidence."

Another silence fell as he studied his large hands, folded in front of him on the desk. Was he even thinking of Grace now? Miriam doubted it. Some great distraction was at work in him, had been at work perhaps the whole time she was here. He was alone with it. "Miriam," he said suddenly, coming back; behind the spectacles his eyes flashed at her, beseeching. "How's Ted doing?"

"Much the same," she said, struggling to come to the new thought. "At times I feel he's a little better. I think his walking helps, but then—"

"I spoke to him last week. Did he tell you?"

"No."

"He was terribly down on himself. For things he'd done over there. Well, he was down on everything, to tell the truth." Again he stared at his hands, palms up now as if to reveal their emptiness. "We prayed together," he said. "Or rather, I prayed. I think he was listening. Does he pray with you?"

"No," she admitted.

"I fear for him."

"I don't know," she said.

"You don't fear for him?"

"He's lost, I know. But there's something in him that isn't lost. I don't know how to put it. When he comes back from one of his walks, I can see it in his eyes."

"The old Ted?" he asked hopefully.

"I don't know what it is."

On the front porch he took her hand in both of his. "Come and see me from time to time, will you, Miriam? And Miriam," he added as she started to turn away, "pray for me, will you?" His request, delivered with a piteous hopefulness, took her aback. She said she would, but her own voice came weakly, and she was glad to get away.

HER VISIT TROUBLED her deeply. She could not understand what he had tried to tell her about himself. Had he told her he had failed to find Christ and was still looking? Or had he merely described the mistakes of youth? And what mistakes? And that comment about different kinds of love—what did that mean? As the days passed, she kept coming back to his insistence that he was *only a man.* In the moment, it had seemed a gesture of clerical modesty—the sort of thing a minister *would* say—but with time she felt a dragging sense of disillusionment. She could not reconcile the man she had just met with the man she thought she had known. She wanted her minister to be above her, to know more than she knew, to demonstrate a more confident faith, and for years, even with the lapse of his war sermons—which she believed he regretted—she felt she had found such a figure in John Scott. Now—his hands on her shoulders, the piteousness in his voice—she felt abandoned by him, and at the same time, assaulted. *Only a man?* It was as if he had stripped off his shirt.

At the same time, she wondered what she could do for him. She turned to prayer, her familiar refuge. Every night for years, no matter what problems she faced or anguish she carried, she always began the same way, with thanks for what she *did* have—small remembered gifts from the course of the day: for the way the sun had gilded a wall; for small acts of kindness she had received or witnessed; for her life. Often, at some point in her thanks, a leap of the heart would come, always unexpectedly; then she might cry out, inwardly, or sometimes whisper into the darkness, her love for God. *I love you, my Lord!* It was the apotheosis of her joy. She saw God as the source of all joy. Perhaps God was joy. Her cry seemed proof as well of God's love for her. To love God was to be loved by Him. This was the core and secret of her faith, uncoached by any theology or minister. All the rest—hellfire, even Heaven itself—was secondary to her. She knew that in believing as she did, she was going against what her church taught: against the tenets of the catechism. At times she didn't care. At other times she suffered from the sense that she was a poor Christian.

After her visit with the minister, the leap of her heart in prayer failed to manifest. It was not the first time. It had disappeared during the worst of her waiting for Ted; and again, at times, during his current troubles. Yet it had always come back, always unexpectedly, a sudden surge of gratitude. Now, hoping for it, searching for it, she waited in vain. Meanwhile, her days felt mired in exhaustion. Life, far more than usual, seemed dreary.

She saw that her sister was not dreary, at least not as often as before. Miriam watched her playing with their brother. They had set up the crokinole board on the porch and were pacing around it, bending to make their shots, teasing each other into missing them, until Grace, reacting to some jostling of Will's, began to chase him around the yard, both of them laughing. She had to admit that at such moments, Grace seemed happier than she was. Watching from the shadows, she was drawn to her sister. She remembered how at times, as a girl, she had envied her. Grace had seemed so much freer than she could ever be—little Grace in her underwear, bolting to run about in bare feet on the rain-soaked grass, impervious to Ada's scolding. And she was spanked, and the storms of temper came. And even then she was freer, somehow, amid those tumults.

10.

The shuttlecock drifted, darted upwards, floated like an inverted parachute towards the lawn, only, at another hit, to fly again. Reaching for a high shot, Grace banged it straight at Miriam, who ducked with a squeal, only to have the bird tumble softly over her shoulder. "I'll have you back for that!" she cried.

Ted was watching the sisters from an upstairs window, a little back from it so as not to be noticed—watching Grace mostly, the ease with which she moved, making her shots with a casual efficiency as if bored with the whole business. In the momentary tightening of her blouse, he caught a glimpse of unstayed curves; in her wide, full mouth, a succour he craved. "Come and see the rain," she had said in the greenhouse, as if speaking to a child. Grateful, terrified, he had approached her down a corridor of leaves.

Below, the bird flew past Mim's outstretched racquet and lodged in a bush. As his wife went to retrieve it, Grace turned and looked up at him, fixing him with such boldness he felt exposed. *You are there and I am here*, her look seemed to say. *This is how things are.* Galvanized, he tried to go on watching, but the thing was impossible now. He had been found out. Excited, chagrined, he retreated down the hall, his cane tapping along the runner to their bedroom. On the bed lay the book he had struggled to read that morning: Gissing's *By the*

Ionian Sea. At some point in the war, the printed page had become an antagonist, its literal meanings clear enough, but the underburden of meaning—what the words did not say but summoned into the circle of felt experience—gone. He snatched up the Gissing, read a few sentences, flung the book aside, and returned to his observation post.

The square of lawn was empty. Their racquets lay abandoned on a chair. His wife's straw hat crowned a nearby table. But joy! Their mixed voices rose to him up the back stairs. They were in the kitchen. Moving to the top of the stairs, he listened to his wife's tale of a dress Mrs. Baker had made for Ada. Apparently, the old woman had used the wrong material. "It looked like— well, it certainly wasn't her," Miriam said circumspectly.

"I saw it!" Grace cried. "It looked like a plate of Brussels sprouts."

He heard words of parting. Footsteps began their ascent. Limping without his cane, he retreated down the hall, considered the bedroom, and descended the front stairs. What was he running from? Panic bore him along, giddily. On the front porch, he was stopped by the sight of Dr. McCrae, smoking his pipe on the lawn.

They smoked side by side, releasing clouds that drifted past the roof of the porch. Secretly bound to the house at their back, he had trouble attending to their conversation. She had slipped her hand into his and for a long moment held it as they watched the rain dancing on the surface of puddles, gusting through the thrashing castles of the trees.

In the street, a gig clipped past, the horse's twisting head fighting the bit. "Patterson's," the doctor commented approvingly. "That was the horse that took the cup in Toronto." *I am here and you are there; and that is how things are,* her look had said. It was still with him, like the after-image of too much sun.

"You said you'd teach me how to shoot."

Will was talking to his father. Ted hadn't noticed the boy arrive.

"When you're older," Alec told him.

"But next year, in Cadets, we're going to shoot .22s."

"A shotgun is a very different thing. It has real kick—put you flat on your back. Anyway, that one you found in the attic, it's in pretty poor shape. Doesn't work."

"Ted, have you got a gun?"

He was looking at Ted directly now. Something in Ted leapt—the boy's words like an accusation. "Not me," he said. "Never want to see another one."

The boy went off. "I wonder what he wants it for," Ted said, looking after him.

The older man went on smoking. "Your leg," he said after a while, gesturing with his pipe. "You've been favouring it lately."

"A little maybe."

"I could look at it if you like."

"Mim's been at you," Ted chortled. The doctor looked at him without expression. Sobered by his glance, Ted spoke candidly: "I admit I've been concerned about it—been pretty hard on it lately."

Perched on the edge of the examining table in his shorts, he looked around the surgery as Alec removed the bandage. The glass cabinet with its trays and cases of instruments. The little oil painting by Paul Davies—a mare and her colt, standing in quiet intimacy in the shade of a chestnut tree. The double doors to the dining room were ajar: a glimpse of red flocked wallpaper. He strained for the sound of a voice.

The little hole in the side of his calf had closed, but the flesh there was hard, hot. It would have to be drained, Alec said, turning away to prepare his hypodermic.

The needle pricked around the spot. Minutes later, at the first touch of the lance, he winced.

"Need another shot?"

"Wouldn't mind one."

"Miriam tried to help me with jobs like this, but it's not really her bailiwick. Fainted dead away once," Alec said, again sliding in the needle. "Gracie, on the other hand—" He broke off.

"She'd make a good nurse," Ted said, perking at her name.

"Or a doctor. Lord knows she's got the brain for it."

"Maybe she will yet. Now that teaching hasn't worked out."

The doctor, intent on his work, would not be drawn. His large hands handled Ted's leg with a gentle insistence. Pus threaded with blood eased down Ted's calf. Alec mopped at it, tossing the wads in a bowl.

A dog suspended in midair. A yellow dog, glowing from the inside in a roar so loud it was like silence. He was flat on his back in a shell hole, watching a glowing dog.

"Are you all right?"

"Yes, yes, fine." He was sweating profusely. "You must have touched a nerve."

As Alec bandaged his leg, he told Ted to stay off it for a few days. "You've overworked it—that wound won't heal properly otherwise."

"Walking's the only thing that helps the—" He broke off, making do with a gesture. There seemed no word for what ailed him; it shamed him even to refer to it. The doctor was watching him closely.

"Shock? Whatever you want to call it," Alec said, "it can take some time to settle. Like a potato when you take it out of boiling water—it still cooks for a while."

He took down a book and removed the bottle hidden behind it. Poured two neat shots. They clinked glasses. "There's an old Irish myth," Alec said when they'd drained them off. His eyes sparkled. "Cuchulainn, you know, the great warrior. It was said that after a battle, he was so heated he had to be plunged into a vat of ice cold water—seven vats of cold water. His body was so hot he just steamed the first ones off. By the end, he'd cooled down."

"I'll give it a try," Ted said.

"There's more than a little truth in it," Alec said. Again he took up the bottle.

"Just a wee bit for me," Ted told him. "I really don't have a head for the stuff. I like it well enough, but with what little sleep I get, it doesn't help; not to mention the mornings."

"Ah yes, the mornings," Alec said ominously, pouring himself a big one.

Later, settled on the porch with an ice pack, he felt breezy, a little drunk—a holiday of the spirit had come upon him, as it sometimes did. Looking up, he saw his wife emerge from the house. His good wife, the wife he did not deserve, fresh in a different blouse and skirt, all cream and brown, new and lovely for an instant, her wide-brimmed hat worn slantwise. Yet those circles under her eyes: his careworn wife, worn caring for him. When she heard her father had seen to his calf, she cried a guilt-provoking *Wonderful!* He gave her so little, she had to celebrate over scraps.

She was off to choir practice, she said. On the street, she turned to wave. He waved gravely back. She disappeared. He smoked a cigarette. He bent his newly drained knee. When he heard the singsong call of a woman's voice, he knew before looking it was Grace.

Shadows on grass. That splash of blue and white moving on his left—Grace, yes, calling for her cat as she searched among the shrubs. He watched lazily, pleasantly buoyed, as she worked her way around the yard, calling in her husky voice for her darling.

"Have you seen Kiki?"

Grinning stupidly, he shook his head.

Under her arms, her blouse was dark with sweat: unlike Miriam, she had not changed. Stepping onto the porch, she saw the pack on his knee but made no comment. Seizing the back of a Muskoka chair, she turned it towards the yard and sat.

A glance gave him a bare arm, resting on the wide, flat arm of her chair. But it was what lay outside his glance that absorbed him; he could feel the heat radiating off her body.

"Aren't we the pair?" she said after a while.

"What? You and me?" He was pleased at being a pair with her, no matter of what.

"Come home with our tails between our legs."

"Is that where my tail is," he said, laughing immoderately. Everything was wonderful. He was terrified of the young woman of twenty-one sitting beside him, and everything was wonderful.

"At least you'll get a medal or something."

"Doubt that very much," he said.

"No medals for me," she said.

"No?"

"I miss my girls," she said after a while. "I miss the look on their faces when they finally understand something."

He nodded soberly. The look on their faces, he did remember that. The listening, the few times real listening happened. "You want to give them everything," he said.

She looked at him suddenly.

"You've felt that? I thought you didn't like teaching."

"I liked it when the student were good. *Was* good. I didn't have many of those. Lost of the other kind. Lots."

"The girls liked me," she said, her eyes glowing. "They'd do things they wouldn't do for Mrs. Bern, at least not resenting it every step of the way." She paused. "Well, that's over and done with. No one's going to hire me now."

"No?" he said. "But if you were a good—"

"I've been thinking about moving to England, if this blasted war ever ends."

"England?"

"It's not here, anyway," she said, flinging out her hand. The recklessness of the gesture shocked him; as if she had rejected everything here, including him; as if anything else would be better.

"I wish I'd been born a man," he heard her say. "Don't laugh, Ted."

"Not laughing." But he had smiled. Before the war, he'd heard her complain about being a girl—tomboy Grace. Kicking against the pricks even then. That time she'd climbed the tree, knickers flashing, Ada in an uproar.

"You men are allowed to do anything."

"We are?"

"While we get to sit and applaud."

"I'll applaud you any time you like."

"Don't patronize me, Ted."

"I mean, you only deserve it."

"I asked you not to patronize me. You don't know anything about me." She turned to look at him, square on—nothing like the look she'd given him from the lawn. She turned away just as swiftly, clearly wanting nothing to do with his compliments, his gallantry; he was left at a loss. "When I saw the soldiers go off, I envied them to bursting. They were getting *out of here.*"

"I should think they regret it now—most of them."

"If they'd given me a gun—," she murmured.

They were looking down the lawn together.

"Anyway," he said. "You did get out of here, farther than most."

"And now I'm back. Check."

Check? "Oh right," he said. Before the war they used to play chess. When she beat him, which she did about half the time, Ada would say, "I'm sure Ted's being generous." But he hadn't been. He'd been fighting for his life.

She was scanning the yard, looking for her cat, he guessed. He supposed he bored her. Her young life, so fresh, so independent beside him. To his eyes she was enviable. The world lay before her, whole; what was the loss of her job compared to this? On the lawn, the shadows of the trees had lengthened.

"So, what was it like over there, Ted?" She had turned to him again, and again her face had changed: not anger this time, but an openness. It was what he had seen on that first day, calmly watching him from behind her flames.

"What was what like?" he said, buying time. A familiar panic had seized him. He didn't talk about the war because he couldn't tell where talk would land him; and besides, no one here could understand.

He stared down the yard to the iron fence above the street. When he saw the river, he tensed. But it went on flowing peacefully, a transparency of ordinary memory laid over the shadow-streaked lawn. "There was this one time—," he said, and stopped, astonished at himself. Beside him, he sensed her waiting. A door had opened. Fields beckoned. And because it was Grace, and perhaps because he was a little drunk, he ventured further. "We'd been pulled off the Line. The whole battalion." His voice sounded raspy, as if from long disuse. "One day we were out marching—ten miles this way, ten miles that. It's what the army gives you to do when they can't think of anything else. We were coming down this hill. A few of the men had started to sing—they were great ones for singing, my lot. I let them go on with it—they'd earned it. Then this river was there. I didn't see it at first. *They'd* seen it. A great hullabaloo behind me—a real mutiny." He grinned. "They wanted to go swimming." He stopped, his throat working. The wide, khaki-coloured river stretched off towards the crayon stroke of the far shore. "So we let them." Kids again. Stripping off their clothes, running into the water. The white, beautiful bodies of his men—

"Did you go in too?"

His gaze found the iron pickets of the fence. "They taught us to keep a certain distance. A matter of discipline. I swam off by myself." He had swum to the far bank, a hundred yards off, letting himself drift under willows where the current was strongest. "There was this ferry upstream. Ran on a cable—silent—back and forth across the river. Full of women going to market. They had a cow with them. I was sure the damned thing would capsize—"

He told her how, swimming back, he had ordered his men out, and how they had dried themselves off with their clothes and gone on, their voices rising with fresh energy. There was much he did not tell her. He saw it with piercing clarity, but he did not tell her because he did not know if he could trust her or trust his experience, and anyway words were too difficult; he was surprised to find the few he had. When he excused himself, she said nothing, but nodded once, slightly, her eyes holding his.

With his cane, hobbling a little, he followed a lane to the Shade River. For a long time he stood looking over its brown water, dimpled here and there with the strength of its flow. It seemed to him that the Shade and the nameless river he had told her of were the same.

TALKING, HE HAD advanced warily, like a man stepping on mined ground. But the ground had held. He credited her—with what? He had been misled so often by his rare "good" days that he mistrusted any sign of improvement. But the experience led him deeper into his entrancement. More than before, the sound of her voice from another room alerted him. Her approach excited him. For her part, she treated him as if nothing unusual had happened.

A patient hunter, he took his cues from her behaviour. If she appeared locked in reverie, he did not break into it. If she was in a bantering mood, he bantered back. If Miriam and Grace were both present, he paid more attention to his wife while remaining covertly aware, a lover in hiding.

He and Miriam had given up trying. Yet now and then, desire slipped past his tensions. Watching Mim come to bed, her breasts free in her cotton gown, he wanted her badly. They kissed and touched, but as before, tenderness led to disappointment. Since adolescence, he had been able to count on getting hard. Now it was as if he had lost a hand.

Miriam was patience itself. She didn't care how long she had to wait, she told him: they would get there eventually. He sensed she *really* didn't mind. She had always been nervous around sex—something in her of the wild animal, trembling when touched. For months after their marriage, she would only make love in the dark. The first time he had seen her fully naked, he had surprised her as she stepped from her bath. Going down on his knees, he had pressed his face into the wet warm softness of her belly.

Around Grace too desire came and went. A flame along the backs of his arms. A stirring in his groin, swift as thought, as swiftly gone. He told himself his impotence was a good thing, insurance against any foolishness. But he raged silently. Christ, what a business! His ease in the world was gone. He jumped at shadows. He tramped the roads like some mad pedlar. And his pecker would not stand up.

But Grace. He craved something he sensed in her—something harsh, cathartic, without pretence. And behind her flames, her calm waiting—but for what?

One morning, thinking himself alone in the house, he noticed her in the library, a small room to one side of the entrance hall. An oval window let in watery light. Her head to one side, she was hunting along a shelf. "Find anything good?"

"Dad asked me to find something for him," she said absently, still searching. Her independence piqued him. He entered the room and began to browse the shelves at some distance from her. A volume bound in red boards caught his eye. *Medicine in the Ancient World.* Flipping its pages, he lit on a passage that drew him in. "Listen to this: 'The Greeks understood that music had restorative powers, and was not simply a source of pleasure and amusement. The physicians of the time would recommend their patients retreat to some temple, where they would listen daily to harp music and eat a suitable diet.'" Bent to a shelf, Grace did not respond. Her very back seemed to repudiate him. "Well," he concluded lamely, putting the book away.

"We don't have music in this house, not any more." Straightening, she turned to him. "Before the war, someone was always at the piano. Or we had the gramophone on. I never liked that thing—the voices so screechy and far away. We used to have dances. I don't know what's happened. Well, it's the war, isn't it? The war," she repeated sardonically. "No one plays that piano any more."

"Well, there's Mim," he said. All week he had heard his wife practising her part of a duet for next Sunday's service. *And the swallow shall build her a nest, where she may lay her young.*

"I mean for fun! We threw parties then. People would take turns playing."

"Why don't we take a bang at it?"

"What—you and me?" she scoffed. "I can't play."

"You *can*."

The upright sat in a corner of the parlour, topped by a square of crocheted lace and a pot of ivy. In the bench they found piles of sheet music: Bound copies of Gilbert and Sullivan in fading covers. Miriam's Scarlatti. The waltz from *The Merry Widow.* "Home, Sweet Home." "The Lost Chord." "Till I Wake." "On the Road to Mandalay." "Red River Valley." The good old songs from the good old days. A hapless sorrow was in him, sweetened by her presence.

Enlivened by their discovery, Grace sat down to the keys. She'd play "Camptown Races," she announced, flipping pages. She had played it as a student, she admitted, which he said was cheating, but she forged ahead, earnest in her sight-reading, glaring at the score like a bull about to charge while the music rattled out under her desperate hands. "Sing!" she cried.

"Not that thing—it's a travesty."

"Sing it anyway! Come on, *Doo-dah, doo-dah.*"

He sang for a bit before she grew dismayed by her own playing. They switched to "Red River Valley." When they got to the lines, "Come sit by my side if you love me, Do not hasten to bid me adieu," he sat down beside her. At once, the music stopped.

"Not that," she said, staring fiercely at the propped score. Abruptly, she got up and started toward the dining room, but quickly came back. "All right, if you're going to sit there, it's your turn. Go on, play."

He played a few chords. His mother had taught him for a while when he was fourteen, but he had rebelled at her discipline and gone his own way. He could play popular songs and hymns with reasonable competence. Now the simple harmonies his fingers released calmed him a little. He found the opening chords of "Abide with Me." When he repeated them, nodding at her, she began to sing. She had sung "Camptown Races" with angry exuberance. Now her voice, a slightly husky alto, bore up the great hymn. He played *pianissimo*, the better to listen to her. That ditch where he had waited in the rain. He had said the words then, like a poem. Believing in nothing, he had said the words. *Abide with me / Fast falls the eventide.* When she broke off, he cried, "Don't stop! Your voice is beautiful."

"I sound like a tomcat."

"Don't always assume the worst of yourself." He flushed, sensing his remark was a step too far.

"I'm tired of this," she said in a smothered voice.

He sounded a last chord, cut it short with the pedal, and stood up. "I've got a few things to do upstairs," he said. She was dismissing him, he felt. Her angry gaze had fixed on the rug.

Stalking past a pot of peacock feathers—what were *they* doing here, in the goddamned trench?—he was sent sprawling by the crack of a Luger. Someone's hand gripped his shoulder. He was on a rug in the goddamned parlour. She got him into a chair, then went off to fetch her father, returning shortly without him. Again she disappeared, coming back with water.

It was nothing, he assured her, shaking as he took the glass. God, let him not start that. She helped him get the glass to his lips. When the cold water hit his stomach, he vomited over her arm.

Helped upstairs, he insisted on going to the WC. Alone, he stripped off his trousers and shirt, took the clean ones she handed through the door.

He had felt he was someone else with her—new, better. Now that she had seen his truth, he felt condemned to it.

OVER THE FOLLOWING days, he sensed a coolness in her. The whole piano episode seemed dismal to him, a snarl of mistakes ending in his banishment. Meeting her in the hall one afternoon, he expected to pass by her, but she blocked his way.

"What's the matter with you?" she demanded. "I feel like you're avoiding me."

"No, no," he mumbled. But he *had* been.

"I promise I won't slam the piano bench any more," she said, eyeing him a bit sidelong.

"Oh that," he said, as if it had been nothing; but his face was hot. It had only been *that*. He hadn't known. "Sorry for the mess."

"That's the fourth time you've apologized."

He did not respond. He felt he no longer had any agency around her, but must wait, in shame, for her direction.

"I have great admiration for you, Ted. And affection." She placed her hand on his cheek. He had an urge, which he resisted, to grasp it and kiss her palm. But he had no sense of her borders any more; he had already breached them once, twice—who knew how many times? He would not take that chance again. Her hand patted his cheek, twice, as it might a child's.

Another bad patch had found him. He walked obsessively. His calf reddened, swelled, leaked a stinking pus. A bluish fragment of shrapnel surfaced and was plucked away by Dr. McCrae, who took the opportunity to drain the wound again and scold him for his carelessness. Changing his bandage, Miriam encouraged more rest. If he could take *a week* off—

"I'm all right," he told her angrily. He could not tolerate being limited; in fact, he was sick with self-loathing. The next day, Miriam tried again. Penitent, he listened. "There's a doctor in Toronto Nan told me about—"

"I'm happy with your dad," he said.

"I don't mean for your leg. I mean for—"

"People like me," he allowed bitterly. He took her in his arms, touching his forehead to hers. "I guess Grace told you what happened."

"No,'" she said, drawing back. "What happened?"

He was sorry he had mentioned it. "Nothing serious, I blacked out for a moment."

"No! Did you hurt yourself?"

"No—" Secretly, his heart danced, that Grace had kept the secret of his misadventure. It was something they had shared *and she had not told.*

FOR ANOTHER TWO DAYS, as much as for Miriam's sake as for his leg, he limited himself to short walks. Down to the post office. Out to the edge of town, where the countryside beckoned—hard not to go farther. Panic in him like a fire. The cool woodlots. The hidden roads overhung by trees—all beckoning. Yet his leg *was* improving. Tearing himself from the temptation, he tramped back to Brockwood.

A few days later he could restrain himself no longer. He tried to sneak out, leaving a note, but Miriam caught him in the act of writing it. They fought. He held his ground; he *would* go, even if—his secret thought, half-pleasant to entertain—he died doing it. As he left, Miriam reminded him of his promise to visit his parents. He'd drop by on his way, he told her—a sop to her disappointment.

He hastened through the centre of town, a route he usually avoided but which led to his parents' neighbourhood. There were too many people on the main street, each one a possible trap. There were too many veterans idling around the memorial to the South African war—torpid, broken men who'd been sent back early, like him. The very sight of them usually repulsed him, but today, their presence slipped his mind. Lost in his obsessions, he was about to cross Mechanic Street when he heard his shouted name and looked up to see them regarding him—half a dozen men lounging on benches or sitting on the granite steps of the memorial, their faces lifted in curiosity and the glee of surprise. He had no choice but to join them.

Their welcome came with rough, joking warmth—a rush of energy transfiguring their despondency. They called him Ted, Teddy. Several had known him from boyhood.

They'd heard he'd been made an officer—was that true? "Lieutenant," he said with a shrug, and for a moment felt like one, an officer before his men, leaning on his cane. For a moment he was there again, where life was simple and you knew who you were.

Slumped over his crutches, here was Carl White, who had grown up on the same street as Ted. *Why hadn't Ted joined the local regiment?* Carl wanted to know. "We're not good enough for you then?"

"Expected to," Ted said. "Then I was in Toronto one day and the damned thing was just there—the recruiting station. I just walked in." No one challenged him. They understood how their lives were governed by chance. Not one of them expected to be where he was now. The man in the wheelchair had lost a leg—Harvey Dowd, who used to work in the plough factory. Shorty Long peered at him with one eye. Mike Stokes, a gleam of metal below his sleeve, looked over Ted's cane skeptically. "So what's the matter with you then?"

"Shrapnel," he said, giving the side of his leg a tap. "Made a mess of things."

"You still get around pretty good."

"Good days and bad."

The others too were looking at his leg. Compared to them, he knew he'd gotten off lightly. Yet he wasn't about to start explaining about the other thing—most of them were probably grappling with it themselves. He was aware of a certain disparity. They were working-class boys like himself. But he'd gone to university. Married Miriam McCrae. Been made an officer. Standing before them in the glaring sun, he was uncomfortably aware of his advantages.

Above, the stone warrior on the plinth continued to hold up his rifle in triumph, a satiric comment on the men at his feet. Conversation lagged. Ted rocked on his heels, picked at the ground with his cane. Yet despite his impatience, he lingered, fascinated by a man on the bench. The fellow had not spoken a word. The lower half of his face was covered with a calico bandana. Above its horizon, brown, glistening eyes watched Ted hopefully.

"I feel I know you," Ted said, taking a step towards him.

The man's answer was more animal sound than language. Ted couldn't make it out.

"Artie Walsh," someone offered.

Stunned, Ted went to him immediately. Artie's hand clamped fiercely around his. He had taught history to Artie: an earnest, hard-working boy, not terribly bright but keen to do the right thing. He had once brought Ted a half-dozen tarts his mother had baked.

"Good to see you, Artie," Ted said, lowering his voice.

From behind the bandana came another animal grunt.

"I take it you're robbing banks these days."

"Trains too!" someone shouted, raising a wave of laughter from the others. It passed through Artie's eyes as for a moment Ted was held again by the old, rough camaraderie of the trenches.

"How are you doing otherwise?"

"O-A," said the muffled voice.

"Okay?"

"Uh-huh."

"That's good then." As they talked, the other veterans added their own two cents. The whole mood of the group had changed. They were quieter now, listening with a kindly attentiveness.

"If I can help you with anything, let me know."

"O-A."

Climbing the hill into the south end, he stopped to slash viciously at a forsythia bush with his cane.

The house he had grown up in had scarcely changed. Bracketed by sagging shutters, three windows overlooked the tiny front yard. He heard his mother's piano from the street. She was playing "Come to the Fair," the gusto of her attack stopping him, his heart momentarily lifted by the familiar tune. In the old days, he and Terry would sing along. *The sun is arising to welcome the day. So it's heigh-ho! Come to the fair!* For a few minutes he stood in the street like a ghost outside the house where he had once lived, spellbound.

"You should come more often," Rose told him, letting him in. "Then I wouldn't have to bawl like a baby each time you do. Your father's in the garden."

"Georgie!" she bellowed, starting towards the back door.

"I'll find him, Mum."

"I'll put on the kettle."

Walking through the familiar rooms—the dining room so crowded with table and sideboard there was scarcely space for their facing armchairs; the kitchen with its yellow icebox and pink walls—he was sickened by a sense of déjà vu. The old life, dead to him now.

To his relief, his father acted as if his visit was nothing special. They stood talking about his garden with a casualness neither of them felt. He had never been able to read George, not really. Something hard there, walled off. His father's father had been hard, Rose had once told him. "Pulled George out of school on his tenth birthday, sent him to work in the fields. And temper! The man was a flaming devil. Went at his kids with a strop."

An animal was eating his plants at night, George complained. Shredding his lettuces, digging up his carrots. "A
bloody raccoon, I should think. I found some scat."

At the table, his mother said in her fierce, direct way, "Are
you getting better then?"

"Well. It's going to take some time, isn't it? Grace is taking
good care of me."

"Grace!" his mother shouted.

"Miriam," he muttered, flushing. "I was just talking to her
sister." This was not true; but he had just been thinking about
her.

"She's a good one, that Miriam. You hang on to her. She
dropped by a lot. Still does," Rose added, a hint of accusation.
"We went berry-picking you know."

"She wrote me about it."

His mother told the story anyway. He heard something Mim
hadn't mentioned. "We made jam when we came back. That jam
there—" She pointed to the jar. "She went up to your room, just
to have a look. I found her sitting on the floor. She was bawling
her eyes out—quietly you know, like the lady she is. I brought
her down to the kitchen. I was bawling myself by then. We had
a jolly good cry. We talked about you, then somehow we got on
to Terry. She would have been nineteen last week."

Ted's sister, dead at twelve. For an instant she was in the
room with them. A lightness passing, and in its wake, the endless coughing and a smell of carbolic acid. They sipped at their
tea, poured from the cozied pot, in silence.

"I could wring the Kaiser's neck," Rose said.

"She would too," his father said, reaching for a biscuit.

"The men who hang around the memorial—are they getting any help?" Ted asked.

"They're with their families, most of them," George said.

"I should think they have pensions," Rose said. She turned to Ted. "You should be getting yours by now. Has it started yet?"

"Not yet," he said.

"Give it time," his father said.

"Time," his mother scoffed. "Time cures all, they say. I don't know," she added, looking bleakly askance.

He forced himself to stay for an hour.

"Where are you off to now?" Rose demanded at the front door.

"Mother," George cautioned.

"I'm only asking." She turned to Ted. "You're not right yet, are you? You can't sit still a minute. You should see a doctor. I know you've got Miriam's dad, but if you went to the city, they might know more about it."

He made his way through the south end, down streets he could have walked in his sleep. A Saturday morning. Kids playing everywhere outside the little houses. From the Flats, the mills' whistles howled, releasing workers from the weekend half-day. He kept getting stopped by people who recognized him. When they asked him to come in, he made excuses, then stood talking with them to make up for his rudeness. The crawl of panic. Knotblades in the brain. Soon others arrived from the mills. Betty Tomlinson. Sam Wishert. Little Meg Kelly. He worked his way along and was nearly out of the neighbourhood when Annie Carter called to him from her yard. Her husband had been one of Ted's best friends—a sports friend, no scholar, but a great fellow to have beside you on a diamond or a frozen pond. Brady had signed up a couple of months before Ted. He was back now, Annie said. Ted hadn't known.

She lowered her voice. "He's in a bad way, Ted. He's lost all the fingers on his right hand, but it's not just that. He can't sleep. Doesn't want to come out of the house. If you could talk with him—"

As he followed her to the house, a boy burst from the back door with a lacrosse stick—their son, Charlie. His mother called him over. Shaking Ted's hand, he glowered evasively before running off. Ted waited in the kitchen while Annie fetched Brady. He could hear the couple talking in a back bedroom. Brady emerged wearing a spectral grin—an aged version of the man Ted remembered. He offered a boisterous welcome, as the men around the memorial had, while his eyes blazed with desperation. He held up his hand—a strange flat paddle with a knobbly end. "Left five good ones in France," Brady said. As they sat at the table, the energy of their talk drained while Annie made tea. She served it and slipped out of the house.

"You've had a bad go," Ted said. His own foot was going like sixty under the table. Maybe they should try vaudeville. The Dancing Fiend and the One-handed Banjo Man.

"The whole thing's a bloody cock-up."

"Seems so," Ted said.

"Nothing seems about it."

For a long while both were silent, held by the thing that could never be described—it was enough to know that the other knew it. Now and then their tea went to their lips.

"Want something stronger?" Brady said, nodding at Ted's cup. Out of politeness, Ted said he wouldn't mind. "Annie empties my bottles when she finds them. She can't find them all though." He disappeared through the cellar door. In a minute he was back with a bottle of what looked like local hooch—an old medicine bottle with no label. He held it under his arm to uncork it and poured a generous shot into Ted's cup. The stuff tasted terrible, a real home job—he sipped a little for Brady's sake.

"They used electricity on me," Brady said. His look to Ted was direct, accusatory. "Trussed me up like a chicken. Couldn't do a fucking thing about it." He gave a derisive snort. "They sent me back after that. Told me I was cured. I knew I wasn't. Something not right in my head. I couldn't think straight. It took this to get me out," he said, holding up his hand once more.

"Well, you're back now."

"Annie doesn't deserve this. I walloped her the other day. Swore I'd never do that."

Ted fidgeted in his chair.

Brady drank, considered. "How'd you get out?"

"Leg, shrapnel." Ted shrugged.

"The perfect Blighty," Brady said. "It's more than your leg though, isn't it?"

Ted shrugged in acknowledgment.

"How you deal with it?"

"I walk."

"You walk! Christ I'll take drink any day." Brady drank, chortled, looked thoughtful. The war was between them, a great, humming blank. It was nothing, and yet it had weight, nearly insupportable. It pressed on their skin, their eyes, their minds. "They made you lieutenant, I hear. They wanted me for corporal. I said I'd do it if I didn't have to wear their fucking pips. A death sentence as far as I was concerned. The fucking Boche—they see those stripes and that's the end of you. I told them where they could put them." The spectral smile came again. "The next fellow they asked took it on. God how that prick lorded it over us. We used to talk about shooting him ourselves. The Boche did it for us. Deprived us of the pleasure." Over the lip of his lifted cup, a gleam of broken teeth. Later, when Ted made noises about leaving, Brady started into stories from their boyhood. There was always one more. Like Scheherazade, Ted thought. Brady would talk forever if he could: to postpone the moment of their parting. But he had to leave: foot going again, the kitchen too small. He got as far as the back porch when Brady jabbed him in the ribs. "Remember that time we put old man Featherstone's outhouse on his roof?" Ted remembered. Tick-Tack night, a week before Hallowe'en. Boys and young men running wild through the dark. Soaping windows. Setting fires.

"Christ, those were the days," Brady said.

TED STRODE UP the Mile Hill road under trees that swept him with ragged nettings of sun and shadow. Far below, the khaki river, spreading through a bend, bore flickered lights among their trunks.

At the top, fields spread streaks of green and bronze. High and higher, clouds piled their hazy ranges, motionless against the blue. It was all before him, the promise of release; except he couldn't feel it, not really. He was chasing it, looking for the door. Past tumbled stump fences he strode; past a farmer cutting first hay; past the switching tails of cows in a fly-blown corner, left right, left right, not marching within the portable safe home of the battalion—nothing of that order—but hurrying on, sensing in the clouds towering at his back a stalking danger. From outside the tattoo of his boots, a dog's yapping startled him. The thing was barrelling down a laneway. It followed him for a while before, duty done, it turned to the leisurely investigation of a ditch.

After half an hour he reached a village. He was drawn to the villages—lonely medieval redoubts in the sea of fields. One moment he was striding between crops of winter wheat, the next passing a house of dressed stone; a school and its abandoned teeter-totter; a church beside its shaded graveyard; a store under its checkered Purina sign; boxcars waiting out- side a mill. Stands of weeds and wildflowers buzzed softly. Peace lay all around, somnolent in the heat, a gift he could not absorb. In the shade of a porch, a woman's bare arms worked a churn. She paused to watch, and when he glanced back, she was still watching.

11.

Over in their corner, Stink and his gang were eating candy. It had appeared the day after he'd given them the money. They ate it before school and at morning recess; at noon they disappeared, returning freshly provisioned. From soiled paper bags, pipes and strings of liquorice emerged; jelly babies, packages of gum; one day they brought a Cadbury's Milk Tray, another the stumps of ice cream cones they nursed while the stuff ran down their wrists. Now and then they lifted their heads to look around with glazed eyes. Realizing he had bought a kind of safety, he dared to venture farther from Beggar.

When the candy-eating ended, they began to show an interest in him again; again he drifted in Beggar's wake. Then one day when Beggar was not at school, they force-marched him to their corner. They wanted to give him a present, they said. They told him to open his hand. Warily, he did as they asked and was rewarded with three blackballs dropped into his palm. They said they'd saved those three for him; they clapped him on the back and called him their pal. They said they'd take him fishing. "Triple hooks," Stink explained. "We put bread balls on them, drop them under the wall there, by Bannerman's dam—we catch these big suckers."

"Huge," Johnny Wilson said.

"We hook 'em underneath," Stink said. "Hook their bellies."

"Hook their eyes!" Jackie Herrendorff put in. "My mother cooks them."

Cooks their eyes? he thought. Stink's cat face grew sly. "So you have to get us more money, okay?"

"I gave you everything," he protested. "Everything I saved up—" This was a lie: he had given them his mother's money, but in their company he would say anything.

"Get it from your dad," Stink said, still jovial. "He's rich."

"Yeah, he's rich!" chimed the others, buoyed by the very idea.

"We used to be rich, but we're not any more," he told them. Panic was in him now—that terrible lightness. "My grandfather lost it all. He got into debt—he couldn't climb out."

Stink's mouth hung open.

"You live in a big house," Jackie said.

He had no answer to this; he had never thought about it.

"Yeah," Stink chimed. "A big house. So you're rich, right?"

"*I'm* not rich. I'm just a kid. *They* have the money."

"Who does? "Stink said suspiciously.

"Them, my mother and father. But we're not rich."

"Liar," Stink said. The change in him was instantaneous. His tongue came out and his face filled with hideous concentration as he seized Will's wrist. Will shouted, but only his wrist existed now for Stink.

"Ow!"

"Shut up," Stink said, glancing over his shoulder. In the busy yard, a couple of boys were looking their way. "Get us another ten dollars or you know what happens."

"Let go of me!"

"So are you gonna do it?" Stink said. Will looked at Stink's crotch. Stink gave his wrist another crank.

"Yes!" he shouted.

Stink twisted his wrist again.

"Ow! I said I'd do it! What are you doing?"

"He said he'd do it," Jackie told Stink.

Stink looked confused. After a moment he let go of Will and patted his shoulder.

"Tell him when to bring it," Jackie said. "The money."

"Yeah," Stink said. "Bring it Wednesday. Ten dollars."

"Fifteen!" Johnny said.

"Fifteen," Stink said.

As he walked away, it seemed a raging fire was behind him, and when he opened his hand—the one Stink had not held—he discovered he'd gripped the blackballs so tightly they had begun to melt.

THE NEXT MORNING, he watched his mother paying the milk-man out of her bowl of change—it seemed she hadn't noticed. Might he risk taking more? On Sunday he watched his father set a crisp, folded bill on the collection plate as it passed through their pew—a whole plateful of money passing under his nose. Somehow, from somewhere, he had to get some. It seemed entirely plausible that Stink's brother would come looking for his family—such an event would be just another part of how things were, along with the deaths of fathers and brothers, and the wounded men around the war memorial, and the Lee-Enfield in the Colonel's hands, and the cold light in Ted's eyes. Something terrible was running under everything like a black river.

ON TUESDAY, BEGGAR CREEDEN spoke to him in the yard. "I hear Stink's been giving you a hard time."

His hands went cold.

"They're blackmailing you."

"Um—"

"They're making you give 'em money."

He looked at Beggar. How did he know?

"Okay. We're gonna visit those guys. After school." The announcement shook him. It occurred to him as he stared at the numbers exercise Miss Roberts had printed on the board that Beggar was going to make him fight Stink. It was the phrase *after school* that had done it, a phrase thrown out as a threat when one boy was challenging another. *After school*, and word would go round that Dick was going to fight Harry; so that *after school* not only Dick and Harry showed up but two dozen boys of all ages, crowding around the patch of bare earth by the bandstand, where for some reason fights happened.

Now he was afraid of Stink and Beggar both.

After school, Beggar was waiting for him in the yard.

"I don't want to fight," Will said.

"C'mon," Beggar said.

In the park, Stink and three others crawled out from under the bandstand. They had what they called their clubhouse in there. Sometimes you saw the smoke from their cigarettes rising from the cracks in the floor.

"I wanta tell you something," Beggar told Stink. "You see this boy here?" He gestured to Will without looking at him. But the others looked at him. Will looked at a tree. "He's my friend, okay? Now I know he's your friend too, isn't that right?"

Stink and his gang looked bewildered. Will thought, *I'm Stink's friend?*

"And I know you wouldn't do anything bad to him, right? Right, Stink?"

"O-*kay*," Stink said ponderously, drawing out the word. He clearly had no more idea than Will what was happening.

"And you wouldn't do anything bad to him, would you, Jimmy?"

"Not me—"

"And you, Ron?"

"I didn't do nothing."

"Good," Beggar said. "So we're all friends. You and me and my friend Will here. *My friend*, Stink. We're all pals. Okay, Stink?"

Stink pulled a face as if he was trying to get something out from between his teeth.

"And friends don't hurt each other, right? Right, Stink?" Beggar said, his smile bright with sudden menace.

"Right!" Stink said, almost shouting.

"Good," Beggar said. "You're all on board. Let's go, my friend," he said to Will.

As they walked away, Will sensed Stink and the others watching across the silence that followed them. He did not understand what had happened, or what had been agreed to; he hardly dared believe he was free.

When Beggar suggested Will come home with him, he said he would; he didn't want to, not really, but he felt he owed it to Beggar and besides, with Stink and the others watching, it was probably safer. He could not quite believe that what Beggar had said about being friends was strong enough to protect him. But as they crossed the park, the silence held, and when he glanced back, the others were still watching.

Beggar lived in the Junction, he said; Will thought of that place of hooting, shunting trains. He said his dad used to do "rag and bones" before he joined up. "Feenie McCoy does it

now—I help him. He's not nearly as good as Da was." He
said his dad had brought home all kinds of great things that
people had thrown out: a lacrosse stick, a bugle, a nickel pistol.
"Da didn't let me keep that. That was okay—I already had
my .22. We can go shooting if you like. One time he found
a lady's hat—just like new! He gave it to Ma. She wears it,
but she says I shouldn't tell where we got it from—don't tell,
okay?" In Beggar's deep-set eyes a shy humour glimmered.
His grin revealed gaps in his teeth—crooked teeth splayed out
with spaces between. "Oh ya, a chess set—all the pieces but
one. We use a chestnut for that one. A knight. Da was teaching
me to play—"

They were climbing the long road towards the Junction, a
way Will never went. Below, on their left, back yards and gardens went by, each with its privy, its bit of garden guarded by
tins on a string. A woman was beating a rug. By a mill, water
skimmed the face of a dam. He felt queerly disoriented. His
river was the Shade; he had only to cross the street and take the
lane through the Bannerman estate; a short run through the
woods would bring him to the placid river behind Bannerman's
dam. But this was a different dam, a different river, smaller
than the one he was familiar with. He did not know its name.
He had no idea where he was.

At the top of the hill, a line of boxcars rumbled past. For a
while they walked alongside the moving train. Between two
houses he saw a gap where two seagulls floated; he intuited an
immense spaciousness below them. It was as if Beggar had led
him into the sky.

Beggar's house was unpainted, the colour of driftwood,
two stories high, with stark, unshuttered windows and a
veranda that sagged—the very look of it saddened him. When

they passed through the door into the strange other-smell of Beggar's life, he wished he had not come. Glancing into a room, he saw a girl hugging her knees on a window seat. He had seen her at school, playing in the Girls' Yard. That girl had been skipping happily; this girl looked very alone in the big room almost empty of furniture. Following Beggar, he entered a smaller room clouded with steam. A pink-faced woman worked a mangle. Hanks of her hair swung past her sweating face as she glanced around at him. Under a table, a small child in a dirty pinafore was howling.

Something smelled good.

"Take Lolly," the woman ordered Beggar.

"What's the matter with Carrie?"

"She's the queen today, apparently."

When Beggar stooped to pick up the child, the woman looked again at Will. Beggar said, "This is Will McCrae, Ma."

"The doctor's boy?"

"Yes, ma'am," Will said.

Beggar pushed past him with the child.

"Barry," she shouted after him. "They've got more laundry at the hotel. You have to pick it up by six. You stay there a second," she told Will. She did something with a wooden spoon. "All right now, so you're Dr. McCrae's boy."

"Yes, ma'am."

"Tell your daddy I'll pay him by the end of the month. He said there was no hurry, but I don't like debt. Can you tell him that for me? Mrs. Creeden, tell him." She was speaking more kindly now, with a look that warmed him. "Would you like a cookie? I just took them out."

"No thank you, ma'am."

"Well, have a look at them before you say no," she said with a wink. She held the pan out to him. Oatmeal. "I had to use molasses—the war, you know—but they're still pretty good." He took one.

As he stood eating it, she spoke of Beggar. "He's a good boy. I don't know what I'd do without him. He's taken it hard, losing his father. He was killed in the war, you know, Barry's father. They were close, the two of them."

When Will caught up to Beggar, the girl from the window seat was jouncing the baby on her hip; Beggar was climbing the stairs. "I'll just get my rifle," he called back. Will was alone with the girl. She was about his age. She smiled at him with a merry shyness. Her hair was plaited tight against her head in a way he liked.

FAR BELOW WILL, Beggar dropped swiftly through trees. Will kept glancing at the gun riding at Beggar's side. In a blaze of sun, he reached an area of flat rock and found Beggar studying the river.

"That's First Rapids," Beggar said, pointing upstream to a flickering line. "Over there's the Willow Woods. There's a big rock in there where an Indian chief's buried." It was a greeny place they were in, shaded by the steep hill at their backs, with the little river slipping away down watery ledges out of sight. "See that?" Beggar said, again pointing. Downstream, a bleached tree trunk lay serpentine on an expanse of pale rock. "I'll set some bottles up." He left Will to hold the gun while he scampered away. The rifle was like a baby brother to the Lee-Enfield that had torn through Will's grip, and in his hands, somehow alive.

Beggar was back in seconds to take the gun and send a considering look towards his work: two clear bottles, one missing
its neck, and another smaller blue one, balanced along the tree
trunk. "You know how to shoot?"

He could only shake his head. It seemed to him that he was
poised on the edge of knowing something he should not know,
and yet he was drawn to it, held less by curiosity than by recognition: somehow, he knew it already.

From his pocket, Beggar took an object he held up between
forefinger and thumb. "Twenty-two long," he said, and Will
saw the small brass cylinder with its pointed grey tip. The bolt
came back, the bullet was slipped into the chamber, the mechanism was closed with the satisfying sound of machined parts
working to perfection. "Now you do it."

Beggar had him do it three times, and each time his hand
loved more the action's sweet, repeated success.

Beggar took back the gun, knelt, aimed it towards the bottles. But though Will watched in suspense, he did not fire.
Beggar spoke of stillness, and aiming, and of the slow squeeze
of the trigger while you held your breath. He handed the
gun back to Will. "All right. Don't be skitty. Take your time.
Fire when you're ready." *His name is Barry*, he thought, and
squeezed the trigger.

The crack echoed around the hillside. The three bottles
stood as before.

"Try again," Beggar said, handing him another bullet.

Aiming, he could not hold the barrel still; it kept making
tiny, indiscreet movements as if changing its mind.

In despair he fired, and on the log one bottle, a clear one,
exploded. "There you go!" Beggar cried. "We'll stop while

we're ahead—that's enough bullets for today anyways. Cost money, bullets."

He followed Beggar upstream along a trail that ran over grassy turf, jogged onto mud flats where Beggar pointed out the skeleton of a pickerel picked clean by otters, rose though a split rock, ambled among the huge trunks of willows, their leviathan crowns hung with dead weeds and a solitary window frame. From that coolness, they emerged onto another shelf, where they sat cross-legged looking over the water. Upstream, a giant elm stood drenched in sunlight. Somehow, in no time at all, he had grown older.

12.

Up and down the slope, the pines stood in their stillness. Occasionally wind soughed through them; then, far above, the great crowns heaved like a sea. But it was their times of stillness that drew Ted most powerfully—the sun-sprinkled hovering of boughs that seemed to hold everything he had lost.

He had come here as a boy. While the shouts of his friends grew distant, he would stand solitary, aware of a presence of which he seemed a part. Once, on his way home, he heard a strange drumming sound. Creeping forward, he saw, in a hollow below, a grouse beating at a log with its wings—lonely as himself yet not lonely in the springtime grove. He had come here again with Mim, before the war. Now, in his travails, he was here again. All around him, the straight, dark trunks stood ranged across the hillside.

His back to a tree, he had a clear view of the flats below, where the main path wandered through the grove. Lower down, the Shade flickered behind trees. He was struggling as usual for calm. In his unknotting back, a little feeling ran. When a machine gun rattled, he sprawled to his side.

Only a woodpecker. Perspiring, he resettled, and the noon hour's slow pulse resumed.

At first, the voice seemed an emanation of his own thought. But here it was again. Someone was approaching along the main path. He could see no one yet. But the voice kept chanting, breaking off for a few seconds only to resume its monotonous reiterations—a woman's voice, he thought, though he could not be sure. Through a space between trees, a patch of grey disappeared, and a moment later, through a larger gap, a woman in a grey dress appeared. She was carrying her wide-brimmed hat in one hand, exposing the dull red cap of her hair.

She was making her leisurely way along, stopping to peer at something in the undergrowth. Now, turning, she faced the heights where he had taken shelter behind a tree. A little path, running past his hiding place, scolded him for his timidity. In a burst of abandon, he rose and flung himself down it.

"What are you doing in my woods!" he demanded as he came up to her.

"I hadn't realized they were yours," Grace said.

"Oh yes, every stick. I've been coming here since I was a kid." He was grinning wildly and felt oversized, awkward. He flicked his cane at the hilltop. "We had a fort up there."

Shading her eyes, she studied the place. "I know all about boys and their forts. They would never let me play with them."

"Well damn their hides," he said. Her laugh gratified him, and he relaxed a little. As she peered up the hill, his gaze travelled over her face, her mouth.

"I would have let you play," he said. She barked a laugh at that. "What—you don't believe me?"

"Of course I do," she said ironically. All this was familiar—the bantering, the play of challenges. They were alone on a forest path.

"Who in the devil were you talking to?" he said finally, flushing.

"When?"

"Just now—talking to the trees."

"I'm a dryad, don't you know."

"So you talk tree-language?"

"In a matter of speaking. Bliss Carman."

"Ah, *him*," he said darkly.

"You don't care for him?"

"He's all right in his place. Someone gave me his poems—over there. Of course I liked them, but it seemed that he'd left out half of life."

"What half is that?"

He didn't answer.

"The half you'd been living, I suppose," she said somberly.

"Not the best material for sonnets in any case."

Again they were silent. He flicked the tip of his cane in the dirt, looked off.

"Are you all right, Ted?"

"As rain," he said, slapping his leg with his cane. "So what was it?"

"What was what?"

"The poem—"

"Something one of my girls brought me. I suppose you'd think it's mush."

"Tell me."

She looked away as she recited the lines. *I heard the spring wind whisper / Above the brushwood fire, / 'The world is made forever / Of transport and desire.* That's it," she said, regarding him sternly.

"Not bad," he said, feeling himself redden; now it was his turn to look away. "Here," he said, turning back at once. "I've interrupted your walk."

"Not at all. I was on my way home."

"We can go together then." He realized he'd forced the situation, but she didn't object, and swallowing his shame and his pride together, he followed her up the path that climbed the hillside. While he grasped at saplings, she rose effortless above him. By the time he arrived at the top, she was waiting for him. "I remember you," he said, breathing hard. "I should jolly well hope so." Her face looked unnaturally pale in the dim woods. When she turned away, he hurried to walk beside her. They went along together, unspeaking, soon leaving the pines and descending a lane lined with maple saplings, sprung up between the rails of a fence. Reaching the river flats, they blinked back the harsh sun. Giant thistles reared barbarous heads. Bees hovered, settled. A smell of vegetable rot was on the air—the familiar stink of the river, drying from sun-baked shallows, a touch of sulphur. Following her along the narrow rut of a cow path, he wondered if he was oppressing her; he had simply announced he was going back with her—given her no choice. The very look of her back condemned him. The hot pasture seemed to him a place of misery. It was the sun, he decided—its power oppressive. She had put on her hat.

When she went off to investigate some debris, he stood in the shade of a sycamore and smoked, watching her circle a heap of brush the floods had left. Stooping suddenly, she picked up some small object. It proved to be a tiny, flask-shaped bottle, still corked, containing an inch or so of liquid. Their heads together, they puzzled over it. He felt they were both acting, faking a relaxed ordinariness that neither felt. Or perhaps it was only him. He feared he could no longer read anyone, not with his two lives clamouring inside him. She pulled out the cork, smelled the contents, tossed the bottle aside.

"Give me one of your cigarettes," she demanded. He tapped one from his pack and gave it to her, laughing to see it wag between her lips. "What?" she objected, nearly dropping it. "I've done this before, you know."

Her cigarette lit, she drew on it expertly before raising her face to exhale, watching him through slitted eyes.

Again they set off, following the rutted cow path. The sun was on his face. He felt a little better now. Yes, following her he was all right. Let him go on like this forever, like the poem said—another of Carman's lies. There was only one forever, and when you knew it you didn't know it. Turning aside, he called to her that he'd catch her up in a minute. He pissed behind a sycamore. Spattering of his stream on the flaking camouflage of its bark, warm cock in his hand—the thing was still good for something. He was pretending with her, he realized; pretending he had a power he no longer had. Yet around her he felt he did have it—or rather he forgot he didn't. Desire stronger than potency: was that a definition of hell? He finished and hurried after her. She had disappeared. He turned in a grove of saplings and stepped, not seeing it, into a cow flap. A nice juicy one. He scraped his foot on clumped grass, sniffed the air around him, and went on.

He found her on a little strip of stony beach, where the river bent in the shadow of a cliff. Hands on hips, staring over the water, she seemed unaware of his arrival. He looked where she was looking and saw the smooth, dim river skimming under the cliff.

She stooped, picked up a stone, flung it sidearm. It nicked neatly along the surface, a series of small white explosions almost reaching the far side.

"Bravo!" he said.

She gave him a quick, expressionless glance.

He sat on a log, smoking, while she continued to skip stones, completely absorbed in her game. Swallows were darting over the river, which had the dim transparency of smoked glass. She continued throwing while he watched her, absorbed. There was no wind. The smoke from his cigarette stood straight up. The flat stones ran from her hand, and he was all right.

She sat beside him on the log, her arms draped over her knees, her hands limp. For some time they looked over the water.

"Is there more?" she said. A faint smile moved her lips, and all at once he wanted to fall on her. All at once, *that* was there, insistent. Or partly there. Just a shiver, really.

"You don't want to hear it," he said.

"But I do, Ted. And I think you want to say it."

He blew smoke, snapped away the butt. The river flowed dark and flat.

"There was this boy," he said finally. He could see everything clearly.

"Yes?"

"We'd left the Line to—recuperate. The whole battalion."

"A holiday?" she said.

"We still had to get up at five. Line up for parade." He gestured dumbly, swallowed hard. "We practised—what you call 'em?—manoeuvres, broke in the new men. Do road work or j-just go marching. I suppose you could say it was a holiday compared to—" He broke off.

"You'd had a bad time of it?"

"There'd been this show near Lens. A platoon is supposed to have forty, fifty men. Mine was down to twenty-four—"

He dug at the ground with his heel. Late summer 1917. He'd been billeted in a village, in a Second Empire house owned by an M. Dupuis, a merchant apparently, the name of his business inscribed in an old ledger he found in a drawer. The family had decamped in a hurry. Boxes of pictures and clothes in the parlour. A rocking horse upended in a closet. His little room was on the top floor, a former servant's quarters. A bowl and washstand. The bed too short for him. Floorboards scored by hobnails. A shelf with books in English left by others. *Fly Fishing on the Miramichi. Glengarry School Days.* A small *Hamlet* bound in leather. Even with the shutters closed, he could hear the grumbling of guns to the north, the horizon lit up some nights by flashes like summer lightning. He told her this because it was harmless: it was something he could still touch, and touching it, he found it to be good. That little room, and the sound of guns like a summer storm passing. And him, curled in the bed that was too short for him, like a child, listening.

THAT MORNING, the morning of the boy, Cam Hunter brought his breakfast as usual; brought him his freshly shined boots. They were soon caked with mud as he trudged up a lane among the battalion's tents. Outside the duty tent, his sergeant, Bob McElroy, was waiting with the names of the latest recruits. New men had been arriving all week. "Bob didn't think much of the latest three," Ted told Grace. "He said they must have scraped the bottom of the bottom for them."

They found the first recruit sitting on an orchard wall. "He didn't bother getting up until Bob put a grenade under him."

She looked at him quizzically. "Just an expression," he said, enjoying her confusion.

"The next chap said he couldn't wait to get at the Boers. The Boers had killed his dad apparently—he was going to make them pay. We didn't bother telling him he was in the wrong war."

The third recruit's tent was empty. "He's just a kid," McElroy said. "Something odd about him—neither fish nor fowl." His name was Hartfield, James Hartfield, Ted saw, glancing at his sergeant's clipboard.

The recruit soon appeared in a crowd returning from breakfast. The soldiers were making a racket, shouting and laughing as if just back from the local *estaminet* and its yeasty ale, their high spirits a surprise to Ted. Since Lens, he'd worried about morale.

McElroy called the boy over—for he was a boy, Ted saw, a slim, fit-looking kid with wide shoulders and a face that might have been a girl's. Complexion like cream; lively, eager eyes under long lashes. Looking nervously pleased with himself, he came to attention.

"At your ease, Hartfield."

"Sir."

"Where are you from, private?"

"Toronto, sir."

"What part of Toronto?"

"The Ward, sir."

Ted glanced at him. The Ward was where he'd wandered that day he'd signed up. Eyes no longer fixed straight ahead, the boy was looking at him with the sort of curious openness only young people can have. There was inexperience there, and trust.

"Very good," Ted said, feeling suddenly at a loss. He asked what the boy's father did.

"He makes toys, sir. For Eaton's."

"I see."

"He used to make them in the factory, but he had an accident. After that they let him make them at home. My mother, she works on the phones."

"At Eaton's?"

"Yes sir."

"You're their only child?"

"I am now. There was Charlotte. We called her Charlie because she liked Charlie Chaplin so much. She could do the walk and everything. We used to laugh like nuts!"

"And what happened to Charlotte?"

"She died, sir."

Again Ted glanced at the boy, his own face hot. "I think that's all for now, Hartfield. You may go."

The boy saluted and started off.

"Hartfield, one more thing."

The boy turned.

"How old are you?"

"Eighteen."

"Of course," Ted said.

"Sir?"

"Nothing. That's all for now."

Ted and his sergeant watched the boy go off.

He was certain the boy had lied about his age. There were kids in the army as young as fifteen, fourteen. He'd heard of one who was twelve. The recruiting officers had gotten less fussy as the army ran short of men. A kid of sixteen or seventeen would walk into a recruiting office, and in the pressure of the moment, give his true age; the officer would suggest he take a walk around the block and think about it.

He couldn't stop seeing Hartfield's face—*neither fish nor fowl*—those eager eyes clinging to his. When he asked McElroy for his impressions, his sergeant spit his wad to one side and said, "He's terrified."

That night, Ted visited his commanding officer in the duty tent. Looking up wearily from his papers, Captain Ross listened to Ted's story in the flickering light of a kerosene lamp.

"It's just bloody wrong," Ted said. "There has to be some way to get him out. We can't have a kid around, screwing things up." He also didn't want to see the kid killed, but he didn't tell Ross that. Already he had a feeling for the boy, a sense of responsibility. He wanted to get rid of the feeling too.

It all came down to a birth certificate, Ross told him, and if possible a letter from home asking for the boy to be dismissed. Ted could write his parents for both. "I wouldn't get your hopes up though. Even if you get these things and send them up the chain, it could be months before you hear anything. If you hear at all."

"Christ, he'll be dead by then." He was sure of this. The boy's very innocence—that trusting look—seemed a guarantee that evil would find him. "Couldn't we transfer him to canteen duty or something?"

"Earlier on, yes. But the brass say there's been too many taking that way out. With this shortage of men— I'll do what I can, but—" Ross turned away to search in a box of papers. At last he produced a couple of pages, but there was no record of Hartfield's home address other than Toronto. "No doubt it exists somewhere. Probably quicker to ask him."

Ted was ducking out of the tent when the captain called him back.

"How are you doing yourself?"

"Still standing," he said, wary.

"They've asked us to pay more attention to how our junior officers are doing. Don't want to wear you out, you know,"

Ross added wryly. "Seriously, Ted, if you ever feel the need to take a few days off—"

"Somebody's complained?"

"No, no," Ross said, too quickly. "Everybody knows your bunch had it hard."

"We weren't the only ones."

Ross did not respond, but he seemed to Ted to be watching him, not as one man looks at another, but as a doctor might look at you while mentally making notes.

That night he found Hartfield and a few other soldiers around a fire. To his surprise, they were singing. Singing was common enough in the army; men sometimes sang as they marched, "the smuttiest stuff you ever heard," he told Grace; or they sang while carrying light rail track, or digging latrines—anything they could bring a rhythm to. Ted's platoon hadn't sung since Lens.

He had heard "It's a Long Way to Tipperary" so often he was sick of its jaunty expression of longing for a place most of them would never see. What they usually sang was the chorus, and he heard it again now, belted out to the strumming of a ukulele. But instead of repeating it *ad nauseam*, which was the usual approach, they paused, and he heard Hartfield's clear, unbroken soprano rise into their silence. *Paddy wrote a letter / To his Irish Molly-O / Saying, "Should you not receive it / Write and let me know."*

THE MEN WERE RAPT. When it came time for another chorus, not a peep rose from them until they were harried by the ukulele player. Each time Hartfield sang a verse, the same spell descended.

Ted felt the pull of the boy's voice too—as he told Grace, you'd have to have been deaf not to. But he was skeptical of those clear phrases with their sentimental conjuring of old places, old loves—they seemed capable of threatening his daily effort to get his men through the war. The boy's voice was subversive, a softness they couldn't afford. Yet he listened to the end. When he led the boy away, they were followed by groans of protest.

They went through the ranks of tents, past other fires, past men writing letters by the light of candles or lamps, past a group who hastened to put away their card game and stacks of coin, past a dog scratching its fleas. They stopped at the orchard wall. Beyond it, dimly lit by the lights from the encampment, trees shorn and splintered earlier in the war raised mutilated limbs. He told the boy, crisply, that he needed his home address. "In case something happens to you, I would have to write to your parents." The boy's alarmed eyes flicked to his.

"I gave them that," he said, suddenly subdued. Ted sensed resistance.

"The information is buried in a file somewhere. We'll be going back to the Line soon. I need it now. In case something happens to you." There was no need for him to repeat this possibility, but he was angry at the boy's deception—he wanted to shove his face in it. Hartfield gave him the address. Ted wrote it in his notebook.

"Is that all, sir?"

"One other thing. You told me you were eighteen. When's your birthday?"

"November thirty-one."

"Only thirty days in November, Private. You'll have to do

better than that." Ted was about to dismiss him, but the boy
looked crestfallen. Softening, he added, "What year then?"
The boy's lips moved slightly as he calculated.

"Hartfield?"

"Eighteen-ninety-eight."

"That's all, Hartfield," Ted said brusquely. Even if he
squeezed the truth out of him, he would still have to prove his
age, for the brass could always say the kid was lying to get out.
That night, he wrote to Hartfield's parents and tried to put the
matter out of his mind. It proved difficult. He paced the floor of
his room. "It's just bloody wrong," he said viciously, to no one.
The arrival of the boy released a wider anger he had kept in
check: anger with the way things were, the stupidity and waste.
Out his window, the night held no answers. A truck, feeling its
way through narrow streets, struggled as it changed gears.

The next day, his men engaged in a training drill that
involved crawling under barbed wire while live fire from a couple of Lewis guns streamed overhead. Ted wasn't required to
crawl with them, but he joined his platoon so he could keep an
eye on Hartfield. He kept a little behind the boy, drawing even
with him from time to time to give instructions. To his relief,
Hartfield performed decently. He didn't stick up his head for
a look around—Ted's big worry—and when he reached the
point where he had to shoot at a target, he fired quickly and
accurately, grinning afterwards at his success. Ted chewed him
out anyway, over some trivial matter. Later, remorseful, he
told the kid he had the makings of a good soldier. "You'll be
all right," he said. In his heart he did not believe it.

As for his other recruits, he wondered if many of them would
ever make decent soldiers. They kept their heads down under
the live bullets, as any fool would; but when it came to shoot-

ing or scrambling out of trenches or just plain hurrying, they
were a ragged lot, passively rebellious under the tongue-lash-
ings Bob McElroy applied, inclined to slack off whenever the
sergeant turned his back. One of them, Rufus George, was a
puzzle to him. He'd come out of the woods; apparently, he'd
run a trap line north of the Sault. He was Native, or part anyway, according to Bob—a lank, slow-moving fellow with dark
eyes that told you nothing, and a way of sharpening his bayonet
that made you think he knew what to do with it. George kept
pretty much to himself, never joining in the games or hijinks of
the others. He was a crack shot, as Ted soon discovered, placing
bullseye after bullseye. But that was the only aspect of training
that seemed to interest him, that and sticking a bayonet into a
straw dummy, which he did with a thin smile of amusement.
Otherwise, he dogged it as much as any of them, said little, and
spent much of his spare time tending to his gear or clicking his
rosary beads.

Most of the recruits were growing sober by now, as they
absorbed the stories and advice of the veterans. But there
remained a naivety about Hartfield—a cheerful eagerness that
seemed to accept good and ill with the same even temper. Was
McElroy right? Was the kid terrified? Even after the recent
rigours of his training, with all their suggestions of danger,
he had remained remarkably composed—or so it seemed to
Ted. Was the boy thick? Did he think all this was a game? Ted
couldn't tell. One thing was certain though: he was terrifically
popular with the platoon. The men fell over themselves doing
little chores for "Jimmy" as they called him, and were quick to
show him the tricks and dodges that made the life of a soldier
easier. They swore less in his presence, Ted noticed, and readily
took him into their activities—a card game, a singsong, a trip

to the *estaminet*. Ted had to admit that the morale of the platoon had improved since Hartfield's arrival. Was he the cause? Ted didn't like to think so. It seemed Hartfield was good for the platoon, yet there was something so unusual in the situation, so unwarlike and off balance, that he worried his men might be losing focus.

Making his rounds one day, Ted noticed Hartfield slip into a tent that wasn't his. Later, he looked in and found the recruit with a sheaf of papers in his hand. Watching him from a cot was Dick Fellows, an East End Londoner who'd just emigrated to Canada when the war broke out. Having no way back to England, he'd enlisted in Toronto. He and Hartfield were rehearsing an act for the upcoming variety show put on by the battalion. "I hope you'll be there, sir," Fellows jibed at Ted. A wiry little man with high shoulders, Fellows knew everybody yet had no close friends. He'd been spending a lot of time with Hartfield, Ted had noticed. There was a gutter aspect to the man, a sly insinuation that he knew your secrets and was quite certain they were dirty ones—he could scarcely open his mouth without this attitude being apparent. Yet he could set the men roaring with a word or a nod. Ted had heard them repeating, with approval, some remark that "Dickie" had made—some black joke about the marvelous decapitating powers of German shells, or the perils of latrines.

At Fellows's remark, the boy thrust his head forward as if he was trying to see Ted more clearly in the dim tent. Ted found something uncannily disturbing in this movement—that long white neck, the face as delicate as a girl's. Ted said he would be at the show.

AS THE DAYS wore on, he noted a new rebelliousness among
the men. Some were slower to obey orders. A fight broke out
between two chaps Ted had thought were friends. Bob McElroy
had trouble breaking it up—"Like trying to peel a rock," the
sergeant said. When Ted applied a firmer hand, a few of his
veterans resisted. He had to have words with a couple of them.
One insisted angrily that Hartfield was the problem. "A face
like that," the man said, "He's a nancy for sure. We don't need
any nancies in this outfit—puts the men off their game." The
man's resentments seemed atypical—no one else had made
such a complaint—yet they inflamed Ted's own suspicions and
gave him fresh fodder for his worries. No, they most definitely
could not have any of *that*—especially if someone in the platoon reciprocated. He thought immediately of Dick Fellows.
Meanwhile the unrest in the platoon continued. Another fight
broke out, and one soldier had to be sent to the guardhouse. He
had worried before about his men getting soft; now he feared
the opposite. A degree of truculence was a good thing in a soldier, just as spirit was a good thing in a horse—but there could
be too much. *Was* it possible Hartfield was in some way behind
the current unrest? He seemed anything but truculent himself,
with his open face and willing manner; yet there was something about the situation Ted couldn't quite fathom. The boy
seemed both serenely removed from events and at the same
time very much in the thick.

MUCH OF THE countryside around the village had been chewed
up by the supply chains that fed the armies to the north and
east. In other areas, fields and woodlots persisted amidst the
damage. You might see people stooking sheaves just as their

ancestors had, while an endless line of small-gauge railcars banged past with loads of troops and equipment. There was an air of disruption and, for him, a sense of sadness as old ways of life were destroyed, the beautiful countryside with its medieval villages and churches chewed up by artillery. The broken land seemed to mirror his own state. He knew he was in a bad way. Until Lens, he had coped well enough, but after that a creeping desperation had taken root in him. So far, he'd been able to control it, but he sensed it was always there. He was not sleeping properly, and in this time of supposed recovery, he knew he was losing ground. Ross had hinted that a longer rest was his for the asking, but although he dreamed of escape from the war, he was unwilling to take time off. Going on, lockstep, seemed all he was capable of.

Walking through the streets of his village, he liked to follow a lane that ended at a stile and a view of fields. There the land had not been broken. He saw pasturelands, isolated shade trees, fields of wheat and oats; and in the distance, a wooded hill pierced by a church tower. Occasionally, he heard bells from that direction. He had never been a strong believer, not in the whole pomp and panoply of what he'd been taught: not as his wife was a believer, or John Scott. Since Lens, he'd given up on God completely, save for the occasional involuntary prayer that escaped his lips *in extremis*. But the tower in the trees fascinated him. One morning, with time on his hands, he climbed the stile and followed a footpath towards it.

The church in the woods was not large, nor was it of the best proportions, its square bell tower too dominant for the narrow nave. What drew him most was the porch, which had been built over the hurrying water of a stream. Nearby, in the shade, two blinkered horses stood hitched to a caleche. In his seat above their flicking tails, an elderly man in a black suit and bowler sat smoking. From time to time, he leaned out to spit. The horses' bridles had been decorated with pink rosettes and a few small bells that tinkled when they swung their heads. The old man wore a pink carnation. Speaking in the gnarled French of the region, he informed Ted that a wedding was in progress. *Les jeunes mariés* would be out shortly. Ted smoked while he waited, exchanging the occasional word with the man and listening to the muffled sounds of voices and organ music from inside. After ten minutes, a man thrust his head from the door and signalled to the caleche. Soon both doors were thrown open as the organ boomed, the bells began their clamour, and the wedding guests poured into the yard, where they turned with a buzz of anticipation to await the bride and groom. Appearing at last, they paused on the porch steps to receive the cries and applause of their well-wishers. Wearing the uniform of a French officer, the groom looked about him, warily expectant, until a little girl approached and tugged at his sleeve. As laughter rose from the crowd, the man let slip a youthful grin. An old woman in a wheelchair waved her hankie. Children dressed in their best ran about.

Watching from the shade, Ted was unaccountably moved. He did not believe in God, but he believed in this pageant honoured by the people of God. It seemed holy beyond any relic or sacred text, this swirling in brief, snatched joy of the generations.

When the groom noticed Ted, he left his bride and walked over. Quieting, the crowd turned to watch. He too was a lieutenant, Ted saw; they saluted, then shook hands warmly, their gazes touching in an intimacy that simultaneously banished the war and acknowledged it. Lieutenant Chabrol. He invited Ted to the wedding feast. Regretfully, Ted declined. He was due back in camp, he explained, offering the man his felicitations and adding that his bride was *très belle, comme une fleur d'été*. The man was not more than twenty: his animated face with its fine, thin eyebrows blushed with pleasure while his bride looked after him, wondering.

Ted watched till the end—watched as the old man brought forward the caleche and the bride mounted into it, helped by her husband, her frothing train gathered around her; watched as the caleche drew off with the wedding guests walking after it through the woods, until the last of them, a little girl who ran back to retrieve a dropped boutonnière, hurried out of sight.

RETRACING HIS STEPS, he was tempted onto a new route by a poplar-lined road. It bore him along a ridge with a view of the fields he had crossed earlier, until a steady stream of trucks drove him into the woods. Soon the tiled roofs of his village appeared, on the far side of a meadow where a large oak stood in the pool of its own shade.

A few steps from the tree, he saw legs sprawling from behind it. Feet turned outward, puttees unravelled. His first thought was that the man was dead.

As he rounded the tree, Hartfield looked up at him miserably. "I'm not good, sir."

"Come on, Hartfield, on your feet now."

The boy clambered to his feet and saluted.

"At your ease," Ted said wearily. Was the boy going to be nothing but trouble? Yet the spell of the wedding was still on him, and he spoke more gently than he might have otherwise. "Now, what's happened, Jimmy?"

"In the latrine. Two fellows—I didn't know them, they must have been from some other platoon. They kept telling me I was a goner. They said one of those big shells—those Jack Johnson things—was going to get me. They said it had my name on it. They were laughing about it."

"They were joking."

"There was something nasty in it, sir. The tall one said I deserved it. We don't like your kind, he said. It's laid me out. Do you think it's likely, sir?"

"What's likely—"

"That one will get me?"

Ted was half tempted to give a soldier's response: *No more likely than getting gassed or cut in half by a machine gun—nothing to worry about.* But he sensed that black humour was beyond Hartfield now. "The thing is, Jim, you have to stop thinking about it. You're a good soldier. You've learned your skills—how to keep yourself safe. Look, we've got parade in half an hour. You need to polish those boots and put your puttees right. Think about those sorts of things. Just keep busy—that's the ticket."

The boy was clearly taking in every word. Ted was aware he was shading the truth. A man might know all there was about keeping himself safe, but only luck could save you in the end. The newspapers talked endlessly of the men's courage. The men spoke only of luck. "Just keep your wits about you. You strike me as the lucky type."

They went through the meadow, the boy stumbling along beside him.

"I don't think I *am* lucky, sir."

"You've made a lot of friends in the platoon. The men like you—they're looking out for you. I would say that's lucky."

"I mean the way I am, sir. The way I was born. *That's* not lucky."

When the boy's eyes found his, Ted blanched and kept going. They were silent until they reached the stile. Ted climbed over first. He didn't wait for Hartfield, but the boy was soon at his side again.

"My dad told me if I didn't come back a proper man, I shouldn't bother coming back at all."

Christ, Ted thought.

"I don't think I *am* a proper man. I don't think it's in me, sir."

"You're still growing, Hartfield. It takes time."

"I don't mean that way. I mean the way I am." The boy had stopped. Turning, Ted met the hopeless candour in his face. Hartfield knew he was different; he knew Ted knew it too: the stark truth was between them. Once more, Ted felt himself at sea.

The boy did that to him, it seemed—carried him to a place where the usual answers did not answer. Struggling, he patched something together. "People change, Jim. Just keep on, do your job—you never know what might happen."

"Sir," the boy said, sounding disappointed.

In the rising heat of the day, the village had a bleak, closed look. The main street, severed by sun and shadow, lay deserted. To the north, the guns were at it again. Earth was being torn up, along with the bodies of men who had sheltered in it. He sent Hartfield on to the encampment by himself, telling him he needed to pick up something at his billet. He climbed to his room, opened the tiny window, and went back down the stairs. What he had needed was to get away from Hartfield. He didn't want to be seen walking into camp with him.

In the following days, he often caught the private looking at him. He'd turn from some task and there would be the boy, sitting in a noisy group of his mates, or with the rifle he was cleaning forgotten in his lap, his plump lips gaping a little as he watched Ted pass by. Ted feared he'd spoken too kindly to him—aroused expectations he couldn't meet. He redoubled his efforts to treat him with the same brisk, matey profession- alism with which he treated the others—a certain distance at its core. Yet Ted would catch himself thinking of him, won- dering how he was doing, or watching him closely when he could not be observed himself. The boy was a mystery to him. Yet he could not have said what the mystery was.

A TREMOR RAN through his hands. His face hardened. He felt worse than when he'd started. Why did he keep on with this business? Why were these stories suddenly there to be told? Beside him on the log, Grace was nodding as if to confirm what he'd said. As if she'd known it all along.

"What happened to him?" she said.

That was his story: what happened to Jimmy Hartfield. He could see the end of it like a small fire on the far side of a vast darkness. He vowed he would never go there.

THE EVENING OF the variety show poured rain. He walked over in his mac to the old market hall, with its stone pillars, high beamed ceiling, and now a deafening cacophony of voices. He found the interior packed with men, the air thick with the mingled odours of tobacco smoke, wet wool, and male bodies. Pushing his way towards a vantage point, he ran into two of his own. There was no liquor on sale, but they'd clearly found some, taking advantage of their relaxed state to clap him on the back and tell him he was a good fellow. They said they were excited to see Jimmy. Jimmy was going to be great, they shouted through the din.

Escaping, he found a less crowded spot, by a pillar. A stage had been erected at one end of the hall, its proscenium arch decorated with swirls of colour and crude representations of high-kicking women in minimal dress. The closed curtain, billowing with the movements behind it, had clearly been stitched up from various scraps of cloth—a Joseph's coat of blues, reds, pinks, and greens, as well as the whites of flour sacks and bedsheets.

He was chatting with a fellow officer when a general cheer went up. A runty chap in a top hat and oversized dress coat had appeared in front of the curtain. He looked, Ted thought, very much like the Mad Hatter from *Alice*, but it was not until the man opened his mouth that he realized it was Dick Fellows. Flourishing a cane, the little man patrolled the edge of the stage, bantering with the crowd in his insinuating way and regaling them with news of the glories to come. He didn't mention Hartfield or any of the other performers by name, though he promised a very special guest who had come all the way from Canada to see them.

All the performers of the evening were soldiers—a fact the audience clearly relished as they recognized their mates in a variety of dress and situations. Ted watched a private from another platoon mimic an officer of a certain swanky type as he strutted about singing boastfully of the girl he was going to seduce that night; he drank liberally from a bottle and ended with a spectacular pratfall, dead drunk, to be dragged off by his heels amid catcalls and gales of laughter. After him came a comic pianist, a Charlie Chaplin imitator, a tenor singing "Under the Old Apple Tree," a cancan chorus line danced by eleven burly men in tutus, and assorted other acts, magical, pseudotragical, sentimental, and gymnastical, all of them introduced by Fellows with a few sly jokes and a deep bow and swing of his top hat.

The mass of soldiers roared. Solitary voices cried out. The hall stank of men, of their bodies and their clothes and their fear: men seething with energy and jostling for relief, determined to bury themselves in the moment while forgetting everything else. Ted sensed a growing anarchy among them, a dark undercurrent that lent a note of impending violence to the celebrations. One performer, a comic who came nowhere near Fellows's level of humour, was lustily booed. Someone threw a bottle. Ted noticed military police gathering at the back of the hall. He was wondering if he should leave when Fellows appeared again. He held his cane aloft as if he might strike them all—and all, to Ted's amazement, gradually quieted. When they were silent at last, Fellows began to speak. He talked of their sisters and mothers and sweethearts, and though he could never entirely banish the satiric edge from his voice, it held a sincerity that was new. Sensing the change, the men remained silent, though now and then someone whooped or cried out. It was time for a very special guest, Fellows told them. She was someone who loved her boys in khaki, someone who had come three thousand miles from Canada just to be with them. Gesturing with his cane, he cried out in triumph: "I give you the lovely, the incomparable, Annie Rose!"

The curtains did not readily obey his command. Only after two or three seconds did they jostle slowly apart.

Standing in a pool of light was a young woman. Below her wide, bare shoulders, a red rose had been pinned to the bodice of her dress.

By his pillar, Ted was electrified. Around him, a palpable stir swept the crowd. The pianist was playing a soft ascension of chords.

Her voice, when it came, was not loud, nor overpowering; only the attentiveness of the crowd made it possible to hear her. They did not move, and she did not move herself, save for a slight heaving of her pale chest as she took her breath, and a slight backward tilting of her head as she closed her eyes and sung the higher notes.

The bittersweet song, familiar to them all, spoke of pipes calling from glen to glen, of roses falling, of return to a dying beloved. By his pillar, Ted seemed to hear the words for the first time, and for a moment he was with his father. They were walking by the Shade while his father told some story. There was light on his father's hand, and he was filled with longing for him. Then his father was gone. Now softness was in him, and sex, and the indescribable sweetness of peace touched by female loveliness.

When she stopped singing, he did not at first notice. Around him, five hundred men had fallen silent. When she brought her fingertips to her chest and slowly inclined her head, they roared as one.

THE MORNING AFTER the show, Ted ordered Fellows to appear. The man seemed even smugger than usual as he saluted in his careless way. Hartfield's triumph was his triumph. All the battalion was talking about it.

Ted had summoned the little Englishman with no clear idea of what he would say. The boy's performance had moved him, upset him, excited him. He kept seeing those wide, white, subtly flexing shoulders that seemed neither a man's nor a woman's. Fellows's appearance filled him with angry indignation.

Grimly, he complimented the private on his job as MC. "I gather you've done this sort of thing before."

"A bit here and there, guv'ner."

"That would be *sir*," Ted reprimanded.

"*Sir*," Fellows said wearily, his face emptying of smugness.

"What brought you to Canada? I would have thought there were plenty of opportunities at home for your talents—more than with us." The inference was not lost on Fellows: *you effete English*. His small eyes darted at Ted. "Well?"

"Circumstances, you might say. *Sir*."

"You're aware that Hartfield is still a boy."

"Half anyway, *Sir*."

"What you did—the dress, the makeup—I consider that an abomination."

"He didn't object, sir. If anything, it was his idea."

"Look, Fellows, I've been to the music halls—I know this kind of thing is common there. He may have gone along with it, but you were in charge, and you knew exactly what you were doing. He's a boy, you're a man—you should never have allowed it to happen. He'll be marked now, among the men."

"The men love him, sir. They'd fair do anything for him."

"This isn't to be repeated, Fellows, you hear me? It's not to be repeated."

"Sir."

"And one other thing: I don't want you—taking advantage," Ted said grimly.

"I don't like the implication, sir."

"And I don't care for your attitude. I order you to stay away from him."

"How shall I put it, sir? That kind of thing—it really doesn't interest me."

"I don't want it happening with anyone else either. If you see anyone paying court to him, I want you to tell me at once."

"So, I'm supposed to stay away from him, and also keep an eye on him?"

"I'm sure you'll figure it out."

There was hatred in the look Fellows shot Ted; and like the sting in the scorpion's tail, a gleam of amusement.

NOT LONG AFTERWARDS, he summoned the boy.

When Hartfield ducked into the tent, Ted kept his eyes on his paperwork. He heard the slap of Hartfield's hand on his thigh as he finished his salute. When he looked up, the boy's gaze was focused on nothing, as he'd been taught, but his face glowed with his new celebrity. To Ted, his success seemed a betrayal of the care he'd taken of him. The boy had run straight into a kind of danger Ted had not imagined, and he had done it willingly, willfully, throwing the ethos of a steady manhood in Ted's face; or so it felt. "At your ease, Hartfield."

"Sir."

"That was quite a show you put on last night."

"Thanks, sir!"

"You're a terrific singer, I won't deny it. Singing is fine, Hartfield, but in the future, no more dresses." Ted scowled at the papers in front of him, touching at them as if searching for something more important than this matter of dresses. But his throat was dry.

"But sir—"

Ted looked up and was pitched back into his feelings of the night before: the sudden warmth, a flood of dissolution. Looking back to his papers, he began to shift them about in his confusion. He felt himself in the presence of a moral fault, something deeply disquieting that he had not felt when two of his men participated in the cancan. They were men on a lark, hairy legs and all. But Hartfield had disappeared into Annie Rose.

"You didn't like that part, sir?"

"It's not a question whether I like it—it's not soldierly. The men have to keep their focus. *You* have to keep your focus. This is a war, Hartfield, as you'll understand soon enough. Not some—" Exasperated, Ted threw out his hand. The boy had sobered. "Listen, Hartfield. I need you to tell me the truth. Did Fellows make you do this?"

"You mean—"

"Dick Fellows—was that his idea? The dress. The bare shoulders—"

"No sir."

"He had nothing to do with it—"

"Well, he showed me how to stand and whatnot. He was a regular bear for perfection."

"And the dress—was that his idea too?"

"I suggested it, sir. You see, sir, I liked it. I've done it before, just not in front of so many—" He broke off, flushing.

"You've done it before."

"Sir." The boy's face dropped.

"Right," Ted said, disappointed. "So Private Fellows didn't make you do anything you didn't want to do?"

"Not at all, sir."

"He didn't—didn't touch you in an unseemly way."

"Not at all, sir!"

The boy looked scandalized. Ted dismissed him. Three days later the battalion returned to the Line.

HE COULDN'T GO farther. Seized by a familiar panic, he lurched to his feet and paced in front of her on the narrow beach until

Grace took his arm and led him towards the town. In a field below, he saw a small child walking in parallel with them. She wore a long dress and a coal-scuttle bonnet that hid her face, a lonely figure whose isolation seemed his own. She seemed to belong to the story he had just told.

13.

The lilacs had turned brown. The fleshy cups of the magnolia were falling apart. Miriam's darning needle worked with a quick, ruthless efficiency. She and her mother had taken refuge from the sun on the porch. Inside her undergarments, the trickles of sweat felt like the scurrying of insects, while Ada's voice, musing beside her, kept dragging her from her reverie. Fundraising for the new hospital had stalled, it said. They were not even halfway to their goal, it said. "It seems everyone's spare change is going to the League."

"Surely that has to come first," Miriam said, peering at her stitches.

"But it's the same need, dear. There's going to be a lot of wounded men coming home—far more than we've had. The old hospital, well it's little more than a house, isn't it. Miss MacMillan saw a rat in the kitchen the other day—"

"I daresay you're right."

"Of course I'm right," Ada said dryly. As her needle continued to weave through the sock, Miriam sensed her mother's disapproval. They weren't so poor they couldn't send their darning to Mrs. Tennant, as they had for years, Ada had often insisted. But for Miriam, mending Ted's socks was a way of staying close to him, and an act of defiance—one of those petty rebellions she was increasingly driven to these days, to her own chagrin. She might be living in her mother's house, but the limits of her accommodation had long been passed. A shift in her mother's tone, or a sardonic smile, could pique her instantly, and while she usually managed to bite her lip, Ada's habit of thinking out loud, with no apparent consciousness that Miriam's attention might be elsewhere, could set Miriam to making accusations in her head. *We have to get out of here*, she told herself, her needle falling still. The thought came frequently these days, and was answered by the usual hard facts. Ted was not fit to teach yet, and his pension had not come.

China clinked as her mother put down her cup.

"What about John Bannerman?" Miriam said.

"When he's already pledged five thousand? I'd be embarrassed to ask." From up the street came the sound of a lawnmower, its blades spinning free. "He might open up for *you* though."

"I doubt it."

"You know very well he's fond of you. He's been keen on you ever since you were in pinafores. Now that he's by himself—"

"He still has his gardener," Miriam put in. "And old Mrs. Wood."

"You know very well what I mean. Servants are hardly company. All on his own now, rattling around that huge place. I should think if you went over there, he'd make you out a cheque on the spot."

"I doubt that very much."

"How long has it been since you visited?"

Miriam sighed, recognizing an appeal to her conscience. She enjoyed the old man's reminiscences but had not visited him for weeks. She had intended to dun him for the League, but before she could, he had brought a cheque to Brockwood.

"I'm sure you could winkle another thousand out of him," Ada said.

"It just seems wrong, trading on friendship for a cause," Miriam said. "I've never been comfortable with it."

"It's the way of the world, dear. You scratch my back, I'll scratch yours. It doesn't mean you can't be friends as well. Everyone—well, our kind of people anyway—understands that very well."

"And the other kind of people don't understand it? I think that's rather admirable of them."

She was not sure Ada had heard. She was rubbing at a stain on her dress, and when she looked up, she seemed momentarily lost, her mouth agape. Her mother had only just turned fifty. Though her hair was greying, she still had the energy of any two women. But in this moment of discomposure, she looked her age. Reaching over, Miriam gave her arm a squeeze.

Down River Street, on the opposite side of the road, the conical tower of the Bannerman mansion thrust above the grey-green cloud of its orchard. How well she remembered the Bannermans' big Daimler parked on the front lawn, its top folded back so that the three of them—John's wife, Martha, Gracie, and herself—could perch on its leather seats enjoying the view as they drove to California. Finger sandwiches. Milky tea. John stopping by with his little bag of humbugs—

"I really must get going," Ada announced. But she continued to sit, her rocker creaking slightly.

"Has Grace come back?" Miriam said after a while. Her sister had left the house late that morning, some hours after Ted. An awareness of their double absence had been with her since.

"*I* haven't seen her," Ada answered, sounding slightly put out. A couple of hours later, hearing the front gate latch,

Miriam looked out her bedroom window to see her sister and husband advancing up the walk. Grace led the way, her hat carried loosely at her side, while Ted trudged behind with his head down, the two of them wrapped in an intimacy she judged had started long before the present moment. When they disappeared under the porch roof, Miriam slipped into the hall. Listening at the top of the stairs, she heard her sister say, "We'll get you some water." Miriam waited a few seconds before following them to the kitchen.

"Oh, you're back!" she cried innocently as she came in. Her mother was there too, making up a grocery list at the table.

"Yes, I've brought the wanderer home," Grace said, almost shouting. Her face was pink, shining with perspiration. Ted was sitting with an untouched glass of water in front of him. He looked exhausted, Miriam thought. "You've tired yourself out," she said quietly, going up to him.

"We ran into each other in the pine woods!" Grace cried. She was busy at the cupboards, opening and shutting doors. "Beautiful out there today!"

"A nice place to idle away the afternoon," Ada said with a touch of sarcasm. Taking up her list, she went out.

Abruptly excusing himself, Ted left by the back stairs.

"You better go see how he is," Grace told Miriam.

"Why, what's happened?"

"Nothing—you know how quickly he can change."

Miriam considered this. "Was he like that when you—ran into each other?"

"Like what?"

"He looks wrung out. He doesn't usually look like that when he comes back from a walk. Usually he looks better— more himself."

"He was talking more than usual—I suppose that could do it. It may be he's a little dehydrated—he's hardly touched his water." Miriam sensed evasion. Grace was peering into the icebox. "We've got that roast beef," she said. At once she shut the icebox door and started towards the back stairs.

"Where are *you* off to?" Miriam demanded.

"Up to my room," her sister said, turning. She looked at Miriam defiantly. "Is *that* all right?"

Taking up Ted's abandoned water, Miriam brushed past her sister and climbed the stairs. She found Ted sitting on the edge of the bed, his cheek clammy and cool to her touch.

"You're not well," she said, with some satisfaction.

He did not respond; she wondered if he had even heard. He was elsewhere, obviously. He was often elsewhere, but this particular absence had hollowed him.

"Here, drink this." He took the glass from her, drank it off, handed it back. Still he would not meet her eyes.

"What's happened, Ted?" she demanded.

He seemed at a loss, as if he really didn't know. Refusing to help him out, she waited. "I don't know," he said finally. "The bottom just gave out."

"I should say it did. Did Grace have anything to do with it?"

He sighed but said nothing.

That night she woke to the sounds of rapid breathing. Turning on the light, she found him crouched on the bed beside her, his hands hovering and shaking over the mattress as if he dared not touch it, yet touching at it too, then jerking back as if it was scalding hot. When she tried to wake him, he fought her off; she had to shout to bring him back. He gaped about as if he had no idea where he was.

Then Grace was there, quickly followed by Alec and Ada.

Subdued in their midst, Ted kept insisting he was all right. Her father sent everyone away but Miriam.

While her father checked his pulse, Miriam got out fresh pajamas—Ted's were soaked. "Your eye," the doctor said, as she brought them to the bed. "You'd better get some ice on it." Ted's flailing hand had struck her.

The next day she set him up on a chaise on the terrace, with a light blanket over his legs, a small wicker table within reach. For the first time since coming home, he seemed actually convalescent, his movements slow, his usual restlessness quenched. The fact that at ten in the morning he hadn't gone off anywhere seemed remarkable to everyone.

Over the following days, the atmosphere in the house changed. People moved more carefully, as if aware of his fragility; though too there was a muted air of hopeful expectation, as if a fever had broken. Gratified that he did not refuse her care, Miriam brought him iced tea, changed his bandage, and massaged his shoulders while he worried apologetically over the black eye he'd given her. She said it was nothing; and truly, in the midst of their unexpected closeness, it was.

Sitting beside him with the latest *Star-Transcript*, she read to him from Nan's "Around the Town" column. *This week the Heighton family of Banfield Street have enjoyed entertaining Mrs. Bosley Hicks, a second cousin twice removed of the current Lieutenant Governor, Sir John Strathearn Hendrie.* Ted barked out a laugh at that—the first she'd heard from him in a good while—and wondered out loud how Nan could keep a straight face writing such stuff. "She doesn't," Miriam said. He was asleep when she finally left.

A few minutes later she glanced out and saw him talking with Grace. Her sister was going on in a low voice in the chair

Miriam had just vacated, while Ted had swung his legs to the ground. Again she caught the notes of an intimacy that excluded her. Certain her sister had wakened him, Miriam went out, and under cover of clearing his plate and glass, suggested strongly that he needed to sleep. In their silence Miriam sensed a united resistance. Going off with her tray, she glared at Grace. A vein of hostility as old as their childhoods had opened.

Later, on the front porch, well out of Ted's hearing, Miriam spoke to her sister.

"When you met him in the woods—the fever started that night. What provoked it?"

In her sister's hesitation, Miriam saw guilt. "Don't you think he's a little better now?" Grace said finally. "Calmer?"

"He's as weak as a lamb."

"Not *that* weak, Mim."

Miriam went to see Ted. He was not in his chaise. He appeared shortly with the framed map of the county that usually hung in the dining room.

"Like to see where I've been," he told her, laying it on the table.

"*I'd* like to see where you've been," Miriam said. Bending over the map with him, she followed his moving finger, yet heard scarcely a word he said.

THE NEXT DAY, she woke at dawn to an empty bed and a note on her writing table. *Back for supper. Love, Ted.* The sudden resumption of his habits took her aback. Of course he would need to walk again—she had noted a growing restlessness. But she had not expected the day to come so soon or to disappoint her so much.

He was back in time for supper, his face filled with colour, a little impatient perhaps—she was used to this—but he made a joke at the table, and when the family laughed, she noted the flicker of a smile in his response and was gratified: perhaps he was improving. That she had caught at such hopes before did nothing to stem their power. She hoped as a bird sings, instinctively.

He walked the next day, and the next as well, and when she offered to go with him—it had been some weeks since she had—he insisted on going alone. Grace had started taking longer walks herself—not with Ted, whose departures were much earlier, but by herself, setting out in mid-morning with a book and a sandwich, returning by mid-afternoon with mud on her shoes and a thoughtful opacity in her manner. The countryside around the town was vast, Miriam reminded herself—fields, villages, and woods stretching to every horizon. The chances of them meeting accidentally were small. On the other hand, if they—

She chided herself for her suspicions. Then one morning, she gave in to a temptation to follow her sister. When Grace left the house, she quickly gathered her things and set out on her trail. But she had waited too long. There was no sign of Grace. Standing in a quandary at the corner of Banfield and River, the thought of the pine woods came to her with a thrill of fear.

In forty minutes she was on the river flats. The grove was just ahead now, a dark mass shrouding the riverbank, the wild crests of the pines stamping the sky. She stepped over a stream and climbed a stony lane, her progress fired by a sense of dishonoured entitlement. She and Ted had often walked to the grove during their courtship; it was *their* place. Now her suspicion that she was being robbed of it produced a sense of fatalism. She was certain she would find them there.

Arriving within the cool, scented gallery of the pines, she glimpsed for a moment the irrationality of what she was doing. Still, she pushed on, wanting what she did not want, hurrying to embrace what she feared. Aiming for the clearing where she and Ted had picnicked, she glimpsed its stronger light ahead. Her breath came raggedly now, excitement flooding her limbs as she crept forward, expecting to see Ted and Grace at any second. Stopping behind a large pine, she heard a voice. It spoke only a word or two, isolate in the stillness of the grove, and so faint she doubted hearing it at all. Peering from behind the tree, she saw—nothing. The little clearing, striped with sun, lay empty.

Taut with expectation, she crossed the clearing, passing the litter of ashes between the firestones. On the far side, she paused in the shade of the grove to listen. Before her, the dim pines descended the hillside. Patches of sunlight trembled. Distantly, she heard the nasal fluting of a veery. Again it came, that reedy song piercing the stillness, conjuring the world's depths, wrapping her in the heavy scent of the pines. At once she was disoriented, swept by desire so strong it left her leaning for support against the trunk of a pine. Slipping her hand past the buttons of her dress, she fumbled under her camisole—

THAT NIGHT, SHE watched from the bed as Ted undressed. She had bathed and put on the light gown she had worn on her wedding night, the brush of her nipples against its soft nap an arousal that fused with the touch of air slipping past their curtains.

In the light of her bedside lamp, his arms were lean, a marbled white, though not so white as the singlet he now stripped off. Still with his back to her, he stepped out of his drawers and she saw his rounded buttocks and long, muscled legs, with

the bandage wrapping his calf and across both thighs the pale
flecks of tiny wounds that had healed, and at once she was
aroused by the thought of what he had seen, what done, drawing on powers she could scarcely imagine.

"Ted?"

"Mmm?"

"Would you like to be close?" It was their phrase for love-
making.

He paused, considering. "You don't have to do it for me,
you know," he said. At once, their past was in the room. They
had not tried for weeks; and even before the war, she had been
skittish. But she had changed, she felt; her experience in the
pines—that breathless touching of herself—had filled her with
new knowledge. She felt ready to share the kind of pleasure
he had enjoyed in the past, in their house on Barks Lane, and
in sharing it, draw closer to him. Yet in his hesitation, doubt
found her.

"I'd like to," she insisted. He reached for his pajamas and
put them on, keeping his back to her. She turned out the light.
When he eased onto the bed, she wriggled close.

"We could kiss, anyway. Come on, kiss me," she demanded.
She lay back on her pillow while he bent over her, nipping at
her lips, teasing her lips, until she dragged down his head to
her open mouth. French kissing, they called it. She had never
liked it. But tonight, for him, she gave herself to it, thinking
herself changed.

He kneaded her breasts, as she had herself that afternoon.
Again, the little currents of feeling multiplied and spread—
tinglings through her breasts and deeper, lower down. He
lifted her gown and began to rub between her legs with his finger. Her back arched as she suffered his touch. She had never

cared to be touched *there*, not so directly. For him, tonight, she would bear it. But she could not bear it for long. She grasped his wrist. "I'm sorry, Ted, not that—please."

For some seconds, he remained frozen on one elbow, head down, his breathing slowly subsiding. "It's all right," he said. "Nothing much happening at my end anyway." He rolled to his back, and for some minutes they lay in silence.

"If you want to smoke, go ahead. I'm all right," she said. But she was not all right; she needed him to stay.

"No, no," he said, "not yet. I want to be here."

He was trying for her sake, she knew, as she was trying for his. But she felt a failure.

When she woke, he was gone. Slipping from the bed, she went to the window. Moonlight had reassembled the yard with its blue and grey metals. He was not in his usual spot by the fence, or by the magnolia. From below came a soft chiming. Twelve o'clock. She put on her robe and left the room, following the hall past her parents' closed door. Turning the corner, she passed the white rectangle of her sister's door and arrived at the back of the house. Below lay the terrace, the lawn, the garden, sculpted in greys and whites. He was not there either. A shadow moved, and a cat—was it Kiki?—trotted swiftly out of sight.

14.

Miriam was alone with her mother in the garden, gathering greens and flowers for the table, when Ada asked how she was doing. It was more than a polite enquiry. Secateurs in hand, she stood regarding Miriam with unwavering directness. There was a power in Ada McCrae—everyone knew that—but there was no hint in her face now of the robust sociability, the brilliant smiles that so often masked her purposes. She was looking at her daughter with a frankness Miriam found unsettling. "Fine, Mum," she sang, moving away.

"Don't turn away from me, Miriam."

Turning back, Miriam offered her mother a look of cheerful, enquiring innocence.

"You don't look fine. You're not sleeping, are you?"

"It'll pass."

"You once said you'd like to move out. I opposed it—given the state of everyone's finances it hardly seemed possible—but I think it would be good for you, for both of you, if you could manage it. We're rather on top of each other here. I admit, the walls *are* rather thin. It can't be easy for either of you. We could help a little—my shares have made more than I expected. But the main thing is Ted's pension—surely it's due."

"That's very kind of you, Mum."

"The Carruthers boy, he came back after Ted and he's already—"

"Yes, you mentioned that," Miriam said dryly.

"You need to find out what's happening—has Ted lifted a finger to find out?"

"Mother, it will come when it comes. We're perfectly capable of taking care of it ourselves."

"Come-when-it-comes doesn't sound like taking care of anything. With an outfit as big as the army, there are bound to be mistakes. He really should look into it. I mean, he surely has the time—he could walk to Toronto and find out."

"Mother! That's hardly fair."

"I'm trying to protect my daughter—fairness doesn't interest me."

Fierce with love, Ada's gaze would not release her. *I will not weep*, Miriam told herself. Since moving back to Brockwood, she had grown steadily more impatient with her mother; she had catalogued her every fault. Now, as she faced her in the garden, there were only the two of them in the world. All else had fallen away.

Ada wasn't through. Almost imperceptibly, she nodded at Miriam as if to say, *There! You understand, don't you?* Miriam turned away and carried her lettuces into the kitchen. *She knows*, Miriam thought, feeling heat invade her face. *She's seen it too.* She went to the window and peered out into the low sun. Ada had bent again to her roses. Miriam was tempted to ask her the details of what she knew, but pride held her back: her reluctance to admit that her marriage was in trouble; and shame that she'd let it founder. Something was happening between Ted and Grace. Until this moment, she'd been able to tell herself, if only half convincingly, that her suspicions were her own invention; her mother's look, her strong suggestion that they move had confirmed them.

After supper, she walked with Ted into the downtown. They crossed the iron bridge to the Flats, turning aside onto the path that followed the top of the flood dyke. To their left the Shade flowed through the shadow cast by the western hills and downtown stores. Ahead, sun flooded the path of beaten earth. They had walked here during the early days of their marriage. The thought of those times weighed on her, reminding her of what she had to lose.

She swung their joined hands—a thing they had used to do. But his arm was heavy in resistance, and she soon gave it up. Ahead, the long sweep of Bannerman's dam poured white water into dark. The scent of oxygenated water was in the air. The dimming sunlight, sloping from the west, brought back the memory of a drowning the previous summer. In the lake behind the dam, a young man had swum to a young woman's rescue. After a struggle, both had slipped from sight. She had seen the boats searching, the men with their long, hooked poles probing the depths under the rail trestle, watched by the families waiting on shore.

Reaching the dam, they started over the iron footbridge that crossed Bannerman's mill race, just where it diverged from the river. When he took out his cigarettes, she paused at the rail beside him.

"Any news yet of your pension?" She spoke with a forced casualness, as if the question had only just occurred. He made no reply but continued smoking as he leaned on the rail. "Ted?" she said, her voice rising as she took his arm.

Sidelong, his eyes flashed at her, and she felt a stab of fear; his eyes could seem more mineral than human.

"I want to talk about your pension."

He took another drag of his cigarette.

"I want to move out of Brockwood, Ted. Soon. We don't have a life there, not the way we should. I know you know that. The whole family—we're too much in each other's laps." She dared not mention Grace, though Grace, suddenly, was there. Defying his silence, she pressed on. "I want to do it soon, Ted. Are you listening to me?" she cried.

"Yes, yes, I'm listening," he said, clearly irritated.

"We need money for that. The army—something that big— they can make mistakes. They could have overlooked you. Couldn't you go to Toronto and talk to the regiment?"

He took in a deep breath and expelled it through his nostrils, looking around grimly as if for escape. "Well?" she said, holding her ground. "For heaven's sake, look at me, Ted."

"There won't be a pension," he said in a low voice.

"Oh!" she gasped.

Flicking his cigarette away, he did turn to her then. In his eyes was the kind of pain that anticipates pain. Yet he was there somehow, the old Ted—for a split second she saw him.

"There was an incident. Right at the end. There was an inquiry. They decided I didn't deserve a pension. They were probably right. I'm sorry." She moved to touch him, but he twisted away.

"An incident—" she said, uncomprehending.

His voice grew rough. "At the end, the last time I was on the Line—"

"What happened?"

"Goddammit, have some mercy!" he shouted. He stalked off, turned, came back. He was breathing hard; his eyes glistened. "I'm sorry, Mim. You don't deserve—I'll get some kind of work."

"Why didn't you tell me sooner? I could have helped."

"I've told you as soon as I could, goddammit!"

She fell silent. They both turned to the river. A man in hip waders was fishing below the dam, his line tugged away by the current.

"What work will you get?" she said, after a while.

"Anything," he snapped, throwing out his hand. "Teaching."

She said nothing. A few days earlier he'd told her he wasn't ready to teach.

His jaw worked. "Or if not that, I'll get something on a farm."

"Yes," she said quietly, wanting only to placate him now.

As they walked home, she struggled to imagine what he had done that had deprived him of his pension. Glancing at him, she saw his face was set in a hard mask and judged it was not the time to ask—if indeed it ever would be. She was afraid of his secret, she realized; and now, seeing his eyes with their shrunken pupils frantically searching some remote space that was closed to her, she guessed he was afraid of it too.

Over the following days, his announcement that there would be no pension harrowed her. Was there no way forward for them then? Did he mean it about finding work? Was he capable of work—of any kind? As far as she knew, he hadn't looked. Did he even want to leave Brockwood? Did he consider her needs at all? At times his secrecy, his failure to confide in her, could raise her ire. Yet, conscious of his suffering, she held back her anger, though now and then it leaked out in a fit of impatience, or hardened into coolness.

Then some kindness would come. He would smooth her hair, or echo her own searching *I love you* with a quick *Love you too*. Then all her doubts would vanish, only to return when he left the room. In her mind's eye, she saw him embrace her sister. She seemed powerless to prevent such visions, which drew her powerfully. There was a new locus of intimacy in the house, and it had a dark, heavy excitement hedged with bitterness and anger.

SHE THREW HERSELF into her work with the League. It was her old remedy—work to keep from thinking, work to do some good in the world, her own problems be damned. She bought groceries for Caroline Best; minded Eileen Kelly's three little ones while Eileen looked after her mother; helped Dora McConachie fill out a government form; took cheques to women who needed extra; recanvassed well-to-do households in the north end. Still, she seemed to move in two worlds at once—down streets and lanes, and through a secret life more real than the people moving past her. In her head, she argued with phantoms. She surprised them at their misdeeds and recoiled from her own imaginings. This was not *her*, surely!

She sought relief in the company of Nan Williams—an escape into normalcy, or so she thought of it. The two friends strolled through the town, talking of family, of their remembered girlhood, of their work, and in the associative drift of their talk, she took flight above the heavy mass of her secret life, which in the light of day, with her old friend chatting beside her, seemed a thing of foolishness and shame. Yet the weight of it did not go away; it was there in their pauses, and in the bleak waters of the Shade, its shimmering surface ambushed by clouds.

Nan did not ask about Ted; this seemed to Miriam an act of kindly forbearance, and she was grateful. Yet she sensed an enquiry would come, and to forestall it, she spoke of Ted herself, announcing that he'd had a few bad days but was noticeably better now. "These ups and downs of his! I fancy I see some progress. I think he does too. He said the other day that he felt almost normal."

She made no mention of Grace, or of her jealousy. Or of her frantic trek to the pines. She only skimmed the cream of her experience, and for a few moments it seemed all there was. Beside her, Nan remained silent. Miriam sensed skepticism—or perhaps it was only her own awareness of speaking shallow truths.

"And his anger?" Nan said.

"Well yes, that's still there," she admitted, adding quickly, "but not so much!"

"Has he been able to talk about the war?"

"A little," Miriam said. "It upsets him to talk about it. I'm not sure that's the best way forward—not just now anyway. The walking seems to help more than anything. Oh look, there's a hawk!"

They had taken a bench on the Lookout, high on the steep hill overlooking the centre of town. The bird was at their level, close enough they could see its feathers ruffling as it hung nearly stationary in the wind. Abruptly, it sheered off, hurtling away over the rooftops. The sight thrilled them, and for a while, taken out of themselves, they were silent.

"You know," Nan said, "Horace envied Ted, when he went off."

Miriam looked at her in astonishment. "I wouldn't think he envies him now."

"No, but Ted went, and Horace didn't. I think a part of him has always regretted it. He holds it against himself."

"It's hardly his fault he failed the medical."

"Of course it isn't. But it's not really rational. It's—I really don't know what it is."

"It reminds me of the day Ted came home and announced he'd joined up. It floored me. I'd thought he was against the war—he'd certainly said he was. It was all nonsense, he said. Then he walked in the door and—" She shook her head.

"Yes, what is that?" Nan said fiercely. "Horace was against the war too—he still is. But there's still this regret. I can sense it."

Below them, the shadows of clouds flooded the rooftops. The hawk had disappeared.

LATER THAT WEEK, Miriam heard news that shook her. Millie Tottle—a woman Miriam knew only by sight—had lost her soldier son, but not in the usual way, to German guns or bombs. Bobby Tottle had been shot for desertion—the first local man to have met such a fate. Out of kindness, Nan and Horace had kept the story out of the *Star-Transcript*. But its rival paper, the *Empire*, published it while keeping the young man's identity back. It hardly mattered. His name was soon on everyone's lips. Some of Millie's neighbours had shunned her, Miriam heard. There had been other cruelties. Miriam went to see her.

Her way took her into the south end of town, into a neighbourhood of small houses where millworkers and their families lived. She had made many visits here, both for the League and to visit Ted's family. Like Rose and George, Millie was English, one of the hundreds of textile workers from the Midlands who had arrived before the war. In this part of town, English accents were as common as Canadian ones. On her visits for the League, over pots of tea, she'd often listened as someone read out a recent letter from Stoke-on-Trent or Wolverhampton, or regaled her with some treasured story from the old country. Yet for all her familiarity with the people here, she had never lost her awareness of herself as an out-sider. A woman she asked for directions eyed her warily before sending her to a small cottage, its back against the Shade.

A swath of fresh whitewash had been slapped up beneath Millie's front window, apparently to cover words painted there, though the letters C, O and W were still dimly visible. When Miriam knocked, it was some time before she heard a bolt being worked. The door cracked open and half a sallow face appeared. "I thought it might be them kids again," Millie said, opening wider. The little woman regarded Miriam sus-piciously as she introduced herself. Millie's face was haggard, her eyes red-rimmed, her bulldog chin jutting defiantly.

"I was wondering if we might talk," Miriam said.

"What about?"

"About Bobby."

The watery eyes brightened. "You have news then?"

"I wish I did."

Millie looked her up and down, and suddenly Miriam was conscious of her clothes. She dressed modestly for this work, in tan jacket and skirt, but still—here was Millie in a frowsy black cardigan, her blouse spotted with food stains. "You work for the League, don't you?"

"That's right."

"I don't need charity, luv."

"Of course not. This is more a private visit."

She followed Millie into a dim, stuffy room smelling faintly of camphor. Behind drawn curtains, the sun silently raged. Millie eased herself into an armchair. Beside her, a small table held a mess of papers, a plate littered with crumbs, an Edward VII cor-onation cup. Miriam carried a chair from across the room.

"I thought it might be them kids," Millie said. There's two of them, the butcher's boy and that other one—Johnson. They won't leave me alone. If my Bobby was here—" Her voice trailed off. "You the doctor's daughter then?"

"Yes."

"They say he's good. Course, I could never afford him."

"Do you need a doctor, Millie?"

Millie stared at her, unresponsive. "They shot my boy for a coward!" she shouted suddenly. Her eyes burned accusingly at Miriam, who instantly felt included in the *they* Millie had invoked—the ones who ran things, who kept their reasons to themselves, who had murdered her son. "He wasn't like that!" Millie cried.

"No," Miriam said in a whisper.

"Nothing like that!"

"No."

"He never did a cowardly thing in his life!" Millie clapped herself on the chest. "I've lost my bloody glasses," she said.

"Can I help you find—"

"That time up at Rainey's store—" Millie was shouting again. "You tell *me* if that was coward's work! He faced up to half a dozen of them—our Bobby did that." She glared defiantly, as if Miriam might understand everything from the sheer force of her fury. "They knocked him off his stilts—the other kids did—teasing him. His dad made them stilts. He was as proud as anything of them. George Rainey, he saw the whole thing. He came and told us about it. 'You can be proud of that boy'— George Rainey said that. 'You can be proud of that boy—he wouldn't back down.' There were six or seven of them, some bigger than him, and he wouldn't back down." Millie fell silent. Her eyes glowed.

Later, Miriam made tea for her. She helped her find her glasses, a search that took them through all the rooms of the little house. Millie showed her Bobby's room, a starkly neat place with an iron bedstead, and on the small dresser, a brush and comb. "I left it the way it was. For when he comes back." On the wall hung a framed photo of Bobby's father with his arm around the boy. A deflated soccer ball sat on a chair. Out the window, Miriam saw a lawn badly in need of cutting, a tree with a swing, the brown ribbon of the Shade: Bobby's view.

Millie showed Miriam a letter from his commanding officer, a Lieutenant Corcoran, who said that Bobby had served admirably for two and a half years. He said that was a long time for anyone to keep his nerve. What had happened at the end was something that could have happened to anybody. He had tried to get Bobby a lighter sentence, he wrote, but hadn't been able to: he had never stopped regretting his failure. He promised to come and see her one day.

Millie brought out the family album. They sat side by side on a horsehair settee, in the suffocating heat. Miriam studied the tiny photographs. Bobby, nine years old, grinning over the fish he held up on a leader. Bobby with a ball under his arm, standing with his pals. Bobby in uniform, cocky under his forage cap, one arm around his mother's shoulders as Millie, her face thrust forward, beamed like a girl.

THAT EVENING AT supper, Miriam told the story of her visit. The family listened in silence. Even Will seemed intent. When Miriam had finished, Ada, passing the gravy boat, said, "Very sad."

"Sad!" Grace cried. "It's horrible!"

Ada turned to Miriam. "I thought we'd agreed that the League wouldn't approach Millie until we decided what was appropriate."

"I went on my own," Miriam said tartly. "I didn't talk League business—though someone certainly should." She felt at the end of her patience—with everything.

"So you didn't mention the League," Ada said.

"She was completely dependent on Bobby's pay—that's stopped now. She has nothing. She's completely on her own." Miriam looked around the table. Everyone was watching her closely. "Millie's a casualty as much as any mother who's lost her son."

"I see that perfectly well," Ada said. "I'm sure we all do. But the matter is complicated—"

"Why would you even *hesitate?*" Grace railed at her mother.

"Because I'm not running the League any more—that's Ann Kerr's job. She needs to bring Millie's case to a vote, and it's by no means certain it would pass. Half the women *at least* are against helping deserters' families."

"In heaven's name, why?" Grace said. "Have we even had a deserter from this town? What do any of them know about it? Nothing, I'd guess." Grace flashed a look at Miriam. For a moment they were allies.

Ada's eyebrows went up. "They worry that if people knew we were helping Millie, it would affect donations. People won't want to give money, especially the ones with men overseas, if they know it's going to—such things."

"Do *you* worry about that?" Grace said.

"I can't stand it," Miriam said, bringing her hand down on the table. Everyone looked at her, startled. "The woman's having a terrible time of it. No one visits her. Kids paint things on her house, horrible things. And she thinks she's going to get a pension. I didn't have the heart to tell her otherwise."

"You mean they don't give pensions to deserters' mothers?" Grace cried.

Miriam shook her head. "Two days ago, I phoned the battalion's headquarters. A chap there, an officer, told me Millie shouldn't expect anything. He seemed sorry about it—not that that does Millie any good. We *have* to help her."

"What's a deserter?" Will said.

"Someone who runs away," Grace said.

"Bobby was a coward?"

"No, he wasn't," Miriam told him. "We don't know what he did." She turned back to the others. "Millie showed me a letter from his lieutenant. Corcoran, his name was. Did you know him, Ted?"

Her husband shook his head. He had grown restless as their argument progressed. "It's a big army" was all he would say. Miriam regarded him with sudden alarm. What nerve had she just touched with her talk of Bobby? She looked at Grace, who averted her eyes, and immediately forgot what she was saying.

"Lieutenant Corcoran," her father prompted. He had not spoken a word during their discussion, yet Miriam sensed he was sympathetic.

"He said Bobby was a good soldier," Miriam went on. "For nearly *three years* a good soldier. Then something happened— who knows what? Certainly, Millie doesn't know. He can't stand it any more. He runs away. Or he won't run forward. He won't get out of bed in the morning. For three years he does everything he's told, and then one day he can't do it any more and so they kill him."

"*They killed him?*" Will whispered, his eyes huge. At that moment Ted lurched to his feet and strode from the room. Seconds later they heard the screen door to the porch bang shut.

AS THE CONVERSATION about Millie limped on, Miriam was restless, charged with anger that seemed futile, given her mother's intransigence around helping the woman. She left the table and went out. Ted was smoking on the lawn.

"*You* left in a hurry," she said sharply, coming up to him. Smoke poured from his nostrils as he ground out his cigarette. "So where are we off to?" she asked. They had agreed earlier to a walk.

"You choose," he said.

"I'll do whatever you—"

"For God's sake, treat me like ordinary man, would you? I'm not an invalid. Everywhere is fine with you. I can never tell what you think, not really. All you do is agree with me."

"All right," she said coldly, taken aback. He had never made this criticism before—it was as if he questioned her care of him.

"So where shall we go?" he said harshly.

She gestured to the north, but really it might have been anywhere. Taking his arm, she paced beside him; he was going too fast for her, as he so often did, but she decided to match him without complaint—she was as good as he. In no time, they reached the countryside. Before them lay the long, straight road between fields crimsoned by late sun. They were headed towards a low ridge in the distance.

"So you'd prefer I picked fights with you, like her?"

"*Her*," he said with withering irony. "Who is *her*?"

"You know very well who she is."

It was some seconds before he replied.

"I enjoy her forthrightness," he said, adding mockingly, "You're not jealous, are you?"

"Of course not."

"I like bantering with her. We've always done it. What's the point of this?"

"No point!" she sang, as if indifferent. But she was filled with rank fury now—from her weeks of self-effacing care, from her suspicions, from her visit to Millie Tottle, from a sense she had given much and received little in return. "I want to move out," she told him, drawing him to a halt. He stared grimly up the road. "I want to move out and I want to do it as soon as possible. You said you'd find work. That was two weeks ago, and as far as I can tell, you've done nothing. If you can tramp about all day, surely you can get some kind of job. I understand it can't be teaching. But *something*, Ted. Working for a farmer. Doing deliveries—out-of-doors work would be good for you. Ted, are you even listening?"

With apparent calm, he took out his cigarettes. She looked at the crumpled pack with loathing: she hated the smell of the things. She saw defiance in the way he scraped a match, lit the cigarette, shook out the flame and took a long drag. He said, "The last time we discussed the subject, you said we should stay where we were."

"Not the *last* time," she said. "Have you forgotten already? Our walk by the river—I told you then I wanted to move out!"

"Why?"

"Why do I want to move out? Do I really have to say? Wouldn't *you* like us to have our own place again?"

"Sure," he said flatly.

Furious, she started to walk away. But she soon turned back. He had not moved, but stood calmly smoking, leaning on his cane. She spoke with icy force. "You don't sound very enthusiastic my dear: our own place—a chance to mend whatever's come between us."

"Nothing's come between us."

Suddenly, not wanting to, she started to weep in frustration. "What we had, Ted, before the war—don't you want that again? Don't look away from me—it's a real question. Don't you want that again?"

"I do," he said, his voice rough. It was all she needed—or perhaps she only feared asking for more. Embracing him, she felt his free arm slide across her shoulders. But he wasn't there, not really. She too was pretending, or hoping. Sick of herself, she broke away.

As they walked on, she tried to give herself to his violent pace, but with a blister coming and her own anger on the boil, she soon demanded they slow down. He did slacken his pace, but she could sense him chafing, a horse held back. They reached the northern edge of the plain and climbed the shallow slope, where they turned to gaze over the farmlands they had crossed. The sun was almost down. Here and there amid the long shadows of trees and buildings were glints of water.

"I'm going to get work myself," she announced. She had pondered the idea in the past; it had returned with sudden clarity. As he continued to smoke, her anger grew. "Ted—did you hear me?"

"What?"

"I'm going to get work."

He blew smoke with a jerk of his shoulders: a stifled laugh? "What—you think I can't?"

"No wife of mine," he said. In the early days of their marriage, she had heard this phrase from him with a certain pleasure; it had seemed a mark of the grown-ups they had become, and a promise of protection, thrilling in its way. Now the phrase was oppressive. "You can forget it," he added.

"All kinds of women work. Grace works!" she threw at him. "The shell factory—it's full of women now—they pay good money too."

"They're not your type," he said.

She knew what he meant. The women there—lower class, rougher. But she knew them better than he suspected.

"And anyway, you wouldn't last five minutes—if they'd even have you. You're not going to work," he said, grinding his cigarette underfoot.

"I'll work if I want to. And really, Ted, if you're not going to work, or can't find work that pays enough—" She watched as he took out another cigarette. "Do you have to smoke those damned things? You smoke them end to end. It can't be good for you. Dad says—"

"Damn your dad," he said, whirling on her. "Just stop your bloody nagging, will you?" He walked off and stood smoking with his back to her, but soon threw down his cigarette. "I half hate the things myself."

He asked if she wanted to go back. In his tone she heard contrition, or as close as he could get to it. She nodded numbly, and they set off down the long slope into the thickening murk of the plain. He was moving more slowly now, for her sake she knew, yet she could feel his impatience, his desire to be off.

15.

Stink and his gang left him alone now, though occasionally they'd look over at him from their corner of the yard with an air of puzzled wistfulness, as if they were not quite sure what had happened. He saw their longing and felt less need to stick close to Beggar. Yet the memory of his time with the older boy—the firing of the .22 and their hour by the river— lived on in him. Now and then they spoke in the yard, Beggar on one occasion promising they'd go into the woods again. But the day never came. When Beggar spoke to some other boy, he watched jealously from across the yard, and when school let out for the holidays, he grieved the loss of his friend. Beggar had a job for the summer, he'd told Will. He was going to work for a farmer called Two-Bit Pete. "He don't pay much, but every penny counts." He wasn't going to have much time off, he said.

So the long schoolless days began. At times he played with other boys. Tiring of chasing a baseball across a sun-baked field, he would retreat to the cool of Brockwood's library, where he buried himself in *The Three Musketeers* and other novels by Dumas, finding in the adventures of their heroes some trace of the thrill he had experienced with Beggar. Alone, he descended to the flats by the Shade, where the summer's crop of thistles made for hard going in his short pants.

As he watched, the snapping turtle lifted its hooked head and fell as still as the rock beneath it. Under a bleaching sun, the remains of a snake lay rotting on the shore. Intuiting something ancient and cruel, he pressed on. Stooping over a shallow pool, he tried to catch small frogs, but they were too quick for him, arrowing away with kicks of their streaming legs. Across the thistled flats the sun beat down in a time neither yesterday nor tomorrow. He returned to his books.

One day his mother interrupted his reading. "There's a very strange boy to see you."

Beggar was waiting outside the back gate. His shirt was soiled, his face glossy with sweat. He'd run down from Two-Bit Pete's, he said, glancing past Will's shoulder. Will's mother, having returned to her chair on the terrace, was watching them.

"Can you come over Saturday?" Beggar said, lowering his voice. "I have to work in the morning, but the afternoon is good. I can show you some things up the river. There's this cave we can go to—"

His happiness was restored in an instant. When Beggar left, his mother called him over.

"Who was that, dear?"

"Beggar Creeden."

"What a strange name! I've never heard you speak of him. Are you friendly with him?"

Sensing disapproval, he hesitated.

"Tell me about him. Where does he live?"

"In the Junction."

"I see. And what does his father do?"

"Um . . . He doesn't have a father."

"I see," his mother said, looking askance.

"He was killed in the war."

"Oh," his mother said. She did not remain silent for long. "What does his mother do then? How does she—"

"She does laundry for people."

His mother nodded slowly, knowingly. "Now, Will," she said gravely, her eyes searching him out. "I'm sure this Beggar—"

"His real name is Barry," he said.

"Yes, well, whatever his name is, I'm sure he's a fine chap in his way, but you see, Will, he's not really our sort." As she talked on about how important it was to choose the right kind of friends, he felt his delight at seeing Beggar pushed down, his anticipation of Saturday pushed down. At once, he was in the woods with Beggar, his cheek to the cool stock of the gun; and now, his mother's hand touching his arm, in a desolate place where there was only the glare of white papers on her table. He scarcely listened as her voice went on, explaining, depriving, reminding him of his grandfather, *the mayor of this town. Reputation*, the voice said. *Our sort of people*, it said. "So, one way to help us keep our good name, and to help yourself along too—we mustn't forget that—is to choose the right kind of friends. Boys like David McNab, or Archie Smith—both from good families. I can't imagine either of them showing up at our gate looking like—like your acquaintance there."

"Beggar's from a good family," he said.

"Well," his mother demurred, while her sad smile said, *That's very sweet, but I'm afraid you haven't lived long enough to understand.*

"He was kind to me."

"Perhaps so. But what did he want? Why was he here?" When he did not answer, she said, "You want to have a happy life, don't you?"

"Sure."

"Well, there you go. I'm sure this Beggar, Barron, whatever he calls himself, is very nice in his way, but being friends with him isn't going to help you. It isn't going to help you grow up in the best way you can, to be the best person you can be. It certainly won't help you get a good position one day, or marry someone you can be proud of. Do you understand?"

He remained silent.

"Will, do you?"

"I guess."

"Good boy. Your mother loves you very much."

When he began to head inside, she drew him back.

"You haven't told me what you and Barron were planning."

"Barry," he said. "He was just saying hello."

"Are you sure that was all? Did he ask you to go somewhere?"

"He's working at Two-Bit Pete's. He had to hurry back."

"Will, I don't want you going anywhere with him. Is that understood? Will, is it understood?"

So it came down to what he knew had been there all along, behind her smiles and her fingers stroking the outside of his arm. She was the only one in the family who had ever struck him, and though she had not done it for years, he felt the shadow of those punishments as a sense of hopelessness: it was futile to resist. Better to give in and return to the warm nest of her approval.

But the nest had not so much attraction as it once had; and although what she said had touched his fear—who did not want to have a happy life?—it had not reached his conscience. His conscience had become a fleeing, lonely thing, hidden in the hills of his resistance. For the moment it was lost, unsure of its loyalty, a fugitive from what he perceived was an injustice.

WHEN SATURDAY AFTERNOON came, he wheeled his bicycle out of the garage, swung his leg over the crossbar, and pedalled quickly down Baird. Something in him grew light as he went along, charged by a sense of panic that was also intoxication at his growing freedom as Brockwood sank behind him; he was going to see Beggar, they were going to the cave. On he went, up Banfield into the Junction, where boxcars rumbled and cattle bawled from the yards: he had escaped into the great world!

Barry was not home yet, his mother told him, turning from her clothesline. "Sometimes the farmer keeps him late. Here's Carrie," she said, and Will saw the girl, her plaits bound to her head in a way he liked. She had just come around the corner of the house. The little one came behind her, dragging a bamboo rake. When Beggar's mother went inside with her basket of laundry, they were alone.

"So you're Barry's friend?" Carrie said, her head a little on one side.

"I guess," he said.

"What's your name?"

"My real name is William, but they call me Will."

"Names are funny," she said. "*Her* name is Laura," she said, pointing at her little sister, "but we call her Lolly. Why didn't we call her Lolly in the first place?"

"Then you could call her Laura!" he said. Her shout of laughter made him happy, as if he could think of anything.

They drifted down the central path of a large garden, adjusting to the slow pace of the toddler. Carrie was behind him a grade, they discovered. Next fall, she would have the teacher he'd just left, Miss Roberts. He wanted to say that he loved Miss Roberts but made do with saying that she was the best teacher he'd ever had; he did not tell her he'd wept knowing he wouldn't have her again, or about Tommy Graham's jeers. There was a boldness about Carrie, an aliveness that infused the things she drew his attention to: the rows of radishes that were her responsibility, the tire swing her dad had put up. She spoke of her father in a way that made him seem alive, and for a moment Will seemed to see the garden as he had seen it: the fence he had made, the scarecrow he and Beggar had put up, its arms stretched like wings over the grey-green rows slumbering in the heat.

AFTER BEGGAR HAD washed and changed, they went into the woods. Will was disappointed Beggar hadn't brought his gun. "I don't always like to carry it," he said. "It's different when you have a gun, you know?"

Will thought he did know, but he liked the difference, the way he had felt with the .22 in his hands, everything he looked at brighter, somehow clearer.

They went the way they had gone before, down the steep bank to the flat white rocks where he had fired the .22, then upstream past the little beach where the pickerel bones had been—gone now—past the willow hung with a window frame, to a place where the river broadened through shallow rapids. Picking their way across, they balanced on ledges, leapt over sluicing narrows, wading the final yards with their shoes in their hands. As they sat putting them on, Beggar said, "Look." A heron was stroking past. Extending its long legs, it glided lower and with a last flurry of wings settled and was there, its neck folded back, standing motionless over the glittering shallows.

They went on through the cool shadows of woods, where giant ferns brushed their arms. Ahead, behind trees, brightness beckoned. They had reached the edge of fields. "Lots of arrow-heads around here," Beggar said. With sudden interest, Will studied a furrow where the wheat grew sparsely. Beyond the fields, thrusting over a line of woods, rooftops had appeared. A church spire. A tall factory chimney. Was it a town? His town? He was happily lost, trusting in what carried him along: Beggar, and the spirit of their day. Along the field's edge, they kept to the shade of enormous maples until another path opened and they plunged back into woods. Now their way ran along the side of a wooded hill, descending through little dells before climbing again. Beggar pointed out a spill of stones the pioneers had picked from the fields. They found a speckled kettle, its bottom rusted out. A garter snake wriggled off the path. Below them, intermittently, the little river appeared, a brown secret in the green woods. When Beggar drew him into the underbrush, he wondered what was happening. Someone was coming along the path, Beggar indicated. Will could make out nothing. A mourning dove was cooing—that sad single note endlessly repeated.

When the boy appeared, Will knew him at once. Stink Henderson was scuffing down the path, entirely alone it seemed, and the dove Will had heard was the sound of Stink crying—sobbing and hooting as he went along, his big face shiny with tears. He disappeared into the dell below them, then re-emerged farther on, dissolving at last in the camouflage of the woods.

"His brother was killed," Beggar said, looking after him. "Les Cook told me. He was in France there. Just like my da." He was staring so intensely at the spot where Stink had disappeared that Will had to stare too. When Beggar said they had to talk to Stink, Will looked at him in disbelief.

"Come on," Beggar said, already stepping out. "We don't want to lose him."

He wanted nothing to do with Stink Henderson, yet he plodded behind his friend, back the way they had come. There was no adventure in the path now, no pleasure at seeing the fields where arrowheads were—everything had emptied except Beggar himself: the promise of the day shrunk to his friend's blue-shirted back hurrying ahead of him.

They found Stink sitting on the felled trunk of a poplar by the rapids. Will hung back as Beggar approached him. Stink looked up with red eyes. "We heard the news," Beggar said. "I'm sorry, Larry. You know Will here."

At Stink's glance, Will looked away.

His heart sank when Beggar joined Stink on the log. "My da," he heard Beggar tell Stink. "About this time last year." Not knowing what else to do, Will stood waiting at a distance while Stink carried on hooting and sniffing. He wished he'd shut up. He wished Beggar would say what he had to so they could go.

Across the pale rock, the river tore through its rapids. "He promised he'd come back," he heard Stink say. "He said when he came back we'd go to Alberta. Me and him!"

When their voices stopped, Will looked over at them. Beggar and Stink were staring at the river now, staring at it as if hypnotized by the charging water collaring rocks and swarming in the eddies. For a long time, neither of them moved. Then Beggar shifted on the log, and thinking he was about to get up, Will perked up. But nothing changed.

In a pique, Will sat down on a rock. From time to time, Stink sniffed or groaned, and still the two went on staring as a shadow swept the river. Suddenly the height of trees shrouding the opposite bank looked foreboding. A lonely boulder ploughed upstream.

When Beggar said he needed to piss, Will got up too, but Beggar told him to stay. So he sat back down, and when Stink sobbed, Will glanced over at him. Stink was looking right at him, his red-rimmed eyes brimming with pain; and for a moment Will saw *him*, Larry Henderson, peering out.

LATER, AFTER STINK had shuffled off, his big legs rubbing together, Beggar said they should go. Will thought he meant go home, but he turned back to the woods. Beggar was somewhere else now, thinking of something else, no longer aware of him as the nameless woods went by, no longer stopping to point things out or reminisce about things he'd done. Will held out hope for the cave. It was just a short walk, Beggar said. Will imagined something spacious, chamber behind chamber, stalactites, secret pools. But when they got there, it was only two big rocks leaned together. A damp, sour smell between them. The smashed china head of a doll. Beggar, his back to him, had stayed down by the water.

"We used to fish here," Beggar said as Will joined him. "My da and me." His voice had lifted, wistful. Will looked at the water swinging through the bend, its brown surface dimpled with little travelling whirlpools that popped up and quickly vanished, a desolation of changing water, never the same thing twice.

HE WAS BACK in time for supper. When his father asked what he'd done that day, he sensed his mother listening down the table. "Nothing," he said. "Rode my bike."

"Don't forget *Monte Cristo*," she said.
"I finished it this morning," he told his dad. So they talked a little of the book, Ted putting in a few words out of his silence. That night, trying to sleep, he kept seeing Stink Henderson's red eyes—the way they'd looked at him as if trying to speak. Along the wall, his curtains wafted out. He could hear the voices of the grown-ups, talking in the dark.

16.

In a dream Grace came to him in a man's shirt, her legs bare. Later that day, he ran into her on the back stairs. As she stopped above him, he read complicity in her look. "The boy," she said, tilting her head a little to the side. "I need to know what happened to him."

Something in him recoiled: his abandoned "story" seemed to lie on the far side of danger. Yet, over previous days, he had thought otherwise. He'd felt proud that in his stumbling, hesitant way, he'd found a kind of coherence—an achievement at a time when he felt he had little. Briefly, he'd glimpsed a way forward. But he was afraid.

She suggested they meet at the Blue Lake cabin.

"We can't hurt Mim," she insisted. He was ardent in agreement. Miriam must not be hurt. He had spent considerable effort assuring himself she was safe. As long as he and Grace kept these meetings a secret then surely she was safe; and besides, what could he do other than talk? Yet he knew he was giving to Grace what he owed his wife. And in truth, it wasn't just the talk he needed, was it? He was in love with Grace McCrae. Without that, he doubted he would be telling her anything.

The lake was a few miles out of town, held in a deep bowl fenced by woods. He waited at the head of a lane lined with maples. He had not walked this way before, but he had been here long in the past, with Miriam's family. Not often, though: Miriam's grandfather used to bring his mistress to this place, she had once told him; it was why she didn't like to come here.

He walked a little, up and down the lane between crops of green wheat. It was a still, overcast day, heavy with humidity. At the end of the lane, the woods that hid the lake had a grey look; the crests of a few white pine, taller than the maples, raised pterodactyl silhouettes. She was half an hour past her time. When a farmer and his team passed along the concession road, he stood out of sight. Finally she came. She was on her bicycle, which surprised him, her skirt flapping, her face pale under the brimmed hat tied snugly under her chin. Her skirt, he saw, was actually a pair of largish trousers made of some light stuff. He thought they looked ridiculous. If she was concerned about not attracting attention, why had she worn them? She dismounted and, pushing the bike, moved quickly down the lane while he walked beside her. "I couldn't get away," she said, catching her breath. "Mim came back sooner than I expected. She wanted to talk."

"About what?"

"We have to get out of sight."

Where the lane faded into the woods, they hid the bike and went on down a narrow path. The air was cooler here. Ahead, in the dim woods, her neck showed pale above the rust-coloured linen of her blouse. Soon water was below them, sending glints through the trees. In another minute the cabin appeared. It was made of squared logs and set back into the hillside, its roof flush with the ground behind, flickering through the woods as they walked. The sense of hollowness at his betrayal had returned. He'd felt it the first time, after talking with Grace by the river, like a door of self-sickening he had to pass through. He wondered: had Archie felt that?

Ted thought they might go into the cabin, but she turned down another path toward the limestone flats above the water. Heat radiated from bone-white rock. "Here," she announced peremptorily. He found her assumption of command amusing. She was nervous and needed things to be exactly so. At her instruction, he hauled two Muskoka chairs out of the woods, brushed them off, and set them on the limestone. She thought the chairs should face each other, but he insisted they face the lake, a few feet apart. He wanted to look over the lake, darkening towards the far shore, when he talked. If he was going to talk—he did not entirely believe he would.

"You're not too hot here?" he said. They had not yet sat down.

"I've got my hat," she said, mugging weakly as she put it on.

"So," he said, looking around uncertainly.

She seemed kidnapped by some thought as she wrung her hands. She looked up, alarmed—as if she had not known he was there. Suddenly she seemed fragile to him, too thin, and taut with fear.

On an impulse, he started towards her. At once, she put up her hands, crying out for him to stop.

"I only meant— You looked frightened."

"I told you. I can't abide surprises. Sit down."

In the low-slung chairs, they were silent for a time. Then she spoke. "After the variety show, you went up to the Line." She was waiting. In the visor of shade under her hat's brim, her eyes were alive. Her attention was like a weapon aimed, and at the same time, like a door opening; and as before, he had the feeling that his story was familiar to her; that she would understand, because she had already lived it.

"Right," he said, wincing.

"With the boy," she urged. Before him the lake was like pounded metal. Unexpectedly, the sensation of returning to the Line came back to him. It was always the same—the fear when you went back. It gathered with the miles. Your death was up there, on the Line, waiting for you. He'd tried to accept this—that his death was there, foredoomed, nothing to be done about it—a trick to banish the fear. Yet something in you hoped—and the fear came back. He felt vaguely nauseated. Inwardly, he renewed his vow not to tell her certain things; it seemed dangerous to even begin. And again, as before, he saw more than he could say.

"We were headed for a new section of the Line—hadn't been there before, knew nothing about it really. They'd shown us maps and photographs but—"

He was speaking to the lake, dull in the noon sun; and to the mass of dark pines on the far shore; and to the dim inlet there, its surface alive with the swarming of creaturely life. But it was all her; her listening had invaded all of it. As before, his voice sounded too high to him, scarcely his. But the words came, a fascination to him, drawn by the pines and the water that was her, moving almost of their own accord, into the hot air.

IN STORMS OF dust, the trucks carrying the battalion passed ragged files of men trudging the other way. Some shouted to the men in the trucks. A few in the trucks shouted back, but most watched the men on the ground in silence. Some of the retiring soldiers used crutches or had to lean on their fellows. They did not march but made their way as best they could, some walking briskly, others hobbling or barely shuffling. Some went by on stretchers, a limp arm dangling a cigarette. Blood-stained bandages wrapped limbs, heads, torsos; their loose ends flapped in the wind from the trucks. "Poor buggers," one of Ted's new recruits commented.

A veteran barked a cynical laugh. "Christ—they're the lucky ones."

They passed houses with boarded-up windows, holes torn in roofs, pastures churned to glutinous mud by the wheels of vehicles. Everywhere trees had been felled for timber, the stumps of former woodlands stretching off indefinitely, stippling the hills, butts glistening with sap. They saw shell holes from an earlier stage of the war. The new recruits pointed them out to each other—a novelty—but there were soon too many to warrant comment. Along the road, lines of poplars stood in varying degrees of distress, some torn in half, others missing only a few branches, others whole, all of them grey with the omnipresent dust.

From time to time they came to a halt. For an hour or more they would wait for some distant obstruction to clear. Eventually the trucks would grind into life again, and just when their momentum seemed irresistible, they would have to stop again. No one complained at the delay.

"And the boy?" she asked.

He had put Jimmy in the same truck as himself, "To keep an eye on him," he told her, explaining that he wanted to make sure the boy didn't screw up. But in truth (he understood this now) he had begun to need Jimmy Hartfield. He needed, as far as it was in his power, to keep him safe. He needed the war to spare him: the war, which had taken everything from so many without regard for youth or goodness or beauty—he wanted desperately for it to spare Jimmy Hartfield. He knew his obsession was dangerous: he must not forget for a moment his platoon. By an act of will, he turned his attention to his men, moving through the truck to talk to them, offering encouragement in tones of confident good cheer. He was acting, he knew. And in their cheerful responses, they were perhaps acting as well. They were going into battle in a state of make-believe. The falseness sickened him, and again his attention swung to the slim figure riding in silence near the cab. At once, he seemed to see everything through the boy's eyes—the felled forests, the shell holes, the lines of wounded men, that stack of coffins by a siding—and these sights seemed more terrible, more shameful, when seen this way. He was sorry the boy had to see them at all—a poisoned gift passed on by the men who had come before him. He felt they were betraying a trust that boys should be able to expect of men: that the world be left to them whole.

They came to the end of roads. It was too dangerous to go any farther by daylight, let alone in trucks. The final approach to the Line must be made by night, on foot. In a dusk thickened by low clouds, they set out in double file, gear clanking. From the northeast came the rumble of guns, a low, steady thunder. Perhaps it was thunder? The new recruits could not tell. Bunching up, the platoon shuffled to a halt in a darkness dampened by sprinkles of rain. Military police ran up and down the line trying to keep order. Men were jostled together as the battalion massed in a crush; elsewhere, gaps had opened that needed closing. The rain came harder now, pinging on helmets. For half an hour they stood in the downpour with their heavy packs on their backs, clutching their streaming rifles. An order came to take shelter as best they could. Men moved slowly to obey—shelter where? They sat on their packs in a field of mud, wrapped in their groundsheets, cursing the order not to smoke.

Ted had lost track of the boy. As he moved among his men, checking to see how they were doing, he searched for him. In the confusion, various units had become intermingled. He found men he did not know, but not the boy.

Just past three in the morning, the rain trailed off. The order came to move out. Down long estuaries between clouds a few stars sailed. The battalion jostled on, stopped, waited, waited some more. They had entered the first communication trenches, leading them ever deeper towards the Line. It was as if they travelled down some sunken country lane—the trench wide and only knee-deep at first, though it steadily deepened and grew narrower, the sandbagged parapets passing above their heads. They were being funnelled underground.

The spectre of a limbless tree appeared above them. Again they were ordered to halt. For the better part of an hour they stood in freezing, calf-deep water. Now came the hammering of a machine gun. "There he is," a soldier muttered as a hush of bullets swept overhead. "Right on time." In the strange intimacy of antagonists, the veterans often referred to the enemy as *he*, no name required. "He's welcomin' us back."

"How does he know we're here?" one of the new men asked.

"Spies everywhere," came the droll reply.

Ted told them to keep quiet.

After a while news came that the guide assigned to lead them through the maze of trenches had not showed up. They would have to wait. Ted asked his corporal to take a headcount of the platoon. The man sloshed away, disappearing into the murk, returning twenty minutes later with the news that they were forty-three. There had been forty-five when they boarded the trucks that morning. "Who's missing?" Ted demanded. "Was Hartfield there?"

The man shook his head. In another twenty minutes the column began to move. The wind had shifted and the stench of the Line found them. The stench of rotting corpses—men, horses, rats, decaying in the mud. You got used to it, he knew, to the point where you no longer noticed, but now, stumbling through the dark, hearing the heavy hammering of the German gun, he thought of the boy smelling it for the first time.

THEY SPENT THE rest of the night in support trenches behind the Front Line, and in the morning took the place of a British battalion. "Each time you come back," he told Grace, "you feel you've never been away. This is where you are—where you've always been. Doesn't matter that you've been on leave, that you've just got a letter or been in Paris—all that's a dream." He tried to evoke for her the place the battalion had found itself in—new in its details, for they'd never been in this section of the Line before, but offering the same cramped, furtive life below ground, knowing *he* was out there smoking and shitting and plotting his surprises. You'd take a peep through a periscope and all you could see past the wire was the same wasteland of shell holes; and oh yes, the charred trees like giant burnt matchsticks, all that remained of some wood to which the French had given some poetic name—Bois d'Or, Bois des Ruisseaux—names that persisted, attached to those ghostly remains, in the talk and plans of the soldiers from abroad. "Of course, the men changed the names to something easier on the

English tongue: Bawder Wood. Raisin Wood. There wasn't a French word they couldn't mangle."

"And the boy?" she said.

His hand trembled as he brought a match to his cigarette. Across the lake a covey of black dots glided. He shook out the flame, blew smoke, shook his head.

"He was killed!" she cried softly.

"Far from it," he said, grinning reminiscently. "Two days after we arrived, he walks around a corner, looking pretty pleased with himself. The men gave him quite the welcome."

HIS PUTTEES CAKED with mud. His left hand wrapped in a dirty bandage. And still grinning from the backslaps and shouts of greeting he'd received as he made his way down the trench. Ted saw him before he himself was seen, time to bury his heart's leap in a scowl. He took the boy into a dugout and demanded he explain himself.

A watery light fell from the doorway, revealing half of Hartfield's face.

"I got lost, sir."

"And how did you manage to get lost?"

"I needed a latrine. Bertie Atkinson—he pointed me up a side trench. I never did find it. Just—went where I was. Then coming back—"

"You took a wrong turn."

"More than one, sir. I couldn't find you." His use of "you" touched Ted with its suggestion of a personal connection. Frowning, he listened to the rest of Hartfield's story. "I walked half the night, sir. There's nothing straight out here. One way leads to ten others." Eventually, he'd fallen in with another battalion, who'd brought him to their section of the Line.

"Australians, sir. They made me feel right at home. Oh, I've got this." He handed Ted a note from one of their officers. It confirmed what Hartfield had told him. Still, one detail bothered him.

"You were two days getting back, Hartfield. You took your time about it, didn't you? What took so long? The Australians aren't that far away."

"Sir," Hartfield said, hangdog.

"Well?" Ted said sharply. The more he sympathized with the boy, the more readily the counterreaction came.

"One thing and another."

"Not good enough, Hartfield. What happened?"

"It wasn't the Australians. They sent me off the next day. It was our battalion—they'd all seen my performance."

"And how did your *performance* stop you from getting back?" He spoke disdainfully. He could imagine how it happened: the soldiers along the Line wanting him to stop for a drink, a story. Perhaps he had sung for them. Perhaps—

"Well, Hartfield?"

"It seems I'm popular, sir," the boy said with a sheepish smile.

"Popularity isn't useful, Hartfield. You shouldn't spend one minute thinking about it, and neither should they. You had a duty to get back here as quickly as you could."

"Sir."

"So what happened—*two days* to cross our lines?"

"I got lost again. Must have taken another wrong turn."

"Look at me, Hartfield."

As he obeyed, Ted saw a protestation of innocence empty the boy's face; it seemed exaggerated. "Jimmy, listen to me."

He dropped his voice. "It's important we tell the truth out here—a lie can have dangerous consequences. Men's lives depend on our knowing and telling the truth. Do you understand that?"

The boy's throat worked. "Sir." Ted was not sure he did. There was something evasive in the play of those eyes. All along, the boy had seemed transparent, naively so. But it was coming clear that he had his secrets, his shadows. In a way, it was a relief. In the dim light of the dugout, Ted felt on firmer ground.

"What happened to your hand?"

"Cut it on barbed wire, sir."

"Let me see it."

He helped Hartfield unwind the bandage, then brought him to the door of the dugout to see the wound more clearly. The palm had been sliced open, not too deeply, but there was inflammation. "You want that cleaned, Jimmy. Corporal Adams will help you."

THAT NIGHT, IN a dugout shared with fellow officers, he felt a little more cheerful than usual. Relief at Hartfield's return was the cause, he knew—another sign the boy had become too important. Yet he hadn't the will to reject such consolation. In the trenches, you took what you could get, and the thought of the boy, grinning at his welcome, put a smile through him.

"That night we had a barrage," he told Grace. "One side would lob over some shells—keep the other chap on his toes. The Germans started this one." He'd been dreaming he was standing on the seashore, with a child's bucket in his hand, watching the horizon grow from a glistening thread to a wall of water, its glassy surface growing taller as it raced towards him. He woke in the roaring heart of the wave. Dirt and stones were pouring down on him. Dirt was in his mouth, up his nose. Coughing and spitting, he fought to reach the faraway voices of men. They grasped at each other's bodies, shouted in each other's ears. Larry Gregoire, Ted's second lieutenant, could not be accounted for. Frantic, they dug for him. At last a hand grasped an ankle, another an arm. They dragged his unconscious body outside, where a miasma of dust boiled through the trench, flash-lit by exploding shells.

Stumbling through the turns of the trench, he groped his way past phantoms cowering in their funk-holes or digging to save their fellows. The roar of exploding shells left no place to hide, erased all thought, left no avenue of escape that did not seem it would lead to madness. Occasionally the barrage relented; then they heard from above the whistling shells of the counterbarrage. In the confusion of dust and smoke, Ted groped his way along the turns of the trench, shouting orders as he went, stopping to help dig a man free. His one thought was for the boy: a clearing in the chaos his mind had become.

Curled in his funk-hole, Hartfield was shaking uncontrollably. Ted put an arm around him, drew him to himself, said things he wished his own father had spoken into his early night terrors.

With German precision, the barrage stopped at five-thirty sharp. Half an hour later the counterbarrage eased off as well. The silence rang in men's ears. They were shocked, disoriented, wary in the grey hour before dawn. Would a ground attack come? Amid the moans of the wounded, stretchers appeared. Men found their weapons and took their places along the shattered parapet, staring out into the mists of no man's land for signs of the enemy.

From above came the twittering of birds.

"WHAT?" HE SAID.

A woman was staring at him from a Muskoka chair.

"I said—did the boy make it through? The look on your face—"

"Yes, yes, he was fine—"

THE PLATOON SUFFERED two dead: Larry Gregoire, his skull crushed by a rock; and Andy Birch, a nervous fellow who was much disliked because his obsessive chatter gave everyone the jitters. His intact head had landed on the duckboard. "Well, he won't be going off his head any more," Fellows jibed. One or two laughed, but most were silent before a death that might have come to any of them. Two others had been seriously wounded. One man, who would probably lose his foot, was carried out to hearty cries of congratulation for his Blighty.

Up and down the trench, they found chunks of shrapnel—cruel, jagged things as large as a man's hand, some larger, still warm an hour later.

Taking a cigarette break outside the ruins of his dugout, he found his hands would not work properly. His old tremor had come back. He'd grown into the habit of not worrying about himself: he did better when he focused on his men. Now fatigue, like a profound illness, flooded his body. He felt he had nothing in reserve. He smoked to calm himself and made a show of chatting with his sergeant. Bob McElroy was one of those squat, powerful men who seem able to absorb any amount of punishment. Even now, he held a depth of calm Ted sensed as a thirsty man can sense water. But he stiffened when Bob asked if he was all right. He was only a little tired, he told his sergeant, and immediately regretted his complaint— weren't they all tired?

Unsteady getting to his feet, he could sense Bob watching, just as Captain Ross had watched him in the duty tent that night, with cool appraisal.

Up and down the trench he went, checking on his men. Finally getting their tot of rum and some warm grub, they were emerging from their stupor. One man, grinning up at him with broken teeth, gave ironic thanks for his deafness—impossible to hear orders now! Another was trying to work up interest in a poker game—"I'm feeling lucky!" But it was too soon for most.

Ted found Hartfield spooning up porridge. Rufus George was with him, the two talking with their heads down. Ted was surprised to see the reclusive George talking with any-one, let alone Hartfield. It seemed a conjunction of opposites, obscurely worrying. He watched as Hartfield, exhausted by his trials, put back his head against the trench wall—that long white throat grimed with dust.

THE GERMAN BARRAGE had not led to a major attack; it was just another harassment, stiffer than most. It had torn holes in their barbed wire defences and collapsed a section of trench wall. Ted thought the battalion might be withdrawn to trenches farther from the Front Line; but word came they must carry on. He had already set a work party to repairing the trench. Now he called for another to go out that night and mend the wire. Within an hour he had most of the volunteers he needed. He was talking to his sergeant when Hartfield appeared. He wanted to join the wiring party.

Ted's first instinct was to turn him down. But with McElroy there, he didn't want to be seen playing favourites and he said yes. "I never know what to do about him," Ted confessed to McElroy afterwards. "His age, whatever it is—he's no man yet anyway."

"He better get there soon," McElroy said grimly; Ted sensed he disapproved of his decision. Maybe his sergeant felt as protective of the kid as he did, as apparently a lot of the platoon did; or maybe he feared the risk to them all of his inexperience. Ted had heard the boy referred to as *Our Annie Rose* by one of the men. The use of the boy's stage name had something profoundly unmilitary about it—the suggestion of a fantasy that Ted felt was dangerous. It was hard to read the mind of a platoon. They lived in each other's laps, practically; but in their thoughts and daydreams they remained strangers.

When the late summer dusk finally turned to night, he climbed a ladder and stepped with twenty others into no man's land. Their faces were blackened; some were armed, while others, heavily gloved, carried wire cutters and hefted bales of barbed wire and iron stakes. No one spoke above a whisper, though occasionally a clank of metal or a sneeze raised a muttered curse. Fog drifted from old craters filled with fetid water, limiting the view and creating an uncanny sense of claustrophobia as objects loomed suddenly from the mist. A flare went up, a high, sputtering light soon drifting down on its parachute. Everyone ducked and froze. As darkness reclaimed the land, he kept stopping to listen and peer. An electric awareness had banished his fatigue.

Distances were strange out here: you couldn't judge them. Distracted by battlefield iron, compass needles frequently lied. In a trice, you could lose the sense of where your own lines were. Once, in '16, he and his corporal—what was the chap's name? Martin? Monteith?—killed in that rail accident—had wandered off course and found themselves on the wrong side of a German forward line. It had taken a bit of doing, and some rudimentary German, to get home: a tale for the officers' mess in the days when such things mattered.

The wiring party set to work swiftly, uncoiling new wire, threading it through the eyes of the iron stakes they had sunk with mallets. The body of a German soldier in a late stage of decomposition had been unearthed by the shelling. One of Ted's men tried to tug a ring from its finger. Finding it was stuck, he clipped off the finger and slipped finger and ring both into his pocket. Ted looked away.

He'd told Hartfield to stick with him. He was there when Ted turned to speak to his men, there when he threw himself on the ground when the flare burst, there when he led a small party forward, puffing at his shoulder. Already he regretted bringing him; the boy's presence made him feel unbalanced, unsure of his instincts, responsible for too much. He needed to set up a perimeter to protect his work party. With Hartfield at his heels, he led half a dozen men up the remnant of a sunken lane. Visibility improved as they reached higher ground, creating a new danger: while they could see farther, they could also be seen. A slip of moon tracked among clouds. Still, it was good to be out where the air was fresher, and a memory of freedom clung to their movements: the freedom of a walk down the street or through a wood; the freedom of knowing you could turn in to a bookstore or a cinema if you chose. The choice a thing they hadn't appreciated until it was gone.

After twenty minutes they took shelter behind a brick wall. No man's land was littered with such ruins: it might be the wall of a house, where a husband and wife had leaned in a private moment. The crypt of a church, where some notable lay. No time for such thoughts now. They were halfway to the German lines. He sent men into the darkness on either side to set up listening posts. All of them but Rufus George were experienced. George fascinated him: the way he cleaned his rifle with such slow, almost affectionate attentiveness; the way he watched solemnly while others joked. At times his wide-set eyes danced with amusement, though his laughter, coming rarely, was a barely audible huffing. He seemed to be striking up a friendship with the boy. George had been among the first to volunteer for the night's mission; had Hartfield volunteered simply to be with him? Why hadn't he thought of this sooner? The whites of his eyes flashing in his blackened face, George listened intently to Ted's instructions. Just before George slipped off, his eyes found the boy.

Ted settled with Hartfield behind the wall. They were alone now, no longer able to hear the sounds of the work party toiling in the dark behind them. No man's land was peaceful, it seemed, save for the scrabbling of rats on sheet metal; the faint dripping of water.

The boy was eager, too eager: twice Ted had to tell him to keep his head down. Marked by the glowing dial of his watch, time moved slowly. Taking out his binoculars, Ted crawled to the end of the wall and settled in a hollow to peer into the murk. A sound of heavy breathing behind him. *Christ, couldn't the kid keep it down?* A rat ran over his leg. For half an hour they lay watching. When Ted passed the glasses to Hartfield, the boy had scarcely put them to his eyes when he dropped his head.

"Holy Mary, sir!"

Ted didn't need the binoculars. Forty or fifty yards away,

revealed by a clearing of the mist, a ragged line of Germans was making its way towards them, stooping as they ran. *A raid*, Ted thought. Already they were too close—he and Hartfield would never be able to outrun them. Gesturing fiercely, he brought the boy along the wall to a hole he'd noticed earlier—a window or entranceway, partially filled with earth. Shoving the boy in, he quickly discovered there was not room for two. Pressing against the base of the wall, he prayed the Germans would go by without looking behind them. They arrived in seconds—grey wraiths hurrying past with only the scuffing of boots to be heard; a faint jingle of gear, quickly gone.

He knew the Germans would be back soon enough, harassed by artillery and machine gun fire from the Canadian trenches: he and the boy needed to get as close as they could to their own lines and take shelter. With luck they might wait out the fight and its aftermath, then slip into their own trenches. But first, he needed to set up a warning flare—the Canadians needed to know what was coming. He searched his pack, his pockets; had he given the flares to Hartfield? The boy didn't have them. Furious with himself, he explained his plan and the two started back, crouching as they hastened towards their own lines. In the thickening fog along the lower ground, objects loomed, bristled, shrank into obscurity. The Germans had undoubtedly posted rearguards—they might stumble on them at any second.

Nearer their own lines, they covered a hole with a sheet of corrugated metal, a couple of logs, the stinking remains of a horse blanket the boy found, trying to make their hideout look accidental, as if these objects had been thrown together by an explosion. They crawled into the narrow space just as the sounds of a fight reached them: shouts, random shots, the chuckling of a Lewis gun, a cry of agony.

240

There was scarcely room for them both; Ted had to cup himself around the boy, from behind, his left arm enfolding him, ready to clamp a hand over his mouth if necessary. "It won't be long," he whispered. "Our chaps will throw them out, then we can go home." As the fight raged on, he guessed the Germans had gotten into the Canadian trench. Men, his men, would be dying; and he had forgotten the fucking flares—

Saturday mornings in their little house on Barks Lane, he lying behind Mim, cupped to the warm breadth of her buttocks, fondling her breasts as he eased them towards love; and her saying afterwards, *Now bring me my tea.*

He was with her and then he was here, in the cold slime of their hideout, shaking uncontrollably in the grip of terror so pure he felt trapped in ice water; while the boy squeezed and patted his hand, telling him they would be all right.

TO GRACE, HE said merely, "We had to stay as we were—not much room in our little shack to turn around."

She was looking at him with glassy eyes. "You loved him, didn't you?"

"Oh hell," he said, looking away. "The kid was a royal pain—"

ONCE MORE THE grey coats poured past them, harried now by machine gun fire. Close to dawn, he and Hartfield slipped past the German dead. A dozen of their bodies were strung on the wire, splayed with blackened faces and outstretched arms, rocking a little on the creaking wire.

It was not so bad as he had feared. Two men in his platoon had been killed, another taken prisoner. Three of his perimeter guards had not returned, though by ten o'clock all but Rufus George were accounted for. Just after noon, he appeared.

"Rufus George," Ted told Grace. "He was only twenty-three, never been in battle, but he was already one of my veterans: one night had done it for him."

Ted took George into an empty dugout to debrief him. "So what took you so long?" Ted said with the hint of a smile. George's answers were curt, gnomic. His mouth scarcely moved. Pressing him, Ted finally got the story. He had set up about a hundred yards to Ted's left. When the Germans appeared, he had had the sense to lay low. While the mass of Germans swept on, two of their number had stayed in the neighbourhood as rearguards. George could hear their voices in the dark, talking with each other. Sneaking up on them, he "took care of them," as he put it.

"You killed them?" Ted said.

"Sir."

"But I heard no shots from that direction," Ted said.

He hadn't used his gun, George informed him.

"What did you use then?"

"Bayonet."

His face was blank with weariness; yet it seemed to Ted it held an undercurrent of sadness.

THE BATTALION WAS withdrawn to the support lines. Life was a little more relaxed here, though they were still living between earth walls, a stone's throw from the Front Line, to which they might be called at any time. Making his way back from the latrine, Ted saw Hartfield coming towards him down the narrow trench.

The boy's face lit up with recognition. They had not spoken since the night of the raid.

"Sir," Hartfield said, stopping to salute. It was Ted's intention to keep going, but the boy blocked his way.

"How are you doing?" Ted asked grimly.

"Very well. How are *you* doing?"

It was too intimate a touch, and seemed a reference to Ted's moment of weakness, a thing that filled him with shame. Yet there was no hint of mockery in the boy's face, no suggestion he now "had something" on Ted. It was simple concern Ted saw, the concern of someone who has lived so long with his own peculiarities that he found nothing unusual or contemptible in the behaviour of others.

"Very well, thank you. The other night—" He broke off, began again. "The other night, Hartfield, when we had to take shelter, you performed very well. We might not have got through it without you."

"Thank you, sir."

"Keep up the good work."

"Sir!"

The boy saluted and went off with brimming eyes, leaving Ted to ponder what had happened. It was his fate, it seemed, to be led by the boy outside the usual dry strictures of military life. He feared this tendency and was often irritated by it—the boy *could* be a pain—but he contemplated this latest encounter with the wonder of someone who has opened a book and discovered a pressed flower, redolent of some forgotten spring.

Afterwards, he relaxed a little in his attitude to the boy. He was still possessed by a desire to protect him, but noticing the affection sent Hartfield's way by the platoon, he became less guarded himself, congratulating the recruit on some little task well done, once even ruffling his hair as he went by. In their way, they were all fathers to the kid, he realized.

Only one thing continued to nag: the boy's relationship with Rufus George. They were often together, Hartfield usually chattering happily while George listened and watched. To Ted, there was something predatory in George's behaviour—in the way his gaze roved over Hartfield's hands, his face, his hair; and in the way he brought Hartfield little treats—chocolate or extra rations he'd picked up, watching with a faint, pleased smile as the boy ate.

One evening, Ted took a break from his duties to smoke. A narrow, well-worn path climbed to an alcove in a ruined wall—all that was left of some unlucky dairy, its name still legible on the spalling brick. As he stood with his cigarette, a tall figure in an officer's uniform clambered up to him. "The Colonel," as the men called Reginald Hardy, shortening his official title of lieutenant-colonel, was the commander of the battalion, despite which he was often in the trenches, as likely to chat with a private as with his officers. Ted had first experienced his democratic proclivities in England during his training, when Hardy had spoken to him one freezing night on the Salisbury Plain. He had run a printing business in Toronto before the war, he told Ted. He kept a sailboat on Toronto Island and liked to run it over to Niagara-on-the-Lake. "Out there you know what peace is. Nobody but you and the gulls." Hardy had endeared himself to the battalion in an incident that had entered its collective memory. The Colonel had kept a horse in England, a fine bay mare he liked to ride in the countryside. One day, he had watched from his horse as the battalion marched past through a seething rain. While other senior officers took shelter, Hardy and his mount kept place, his dripping hand held in rigid salute until the last waterlogged soldier tramped past. The gesture had won him a world of loyalty. Hardy was one of them, the men said, omitting him from their general mistrust of the brass.

Hardy's visits to the Line had also earned him a reputation for recklessness, for he seemed oblivious to danger. Talking with him once on the Line, Ted had been aware of the Colonel's exposed position, yet he went on smoking and talking as if it were a sunny afternoon in Hyde Park. With a forbidden touch to the man's elbow, Ted had managed to ease him, still talking, to safety.

Hardy had lost weight since then, his face behind its trim moustache hollowed with fatigue. Ted struck a match, and holding the hand that held it, brought the flame to Hardy's cigarette. They smoked in silence. A section of canal lay like a gold bar in the mist. For a few minutes they were simply men, enjoying what they might have enjoyed had they met at the rail of a boat in peacetime. Yet Ted could not entirely give himself to the moment. Hardy was still his superior, and Ted wanted something from him.

When he began to speak of Hartfield, he sensed the other man's attention sharpen.

"I understand we're short of men, but I think it would be good for him, good for the platoon, if he could be transferred behind the lines."

Hardy blew smoke reflectively, taking his time—and perhaps indicating displeasure that the chain of command had been disrespected.

"Why good for the platoon?"

"A lot of energy goes into taking care of him, sir."

"You gave him a good report—that raid."

Ted allowed that he had.

"So he's adapting then?"

"To a point, sir."

"How to a point?"

"As I mentioned, he's very young, sir. Far younger than anyone in the platoon. Fourteen, fifteen, it's hard to tell. It's no place for a boy. There's an innocence about him, sir. A goodness. He's not got the makings of a fighter." He felt his face heat, knowing he was showing too much of his private heart, poor coin in the military.

"Hardly an argument to persuade the brass."

Ted paused: was the Colonel referring to himself?

"I gather no one here knows how old he is."

"I've written letters to find out, but no. It's not just the war, sir, but—I'm concerned he might be—interfered with."

"You mean sexually."

"Yes sir." He had no proof of his allegation. But he was throwing all the reasons he could think of at the Colonel, hoping one might stick. Grinding out his cigarette, Hardy said he would look into the matter.

TWO DAYS LATER, Ted was told by Captain Ross that he was being given ten days of mandatory leave. "Not a working leave—you can go where you like, as long as you're back by—" He handed Ted a permission paper with the date and time of his necessary return. It had been signed by Lieutenant-Colonel Hardy. Ted's first reaction was anger: Hardy's decision seemed a betrayal of their conversation. He had clearly been evaluating *him* the whole time.

He was reluctant to leave his men and didn't think he

should have to. In truth, running his platoon was the only thing he felt capable of any more; he was so bent to the wheel that he had become fused with it. Yet as his leave approached, he found himself thinking more favourably of it. He had been haunted lately by a growing conviction that his luck was running out—it was the nature of the beast, and he'd had more than his share. He began to look forward to his leave, not so much with an anticipation of pleasure as with a sense that he was cashing in his chips before it was too late. As the day grew closer, he became desperate for it. He had to chide himself for losing focus.

Another officer advised him where to go. His train tore through the *bocage* country of Normandy, whistle shrieking under hedgerows that seemed almost a repetition of the trenches, so high and close they loomed, only these were green, while below them the verges streamed with wildflowers.

The little *auberge* had been a residence, its casement windows looking across a meadow to a small chalk river that slipped away into the darkness of evergreens. As the only guests, he and a recuperating British lieutenant—the man had sustained a serious head wound, his bandage slanting across one eye, lending him a piratical look—fell into easy companionship, superficial in some respects, but drawing on the assumption of a common experience that lent meaning to their pauses. Outerbridge was a keen fly-fisherman, and though he showed Ted how it was done, Ted found he had little of the patience required; a tangle in his line generated more angry frustration than the game was worth. Better to follow the whims of the little river unencumbered by rod and creel, its clear waters pulsing through woods and water meadows, sifting over sandbars, pausing in the iodine depths of a pool where trout hovered, their gills slowly fanning. How thin life had become on the Line; he had not known it until he got away. Now the world tended towards depth again, though the discovery was not an unalloyed joy. The little river beckoned sweetly but held terrors. Sunlit stones spoke of dead faces.

Still, over the days, his tensions eased somewhat. He found himself looking forward to the next discovery: that small chateau on the brow of a hill; his evening meal of trout. But the countermovement continued too; long-repressed emotions surfaced: dread, and a heavy sorrow. These things too belonged to the world's depth. His mood could change in a second. Scenes from the Front were never far away; he feared he had been permanently imprinted by that landscape of death. Yet at the same time, he missed his men, the sense of life simplified to a common purpose. He felt he had abandoned them, the boy especially. What right did he have to be here, safe, while they, just as deserving, trudged on without him? There was a strange sense of unreal lightness in his position, a nauseous sense he had been yanked from his natural element, like the fish that lay gasping in Outerbridge's creel.

Over dinner, he spoke of such feelings to the man. By way of answer, Outerbridge ordered a second bottle of wine. As they drank, he told the British officer about Hartfield: about the difficulty of his age, about Annie Rose, and about his troubling friendship with Rufus George. Behind the smoke of his cigarette, the British officer grew still, his one eye watching Ted closely.

"There's something happening between them. It might be friendship. It might be more than that. If it is more than that, I worry about the effect on the men."

"What do you imagine the effect might be?" Outerbridge said, knocking the ash off his cigarette.

"You know—*that*," Ted said, feeling the heat in his face. "No one else can have his wife or girlfriend there. It could make for bad feelings. I just have an uneasy feeling about it. I worry about the boy especially. He's admitted to me he's—well, like that."

"And this George fellow, he's—*like that?*" The solitary eye seemed to laugh at him.

Ted admitted he didn't know. "He's hard to read—a good soldier, a natural soldier you might say. But he's pretty opaque. He seems quite fixed on the boy."

"How old is he?"

"George? Twenty-three."

"And the boy is fourteen, fifteen, you guess?"

"Maybe younger."

"And how does he react—to this *interest* in him? Let me put it this way, how do they get on? Are they comfortable with each other?"

"I would say so, very comfortable," Ted said. He was beginning to feel foolish. Something obvious was surfacing, though he couldn't make out what it was. Outerbridge's bandage, covering his other eye, seemed to hide skepticism, perhaps mockery.

"I wouldn't worry about them," Outerbridge said, twisting out his cigarette.

"Easy to say," Ted said with a smile.

They talked of other things. Before they parted in the upstairs hall, Outerbridge said, out of the blue. "The boy, you know. This might be the only chance in his life to love someone—love, you know?" The eye looked at Ted with a scalding directness. "He should have that, don't you think?"

HE DID NOT tell Grace about this conversation with Outerbridge, but in a pause, held by the feathering of the lake in a breeze, he remembered it. Grace turned to him, inquisitively. From down the hall came the sound of Outerbridge's door clicking shut.

THE NEXT MORNING, the sun on his face, he felt his skull had been smashed in. Would he ever learn that he couldn't drink? Outerbridge was gone, as he had said he would be: driven to an early train by the patron's son. Alone in the little hotel, he spent the day recovering. The next day he wrote to Miriam, struggling for an optimistic note that belonged more to his early days at the *auberge* than to the present. He was lonely, and oppressed by the prospect of his return to the Line.

As his train carried him back to Paris and a second train bore him north, he gazed out the window as the stone houses of a cemetery floated past. Poplars in martial rows. A child crossing a field. All the lonely integers of his descent to the only reality. Down the aisle of his nearly deserted car came the scratching of someone's pen.

HE CAUGHT UP to his battalion during one of its regular retirements behind the Line. Ducking into the duty tent, he took Captain Ross by surprise.

"You're not due for another day."

Ted could only shrug. In truth, he felt he was back where he belonged, though the place had not entirely claimed him yet. Let him get busy and forget. He looked hard at Ross when the captain told him that the Colonel had been killed. "Careless once too often," Ross said, shaking his head. "He used to speak of a sniper who had it in for him—as if there was only one, as if, you

know, the guy would inevitably get him." The news touched
Ted, but faintly, and he knew it would be stored away where all
the other deaths had been stored, waiting for their time.

He asked after the boy. Had he been transferred? "I've seen
nothing about that," Ross said.

"The Colonel didn't say anything?"

"Not to me."

"Any casualties?" Ted said, still thinking of the boy.

"Not while you were away."

He went out into the sun. Naked from the waist up, two soldiers were wrestling as their mates cheered them on. Money
was being exchanged. It vanished as he passed. His platoon had
taken over a barn, Ross had told him—he saw its roof of red-
dish tiles above the trees, a line of pigeons dotting the ridge.
He ran into a half-dozen of his men. The enthusiasm of their
welcome buoyed him a little.

The barn, when he looked in, was empty. Pallets lined the
floor in tidy ranks, the dim air smelling of men and fresh hay.
One of his corporals was there, Jones. When he asked where
Hartfield's pallet was, and where George's, the man looked
around and pointed. The two were side by side.

Outside, Ted turned a corner and saw Hartfield. He was
standing between two of his mates, listening to them talk. He
looked downcast, worrying at the ground with his foot, but
when he glanced up and saw Ted, his face filled with a radiance
that seized Ted like a physical force.

17.

She had taken up the idea of a job as a weapon—a declaration of independence from the frustrating demands of his condition; and when he forbade her to work, from his authority. All her adult life she had honoured the supremacy of men; it flowed from scripture, she believed. It flowed from Eve's sin in listening to the serpent, and in tempting Adam. But her threat to find a job had flowed from some other place in her, and she was aware of the contradiction: her skepticism and reserve, hardening at times to resentment, long felt but rarely expressed, though now it came alive in her again, lending fuel to her campaign to leave Brockwood.

Two days after their fight, she walked up to the Junction to see Clarence Martin about a job.

Under its sawtooth roofline, Martin Munitions crowded a back street a stone's throw from the fields. Before the war, the factory had made ploughs and other farm equipment, with little financial success. But the switch to artillery shells had catapulted the business to a new level of prosperity.

Miriam had known the Martins all her life, a family of four daughters and one son, Hector, a well-meaning young man who had courted Miriam in the days before Ted. Hector had never really attracted her, and she'd had an uncomfortable time holding him off while trying not to lose his family. She had been especially close to Dora, Hector's younger sister, but their friendship had not survived Miriam's refusal of her brother. Only Clarence Martin, Hector's father and the head of the firm, had remained friendly, receiving her with an element of gallant flirtation she found onerous.

She passed through the clacking of typewriters and entered a long corridor she had travelled before, for the League. Hearing Clarence's voice, she stopped at once. He was berating someone—angrily insisting that he would *never, not in any circumstances*, have asked the person to send a certain letter. "But sir," a familiar voice piped up, "you asked me to send it last week."

"Absolutely not!" Clarence thundered. Miriam was about to retreat when Clarence rounded the corner with fury in his eyes. "Ah yes, Miriam," he managed, red-faced. "So good to see you. Yes, good. Good. Just wait in my office, will you? I'll be back in a moment."

"I could come another time, Clarence."

"No, no, you go in. I'll be with you in a minute." He called back to his secretary that Miriam Whitfield was here; could he see if she needed anything?

Alone with the young man, who sang with her in the church choir, she immediately apologized. "Dear Joseph, I'm afraid I've come at the wrong time."

Joseph sent her a bleak smile from under his eyeshade. "I'd say your timing was excellent." They chatted a little, struggling to ignore their mutual embarrassment. Declining Joseph's offer of tea, she took a chair in Clarence's office. A large Union Jack, new since her last visit, had been tacked across the wall behind his desk.

"I suppose you've come to dun me again for the League," Clarence said as he strode in, all cheerful bonhomie now.

Taking the big leather chair behind his desk, the large, floridly handsome man, clearly in the prime of life, smiled at her in his faintly suggestive way.

"Actually," she said, steeling herself, "I've come to ask for work. Office work would be best, but—well, anything you have, really."

Determined not to falter, she met his gaze. Clarence was dumbfounded, she saw. He simply had no means to comprehend her request. Into his silence she felt compelled to pour more words. "It's for Ted and me. He isn't able to work yet, and— Well, you're aware we've been living at Mother's—we simply want our own place. To pay for our own place—that's important to us."

"Right," he said, looking down at his desk as if some solution might lie there.

"I've seen your ads," she said. "You need women."

"Are you thinking of something in the office?"

"Yes, as I said—"

"We don't *have* anything in the office, not right now. All our openings are for the factory."

"I'd be fine with that—the factory." She felt uncertain of this—what did she know of factory work?

"Miriam," he said with a faint, knowing smile. "The work here—it's not for someone like yourself."

"You think I couldn't do it."

"I'm sure you could do it, physically. But—your background, the way you've been raised. These are pretty tough women, Miriam. They're not really—" He groped for the right words; it was as if she had asked him to say what was understood but should never, on any account, be said.

"My kind?" she said, challenging.

An open hand allowed this was so.

"I've been in their houses, collecting for the League. I know very well what they're like. They're tough, yes, but they have to be: so many children, their men away—all that. I'm good friends with some of them, you know," she added, aware she was stretching the truth. "They're good women. Salt of the earth."

"Let me show you what we do here, Miriam," he said. "You can see for yourself."

"Are you offering me a job, Clarence?" She was astonished at her temerity—at the smile of defiance she felt rising to her face. Clarence did not answer her but stood up and gestured in his gentlemanly way towards the door of his office. It seemed more an order than a suggestion.

As she went with him down the corridor and through the clacking of typewriters, he kept her arm, holding it lightly at the elbow to steer her. It was how he had always acted around her: shepherding, suggesting, gently guiding. Yet there was something in him that was not gentle—a hardness, forever pushing.

Now he swept her into a smaller room—a kind of cloakroom lined with wooden boxes. In the boxes were pairs of shoes—scores and scores of shoes, mostly women's. Above, hanging from hooks, were a number of women's hats and jerseys. The roar of machinery came to her like the sound of violently rushing water, slightly muted. She sensed she was willfully risking something important, something she had always depended on—but what? He was telling her to take off her shoes. He was slipping off his own shoes, and now, having put on a pair of wooden clogs, he set about finding clogs that fit her. A pair in hand, he knelt before her, like a shoe salesman. When he gestured for her foot, she rebelled. "I can do it myself, Clarence."

Apparently amused by her sally, he watched with folded arms as she put them on. When he asked if she had any matches, she fumbled through her reticule; sometimes she carried spares for Ted. "Don't want you blowing the place sky-high," he said, grinning as if the prospect pleased him.

They pushed through another door, into a din so loud she had to resist putting her hands to her ears. Before her was a vast hall filled with whining, slamming machines. Coils of metal curled from the blades of lathes. In a corner, other machines, each watched over by a woman in trousers, punched holes in metal plates. Around long tables yet more women were assembling parts. A woman shoved along a cart while another rode high on a small tractor, pulling a train of empty trollies. How serenely in command she looked, perched up there with her hair bundled under a peaked cap, giving a toot on her horn!

A man—some kind of overseer—patrolled the aisles, stopping to inspect, to correct. A fellow in a cloth cap—she recognized Arnie McTavish, from the Flats—shoved along a push broom. But it was the sight of the women that overwhelmed her—an army of women involved in the exercise of some great and complicated power. In the first rush of impressions, she felt she had glimpsed something elemental, as if the earth had opened to reveal its secrets, and at the same time something she had once known and long forgotten—a power, a feeling, and for a moment she was walking with her friends, all girls, that glorious spring day they had escaped from Watson College and taken a streetcar to the lake: eight or ten of them, striding spread out across a beach, laughing and talking and feeling in the strength and pride of their joy as if they owned it.

A clacking sound, scarcely heard in the roar, brought her back. It was the slap of clogs, she realized, beating on the cement floor. Hers were clacking too as she moved with Clarence down the aisles. She liked the feel of them, her stockinged feet free under the leather cowls, and again she knew the old joy as she and her Watson friends advanced across the deserted beach, their bare feet free in the cool sand, sharing a sense that they had found in each other what they would never find elsewhere.

As Clarence took her up and down the aisles, women looked up at her blankly—she scarcely recognized any, not in their dusters, their hair hidden under caps. Now and then Clarence shouted in her ear about some procedure. Abruptly, he plucked a mechanism from a woman's hands—a type of fuse, he told Miriam. He gave it back to the worker without a word. Miriam nodded and smiled at the woman, whom she knew by sight, but the worker turned away without response.

It was uncomfortably hot in the factory—sweat was streaming and prickling under her camisole. And a headache was brewing: the noise was truly demonic. How did the women stand it? Their faces bathed in sweat, they worked with relentless concentration, unable to enjoy the companionable talk that might have flowed in a quieter workplace.

Now Clarence took her through another door, into a vast hall open at one end to the blazing sunlight of the railyard. It was quieter here, an immediate relief. Around her, flats of finished shells awaited shipment—hundreds of shells in dull, brassy metal, standing in perfect ranks like soldiers. It was sobering to come upon them; the women's marvelous labour ended in this— this vision of deadly power. Of course she had known, but the sight of the actual shells stopped her. She had to touch one.

"Impressive, aren't they?" Clarence said. He was watching her with that same complacent grin. "Every one's got some Boche's name on it."

They passed through massive wooden doors, then a second doorway covered by a heavy rug. The factory sounds faded somewhat. Before them, a series of tall wooden boxes stood on legs several feet above the floor. Around the boxes, women were perched on high stools, their hands and forearms thrust through holes in the canvas covering the openings. Heavy dark gowns shrouded them from shoulders to feet. Their hair was hidden by close-fitting hoods. The hot air was filled with a fine yellow haze. There were no men here, but a stout woman in a belted uniform and peaked cap, her hands clasped behind her back, slowly made the rounds. They were packing shells with TNT, Clarence explained, pointing to racks of open-mouthed shells. She walked with him, slowly clacking around the boxes and the women who served them. She hated that she was observing them like animals in a zoo, but she could not stop looking. Their faces, shining with sweat, had a yellowish cast. An older woman leaned out to peer at her and Miriam saw that her mouth was ringed with yellow, like a clown's.

When the tour was over, Clarence invited her back to his office. She sensed his impatience, and in truth she only wanted to escape, to tend to the pain pincering her forehead. Yet she followed him down the corridor with its framed drawings of artillery shells and the weapons that used them, past Joseph's empty desk, into Clarence's office. He closed the door behind them.

"Miriam, I've been thinking." He was speaking from behind his desk now, touching at objects—a glass paperweight, a ledger, a little photograph propped up with its back to her—as if they were an essential part of his thought. From somewhere in the factory, a siren howled. "It would be unkind of me to let you work here. Perhaps in the future, when something comes up in the office—perhaps then. But not in the factory, no. It would be on my conscience to let you work there. I'm sure you understand." Blue, friendly eyes came up at her over the rims of his spectacles, but the pushing, the hardness, was still there.

Disappointment fought with relief. She really did not know how the women stood it. For the sake of the trouble he'd taken, she expressed regret. But she would not allow that he had been right, that this was no place for her, though in her soul she knew that it was so. She was fortunate beyond measure that she did not have to do such work.

He did not walk her out, as she half feared; but before she left, he insisted on writing her a cheque for the League.

Outside, she saw that the women were on their break, chatting over their lunches on benches ranged along the factory wall. Noticing her, they fell silent. It was excruciating for her to walk past them; only one responded, weakly, to her greeting. "Come to see how the other half lives, have you?" a voice cackled behind her, to muffled laughter. Some distance on, Miriam turned to them—she simply could not walk away—and saw them watching her out of a stillness that seemed more curious than judgmental. Instinctively, she bowed her head to them, before going on her way.

BEHIND BROCKWOOD, HER sister's bicycle leaned against the elm, its tires white with dust. Inside the house, a precarious stillness reigned through its cool rooms. Upstairs, through an open door, she saw Grace sitting slumped on the edge of her bed.

"Are you all right?"

A wan face turned to her.

"Honey?" Miriam said, going to her.

"Just tired."

"I see you've been riding your bicycle. Don't overdo it, you don't want to—"

"I'm all right, Mim," Grace said, almost hostile. Rebuffed, Miriam went on to her own room. She lay down but could not settle. She paced as her headache tightened its grip. Half glad of the pain, she received it as the just reminder of her ignorance. The shell factory women had made her conscious of her own freedom; even in straightened circumstances, her life was far more pleasant than theirs. Yet she envied them: their confidence among their machines; their easy camaraderie on their noon-hour benches. And yet, what had their labour produced but that cold forest of shells—grief to other mothers who across the ocean were engaged in the same work? It was as if the world were founded on a terrible misunderstanding—a tragedy of misspent virtue.

HAVING PUT TO bed that week's issue, Horace Williams was in a receptive mood. He listened as Miriam struggled to describe her visit to the factory. On his desk sat a plaster bust of Abraham Lincoln, familiar to her since she and Nan had visited here as schoolgirls, when Nan's father owned the paper.

Horace was fond of her, she knew, as she and Ted were fond of him and Nan, who were among their closest friends in the town. This fondness was in his face now, but so was an estimating coolness that undermined her confidence a little.

"What they do up there, the women, it's extraordinary," she concluded lamely. "You really must do a piece about them."

"It does sound extraordinary," he said. "You've given me a lot of vivid pictures, but I have to ask, Miriam: what's the story?"

She was taken aback; she thought she'd just told the story—

the story of her visit. "Well, the women," she said. "What they can do. They're really quite magnificent. If you could show that . . ."

"Magnificent isn't a story. There would have to be some sort of angle. A common thread."

"It's the irony, you see—they're doing this very hard work, and doing it well, and on the other side German women are doing the same thing—and it's all about killing each other's sons. If you could point that out . . ."

He was shaking his head. "Miriam," he said gently, "You are right, absolutely right—that is the terrible, ironic truth, but— how shall I put it—after the soldiers' letters, we lost so many subscribers, faced such outrage, that we can't afford another risk like that." She was about to speak, but he went on. "The other thing is, it's war work—we couldn't reveal anything too specific. The packing of those shells, for instance, or the work on the fuses."

"But that's so important."

He swiveled in his chair a bit, considering. "Let me put it this way: We're rather walking on eggshells around here. Legally speaking, we're not the same country we were before the war. The government—I should say the cabinet—has the power to pretty much do as they please. They're particularly down on newspapers—at least the ones that don't offer one hundred percent support—which as you know, we haven't done. Something like this, involving war work, I'd have to look at it very carefully."

She was subdued. What she heard in his voice was refusal, couched in the kindest terms. There was a wall, invisible as numbness; you never knew when you were about to run into it, and when you did, you were reminded. *Not here, not now,* they told you. On Horace's desk, Lincoln continued to brood. As a girl she had thought, *God must look like that.*

"Look, Miriam, why don't you try writing the story yourself?"

She looked up in surprise. Years ago, after reading a piece she'd written for her school yearbook, Horace had told her, playfully she'd thought, that she should be writing for the *Star-Transcript.* It had become a standing joke between them. She had never taken it seriously.

He was looking at her now with a frankness that called her to account. At once, the wall was gone, and she was taken aback.

"I'm not a writer, Horace."

"That yearbook piece—"

"You mustn't go on about that—it was years ago."

"Are you telling me you didn't write it?" His level gaze continued to hold her with a seriousness that demanded she meet him equally.

"Well . . ." she said.

"Write something up for us. If we like it, we'll publish it— as with any other contributor. If we don't, or if we feel it's too dangerous, we won't. No favouritism, all right? We might have to edit it, trim it a bit, but again, it's the same as with anybody else. We can't pay you much—"

"I don't want pay," she said. "I don't want to get you into trouble, either. I don't think I should do it."

"Writing a piece isn't the same as publishing it. We'll cross that bridge when we come to it."

TED APPEARED JUST as they were sitting down to supper. He looked exhausted and said little. Staring at Grace's empty place, he fell into a brown study, then abruptly alerted to the sound of a door closing on the second floor. Weary of such games, Miriam tried to put his obsession out of mind.

That evening, sitting alone in the gazebo, she made some notes recalling her visit to the shell factory. Knowing they were only notes freed her a little. *Clogs—the sound they made. The woman driving the train—her kerchief. Sitting up there like a proud little general. Reminded me of that woman I saw last year in Toronto, at the fair, riding her horse. Back straight as a poker. No expression. No apologies.*

THE NEXT DAY, learning that the League under Ann Kerr had decided not to help Millie Tottle, Miriam lashed out at her mother as if she were at fault. Ada accepted her apology but wanted to know, once again, if Miriam was all right. "Not particularly," Miriam allowed sullenly, bringing their conversation to a close. There was a rawness in her that she didn't want to hide.

That evening she crossed River Street and passed through the gates of the Bannerman estate. The light, streaming from the west, pierced the great maples and elms of the park, throwing quivering streaks across the decorative battlements of the house.

John Bannerman himself answered the door. She had long been on warm terms with the old man and was conscious she was about to trade on his good graces. She had criticized her mother for such tactics, and scorned Ada's argument that they were "the way of the world." Now, as she followed his slight, limping figure through the house, guilt found her. In truth, she had no idea how she was going to reconcile her purpose in coming with her affection for him.

Under high ceilings, in rooms lit only by the fading glow in the west, they passed marble-topped tables, ornate lamps, chairs and divans covered with sheets, a standing clock stopped at five after three, soulless occupants of rooms no longer lived in. Since his wife's death, John Bannerman, owner of the town's largest mills, was still driven each day to work, but he had pulled back the boundaries of his home life to a small study by the kitchen, where he now offered her an armchair.

"I think that's your place," she said with a smile.

"No, no, this is mine over here," he said, indicating a chair she knew had been his wife's.

Would she like tea, he asked, as both of them continued to stand; and perhaps some biscuits—his sister had just sent shortbread from New York. She had just eaten, Miriam said, thanking him. Noticing her attention to the framed photographs on the wall—weren't some of them new, she asked—his hand extended from a frayed cuff to point out the scenes from the mission school he supported in Korea. Ranks of children, dark hair bobbed, grinned from their desks. Others posed by a pommel horse in a new gymnasium. A dozen teachers stood smiling in a row, as if about to meet some dignitary. "There's Ginny," he said—Ginny MacFarland, a local girl Miriam had known in school, who had travelled as a missionary to the East. She had been a favourite of Bannerman and his wife, almost a daughter to the childless couple. John Scott occasionally read out her "Letters from Korea" to the congregation. Miriam peered at the young woman gazing calmly from behind her glasses, her clear, earnest face emanating the spirited kindness Miriam remembered.

As he described the work of the Korean school, he became animated, his gnarled hands gesturing, his eyes glowing.

They had sat some time talking before Miriam found her nerve. "I wonder if you know Millie Tottle in the Upper Town. Years ago, she worked for you."

"Number Six mill," he murmured reflectively. "She was a cutter."

"Was she!" she cried, taken aback. He had hundreds of workers. "Her son—"

"Yes, a terrible case. How is she doing?"

"Not very well, as you can imagine. On top of losing Bobby, she's not going to get a pension—because he deserted, you know. Or at least they say he did. Now the League's refused to help her."

She could not tell what he was thinking. His eyes had fixed her with no trace of emotion—was he even hearing her? "She can't work any more," Miriam went on. "When she left the mill, she cleaned houses for a few years—I heard she did quite well out of it—you probably know this already," she added, a little intimidated by his silence. "The thing is, she can't work any more—arthritis—"

She paused.

"How much does she need?" he asked simply.

The quickness with which he offered stopped her. So many must come to him—he must know what they wanted before they opened their mouths. He must have known about her too. She felt transparent, exposed in her use of him. And yet he seemed without resentment. For a moment, she couldn't speak.

"I haven't had that conversation with her," she managed finally. "I need to find out what her resources are—they can't be much. But then, her needs can't be much."

Feeling she had come ill-prepared, she said she would make enquiries and report back to him. They talked for a while of other things. Beside his chair was a pile of books, his Bible topmost. Bits of paper were sticking out of it where he'd marked some particular page. Most of them were in the New Testament, she saw. He gave so much—to the church, the mission, the new gymnasium he'd built downtown—yet his shirts were frayed; he took his own lunch to the mills in a paper bag. Could he even afford what she was asking?

Leading her back through the house, he stopped at a painting in a massive gilt frame. Across water flecked with gondolas shone the pale dome of St. Mark's. "Martha loved that one," he told her. "She wanted to go to Venice, but I was always too busy. With the mills, you know."

He gestured, wondering, at the great room. "I built all this for her. I thought it was what she wanted. It seemed to please her, but one day, I understood—I understood she was pleased for my sake. She simply wanted me to be . . . to be . . ." His eyes had grown moist. He could not continue. They went on into the front hall. As he saw her out, his voice came in a whisper. "God's blessings on you, dear."

She turned at once.

"And on you, John." It was the first time she had addressed him by his Christian name.

For a moment, shyly, he brightened.

SAYING SHE'D PUT on the kettle, Millie hobbled out, leaving Miriam alone in the low-ceilinged room. A colour picture of George V, snipped from a magazine, had been framed and hung on a wall. Above his chest with its encrustations of medals and braid, his eyes were deeply circled; yet for all the weariness of his face, it had a pinkish, boyish cast under his tidy cap of hair, parted down the middle.

When the kettle's strident whistle went on for half a minute, Miriam got up and went into the kitchen. Millie was sitting at her table in a trance. She looked up as Miriam poured boiling water into the pot.

"What I don't get," she said, "is why they wouldn't give him a second chance?"

"That would have been right, yes."

"People get tired. When I had Bobby, his dad was away on the railway. I was half nuts I was so tired. All he did was cry. You'd do anything in that state. The ideas I had then. They'd have locked me up if they knew. You have kids?"

Miriam shook her head.

"Why not then?"

"I guess it just—well we'd only been married for a bit when the war came, then Ted was off—"

"He's in the war then?"

"Well, he—"

"Is he all right?"

When Miriam nodded, the little woman's eyes searched her face so hungrily she felt disbelieved. "Actually, he's been wounded, they sent him home. He's pretty shaken up."

"But he's alive, girl! You've got that."

"Yes," Miriam said quietly. She wondered how to begin. "Millie—do you need any help, with money?"

For some seconds, Millie looked stolidly at Miriam.

"You say you're from the League?"

"I work for the League, yes. But today I'm—"

"Because I won't have charity. I got Bobby's pension com-ing—Matt Thompson at the church said so. Another month or so and you'll be all right, he said. Matt Thompson."

Millie got up and stomped off. In a minute or two she was back with a sock, shaking its contents onto the table. "How much is that?" she demanded. Miriam did a rapid tally of the change and few bills.

"About twenty dollars, I'd say."

"Twenty-two dollars and fifty cents. And I've got forty more in the bank—what's left of what Bobby sent." She pushed forward a bank book. "So I think I'm all right—do you think I'm all right?"

"How much do you spend a week?"

"Good Lord, I don't know—a few eggs, bread, cream for my tea. I told you I'm not interested in charity."

"Millie, there's something I have to tell you."

At her shift in tone, Millie looked at her, defiantly suspicious.

"Because Bobby was a deserter, there won't be the usual pension for you. In fact, there won't be anything. Army rules, I'm afraid—I phoned the regiment. It isn't right, I know. In fact, it's terribly wrong. I'm sorry, Millie."

The little woman went on looking at her as if she hadn't spoken. Slowly, her face knotted in anger. "But he weren't a deserter!"

"We know that Millie. But the army doesn't."

"The army's wrong! You go and tell them they're wrong!"

Miriam did not answer, and Millie's gaze returned to the depths, where it roamed furiously over a landscape of injus-tice. Her mouth began to work, silently at first. "So they take away my son and just for good measure, they make a pauper of me!"

"I'm sorry, Millie. When your money runs out, or a little while before that, we'll make sure you have what you need. There are people in town who don't want you to suffer any more than you have. There's help for you, Millie."

"I think I'd like you to leave now."

"Of course, Millie."

When she squeezed the old woman's shoulder as she passed, Millie's voice came snarling back at her, "You come down here out of your fine houses and ask us to give our sons to your damned wars and then you make a pauper of me. *For King and Country*, they said. It's all bollocks, Missy. Bollocks and lies!"

"It is, Millie. I agree with you."

"I told you to get out."

To have her efforts thrown back in her face was painful, yet she could only think Millie was right. She let herself out.

MIRIAM CONTINUED TO make visits for the League, to shop and cook for her family, to adjust herself to her husband's shifting moods while keeping his clothes washed and mended, all the while struggling to raise herself above the turmoil of jealousy and suspicion that kept engulfing her.

Her exhaustion deepened until it became a state of mind. It was harder to get out of bed in the morning, harder to show a pleasant face. Her days were undermined by a sense of futility. Her dreams were full of obstacles: a bridge broken off in the middle; a wall perforated by tiny windows where distorted faces leered down at her.

Ted was on the road again—somewhere *out there*, traversing the vast sea of fields and woods around the town. Grace was housebound with a cold—consolation of a sort, though this morning Miriam found herself less oppressed by jealousy of her sister than by longing for her husband, her mood sparked by a photograph that had tumbled from a book. It was not the posed wedding photo she kept on her windowsill, but another taken at the time by Nan, a small snapshot that had caught the two of them laughing on the church steps. They looked positively silly—she in her white dress, lunging forward with her mouth open, Ted swinging his head sideways, gaping too while looking like anyone but himself—an undiluted happiness.

Wild with sorrow, she left the house, only to stop halfway down the walk. What was she doing? She had little chance of finding him. But she was already moving again, out the gate, north past the high school, not knowing why she should be hurrying this way and not another. She had slept poorly the night before and now the sight of the fields, stretching off to the crayon stroke of distant hills, filled her with despondency. It seemed hopeless to go on. Yet she could not abandon the sight of the dusty white road, as straight as a dressmaker's yardstick, narrowing to the north. It was the road they had walked the evening of their quarrel, and perhaps some tincture of possibility still clung to it, for even in quarrelling is a kind of intimacy. Nearby, a cluster of oaks proffered cool respite from the summer's heat. A bench had been placed there by the farmer.

She sat in an entrancement of despair. Voices told her she must be up and doing. After some time they stopped. The shadow of the grove, laid on a field of oats, gradually shifted to the east. A figure walking up the road was passed by an undulating flock of sparrows. Above the distant Reid Hills, cumulus piled its hazy mountains, nearly as pale as the sky itself. That she was waiting did not occur to her; yet she sat with a sense of her husband.

18.

Her father was turning sixty. Unable to think of a gift, Miriam approached her mother for suggestions. "I can't think of anything he'd actually want," Miriam said. "I don't want it to disappear into a drawer like everything else." As Ada pointed out, he wore the ties Miriam had given him, and the new putter she'd bought five years before still served him on the links. But Miriam wanted something special, something to take him by surprise because it answered a need he had not been aware of; and to show him, as a sign of her love, that she knew him well. Ada wondered about a subscription to *National Geographic*. Miriam thought not, but her mother's suggestion triggered another idea. "He loves that little painting by Paul he keeps in his surgery," Miriam said. "I could get him another, to make up a pair."

"A pair of what?" Grace said, entering the kitchen.

"Something for Dad," Ada explained. "For his birthday. Miriam thinks a painting by Paul would be good."

"To go with the one in his surgery," Miriam said. Feeling protective of her idea, she was sorry her sister had appeared.

Grace was immediately enthusiastic. "We can go together on it—would you mind, Mim?" Miriam had imagined that she and Ted would pick out the picture together, an all too rare expedition for the two of them. She said she wouldn't mind.

Paul Mirani Davies was a family friend who'd had considerable success as a painter of horses; he'd exhibited a large one, "Reveille," at the Chicago World's Fair. Miriam contacted the painter, and later that week the three of them climbed the steps of his big cobblestone house, passing between pillars into the deep porch where Paul was waiting—a slight, dapper man in his fifties, a little slowed by arthritis, his large dark eyes playing mostly to the women as he explained that his studio—it was in a belvedere on the roof—was too hot for comfort these days and he'd been working on the veranda at the back of the house. "I've put out some paintings there, if that suits."

"Of course," Miriam and Grace said at once. They were a little in awe of him. With Ted following, the sisters chatted with the painter as they moved down the broad hall, past an empty wheelchair draped with an afghan. It belonged to Paul's father-in-law, old Cyrus Cain, the mill owner who had built the house a half-century before. An open door gave a brief glimpse of Cyrus's bed, moved downstairs for convenience. A sickroom smell pervaded, and it was a relief to step onto the veranda with its cool river breezes.

On an easel, a large unfinished canvas had been set. Several horses stood together in a pasture, under a sky that took up more than half the picture—several bays and chestnuts, a silver mare, a colt—all so alive in the casual, unpeopled solitude of their gathering that Miriam cried out in pleasure. As she and Grace exclaimed over it, the painter stood studying it himself. "I'm planning to put a figure in—right about here," he said, indicating a spot in the centre of the group. "He'll be putting a bridle on the stallion."

"No!" Grace protested. "The horses are so wonderful on their own. Do you really have to?"

"It does seem a shame," Miriam agreed. The horses seemed free without humans and their bridles and bits, as if the world had been made for them alone.

"Oh my dears, my dears," Paul crooned, darting an amused glance at Ted. "This is a commission, you see—he who pays the piper gets to decide what's in the picture, and if it's himself he wants, who am I to quarrel?" Paul shrugged, as if helpless; but his smile was complacent—this piper liked to be paid.

"Your horses are so convincing," Ted said. "You must have grown up with them."

"No more than anyone else. I suppose I've always preferred them to people," he said, drawing a sardonic chuckle from Ted.

Paul had leaned several unframed smaller paintings against the railing. He picked one up and placed it on an empty easel. A young woman in a skirt rode side-saddle beside the young farmer walking at her side, gazing up at her with the devotional look of courtship. The painting, which Paul had entitled "Harvest Love," reminded Miriam of some medieval romance: a knight and his lady, highly idealized. She did not think her father would like it much. When their eyes strayed to other paintings, Paul took away "Harvest Love," swiftly replacing it with another.

As the showing continued, Miriam and Grace did most of the talking. Ted made a few comments, but once all the paintings had been seen, he retreated down the porch to smoke. The sisters had differing opinions, they changed their minds, they hesitated as paintings reappeared and were replaced. Miriam had a growing sense that, for Grace at least, they were in some kind of competition. When Miriam was enthusiastic, Grace would shake her head and drawl, "No, I don't think so—I think Dad would prefer the last one." But when the last one was returned to its place, it no longer pleased her as much.

Growing up, Miriam had imagined herself her father's favourite; she knew Grace felt the same about herself. They both had preferred Alec to their mother, perhaps because he demanded less of them; his remoteness contrasted favourably with what they took as Ada's intrusiveness, allowing them to invent the father they needed.

Down the porch, Ted loitered with his cigarette, its smoke drifting into the trees that screened the river. His stolid removal from the viewing irritated her. It seemed discourteous to Paul, discourteous to her, and as Grace kept glancing at him to gauge the effect of some remark, Miriam was half tempted to chide her. Though what would she say? *Stop looking at my husband? Don't worry, he's still there?*

An hour passed, and they were no nearer to a decision. Paul was growing impatient, Miriam sensed, though his courtesy did not falter. On a table, his jars and tubes of paint, along with brushes in tin cans, stood waiting in a strong odour of turpentine. A large palette was smeared with colour—rapidly hardening, no doubt. She regretted keeping him from his work and began to assert herself more firmly. Finally, she managed to narrow their choice down to two paintings. Miriam favoured the forge scene—the perfect match, she said, for the one their father already had. A huge sycamore shaded the forge, while two Clydesdales stood tethered outside. Grace favoured the view of a covered bridge. It was more freely painted than the other, the bridge's red side made brilliant by late sun and contrasting starkly with the roiled blacks and greys of an approaching storm. A lone buggy, its hood raised, was climbing the ramp to the bridge. The driver was indicated minimally—a pale spot of paint for his face, a smaller dot for the hand that held the whip.

The horse, a black, had wrenched its head around, revealing, within its blinker, a hint of frenzied eye. Miriam had thought this painting clumsy, almost amateurish in its broad strokes, and lacking the peacefulness of the other. Neither sister would give way. They asked Paul's opinion. He shook his head and said both were good. "Like asking a parent to choose between children," he said with the indifferent tone of someone who has said the same thing once too often. Grace called Ted to come over. Miriam sensed his reluctance as he threw away his cigarette.

"Which one do you like?" Grace said. She had taken down her favourite and was holding it in front of her for him to see, while eyeing him rather coquettishly. Beside her, on the easel, was Miriam's choice.

"You have to choose," Grace demanded.

Disdaining to play this game, Miriam did not touch her painting, but standing beside it she was conscious of what Ted was suddenly faced with; conscious too that she felt dowdy and rather plain.

Ted met her eyes—a fond yet nervous touch. He smirked at Grace. He shook his head and said, "Like Paul says, they're both good. You'll have to figure it out. Alec's your father, not mine." A few minutes later, he announced that he was leaving. Miriam watched his back retreat down the veranda stairs and around the corner of the house.

Looking grim, Grace set her painting back on the easel, threw off a brief, satiric smile directed at no one, and turned away to the railing. Looking again at the two paintings, Miriam saw in a flash that the one her sister had chosen was the better: there was really no comparison. "Now that I look at them again," she said, "I think yours is better—really. It's got such a strong mood—the whole thing is—I don't know, *alive*." This felt insufficient; but it was as close as she could get. She felt a little ill at this wrenching volte-face. She looked again. Yes, the nervous horse, the advancing storm, the mysterious driver with his whip—it was not only the better painting, but it caught something of her father, the thing that danced in his eyes when he got off a riposte he was pleased with—the thing no one could get close to, at least for long. Here was his past as a young doctor, in the days before cars.

"You don't have to say that," Grace said, over the railing.

"Of course I don't. Except that it's true," Miriam said. "I thought at first it was too rough, but that light on the bridge—wonderful."

So they agreed. As Paul took down the painting and looked at it, Miriam sensed disappointment in Grace, or perhaps it was only indifference, all her energy fleeing once their combat was over. "It's a favourite, truly," Paul was saying. "The gods were with me the day I painted this one. But it's not the sort of thing most people can appreciate—a little too wild for them, I'd say," he added with a flirtatious glance at them both. He immediately sobered. "Though compared with what they're doing in Europe right now, it's rather tame, really." He seemed reluctant to give up the painting, staring at it for a few seconds longer. He would have it framed, he said; they could pick it up in three or four days.

As he escorted Miriam and Grace back through the house, they found Cyrus waiting in his wheelchair. The builder and owner of mills was unable to walk now, and not always in his right mind. One eye was half-closed; one of his large hands, no longer working, lay nested in his lap. Under the crown of white hair, as vigorous as any young man's, his good eye watched without expression as Grace and Paul, briefly greeting him, passed down the hall. Miriam stopped to talk with the old man. When she emerged a few minutes later, neither Grace nor Paul could be seen. Only there was a man there, the near giant the Cains employed to look after their horses and tend their gardens. Rearing up in his shabby frock coat, with a clutch of roses in his massive hand, he nodded at her while his face remained stolidly unexpressive, his eyes avoiding hers as she passed.

THE DOCTOR'S BIRTHDAY fell that year on a Saturday, and he was under strict orders from his women to honour the holiday. No babies must be born on that day, or the previous night, either; none of his patients were to break their legs or come down with chickenpox; and his office door must not be opened on any account. Alec promised to see what he could do.

On the day itself, dawn offered a cloudless sky. Peering out the window as she dressed, Miriam noticed Sandy Robinson trimming the edge of a flowerbed. The front lawn, cut the day before, gleamed with dew. Ted had already gone off, to "grind off the rough edges" he'd said, in sardonic acceptance of the day's festivities. Miriam hurried downstairs to prepare for the arrival of Mrs. Teale, charged with making sandwiches for forty. Miriam herself would bake the cake.

Ted did not get back in time for breakfast, as he'd promised, and after stretching out the meal for as long as they could, the family gave the doctor his presents. Ada presented him with a silk scarf, which he promptly wound around his neck, flinging the long end over his shoulder with a panache that set them laughing—they so rarely saw this side of him. Miriam watched intently as he picked up the wrapped painting. Grace, she saw, was also on tenterhooks. At her end of the table, Ada was saying, "I think the girls made a wonderful choice this year."

"It's from Ted too," Miriam quickly put in. The doctor studied the painting. "It shows best at a distance," she added.

"Here," Grace said. She got up and took the painting, stepping back to hold it for his perusal.

"We thought it would remind you of the old days," Miriam said.

"A match for your other one, of the two horses," Ada said.

Will got up to better his view.

"I like it," he said, standing beside his father.

"So do I," the doctor said warmly, and his hand came up and rubbed his son's back. "Very much." As he turned to thank them, Miriam caught the glitter of unspilt tears and felt a rush of love and relief. Her face shining, her sister turned away to set the painting on the sideboard.

"It was Grace who recognized it," Miriam said on a sudden impulse. "She saw how good it was—that helped me see it."

"*Well,*" Grace said, demurring.

"It's true," Miriam said gaily.

A few minutes later, Ted arrived to the news of the present's success. His hand touched Miriam's shoulder as he swept behind her chair.

After breakfast, Miriam and Ted moved chairs onto the front lawn, attentive to how the shade would fall as the afternoon wore on. When he left, she paused for a few seconds at the bottom of the lawn, looking with satisfaction over its clusters of chairs, its passages of sun and shadow, a little world put right. In her exhaustion, fruit of another restless night, she half regretted that people must come and spoil it.

A FEW MINUTES after two, their guests began to arrive. They were mostly old friends of her parents, including the mayor, Rudyard Collins, and his wife, Cecilia, her vast hat ringed by tiny roses. The Reverend Scott came, bearing regrets from his wife and a small package, which was added to others on the porch. To Miriam's delight, John Bannerman appeared. He'd seemed reluctant when she'd asked him, but he had put on a white suit, fixed a boutonnière in his lapel, and brought news of Millie Tottle. After Miriam had passed the name of Millie's bank to him, he had spoken to the manager about making monthly deposits, he told her, adding with a wink, "All on the q.t., of course." Horace and Nan Williams arrived with their two boys, who promptly ran off to look for Will. Sandy Robinson was there with his wife, Hettie, pushing her wheelchair from around the corner of the house.

The cook's nieces, Julia and Estelle, circulated in the growing crowd, offering sandwiches and carrying away plates and cups. At three, Ted's parents came, Rose in a dress of blue-and-white paisley, George in his Sunday best, his chin nicked by the razor. "You'd think he'd been in a fight," Rose told Miriam, eyeing the dab of sticking plaster.

"Well, I have, haven't I?" George said, adding, with a finger aside his nose, "Don't worry Mum, mum's the word."

In her element, Ada cruised among her guests, welcoming here, giving orders there, pausing to support a story told by one of her oldest friends. She too wore a great hat, with more aplomb than any woman present, Miriam thought; there was impressive consanguinity between its rakish tilt and her handsome profile.

Alec moved about as well, though not frequently enough for Ada's taste. When she judged he'd spent too long with one of his cronies, she'd sail by with a reminder that so-and-so was waiting. With his straw hat pushed to the back of his head, he was resistant to these hints, particularly if he was enjoying himself. Miriam too circulated, sharing the hostess duties with her mother while remaining aware, peripherally, of her husband. Now he was on the porch with a cigarette; now, looking wary, he was chatting with John Scott. She knew what these social engagements cost him, so when she saw him with Horace Williams, Horace doing most of the talking while Ted listened with his head down, worrying at the lawn with his shoe, she went over to join them. Horace was holding forth on the subject of conscription, a topic that had enflamed passions around the town.

"I wasn't in favour of the war, any more than you were," Horace was saying, sparing Miriam a nod. "But now that we're in it, we have to win—anything else is unthinkable—so it's a matter of everyone contributing."

"Why do we have to win?" Miriam said. Ted looked at her askance, while Horace simply stared. Flushing, she held her ground. "I mean, as long as it's over."

"Well, the mothers of the fellows who've been killed," Horace said, finding his voice, "the families—we can't tell them it's all been in vain."

"So you'd rather that German mothers felt it was in vain."

"Of course I don't wish suffering on anybody, but—" Horace flashed a look at Ted, who looked away.

"I think everyone should lay down their guns and go home." She had spoken with an anger that surprised her. "Anyway, no politics allowed today. You two be good—I've got my eye on you." Her forced bonhomie felt sterile to her. Leaving them, she went to greet a late arrival.

As the shadows shifted around the trees, lengthening through the afternoon, and the shadow of the house crept down the lawn, the party murmured on to the tinkling of glass and porcelain. Some of the guests had settled in chairs. Others sat on the porch or stood in little conversational groups, visited now and then by Julia or Estelle offering sweets, tea, and lemonade. Miriam's father had disappeared. The next time she saw him, shaking with merriment beside the mayor, she was certain he'd taken a nip in his surgery. Here and there laughter burst out, or a child ran by. Crows started cawing from a tree as Kiki passed below. A reticule was lost and found.

Miriam's headache came with a nagging sense she had overlooked something important. She felt off balance as the effort of playing hostess alongside Ada began to tell on her. When Ada whispered to her that Mrs. Wimmer needed attention, she trekked dutifully off to attend to the old lady and was soon stuck on a chair beside her, listening for the fourth or fifth time that year to her complaints about the church choir. "It's not you," Gloria kept telling her, patting her hand with her own cold, heavily veined, and much beringed one. "Your soprano is one of the few bright spots. If I may say so, you rather remind me of myself when I was younger. But half the bass section can't even read music. Two of them—that Harrison fellow, and that other one, the tall one—don't even notice when they're off-key. It's a scandal, really."

"Well, with the war—" Miriam began.

"Oh yes, the *war*. I don't disagree, but you would think the chaps that are left would learn to read music at least, considering what our soldiers are doing."

Miriam's chair was in the sun. A thin pain stretched over her scalp to a point above her left eye. She was too warm, her under-garments damp, and something in her no longer cared. For the next hour, forcing herself through her duties, she felt mired in a growing discomfort. Her time of the month was approaching, she sensed. She needed to eat something. She snatched a couple of tiny sandwiches from a passing tray, wolfed them down with her back to the crowd, and had just returned to the fray when Ada buttonholed her with the news that the children were running wild. Chasing each other through the house, they'd broken a pitcher, she said. Miriam suggested she try Grace: "She's so good with kids." Her mother responded that she had no idea where Grace was. Miriam enlisted Nan and they went to straighten things out. They rounded up the children, redirecting their energies into a game of Simon Says on the open stretch of lawn between Brockwood and its north-ern neighbour. Leaving them in the charge of one of the older girls, Miriam and Nan went off together. Miriam would have preferred to be alone, and when Horace called for his wife to join a group, Miriam took the opportunity to escape.

In the back garden, she lingered under the elm. It was cooler here. In the smell of earth and flowers, she came to herself a little, touching the trunk of the great tree as she moved toward a short walk that formed a kind of alcove between the old sta-ble and the vegetable garden. There was a bench here, where Sandy Robinson liked to sit with his cigarette; a fence weighted with vines screened the street.

She had sat for some time with her back to the wall when she heard, like the delusions of fever, the garbled sound of people talking. The voices were coming from the other side of the fence—from the street.

"Do you feel better now?" Ted asked.

"I was going mad out there," Grace answered.

"It's not easy, is it—"

"I'm tired of the secrecy, Ted. I want to tell her."

"I've told you, that's not a good idea. If we don't want to hurt her—"

"Of course I don't want to hurt her. What do you take me for? But what we're doing—the secrecy—it's not right. I can hardly face her any more."

"I can't see any harm in it. It's not like we're—I don't know, planning to run off together—"

"Don't even joke about it."

"We're not harming anyone. I think it's even helping me. You know, I didn't want to start, but now that we have—"

The voices drifted away, soon falling silent altogether.

There was still the rest of the party to get through; and the evening's meal on the terrace with Ted's parents and the Williamses. Across the table, looking grim, Grace evaded Miriam's gaze. When Ted asked in a whisper if she was feeling ill, Miriam got up and left. She paced in their room, furious that he hadn't followed.

After ten minutes he came, stopping when he saw her. She faced him across the bed.

"What you said to Grace, what you both said—I heard it, Ted. I was behind the fence, by the stable. Ted, do you hear me? Are you thick? *I heard what you said, you and her.*"

He had fallen still. In the dimness of the room, she could not read his face. She imagined him furiously thinking up excuses, and she snorted in derision.

"Miriam—" he implored, starting towards her.

"Don't you move!"

He obeyed.

"How long has it been going on?"

For a long moment he was silent. The sound of laughter reached them from the terrace.

"I don't know," he said tentatively.

"You have to do better than that, Ted."

"It started by accident. It was that day in the pine woods. I ran into her in the pine woods. You were there when we came home."

"Little suspecting," she said bitterly.

He paused for a long time while she waited. She wasn't going to help him out, not now, not any more.

"It's not what you think, Mim—"

"Don't lie to me, Ted. Ever since you came back, all I've had from you is secrecy and lies. You let me think a pension is coming, and then you tell me it isn't. You tell me you made mistakes, but you don't tell me what they are. You disappear for hours every day and say almost nothing about where you've been—and now this. Who are you, Ted? Because I have to say, I have no idea any more."

She turned away in disgust. He was slippery, slippery. Had he always been so? Had she been fooling herself? Had she made him up—the good Ted, the Ted who cared for her? In a sudden access of violence, she began to pace, up and down the space between the bed and the window. Suddenly, his hands grasped her shoulders.

"Don't touch me, dammit!" Charged with anger and disgust, she struggled to writhe away. But he wouldn't let go. Tears she resented as they fell coursed down her cheeks. She would not look at him, as ardently as he begged her to.

"Mim, listen to me!"

Breathing hard and still refusing to look at him, she listened.

"You seem to think that Grace and I—that we're lovers."

"And you're telling me you're not? Do you really have such gall?" She did look at him now, in her fury.

"You know I can't be anybody's lover."

"Ted, I'm not blind. I see the way you look at her, the way you follow her around. Everyone's aware of it. The way you talked to her today—there's an intimacy between you." She was searching his eyes now, her gaze going wildly back and forth between them as if one might prove honest. "You've tried to p-please me with your hand," she stuttered. "Does *she* like it? Your hand?"

"It's not like that," he said.

"What is it *like* then?"

"I tell her stories, about the war."

"You must think I was born yesterday."

"I don't tell her everything, but—she was interested," he concluded with a shrug, as if the matter was trivial.

"*Interested*," Miriam said with rough sarcasm. "I'll bet she was." When she twisted against his grip, he let her go. She went to the window. On the lawn below, the abandoned chairs sat in silent colloquy. One had fallen over. "You tell her *stories?*" she said after a while.

"Yes."

"About what happened to you?"

"Some things. Not all."

"How can you expect me to believe you, Ted, after everything else?" She spoke more calmly, though when he said nothing, her momentary hope failed. Glancing around, she saw him staring, eyes glistening, as she had so often seen him stare, into some deep space before him, gone from her. "Well," she said more softly, "how can I?"

"I can't make you believe anything," he said quietly.

"You've fallen in love with her, haven't you?"

He dropped his head.

"I can see you have. Everyone does. I can't say I've gotten used to it. But it doesn't surprise me. In fact, I've watched it happen. Do you really only tell stories, Teddy?"

"I've never actually touched her. She doesn't want it."

"But you want it," she said.

He said nothing. With his tear-stained face fixed helplessly on the floor, he seemed very young.

LATER, SHE LAY beside his dim, sleeping form as the sounds of the night harried her: the rumble of a train on the trestle, a cat's yowl—isolated cries that subsided into the enveloping dark, leaving no trace. She had believed what he'd said about not touching her sister; in the dark she was no longer sure. She believed he had told Grace stories of the war, but had stories been the main thing, or a minor truth he'd thrown out as a diversion? In the night, suspicions became facts that she struggled to undo. Had he really told Grace about the war merely because she was *interested*? Hadn't *she* been interested? Hadn't she tried, in all earnestness, to coax his stories from him? He had confided to her sister the hardest, most intimate secrets of his existence; it seemed a betrayal as bad, perhaps worse, than anything they might have done with their bodies; they had touched each other's inner selves in an intimacy that ran deeper than the touch of hand or breast. They had participated in the opening of secrets, and they had done it behind her back *because they had not wanted to hurt her.*

She rejected this motive savagely: she didn't want their protectiveness, their care—not that kind, that posited a false thoughtfulness that was only an excuse for their indulgence, for their greedy slavering over *secrets*.

Sliding from the bed, she parted the curtains and looked into the night. A movement in the street caught her eye. A man was there, standing on the other side of the fence that bordered River Street. He held the lapels of his jacket closed at his throat as her gaze caught his. Clutching her own throat, she watched John Scott turn and hurry away.

EARLY THE NEXT morning, she woke to the jingle of her husband's belt. Instantly the turmoil of the previous night reclaimed her. She sat bolt upright and grabbed her brush, tugging it violently through her hair. The room brimmed with sunlight. "Did you change your bandage?" she asked tersely.

He was roaming about, scanning the floor.

"Ted," she said; she had to say his name twice before he stopped. "I have to know something—"

He looked at her as at some stranger he had little patience for.

"Do you have plans today—to see her out there?" *Out there*: the entire world that lay beyond this room—streets and roads and paths she could no longer trust.

Again he started to move about, searching. Had he even heard?

"Ted—" She had lowered her voice, conscious of the sleepers through the wall.

"What?"

"Are you seeing her today?"

"Lord, I don't know."

His answer put a chill through her.

"So you have *plans*, the two of you?" She was trying for a note of scathing sarcasm, but her voice trembled. She slid from the bed and seized his arm. "This is horrible for me, Ted. You have to realize that. You have to pay attention."

Stooping suddenly, he fished a little jackknife from under the bed, slipping it into his pocket. "Miriam, I know you may not believe me, but you have nothing to worry about. I love you."

"Love isn't just words, Ted—some kind of feeling. It's what you do and—"

"For God's sake, I'm not a child," he said angrily as he strode from the room.

SHE STOOD AT the bedroom window, waiting for him to appear on the front walk. But the walk remained empty; in the daylight, the abandoned chairs looked forlorn. She supposed he'd left by the back door. But it was just as possible he was still in the house. Repressing an urge to rush downstairs—she *would not* run after him—she set about dressing and making their bed; she tried to read her Bible as she did most mornings, but her concentration was gone. In the hall, the sight of her sister's door stopped her. *I have to talk to her*, she thought. But the door was closed, its stark white rectangle thick with the silence of sleep.

He was not in the kitchen, drinking coffee or making himself a sandwich to take with him—a disappointment that, like his failure to appear on the front walk, seemed a personal affront. *What right has he to—?* She went into the garden. There were his footprints, on the dewy bricks of the path. She followed them through the gate, where they disappeared in the dust of the road. For twenty minutes, she stalked the streets, searching for him.

In the kitchen, her mother greeted her cheerfully. "Well, you're up with the robins!"

"Beautiful out there," Miriam said in a deadened voice, passing swiftly to the sink.

"Are you feeling all right? You left so quickly last night."

"Yes, yes, I'm fine."

"Everything all right with Ted?"

"Is Gracie up yet?" Miriam said, filling a glass.

"Not that I've noticed," Ada said irritably. "So things with Ted—"

Miriam left without answering. Upstairs, she saw that Grace's door was still shut. In their bedroom, she lay down in her clothes.

In her dream, a bell was clanging from inside a cupboard; she woke to the bedroom flooded with sun. She had slept for well over an hour. Hurrying down the hall, she saw that Grace's door was open, her bed made. Downstairs, Ada told her that Grace had set off half an hour before, on her bicycle, with no hint of where she was headed.

19.

His way took him into a low country between hills, through a woodlot that pressed close to the road. Between drowned trees, green water gleamed. Then the road bore him up and he saw the woods that hid the lake.

He had begged her for another rendezvous; when she refused to commit herself, he had told her he would be there by nine. A little before nine, he skirted a field of rye, then plunged into woods where a stream slipped among cedars, winding among hummocks of roots and old needles, sluicing over a ledge, gleaming above pebbles—the riches of the wild world that he seemed to be failing with each step. He felt he was striding towards his own dissolution. In some way, he craved it.

In a sudden onslaught of light, the lake appeared. On its far shore, the white chinking of the cabin pierced the screen of trees, above the white strip of the shore. A green canoe lay overturned on the rock, just below the cabin. The sight alarmed him: the outside world had broken in. A moment before, all that had existed was himself, Grace, and Miriam—Mim's presence fading as he neared her sister. Now, others were here, a threat. Wary, he circled the lake and approached the canoe from the woods. Its hull was dry; a spider's tightrope linked it to a boulder. There was no sign of paddles. He climbed to the cabin. Its door was closed, as he and Grace had left it; inside was a heavy smell of must, a roll of ancient canvas on the rusting stove.

He had taken out his cigarettes when he heard footsteps pass outside. Through a ragged hole in the filthy window, he watched her descend to the shore. Smoking, he followed. Her back to him, she was facing the lake. Wary of surprising her, he stopped at a distance. At once, she whirled, her face white with panic. They were a pair, she had said.

"Give me one of those," she demanded, falsely hearty. She looked like she hadn't slept. He held a cigarette to the tip of his and passed it to her. He could smell her, some soap she used, and the acrid smell of her fear.

"Whose canoe?" he said.

She exhaled before answering. The canoe belonged to the local farmer, whom the family allowed to fish and swim in the lake, she told him. Other people had used the place "for donkey's years."

He drew in smoke, released it. She threw her half-finished cigarette away. Their past was between them, he felt—the hours of storytelling and also the other, unspoken things, the charged silences; he had never been sure how she felt about him. Perhaps she was as uncertain as he was. "So where shall we sit for today's lesson?" he joked, looking around. In the moment of his inattention, she came towards him, stopping within inches.

"Ted," she said. Her fingertips came up and rested on his chest. Her eyes found his, all earnestness now—a sharp, panicked searching that cut him to the quick. "Are you sure this is all right with you? What I've been asking of you—I don't want it to harm you."

"I'm all right."

"You're sure?"

Her face was so close. His eyes devoured her mouth. Did

she want him to? It was she who moved first, pressing into him while keeping her hands on his chest between them. "Just hold me," she said.

Awkward, he circled her with his arms. She felt frail, bird-frail, yet there was something determined in her, her arms bundled between them to protect her breasts yet unable to prevent the desperate current of her energy from reaching him. When abruptly she pushed back, he let her go.

She walked off a few steps, stopping with her back to him. Facing him once more, she struggled to resume her old, ironic manner. "So, shall we get out the chairs, Lieutenant?"

"Are you sure *you* want to do this?"

"Of course," she insisted, raising her face in challenge. Uncertain himself, he looked around. The upended Muskoka chairs lay in the woods where they had left them. They dragged them onto the limestone. When they had arranged things to their satisfaction, she lit another cigarette. There was too much self-consciousness in the air for him—too much nervous ambiguity. He was tense, feeling he was expected to perform. He got up and walked away. "Back in a minute." In the woods, he peed behind a tree. Coming back, he saw her sitting, her arms along the arms of her chair. He had the queer sense that she had been thrown back in the chair, as if an explosion had picked her up and tossed her there; and suddenly he knew what had been in front of him all along.

Taking his chair, he joined in her silent perusal of the lake.

"Something bad happened to you, didn't it?" he said. And when she did not respond: "Maybe today you could tell me yours."

She did not answer, not right away. He saw that her chest was heaving. "Not today, Ted—" she said, her voice small.

"But it was something—something like mine. You said we were a pair." She did not answer him, yet in her silence he sensed affirmation. All right," he said, "I'll start." He felt calmer now, assuaged by a sense of equality. It was why he'd been able to talk to her; it had happened to them both.

AROUND THE BATTALION'S encampment behind the lines, in fields scarred by the passage of men and vehicles, their training proceeded. "There was a different philosophy in effect," he told Grace. "After the Somme they knew they had to change their approach. So many officers had been killed in attacks, and the men were left in a state of confusion. So they taught everyone how to take responsibility in the field. Corporals and sergeants could take over from lieutenants, and if none of the NCOs were left, the men could run the show themselves. It worked, after a fashion."

"It didn't always work?"

"Nothing always works, not in the army. But it worked better than what we had, or so they tell us." He blew smoke. It was not too late to stop, but her silence was a poultice, drawing his poisons.

AFTER THE LONG days of training, his men amused themselves, some fishing in a stagnant canal, while others wrote letters home or took themselves off to play cards. One rainy evening, Ted came across Hartfield, George, and two others, talking under the overhang of the shed where they were quartered. As usual, the sight of the boy unsettled him a little. He never knew quite who he was with Hartfield: officer, man, brother, or father—or something that had no name.

Roly Jenkins was holding forth on the subject of Ypres—

Wipers, Jenkins called it, using the English corruption of the Belgian name. Jenkins had been at Wipers in "Fifteen," well before Ted had arrived on the Line. "A bloody fuck-up," he said, pausing to shoot tobacco juice. He turned to the boy, who was listening intently. "The Boche had the high ground on three sides of us—it was a fucking shooting gallery, pardon my French. Picked us off at will. Pray God we never have to go back." Jenkins threw Ted a glance, as if he might confirm or deny this possibility. But Ted knew no more than his men. As far as he was concerned—and the opinion was general—they'd be heading back to Lens before winter. They'd taken Hill Seventy, but they hadn't managed to take the town at its foot. "Christ, the mud!" Jenkins said, to no one in particular. "You're sitting in a fucking swamp, and when it rains you're up to your nuts in it." He shook his head. "Pray to Almighty God—"

"I heard they begged the General—who was he then—the top guy?" Archie Stokes put in.

"French," Jenkins said.

"Yeah, General French. They begged him to pull back—there was better ground behind the salient, eh? He wouldn't do it though—wouldn't give an inch to the Boche—British honour, I guess."

"Their honour, our asses," Jenkins said.

George's gleaming eyes remained fixed on Jenkins; he had clearly been stirred by the veteran's tale of hardship. But Hartfield looked at Ted as if to say *Is that true?* Ted looked away.

On quiet nights they could hear the rumble of guns from the north—it was Wipers, the men said. The British had been extending the salient through the summer. Hearing the duelling guns, like a storm without end, and seeing the faint flashes throbbing at the horizon, they thought of the men cowering under a rain of shells or following a creeping barrage across no man's land, hugging that wall of exploding shells that could kill you as quickly as any German gun if someone screwed up; and of the men going deaf by their guns or reduced in an instant to a spray of pink, nothing to be found of them on this earth but their pants buckle or a tooth. In other words, they thought of men who'd done what they'd done, seen what they'd seen, yet it seemed worse because it was Wipers.

Meanwhile they continued with their training—prelude, everyone thought, to an autumn attack on Lens, on the Belgian frontier. Amid the buildings of an abandoned village, they crept under walls, squinted for possible booby traps, scratched their asses, wondered what the kitchen would serve that night, fixed bayonets, ran shouting at straw men, worried over infected blisters.

Hartfield continued to perform well, Ted thought; there was a new seriousness about him—was that George's influence? Yet George was more contemptuous than serious. Ordered to run, he merely loped, trailing behind the others. Had Ted not valued his fighting abilities, demonstrated on the night of the raid, he might have chastised him more severely than he did. In his mind, he placed him among the platoon's handful of "hard men" who enjoyed fighting. It occurred to him that Hartfield was safer in George's company, but it was just as possible—wasn't it?—that George would lead him into danger. As for Hartfield's enthusiasm, it seemed unaffected by the cynicism of his friend. Ordered to run, he ran with all his heart. He joined in singsongs as readily as before, his unbroken voice rising in all its purity, while George, sitting beside him, smiled enigmatically into the fire.

Ted imagined Hartfield maturing as his time with the army extended—rounding into what he thought of as a more normal manhood. It was his hope for the boy. And in certain ways, Hartfield fulfilled this hope. He was sharper, more observant; he handled his rifle like a soldier; and he had put on muscle. Yet in the way the boy would let his hands hang limp at the wrists, and in the luxuriant way he stretched, throwing back his head, Ted glimpsed Annie Rose. Was it his imagination, or had such mannerisms increased since he and George had formed their friendship?

One evening, walking by the canal with Bob McElroy, he brought up the subject. "How do you think Hartfield's doing?"

"Pretty well. You?"

"Does he seem girlish to you?"

McElroy looked distinctly uncomfortable. "Don't think it matters," he said. "Don't think it matters to the men either. The boy is what he is—they understand that pretty well. Anyway, they've got more important things on their minds."

Ted felt rebuked. Nominally, he was McElroy's superior, but he looked up to the man, who was a decade older. In remarking that the men had more important things on their minds, he'd in effect told Ted he should be thinking of more important things too.

The next evening, out for a walk, Ted found Hartfield sitting on a bollard by the canal. He was bent over a book. Ted had never seen him with one.

"What have you got there, Jim?"

Taken unawares, the boy shot to his feet while the book tumbled to the ground. "Sir," he said, saluting.

"What's that?" Ted said, indicating the book. Hartfield picked it up and handed it to him.

Expecting the kind of smutty novel popular among the troops, Ted turned back the cover. The little volume was a school poetry reader.

"I found it in the barn, sir. Corporal Wright said I could keep it." On the inside of the cover the name E. S. Miller had been printed in blue ink. "It must have belonged to one of the chaps who was here before us."

"You like poetry then, do you?" Ted said, handing it back.

"I didn't think I did, not much anyway. But there's lots of good ones here. There's one makes me feel I'm on the river again. Me and Eddy Watts—we used to camp down there on the Don."

"Which poem was that?"

"May I, sir?" He took back the book and fumbled through its pages. The boy's youthfulness seemed especially strong just then; Ted got that feeling of drift he sometimes had around the recruit, a sense of walls and borders dissolving. The boy frowned in concentration as he turned the pages. "Here it is."

Ted took the book back. The poem was "Canadian Camping Song" by Sir James D. Edgar. "Ah yes!" he cried, delighted. "We had to memorize this one." Without looking at the page, he began to recite: *A white tent pitched by a glassy lake, / Well under a shady tree— / Or by rippling rills from the grand old hills, / Is the summer home for me. / I fear no blaze—* His throat crammed suddenly with grief, he broke off. "Very good, Hartfield," he managed. "Carry on." He pushed the book into the boy's hands and left.

He walked quickly along the canal, as if he had some purpose that way, but sensing Hartfield's eyes on him, veered right, into a copse, and kept going until he emerged in a field-corner where stones had been dumped. The broad field had been chewed up by training manoeuvres; at a distance, a long, low berm showed where a practice trench had been dug. Nearby, hidden in long grasses, crickets were chirping. A lark whirred skyward. Weeping, he watched as it pulsed over the field and disappeared against a pink cloud. There were so many ways to die. You could die without dying, with a blank stare. You could die without a mark on your body from the concussive force of a shell. You could die with your guts in your lap, or in the hurricane of tiny blades that was shrapnel. Out here, death was a way of life. You knew it was evil and yet you participated anyway, believing you had no choice.

His desire to live—his desire to have Hartfield live—was blown to white heat. The boy's openness, his enthusiasm, everything in the boy that still lay unspoiled before the great prospect of life—all that had once been his now belonged to the boy, and the boy *must* live.

It was half an hour before he felt composed enough to return to the encampment.

THE NEXT EVENING, he watched Hartfield approach. Almost, he wanted to turn away. But he held fast, striking a crisp note he hoped did not sound too friendly.

"How's the reading going, Private—read any more poetry?"

"That one I showed you—that you knew? I'm getting it by heart."

"Good for you, Hartfield. It helps to have a poem or two in your head. To say to yourself when you can't sleep."

"I sleep like a log, sir."

"Good for you. Now, I have to get on—"

"Sir?"

"What is it, Hartfield?"

"Sir, my poetry book—I'd be pleased if you didn't mention it to Geordie."

"Geordie?"

"Private George, sir. He doesn't like me reading poetry. He says it makes me soft."

"You're free to read what you like," Ted said. "In any case, poetry doesn't make you soft. Some great poets were also soldiers. Aeschylus—he was one of the greatest poets of the ancient Greeks. He fought against the enemies of his country, like you. He was prouder of that than of all the prizes he'd won for his poetry." As he spoke it, the dry name, Aeschylus, came alive for him. The man had lived, had known what he knew; and for a moment he was moved by a sense of their connection across the ages, a sense informed, too, by the flaring of interest in the boy's eyes. Aeschylus. Him. The boy. For a moment they stood together.

THE NEXT AFTERNOON was spent marching. With sixty pounds of gear on each man's back, the whole of B Company—three platoons in all, including Ted's—threaded its way through towns, past military convoys and clusters of curious children, past women on their way to market, and, emerging on the other side, past labourers swinging their scythes in unison through a field of grain. Captain Ross rode at their head, his back starkly upright above the swaying buttocks of his horse. It was unusually sunny for that September, which had had more than its share of rain. Feet burned. Straps cut into shoulders. Empty canteens were refilled at village pumps. Ted carried no pack yet moved in a trance of fatigue. It was something he was used to: the hoarding of the small core of energy that insomnia had not taken from him. Habit and will did the rest. And singing,

for at times the men broke into song, their single rough voice
bellowing out the lyrics to the beat of their marching.

You'll see from the La Bassy Road, on any summer's day
The children herding nanny-goats, the women making hay.
You'll see the soldiers, khaki clad, in column and platoon
Come swinging up the Bassy Road from billets in Bethune!

There was an angry joy in these outbursts that seemed to
sweep him along, momentarily glad to be part of this vibrant
column, glad, even, to be alive as he caught, just, the boy's
pure voice carolling above the masculine uproar, a lark above
the storm.

At last, they swung back towards camp, descending a hill
onto a stretch of water meadow. "It was a sweet evening," he
told Grace. "The sun low, cattle grazing." Church bells were
announcing the Angelus. It was the sort of evening that men
who make war desperately need, and which breaks their hearts
when it comes. "I was walking near the front of the column
when I heard shouting behind me. A mutiny, it sounded like—
the men wanted to go swimming. There was a river on our
right—I'd barely noticed it. Luckily, Ross was in a forgiving
mood. He bawled them out and then let them go in."

"Oh!" Grace cried, sitting up in her chair. "Was this the
time you swam across the river?"

He looked at her in incomprehension.

"You know, the men wanted you to go in with them, but
you swam off by yourself? The women in the ferry?" she
added, prompting. "You told me that day Dad fixed your leg.
We were sitting on the porch."

"Right," he said. "I guess we can skip this bit then."

"No, don't. I hadn't realized the boy was there. I didn't even know about the boy at that point. Did he go swimming?"

"I believe he went in with the others—I don't really remember. I do remember the women in the ferry—they'd been babbling away, and when they saw us—you know, over a hundred young men with their clothes off, sporting downstream—they went dead silent."

"You didn't tell me that bit!"

"I suppose I was honouring your female delicacy."

She gave a hoot of laughter.

He remembered perfectly well that the boy had gone swimming. Returning from the far bank, he had treaded water as he watched his men at their horseplay in the shallows, Hartfield's slim, pale form among them. At that moment, they were all boys: the beautiful naked bodies of his men, at play in the river.

ON THEIR NEXT retreat behind the lines, they found their training had changed. They no longer fought mock battles in the abandoned village. On sloping ground fringed with wild grasses, they practised attacking pillboxes mocked up in cardboard and wood—frail imitations of the concrete defences the Germans were increasingly depending on. Ted knew something was up—they all did, the air thick with rumour. One night, a few dozen officers were summoned to a schoolhouse that served as the local battalion headquarters. They crammed themselves into student desks, a crowd of weary-looking veterans, skepticism in every eye. Some took off their sidearms and placed them on top of the little desks where generations of students had carved their initials. Ted's finger idly traced a deeply gouged O as he looked to the front of the room. A cluster of staff officers were talking together with an air of collegial preoccupation. Behind the teacher's desk, the major in charge of C company, C. D. Hicks, said a few words of welcome, then turned to introduce a barrel-chested man in uniform: Lieutenant-Colonel Banbury, the new head of the battalion. It was he who had replaced the popular Colonel Hardy. There was a rustle of interest as he stepped forward to speak. Unlike his predecessor, Banbury had rarely been seen on the front lines. Few of the junior officers in the room had spoken with him. He had a reputation as a martinet, and as he paced before them with a smile of prim self-satisfaction, slapping his riding crop against his leg, he did little to change the general bias.

He explained that the battalion, along with others, would shortly be shifted to a new front. He said he was not at liberty to divulge the location just now, but the officers would know soon enough—"If you haven't already guessed," he confided with a wink. Getting no response, he mustered a more earnest face. "The top brass feels that we're on the verge of a break-through, so every man needs to give his utmost. The light is at the end of the tunnel, but we have to fight like never before to seize it." Ted was certain that most if not all of the lieutenants and captains in the room were little impressed with this speech, which in one form or another, they had been hearing for the last two years. But the lieutenant-colonel was not through. "You know, speaking candidly, wouldn't it be a good thing—a great thing—if we could finish the job before the Yanks get here? It's been our fight from the beginning. Let's give a push and finish the damned Boche off without them!" Behind him, his support staff growled their approval; one or two applauded. The officers in the room remained silent.

Not long afterwards, the roads to the north were packed with thousands of men as all four Canadian divisions set out on roads thick with glutinous mud—an endless train of trucks, wagons, limbers, horses, mules, and munitions wagons crawling through the driving rain and frequently getting stuck, heaved at by men and exhausted horses that soon came to look as if they were made of mud themselves. It wasn't long before the veterans soon guessed their destination. "It's bloody Wipers," Riley Jenkins muttered, as another filthy dawn revealed familiar landmarks.

Over the following ten days, Ted and the other junior officers were brought into battalion headquarters to study maps and aerial photographs set up on easels and marked with the routes of their own units in the planned offensive. The British campaign to extend the salient—the bulge in the Line they had occupied since 1915—had taken the low ground between the Ypres salient and the Germans on the opposing ridge, topped by a village called Passchendaele. The village itself had been obliterated by artillery—in the ariel photos Ted saw a smudge of ruins scarcely distinguishable from the ground they covered; but the ridge and the name of the town remained. The job of the Canadians, brought in for the final push, was to take the ridge and hold it.

"We used to joke about the maps with all their little arrows and lines—where we'd get to by such-and-such a day, such-and-such an hour," he told Grace. "The dots where the enemy pillboxes were. The names where the farms and woodlots were or used to be. It was all so neat and looked so easy. But we saw only dead men."

"Why didn't you refuse?"

He did not answer her. The question seemed to arrive from a place of radical innocence. He had never thought of refusing, not then; he had never thought of running away, though he had often wished himself elsewhere.

One day Ted and several other platoon commanders were taken to a vantage point where they could see the vast tract of low ground that had been retaken by the British and Allied troops. In the distance was the dim seam of the ridge where the Germans were. But what held him was the low ground itself, a vast and utterly lifeless moonscape of shell craters—thousands of them it seemed—filled (if the nearer ones were typical) with a grey scum of water scarcely distinguishable from the grey-brown land. "In the other bits of no man's land I'd seen, there was always something to tell you what had been there—the remains of trees, a bit of grass, wildflowers struggling up. A red streak of poppies—the poppies were unkillable, it seemed. But there was nothing here. If was like the end of life—something Dante might have imagined."

The Front stank everywhere, but here the stench was thicker and more repugnant than anything he had known as over the course of years the rotting potpourri of dead men and dead horses and dead rats was churned up and churned again by endless barrages. Even as he stood watching, feeling that at any moment he was going to puke, the whining and hissing of German shells never entirely ceased. Here and there geysers of mud and filthy water shot up as yet another one landed. Their guide told them: "It's actually pretty quiet now. Old Fritzie must be taking a rest." He pointed out the slim track of duck-boards vanishing into the grim distances—it was where the Canadian troops would have to walk to get to the foot of the ridge. "You'll go in at night," the guide told them. "Mind none of your men step off those boards—all that equipment on their backs, they'll sink like rocks. That ain't ordinary mud. Fall in that stuff and it's goodbye Picadilly. Only good thing about it is that it eats Fritz's shells too. Half of them bury themselves in that crap before they go off. They're getting wise to that now. They're setting the fuses to go off before they hit." The little man grinned with the few teeth he had left; he sounded Australian, and his small eyes held that intimation of crazy humour Ted had met so often in the trenches—a black delight in the sheer awfulness of a situation, a ruinous laughter at the world's end. He had more to say. "The big barrages start at night. They've got our duckboards nicely zeroed in. We rebuild them, they shell them. Whether or not they shell the bit you're walking on," he shrugged, "matter of luck."

Back in camp, Ted found Captain Ross. Taking the man aside, he demanded that Hartfield be excused from the attack.

"Put him in the clink, set him peeling potatoes, tie him up—anything. You know it's not right that he's involved in this. This will be worse than anything we've seen."

Ross scowled and looked around: a man torn between his moral instincts and his duty; a man who hated to be put on the spot. Ordering Ted to stay where he was, he disappeared behind a wall and was back in minutes with a folded paper. It was an order to send Hartfield to a unit behind the lines that made duckboards. "This will probably cost both of us our heads, you know," Ross said. At that moment, he too had the fierce humour of nihilism in his eyes.

That night, Ted took the news to Hartfield.

They stood together in the dark behind a line of tents. The boy was crestfallen, then furious. Ted clapped him on the shoulder and told him he would see plenty of action one day. But not now.

"Why?" Hartfield cried angrily.

"Orders," Ted said. "We don't have a choice. I'll tell Corporal Evans to take you to your new unit in the morning."

"And what about Geordie?"

"Who?" Ted demanded, knowing perfectly well.

"*You* know. Private George."

"What about him?"

"We, we—"

"Come on, Private, out with it."

"We've taken an oath, sir."

"And what oath is that?"

"To look after each other." He was glaring at Ted now, roused beyond any sense of rank or propriety. It was a side of him Ted had never seen. Taken aback, he wondered if he was making a mistake. In the boy's anger he glimpsed something aggressive, independent. Maybe he *would* be all right in a fight. In any case, it was too late now. "Well, he'll be glad you're safe then, won't he? He won't have to worry about you."

"But I'll worry about *him*!"

"He's a good soldier, he'll be all right."

"There won't be anybody out there who loves him!"

The boy's tears were coming now, tears of frustration and rage while he kept stolidly to attention. Shaken, Ted embraced him and knew, as if from far away, the familiar pull of warmth and bodily comfort. But the boy remained stiff in his arms.

THE NEXT MORNING, Hartfield was gone. Ted marched his platoon into a field corner and put them at their ease under the remains of an oak, its mutilated crown shading only half of them. When he told them they were going in that night, a stillness gripped them, every face intent as he sketched the long trek to the ridge. No cigarettes—no matches or lights of any kind. They would be able to see "in starts" by the light of the guns firing from Allied batteries around them, and from the explosions of German shells. If a man fell off the duckboard, no one was to go in after him—they must try instead to reach him with a hand or an extended rifle. If they couldn't, then they had to keep on. Busying himself with his duties, Ted had largely managed to keep his own fear at bay. Now it pressed behind his words, behind his face and chest: a fantastic giddiness he feared was visible. Before him, the faces of his men had the stillness of a photograph. Who would be missing on the morrow? To one side, McElroy kept sternly erect, his focus inwards. "Try to get some sleep this afternoon," Ted concluded. "There won't be any tonight."

Later, he found the men among their tents, busy writing letters, cleaning and recleaning their guns, giving away money—all the usual preparations of men going into battle. Now and then some bout of hilarity erupted, relieving the tension. Many went off to the services offered by the padres. The familiar words of communion. The cup tilting to the lips. The wafer on the tongue. And for altar: the pure white of a cloth draped over an ammunition box, an almost domestic touch, reminiscent of the clean sheets of home. Ted wrote a letter to Miriam and gave it to McElroy "just in case." He took the sergeant's letter to his own wife, slipping it into an interior pocket. They shook hands, and he went for a walk. A distant group of trees drew him. In a few minutes he was looking up into fluttering clouds of leaves. He touched their trunks and for a moment smelled clean, fresh sand. As a boy, he had once travelled with his family to Lake Erie for "a day at the seaside," as his mother put it. There had been poplars there too, glittering among the dunes.

THEIR FACES BLACKENED, they went in at 01:30 hours. The slipperiness of the duckboard came as a shock. Burdened by their heavy loads, men cursed as they jostled together, while NCOs struggled to keep order. Ahead, as promised, the night was rent by explosions—the flash of Canadian artillery ensconced in the mud while German shells, whistling and screaming, ended their flight in eruptions of mud or blasts of white light. Now and then, through clouds, a faint moon ghosted, while a misting rain fell on helmets, making them shine in the intermittent light. At the head of his men, Ted tried to keep the platoon in front of them in view. At times the murk closed thickly and it was all he could do to stay on the wooden track. Then the track would end, and their feet knew the viscous grip of what passed for dry land; then they were back on the boards again. A huge explosion up ahead was quickly followed by a concussive wave that brought everyone to a halt. Distantly, other shells went on exploding. In the small, dark world of the platoon, an expectant silence reigned. Soon they heard faint wails of terror, quickly overborne by shouts calling for stretchers. The order to halt came down the line. But they had already halted and stood now in a deepening awareness of their exposure. Another shell like that one, and— All around them, near and far, as if to remind them of the lottery they had entered, the explosions and flashes of guns continued. They were suspended in a darkness where the only light signalled death. On the left, oily water gleamed. No telling how deep it was. No telling where they were. No one spoke. Even the black-humour artists had shut up. Ten minutes grew to twenty by the light of Ted's watch. He feared they would not make the ridge before dawn: sitting ducks on the duckboard.

Stretcher parties crowded past. The platoon shifted as close to the edge of the duckboard as they dared. Their heavy packs, crammed with extra ammunition, were brushed by the men going the other way, dim forms carrying stretchers where the wounded moaned under blankets and a bandage showed white and was gone.

Again they moved on, shuffling at first until adequate spaces for walking opened up. Now there was water on both sides. A shell flash showed a mass of floating—but what was it? A swollen mass of uniforms with men in them. German or Allied? Impossible to tell, and now, in the plodding heart of their fear, not mattering. Farther on, a corpse's bare backside thrust up where a shell had unearthed a hasty burial. A dead horse lay on its side, grinning. Such things appeared and vanished like scenes in a magic lantern show, not mattering, not mattering. *Only let me live. Let me live a little longer. If I live I will give you. I will build you. I will never say that again to you, never again will I say it I will bring you lilacs from the lane.* They passed one of their own guns, and its crew were men of mud, emerged from underground to feed the thundering behemoth in their midst: a white burst at its muzzle and they saw themselves, a mass of shuffling helmets, troll-like under their loads.

The cry of gas brought everything to a halt. They fought to get their masks out of the boxes on their chests. *What do I do with this goddamned strap? I should have paid attention.* They were aliens now, peering from insect eyes. From inside his mask, Ted listened to the ghostly sounds of his own breathing.

The self-haunting enclosure was intolerably hot. His eyepieces kept fogging up. Then the all-clear came and they stripped them off. Still they waited. Word came back: a section of the duckboard had been blown out. Some of the men wanted to sit down. Ted wouldn't let them: sit with that load on your backs and you'll never get up again. Again they moved forward. They came to the gap blown out by German shells. "Go to your left!" a voice called from the dark. By another flash they saw men struggling in shallow water—or was it mud? Ted stepped gingerly into the fetid ooze. There was a rope to hang onto, stretching off to God knew where. The mud came only to his knees: it wasn't too bad, he thought at first. But it deepened, its grip formidable. Each step was a struggle that grew strangely personal, as if the stuff had it in for you. Yet the Australian had been right, the mud smothered the shells falling nearby. They heard the squelch as they went in, and almost instantly the thud of a harmless explosion. After a few minutes, the bottom grew hard. He felt himself sliding, coming to a stop waist-deep in icy water. Somewhere to his left, a voice was calling for help. He went on. Then, abruptly, he was up to his armpits. He felt for a foothold and found a spongy texture under his boots. He pressed off quickly as it sank farther beneath him. Then he reached something hard, like cement or metal, and within a few seconds was sloshing through shallows towards a crowd of men helping one another back onto the duckboard.

As the platoon tramped on, Ted glimpsed higher ground ahead of them. They were nearing the ridge. And there, past it, was the sky—it had grown lighter. A runner appeared, on his way back to some command post. He stopped by Ted to catch his breath. When Ted asked him what was up, he pushed on without answering.

They left the duckboard and after a few more minutes felt solid ground beneath them. They seemed to be climbing now, up a slight incline. Now, in the shell flashes, they saw Canadian insignia on the shoulders of the men they passed. They were passing through the ranks of another division prior to taking their positions nearer the top of the ridge. With the sky lightening, half the platoon fell into what passed for a trench, a shallow thing only three or four feet deep. Ahead: the torn remains of a wood, a stream like a smear of blue oil, and the dimness of the ridge where the Germans were. As they rested, German shells kept falling behind them, in the morass they had passed over; while from the darkness ahead came the pounding of heavy machine guns, the bullets streaming overhead, searching them out. As he consulted his map, Ted was interrupted by an NCO, who slid into the trench beside him. "Sir."

"What is it, Corporal?"

"It's about Private Hartfield, sir."

The name seemed to come from another life. "What about him?"

"He's here, sir."

"What do you mean, *here?*"

"He just popped up, sir. He's over there with his pal George. What should I do?"

Ted paused for a moment. "Don't do anything. We'll deal with it later. He'll attack with the rest of us."

"Right," the corporal said, and pushed off.

And the devil take the hindmost, Ted thought, in his fury.

HE HAD STOPPED speaking; he had stopped feeling. As if he were there again, on the riven slopes below Passchendaele, except this time he knew how it ended.

"What's the matter?" a voice said nearby. He looked up and saw her—a woman in blue, in the deep chair, her pale face fixed on him from under her hat-brim, a stranger.

His voice came narrowly, from somewhere else. "I've come too far. I promised myself I wouldn't—"

"Did he die?"

"Goddamn you, woman! What's the matter with you? It was a goddamn war! Have some decency, goddammit!"

She went still, a small animal sensing danger. He buried his face in his hands, and when she tried to speak, he bolted for the woods, the trees a green blur swallowing him. Then he was lying face down in the dirt, legs kicking as he tried to walk into the ground, walk away, walk under, walk underground. A warm hand was on his back—or was it blood? Someone's voice was begging him to stop. He rolled over and saw, past her face, the blue sky between treetops.

MUCH LATER, THEY walked back together, in the exhausted aftermath of their distress, the wheels of her bike turning between them. At a crossroads, men were burning lime on a hillside, smoke pouring from the stone kilns. They stopped with the bike.

"I've been selfish, Ted. I pushed you too far."

"He was wounded—the boy. Horribly wounded, there was no hope. He begged me—" Attacking, he and some of his men had been held up by an enemy pillbox. By the time they caught up to the others, the German mortar shell had done its work. Rufus George lay dead, along with two others. Jimmy Hartfield was sprawled nearby, thrown against a fallen tree by the blast. At first Ted's mind refused what he was seeing—it seemed the boy was tending a wounded animal. Then he understood. Jimmy was struggling to gather his own intestines.

Standing with Grace at the crossroads, Ted saw it all clearly. It was as if he had passed through a storm into its calm centre. "He died," Grace said, scarcely audible. "I shot him," he said, feeling the tears course down his cheeks. In her face, he saw the boy's frantic eyes begging him to do it.

20.

Miriam plodded through her morning. She left the post office without her keys. In Effie Gray's kitchen, she called Effie Grace. Ten minutes later she nearly walked in front of Dr. Dunton's Ford. Grace and Ted were together, she was sure. In the past, she might have gone looking for them. Now a fatalistic torpor kept her in town. Still, she could not help glancing down side streets into the country—that grove tucked into a hillside might hide their happiness, that windy line of poplars.

On the way back to Brockwood, she turned aside to the bowling greens. She had often come here to read Ted's letters. Now she was drawn again, as if to bury herself in that simpler time: when he was away, all she craved was his safety. Now nothing was safe.

A solitary bowler stood on a green in his shirtsleeves, watching his just-released bowl. It travelled in a shallow arc towards others, knocked among them with a soft collegiality; then all were still. She reached her favourite spot, a bench on the east side. There were trees at its back, but she had come too late for their shade. She sat anyway, with the sun in her eyes.

She tried to pray, but the very idea of God seemed burned to a nullity, everything too bright, too sharply edged, a barbarism of light on the cropped lawn. Under her dress her body shrank from the heat, the chafing of an undergarment. Dear

Lord, she murmured, but her prayer, spoken without spirit, primed no response from her heart. What was God? She had never imagined him visually. The illustrations in her Bible, and the reproductions of the creation of Adam pondered in Brockwood's library since childhood—those reaching hands almost touching, that Herculean nakedness shaped by Michelangelo—had never moved her. Her God lived in the darkness of intuition. Her heart's leap to Him was secretive: a shy, wild animal. It had been weeks since she'd known its joy.

God had abandoned her, she felt; or perhaps she had abandoned Him, her faith not strong enough. If to love God was to know oneself loved by Him, was to lose Him to lose oneself? She felt she had lost herself. Something essential, something that united all things in love, was gone. Now, there were only things in their absurd separateness. That heap of cuttings left by the groundskeeper, buzzing with flies. That handkerchief hanging from the bowler's back pocket—absurd fragments of a lost whole. Without love of God, there could be love of nothing. On the green, bowls fell wobbling to their sides, lay motionless in the brutal light.

From where she sat, she could see her church down the lane. Its pyramiding roof oppressed her with its suggestion of ponderous weight, a thing of suffocation and duty. What was duty without love? Better than nothing perhaps, but its touch was cold.

Obscurely prompted, she got up and, with a dull nod to the bowler, walked back to River Street. She paused to let a car rattle past, then crossed the street and started the long ascent to Brockwood. Fifty yards ahead, two people were also climbing the hill. She knew them instantly. It seemed as natural that they were there as that railway bridge, under which they now passed, or the red letterbox drifting past her. The couple walked slowly, heads down, the wheels of Grace's bicycle turning between them, and it seemed to Miriam that their measured pacing signified an intimacy as old as time. They had always been just there, climbing the hill in front of her, while she followed unnoticed.

By the time she reached Brockwood they had disappeared. Before her, the façade of the house gazed down upon the lawn with a changeless indifference. She felt the place no longer hers. On the porch, a shapeless lump transformed itself into a cat. Claws tearing at the jute mat, Kiki stretched. Letting herself in, she heard Grace's voice from the kitchen. Then Ted's voice spoke and was answered by her father's. At once, the idea of other people was anathema. She was about to turn away when something brushed her leg. Kiki had come in with her. The touch of that other life deflected her, and she followed the cat to the kitchen.

"There you are," her husband said, looking up. The kindness in his voice seemed far away, a memory only.

"Hi, Mim," Grace chirped casually, turning to the counter.

Her father's tongs hovered over a pan of boiling water; he was sterilizing instruments. Grace was pouring herself a glass of ice water. Miriam opened a cupboard and took down a glass. At the table, Ted massaged his forehead.

A bell jangled faintly from the dining room.

"There's my patient," the doctor said, turning off the gas. With a worried glance at Miriam, he left. Into the silence that fell, her old self might have spoken to break the tension—to take care of *them*; but she no longer cared about them or about herself. She filled her glass and went out into the garden.

At the table that evening, she said little. Grace was not there—feeling poorly, Ada said, adding, in a tone of humorous disapproval, that whatever was ailing her girls, she hoped it wasn't catching. Her father gave Miriam a look of worried affection that filled her with shame. He had long depended on her to be happy. She deserved no one's love.

Later, Ted helped her with the washing up. "I'm going for a walk," she announced, putting aside a pot. She did not feel like a walk, but she needed to be alone.

"Do you want company?" he said. Briefly, she felt the old tug. But she went alone—up Jane Street towards the declining sun, then back down Banfield—a shorter stroll than she'd intended.

They were mostly silent with each other that evening. Ted kept darting questioning glances at her. At last he asked her what was wrong. "You don't seem yourself."

"I hadn't thought it mattered to you," she said.

"Of course it does, darling." He took her in his arms, but sensing her lack of response, stood her back from him, holding her shoulders.

"I'm very tired," she said, evading his gaze.

Later, she slept a little, then woke to an empty bed and the smell of cigarette smoke. At the window, she saw him smoking at the fence overlooking River Street. The sight, so common now, filled her with wonder. She had married a man who smoked in the middle of the night. Who told his secrets, and perhaps hers, to someone else. Who was kind to her when he was able; and lived a million miles away, with a war that had never stopped. The small red planet of his cigarette rose, glowed, and fell; rose and fell. She loved him a little then, but it was the love of old she knew, as if she loved him across a gulf of time, nostalgically.

Back in bed, the sense that something was wrong kept her awake. Wrapping herself in her robe, she stepped into the dark hall. Her parents' bedroom door was shut—a ghostlike whiteness behind which their snoring played its ragged counterpoint. Will's door stood a little open. Peering in, she could hear the regular hush of his breathing—the suspirations that came at long intervals, as if he'd been holding his breath. A faint cry alerted her. It might have been a nighthawk, she thought, or some quarrel between cats. It was then she heard the sounds of struggle—of sheets being fought and flung, kicked against in a sudden hollowing of air; and that cry again, muffled as if by a hand. She went swiftly to her sister's room and fumbled on the light.

Entirely naked, Grace was writhing on the floor. Miriam's eyes flew at once to the darkness at her crotch. It seemed in the shock of first sight like some animal battened there—the furry thing her fluttering hands struggled to remove.

As Miriam knelt to her, Grace's eyes rolled up with a look of frantic disbelief, like the eyes of someone drowning. Then she was gone again, whimpering through gritted teeth as she twisted this way and that while Miriam grasped at her wrists, tried to subdue her shoulders, spoke, shouted into her terror; nothing broke through.

When Alec and Ada joined her, they soaked towels in cold water, holding them in place against Grace's heated body while she fought them off. Gradually she calmed, though once, in a dying flurry, she kicked off the sheet. And again Miriam saw the wild mass of her sister's pubic hair, the skin scratched raw above it.

In the doorway, Ted stood gaping until Ada noticed and sent him away. Later, in their room, he asked Miriam what had happened.

"She's had some kind of fit," Miriam snapped. The crisis had roused her from her torpor. He and Grace had been together, then *this* had happened. He was at fault—how or why she did not care. He had brought the contagion home with him. Subdued, he frowned at the floor. "Well?" she demanded. "You were with her. *You* tell me what happened."

He shook his head.

"Come on, Ted. You must know *something*."

"I told you, I was telling her about the war. I never expected—" He seemed perplexed, and guilty, guilty. But he spoke again. "Something's happened to her, Mim. She's been damaged in some way."

"Obviously, Ted."

His eyes full of suffering, he looked at her. "I mean, I think she came home that way, from Toronto."

"You weren't here when she came home. What would you know about it?"

"I just know something's happened to her. Something— before me. She as much as admitted it."

She shook her head; she was in no mood to consider what he said.

IN THE FOLLOWING days, all her thoughts were for Grace. Now and then, a sort of mania seized her sister's glance. And she was thin, too thin—the crisis had shown them the stark press of her ribs under alabaster skin. Miriam's father said it was critical that she gain weight.

Miriam and her mother cooked various dishes to tempt her, but she was indifferent to most. It was a triumph if she got a few bites down. One afternoon, Miriam tried reading to her from *Adam Bede*, a book her sister had loved. "Too many words," Grace said from her bed, stopping her. She was weak, and the fevers kept coming, sometimes with little runs of delirium, though in general, as the days passed, she seemed to gain strength. She no longer kept to her bed but sat at her window with a blanket over her knees, gazing at the foliage of a maple and a scrap of sky—all that she needed or could tolerate of the world—or drifted through the house in her robe.

For Miriam, nursing her sister became an obsession, to the point where Grace upbraided her for hovering. Miriam felt the rejection keenly. One afternoon, the sisters were sitting in Grace's room when Grace spoke into their silence.

"Ted never comes to visit. Is he all right?"

Miriam did not respond at first, the comment raising so many conflicting feelings that she could not sort them out. "He's very concerned about you," she said finally. "I've told him it's best to wait until you're better."

"You told him not to come!" Grace cried.

"I *suggested* it might be best—"

"Well, it isn't!"

"But Grace, surely it was a natural thing for me to think. When you had your—your attack—you'd just been with him. I thought—"

"Well, you thought wrong. Ted had nothing to do with what happened to me."

There was ambiguity in the way Grace put this. Was she referring to Toronto, or to more recent events?

"I'm glad to hear that, but—"

"But what?"

"Ted—with his own troubles, he can be blind to other people's, and in your condition—"

"My *condition*," Grace said dismissively. "You're babying
me, big sister."

"Gracie, you've been very ill. Surely—"

"I'm better now—I can handle a visit. I *want* him to visit."
She paused for a moment before adding. "Are you trying to
keep us apart for other reasons?"

Miriam flushed, feeling caught out.

"Because I want you to know, there's nothing like *that*
between us."

"Like *that*," Miriam said, with sudden bitterness. "Whatever
it was *like*, it wasn't good, Grace. You stole an intimacy—you
broke into what we had. The least you could have done was—"
She cut herself short. Her sister was conferring with her tree
again—was she hearing her at all? Now Grace's voice came
almost wistfully, as if she were trying on an idea. "I love him as
a brother, I suppose, and as a friend. But the other—no."

"Not even a little bit?" Miriam said with biting sarcasm.
The silence that followed was excruciating for her. "*Grace!*"
she demanded.

"I don't know," Grace said finally, to her tree.

What Miriam had gained a moment before, she felt slip
away.

"You understand why that's hard for me?"

For some seconds, Grace went on studying her tree while
Miriam gripped the arms of her chair. Suddenly, Grace turned to
her, eyes glittering with unspilt tears. "What he's been through,
Mim—you *have* to love him. I can't do it, not like you can. You
were made to love him. He won't get through this without you."

Suddenly, where there had anger and bitterness, Miriam experienced astonishment, confusion, and within moments the realization that Grace had just given him up—or maybe had never claimed him, not really.

There were tears then, and an embrace that lasted until Grace, complaining that Miriam's hair was in her mouth, pushed her away. Miriam left the room in a state of confusion. Her sister had loved her husband, of that she was sure, perhaps loved him still. Yet something had changed. Miriam walked with a lighter step.

She saw Ted before he saw her; he was in the gazebo, bent over his walking shoes as he cleaned them. In a flash, she saw the man she had loved—something boyishly earnest there, forelock drooping as he worked with the concentration with which he did everything.

"I've been watching you," she said as he looked up. "Loving you," she added. It was her half of an old, ritual exchange, yet it seemed fresh to her. And perhaps it did to him too, for he lit up immediately—something grateful there. She sat beside him while he worked. There was self-consciousness between them now, an awareness that something precious but fragile had been summoned. It seemed dangerous even to speak. They traded trivialities, though each word seemed weighted. After a pause she said, "Gracie says she'd welcome a visit."

He worked at the shoe a little more.

"I thought you didn't want me to—"

"She's better now. I think it would be all right. Ted, look at me." He turned to her. "Go and visit her. It's all right." She was aware she had evoked the trust between them, the trust that had been lost and only now had put up a single, tender shoot. At once, she felt the risk.

She was stripping the sheets off Grace's bed the next morning when he appeared. A bit awkwardly, the three of them bantered. When Miriam left, leaving the door open, silence descended behind her. Half an hour later, moving down the hall with an armful of laundry, she heard their voices. And again, as in the past, she caught the notes of an easy intimacy. She had her own intimacy with Ted, but the notes she heard now were in a different key. A flutter of her old jealousy came back, along with a sense of exclusion. She refused to glance in as she went past.

He sat with Grace every day, for half an hour or so. They did not talk much, as far as Miriam could tell, but simply sat with only the occasional word or phrase exchanged—words she strained to hear while catching only fragments. Someone called "the boy" was referred to more than once—were they talking of Will? She still found it hard to suffer their closeness, but felt it was the price of a new constellation of trust between the three of them.

She found that the less attention she paid her jealousy, the less it bothered her. Still, Grace knew things about Ted she did not. Things about the war. She clung to the hope that one day she would learn them too. Grace had some gift it seemed: she could draw things from him that Miriam could not. She told herself she should be grateful.

There were setbacks for Grace, more runs of fever, more outbursts of unreasonable temper. Her middle-of-the-night prowls, reminiscent of her return in the winter, resumed—was Ted the cause? Miriam was about to suggest that possibility to Ted when he spoke of it himself. He made an attempt to visit Grace less, but she rebelled at his absences and seemed worse, so with Miriam's encouragement, he resumed his visits.

As the family's concern deepened, Miriam's father wrote a man in Toronto—a colleague he had known in medical school—asking him to "take a look" at Grace. The phrase, spoken by Alec over the dinner table when Grace was absent, caused Miriam to bridle. It suggested an inappropriate casualness, an almost touristic staring. "Has Grace agreed to be *looked at*?" Miriam demanded, not bothering to hide her irritation.

"I'll ask her, of course," Alec said, bowing to his soup. In fact, Miriam was relieved he was bringing in someone. She was as baffled as anyone by her sister's state.

"He's supposed to be very good," Ada put in. "He's as much a doctor of the mind as of the body. Isn't that right, Alec?"

"He's a student of psychology, yes. But he's a fine diagnostician, too, one of the best."

Alec must have consulted Grace because later that week, Grace told Miriam that she had agreed to meet this "medical chap Dad wants me to see." She spoke of him flippantly, as she sometimes spoke of John Scott. "His name!" Grace cried. "Have you ever heard such a name?" Miriam hadn't heard the name at all. "Joseph T. Goodenough," Grace told her.

"How's it spelled?"

"Just like it sounds. Goodenough!" Grace crowed. At once she grew sober. "I hope he's better at his job than that." Miriam was encouraged by Grace's openness to seeing the man. It suggested that for all her defiant protestations that nothing was wrong, she was aware that something was; that her suffering might have a practical solution.

Dr. Goodenough arrived one Tuesday on the one o'clock train—a slim, pink-faced, sombre-looking fellow armed with the usual black bag. Over lunch with the family—Grace was present too—he spoke of his boyhood on the farm. It was a point of contact with Alec, also a country boy, and as the two of them traded anecdotes, everyone relaxed. Miriam thought it an encouraging sign that Grace laughed with the rest.

After lunch, Grace and the doctor went into the library and closed the door. After forty-five minutes, Miriam heard her sister shouting. Then the shouts subsided. A few minutes later, Goodenough emerged looking slightly pinker than when he'd gone in, and more thoughtful, closing the library door behind him. Almost immediately, he and Alec and went off to the surgery. As the silence behind the library door continued, Miriam knocked and went in. She found her sister sitting on the empire divan, staring into space. Seeing Miriam, she got up and brushed past her to the door.

Miriam, Ada, and Ted watched from the front window as Dr. McCrae walked with his colleague to the street. For a few minutes, they stood talking by the gate. After a final hand-shake, Joseph Goodenough went off to catch his train. When Alec started back to the house, the watchers had shifted to the porch, eager for his report.

"Well?" Ada demanded, as he reached the steps.

"I have to consider what he's told me," Alec said gravely; he seemed displeased to find them there.

"But you can tell us *something*," Ada said.

"He's of mixed opinion, shall we say."

"I'm not of mixed opinion," a voice said. It was Grace, emerging onto the porch in a baggy skirt and long-sleeved blouse, its buttons fastened unevenly. She had changed her clothes.

"Grace, you mustn't," Ada said.

"It's all right, Mother. I won't break." But her pale face shone with perspiration, and as Miriam moved to her side,

Grace grasped her arm and held it fiercely. "I didn't like him. I didn't like him at all. I didn't like his questions, and I didn't like the way he examined me. It wasn't right." Miriam felt the involuntary jerk of her sister's hand.

"Don't upset yourself," Alec said softly. He looked at the others. "That was one piece of his advice I agree with—we have to proceed quietly."

"We've said that ourselves!" Ada challenged. "He came all the way from Toronto to tell us that!"

If there was going to be a family quarrel on the porch, Miriam thought that Grace was best out of it. She started to draw her off, but Grace resisted. "I'm not a baby," she snapped at Miriam, pulling her arm free. She addressed them all now, with something of her old fire, while they worried it might consume her. "I know what that Dr. Goodenough of yours was up to. I could see it in his eyes. He was thinking I belong in the nuthouse."

"No, no," everyone crooned.

Grace laughed sharply. "I see you agree with him."

"Gracie, come away. You're just upsetting yourself," Miriam said.

"I just want you to know that if it ever comes to that, I won't go. Do you hear me?" She glared at them, challenging, while their gazes fell.

"You're not going anywhere," said Ada, who was the first to recover. "You're my girl, and they'd have to go through me first. Anyway, you're not like *that*. Never have been."

"Dad?" Miriam said, turning to her father. "We need to—" She wanted his help bringing the conversation to a close.

"Yes, well," he said, clearly not understanding. For a moment a spirit of irresolution held them all.

THAT NIGHT, MIRIAM was again drawn by sounds from her sister's room. Grace, in her gown, was fumbling to lift her window sash: the thing was stuck, it seemed. Her curses as she banged at it brought not only Miriam but Alec and Ada. "I can't *breathe*," she complained. "I need some air in this place." It was a hot night—no one had been sleeping well; but Miriam could only think how far down it was to the ground. "Go on then, back to bed," Grace told them. After Ada and Alec left, Miriam lingered. "You too," Grace said.

"You don't want me to stay?" Miriam said.

"No, dammit. I want to get my window open."

Together they forced up the sash. When Miriam left, she found Will in the hall. She went with him to the door of his room.

"Could you sit with me?"

It was a request he had not made for years. Miriam settled in a chair beside his bed while he lay in silence, his face dim against the pillow.

"Have you said your prayers?"

"Yes."

"Did you remember Gracie?"

"Yes."

"Good. Go to sleep now." She thought he was on his way out when his clear voice came again.

"Is Gracie going to die?"

"No, no," she told him, startled by his question. "Whatever makes you think that?"

"That doctor came to see her."

"He was just helping Daddy. Doctors often talk with each other, when they're trying to figure out what the problem is."

"What did they figure about Gracie?"

"That she needs rest. And quiet. Then her body can mend itself."

"But what's wrong with her?"

"Ah, she's very tired and weak, you know."

"Why?"

"Well, we're not sure about that. She's getting stronger, but it's important that she rest. And it's important you rest too. Go to sleep now. I'm watching."

He rustled under the sheet.

"Just being with her helps," she said. "When you visit her, that helps. I'll be quiet now."

"Is she supposed to stay here?"

"What?"

"Is she supposed to stay in the house?"

"What do you mean?"

He had fallen silent.

"Will?"

"I promised not to tell."

With Miriam's coaxing, he did tell. Will had been in the back yard when Grace let herself in the gate. "She said she wasn't supposed to be out. She told me not to tell. Please, Mim, don't tell her I told."

"Will, listen to me. If you notice her going off like that again, could you tell me? Or Mum or Dad? She's probably just taking a walk through the neighbourhood, but tell me, all right? She shouldn't be alone. It's best if someone goes with her."

"Why?"

"It just is." Sensing this was insufficient, she added, "We don't want her to tire herself out. That might make her sick again."

She could sense him thinking in the dark. "But Mim, even if someone goes with her, couldn't she still get tired?"

"Yes," she fumbled. "But then they could help her home. They could even hurry home and get Dad, with the car."

It was some minutes more before she heard the measured sounds of his breathing. Returning to her room, she found Ted pacing. He had heard the commotion but had not followed her. When he asked her what had happened, she felt his position as an outsider, and something of his shame: too aware of himself as a problem, a disrupter, to follow her to Grace's room.

GRACE SEEMED a little better. Now, in the mornings, she would dress, eat a substantial breakfast—though not as substantial as Ada would have liked—then spend the day at ease around the house, reading, walking about the yard, doing a bit of gardening. The person who most enlivened her was Will. He would bring her little presents from his forays into the woods, where they had used to go together: an unusual stone, a jar containing a few bugs and a bit of greenery. They played chess, and once Miriam overheard him reading her a story out of *The Boy's Own Annual*.

Her father said nothing more, at least to Miriam, about what he had learned from Dr. Goodenough. If he had confided to Ada, she gave no hint of it. One afternoon, Miriam ran into her father in the back garden. He had just returned from a round of golf, whisky on his breath. She drew him into conversation in the gazebo.

"What did Dr. Goodenough tell you about Grace? You've never really explained."

He had bent to slip a ball into the pocket of his bag. Now, not answering, he stood the bag in a corner. "He couldn't find any organic cause," he said finally, to the yard. "No hint of a tumour or underlying condition."

"But what about the fevers?"

Alec cast her a narrow look. "Yes, that's what I asked him. He said they could be caused by something emotional—you know, some kind of crisis she's had that she hasn't been able to get over. I've seen cases like that myself."

"What kind of crisis?"

"Some shock to the system."

"Like getting fired from the school?" She was thinking of Ted's words about something happening to her sister. *Something before me.*

"Possibly."

"I've wondered if it's—you know, a love thing."

"A love thing," he echoed contemplatively. "I've wondered about that myself. Do you know if she's had a sweetheart?"

"Not that she's ever told me. But it has to be something that happened in Toronto—we know that much, surely. She wasn't like this when she left us at New Year's. Then three weeks later—"

"She's still not told you anything about what happened?"

"No, and she won't tolerate my asking, not any more. It upsets her too much."

"If it was a love thing—"

"Yes?"

"It must have been something more troubling than a boy-friend leaving her."

"What do you mean?"

Clearly uncomfortable, her father shifted on the bench, wincing before he spoke.

"Sometimes men, well, they presume too much of a woman. They—how shall I put it?—try to force certain things."

It took her a moment to understand. "No! Do you think—"

"I don't know what to think," he said. They were silent for a while.

"*She* believes Dr. Goodenough thinks she is mad," Miriam said. "I haven't been able to persuade her otherwise. But Dad, really—what did he say?"

"He did not come to that conclusion," her father said, reddening; she was immediately suspicious. "But he did have some concerns about her stability."

"And what do you think?"

"She's always been unusual. I think that's a long way from insanity."

She heard his opinion with relief. Still, she had a connected worry. It had to do with Aunt Mary, her father's sister, whom she'd never met. Alec rarely spoke of her, and when he did, he would call her "poor Mary." She had spent years in a sanitarium. Once, on a family trip to his parents' farm, he had driven them past the building without comment. Miriam only learned what it was later, from Ada, who cautioned her against asking Alec about his sister. It was a brick building, three stories high, with heavy mesh grills over the windows and two Doric columns bracketing the front door, oppressive in its severity. Mary had died when she was twenty, her mother told her. She had never been "right in the head."

"Dad? How did Mary die?"

"She drowned," he said after a while, in a voice unlike his own.

"Could you tell me about it?"

It was a long time before he spoke. "She was home with us, for her birthday. She went for a walk and she didn't come back."

"An accident?"

"We never knew."

The silence that engulfed them seemed to spread, holding now the garden of late summer and the lawnmower someone had left on the path. Then her father spoke again. "At the time of Mary's troubles, I was only a boy. But whenever I was with her, I never felt there was anything wrong with her, you know. I loved her. I felt she understood me."

AS AUGUST WORE on, Grace was clearly gaining strength. Her walks around the neighbourhood with Miriam or her mother grew longer, while she chafed at their "chaperoning." Sometimes Will tagged along or surprised them by popping out from behind a tree. People's worries for her, while not disappearing, were assuaged by a sense of routine and by her rising spirits. There was colour in her cheeks now, and she had put on weight.

One afternoon, Miriam was on her knees in the parsley bed when John Scott let himself into the yard. They had not talked since the night when she'd noticed him looking up at her window. She still sensed the event between them, with no idea what—if anything—it had meant.

He announced that he had come to see Grace. Miriam was taken aback. Ada had asked him to come, he added quickly. "Apparently, the lady herself is open to a visit." Realizing she was powerless to stop him, Miriam advised him to proceed carefully. "If you notice she's getting agitated, best if you—"

"Fold my tents like the Arabs—"

"Thank you for understanding."

"And how are *you*," he said warmly.

"Very well, thank you."

As he stood hesitating, she was aware of his goodness, not as a fixed quality but as something he was searching for, not something he thought he had. She liked him the better for it. After he went in, she tried to continue with her work, but her attention was divided now. After forty minutes, she was about to investigate when she heard the minister in the kitchen. Apparently, he was talking to Ada. After a few minutes, he came out, looking distracted.

"John?" she said, approaching. "How did it go?"

"Yes. Well, I thought—she was quite—congenial. Of course, I haven't seen her for some time. Her eyes—" he said, hesitating. "Well, they were always bright, weren't they?"

"What do you mean?"

But he was already hurrying away. Miriam went immediately to her sister's room, where she'd retreated after talking to the minister in the library. She found Grace sitting on her bedroom floor, cutting out pictures of dresses from the Eaton's catalogue. She hadn't done this in donkey's years, she said. Her eyes *were* unusually bright, Miriam noticed.

"How did it go with John?"

"Well, he didn't preach at me, thankfully." Grace put down her work. "I had a funny feeling he was afraid of me."

"What do you mean?"

"He was awfully nervous. If he wasn't looking out the window when he talked, he was staring at my bubbies."

"Your bubbies," Miriam said, chuckling.

"I had half a mind to show them to him."

"You wouldn't!" Miriam cried, scandalized into laughter. Grace shrugged and went on cutting.

Miriam soon left and did not see Grace again until she came late to supper on the terrace. As usual, the family pretended not to notice Grace's tardiness—they were glad to see her at all—though Sandy Robinson, who had brought his wife in her wheelchair, remarked that late was better than never.

There was cold chicken, a salad from the garden and another of potatoes and mayonnaise. The murmur of their conversation was subdued, under an air of self-consciousness, yet as the meal wore on and Ada let loose with one of her drolleries, their spirits rose. There was laughter when Will challenged Miriam to a race after supper, and Miriam insisted she could beat him running backwards. Will said he could beat *her* running with a bag on his head, their sparring giving rise to a whole series of absurdities. After a pause, Ted remarked that he'd never run faster than when "old man Cox" had chased him and his pals for soaping his windows: "He turned out not be so old after all. We thought forty was old in those days." As always, when he spoke, people paid attention—he spoke so rarely. Miriam thought him a little more at ease than usual, though he soon fell silent again. He sat next to her, so she could not tell when he was looking at Grace. Grace rarely looked at Ted, though when she did, her gaze filled with tenderness, Miriam thought. Above, leaves trembled among the branchings of the elm, gilded by a low sun. The crickets of late summer were chirping, a touch of autumn in the air.

After ice cream, flavoured with ginger and scooped with a wooden paddle from the churn, the party dispersed. The Robinsons wheeled home, the doctor retired to his surgery, Ada said she was going to write letters, and Miriam, after begging off from the race with Will—she was too full of supper, she said—did the washing up with Ted, then set out with him for an evening stroll, leaving Grace and Will on the porch with the chessboard. When Miriam and Ted got back half an hour later, the two were no longer there. Miriam thought nothing of it, assuming Will had been ordered to bed and perhaps Grace had retired too.

At the dining room table, her mother was still busy with her letters. She kept up a wide correspondence with women she'd known at Watson College. As Miriam stood chatting with her—Ted had gone on to their room—Dr. McCrae emerged from his surgery. "Alec," Ada said. "You remember Flora MacDonald? Apparently, she's married some chap with gold mines."

"Lucky her."

"I don't know," Ada mused. "Leona Haggart's met him and thought him rather a stuffed shirt."

Miriam left them talking. Upstairs, neither Grace nor Will were in their rooms. She went back down to her mother. "I thought they were on the porch," Ada said. "I was just thinking I'd let him stay up too late."

"They're not there," Miriam said.

She and Ada looked through the house and around the yard. They peered down River Street in both directions. Lights were coming on in the houses. "Probably they've gone for a walk," Miriam said.

"Well, they've picked a poor time for it," Ada said. "She knows he's to be in bed by nine."

In another ten minutes, neither had appeared. Noticing Hilda Barber on her veranda, Miriam crossed the road to speak to her. The old woman had noticed Will earlier, she said. The boy had entered Bannerman's back lane, at which point she lost sight of him. "Grace wasn't with him?" Miriam asked.

Hilda looked confused. "I don't think— I might not have—"

"How long ago did you see Will?" Miriam cut in.

Hilda fumbled at her choker. "I think there was still a little sun in your spruce there."

Miriam left thinking Will and Grace were probably together, and that the old woman had momentarily averted her attention. Back at Brockwood, Ted and Alec had joined Ada in front of the house. The news that Will had headed down Bannerman's lane and might possibly be alone galvanized their concern: the lane was Will's favoured route to the river, but the thought of him heading down there at night was disturbing.

And where was Grace? Miriam intuited disaster and had to scold herself for leaping to conclusions. And perhaps her family were governed by similar feelings, for there was anxiety in their deliberations. Ted paced restlessly as the others talked. When it was decided that he would take the most powerful torch and search the river paths to the north of the town while Alec and Miriam searched the nearer woods and flats below the Bannerman estate, he retrieved the torch and immediately stalked off. Meanwhile, Ada would stay home, and ring the old sleigh bell if the missing ones appeared.

Miriam and her father went silently down Bannerman's lane, past the outbuildings of the estate—the stable, the gardener's cottage, sundry barns and sheds—soon reaching the woods that covered the riverbank. Their torches played on the trunks of trees as they descended the steep path, passing into the cool atmosphere of the river. She had made this trek many times as a girl, yet the woods had grown strange to her, a thicket of possibilities scarcely dissipated by her narrow band of light. They reached the bank, covered with lank grasses. There were slabs of cement here, sloping to the river, placed by John Bannerman for the ease of swimmers. Just beyond, a secret revealed by their fleeting beams, the Shade eased towards the dam, invisible past the towering stone pillars of the rail trestle, though they could hear the steady hush of its waters. They called into the night and stood listening for a response that did not come. Again and again, their torches flicked over the river, and again they saw, in the weak ovals of their lights, the dull, malevolent water.

Alec would go south, he said, under the rail trestle and into the woods below the bowling greens. Miriam would search to the north, over the flats and across the athletic field. She soon reached its ghostly expanse. On the far side, the shadowy grandstand loomed like an abandoned hulk. To the south, behind her, her father's voice called. Had he found them? She stood uncertainly. A train was shrieking from the countryside. Moments later, it broached the trestle, filling the valley with its thunder, seeming to travel through the air behind the gleaming shaft from its headlamp. Now the engine disappeared into the high, wooded bank, while the long chain of boxcars continued to rumble over the trestle behind it until the last of them had vanished, their clamour subsiding to the chirping of a solitary cricket. Her father was no longer calling. Moving on, she ran her torch over the water's edge. When a deer bolted, she cried out. Its white tail bobbed twice and was extinguished by the dark. She had passed beyond the boundaries of the town. Above her, through woods, she glimpsed the dark humps of fields. Ahead, along the river, were more woods—miles and miles of cedar bush following the river. There were abandoned gypsum mines in the bank up that way. Will had been warned never to go near them.

Again she called, and caught an echo from up the river—or had someone called back? It came again—was Ted calling? Had *he* found them? But the voice had fallen silent.

At the sharp ringing of a bell, small yet clear, her heart leapt. The sound had come from behind her, a frantic ringing. She made her way quickly to the bathing place, where her father soon arrived. They climbed the steep bank together.

Ada was on the front lawn, with Grace. They were arguing. Both were in tears.

"Thank heaven you've come," Ada said, rushing to them.

It took Miriam some seconds to understand what had happened. Seeing Grace appear on the street, Ada had rung the bell. In her initial excitement, she had not realized that Will was not with her.

"I told him I was going for a walk!" Grace cried. "I told him it was time for bed. Then I went off—"

"He must have followed you!" Ada shouted.

Miriam looked at her sister.

"He did," Grace said. "Oh God, what are we wasting time for? Let's look for him—"

Alec confronted his younger daughter. "Grace, listen. We have to understand. You say he followed you—"

"I didn't notice until we were at the bathing place. I sent him back."

"Well, he never came!" Ada thundered.

"He probably kept following Grace," Alec said. "We'll go over the same ground. Ted may not have heard the bell— probably a good thing. It would mean he's still searching." He insisted they not set out until he had fetched extra batteries. "Ada, if you could call the Macphersons. Chet Munn too. Tell them what's happened. Now, Grace, where did you walk to?"

Grace said she'd walked as far as the ruins of a bridge a mile outside of town—"The Abutments," people called them. Then she'd left the river and returned by road. In the light from

the house, Miriam noticed that her sister's skirt was wet from
the hips down, her shoes coated with dry mud. "Are you feverish?" Miriam said, reaching to her forehead. Grace pushed her
hand away but trooped obediently inside when Miriam insisted
she change her clothes. Miriam was about to follow her when
she looked again towards the street, its feeble gas lamps glowing at intervals through the dark. No one was there.

21.

August 1928. In the afternoon heat, the trees on Brockwood's lawn are still. On the porch, a clipboard on her knee, Miriam works on her column for the *Star-Transcript*. It's a portrait of Anna MacMillan, the nurse who became the first administrator of the new hospital Ada had helped found. Anna had died earlier that summer, during a minor surgery, a loss to Miriam personally, for in the course of writing an earlier column about Anna and her work, the two women had become friends.

Miriam is having trouble getting the tone right. What she's written seems too formal, too much the standard obituary; she's failed to catch Anna's generous spirit—those mornings when she bustled into the hospital with strawberries from her own garden, a treat for patients and staff. It is one thing to put down the bare facts, quite another to give the reader a feeling, however momentary, of Anna's presence as she moved down the halls, knowing everyone, stopping to chat. Miriam slides the pages she's written under the thickness of empty pages on her clipboard and thinks how to start over.

Perhaps the man has been watching her for some time before she notices: a thickset fellow of middle age, wearing a straw hat with a coloured band, standing at the gate. When their eyes meet, he takes this contact as permission, for he lets himself in and starts up the walk, heaving himself along with a pronounced limp. He wears a prosthesis, she realizes, his left

leg held stiff. Standing as he nears the porch, she has a growing feeling she knows him. Removing his hat, he offers a gruff
good afternoon, and asks if she is Mrs. Whitfield.

"Yes, I'm Miriam Whitfield," she tells him.

"Bob McElroy. I—"

"I thought you might be!" she cries. "Come up, Bob, come
up!"

With some difficulty, refusing any help, he mounts the steps
while she waits. Blinking away tears, she fusses to make sure
he has the most comfortable chair, and when he eases into it, he
says, "So this is where he lived—"

"Before the war we had a cottage at the other end of town.
When Ted left, I moved back here—my parents' house. Ted
lived here too, after he came home. Can I get you anything,
Bob? A glass of water?"

He seems not to hear. As he goes on looking down the yard,
she looks too, and for a moment she seems to see the view as
Ted saw it: the great trees standing in their own shadows, the
place by the fence where he smoked, a world at peace, strange
to him after what he had known. Bob McElroy produces a
calico handkerchief from his pocket, mops vigorously at his
face. "Excuse me, ma'am. I'm sorry I didn't write a longer letter. You wrote me such a good one, but I'm not much of an
author." He has turned to her now, his forehead marked with
the welt his hat has left. "Your news was a shock."

"I'm sorry, Bob. And I'm sorry I couldn't have told you
sooner. I'd only just found your address among his things—"

"Getting through the war, you think you're safe, but we're
never safe, are we, not in this life." Making an effort, he rouses
himself to a more cheerful key. "So I found myself in Toronto,
you know—we have a daughter there now, she's teaching high

school—and, well, I didn't realize you were so close. Then I saw the schedule, and I thought I'd pop out—to see where he lived, you know, the town. I didn't mean to bother you, Mrs. Whitfield, coming unexpected like this—"

"I'm very glad you've come, Bob. And by the way, please call me Miriam."

"He was one of the good ones—never asked any of us to do anything he wouldn't do himself." He is moved, she can see, unable to say more as he looks away.

"He cherished you too, Bob," she says quietly.

It is a while before he turns back to her. She sees he has wept, the tears shining past the handkerchief he clears them with. "So sorry," he fumbles. "I promised myself I wouldn't—"

"It's all right, Bob. Listen—you've come a long way. Can I offer you tea? Coffee? You must be hungry—"

Water and a biscuit are all he wants. When she brings them to him, he is staring again over the lawn. She sees his powerful shoulders, distorting his light jacket, and remembers what Ted called him. *My rock.*

He takes a few sips from the glass and dispatches the biscuit. Takes out the handkerchief, blows his nose.

"It was the flu, you say—"

"Yes. The fall of '18. It was very bad here. We lost almost as many to the flu as to the war. Ted was helping my father. The doctors had turned the armouries into a hospital for the worst cases—"

"Your father's a doctor?"

She nods, refraining from correcting his tense. "Ted worked as an orderly. He was helping Dad. They were down there night and day. That's how they caught it."

"Your dad's all right?"

"We lost Dad too."

"Oh Miriam. What a world."

They are silent for a while. She has questions, but it is too soon to ask them.

She points out the spot where Ted liked to smoke. She tells him about Ted's walking. "I was forever darning his socks, he wore them out so fast." She asks about Bob's family. He has three grown children. The eldest, Frank, has taken over his fishing boat. A married daughter lives nearby. He seems proudest of the girl who has become a teacher. "Jarvis Collegiate," he tells her. "I never saw a school so big—you could hide a battalion in it."

Miriam tells him Ted had tried to go back to teaching that fall, the fall he died. "He wasn't ready for full time though—his nerves, you know. He'd just go in when a teacher was sick. He liked the physical education classes best—it allowed him to move around a bit. He was never quite himself again. He had good days, but—" Again they are silent. "My sister's a teacher," she tells him, brightening. "Grace. She teaches English and phys ed. She lives with us here. Her husband took over Dad's practice. I'd introduce you to her and Mum but they're out right now."

They sit talking while the sun slowly extends the shadows on the lawn. He has slipped into another reverie; the habit reminds her so much of Ted that her husband seems almost present. "You talk about getting our old selves back," he says. "I don't suppose any of us have managed that."

"No," she says soberly.

He slaps his bad leg. "Not just things like this, but—there were times out there, we stopped being human."

She waits for him to say more, but no more comes. "Bob," she says softly, "I know what happened at the end, when Ted was wounded. I know about the boy, Jimmy—how he died at the end."

"Ah," he says, shifting uncomfortably.

"I think Ted never got over that—the boy's death."

"He cared for that boy. We all did."

"Can you tell me anything about that?"

"About what, Miriam?"

"About how it was between Ted and the boy—before the end."

It was Grace who told her what had happened, after Ted's death. The sorrow of it has been with her ever since, thinking of what he had to do, and how it must have burdened him. She has asked her question as tactfully as she can; it has been swallowed by another silence. "My sister— Ted could talk to my sister about the war, more than he could me. She's told me a few things, but—"

He turns back to her, his words uncertain now. "Yes, a boy. He was far shy of eighteen. Ted tried to protect him, but he—he wasn't able. *We* weren't able. I don't know exactly how to put it, Miriam. That boy—he was the soul of the platoon. It hit us hard, what happened to him. Of course, there was no time to think of it, not then."

"I see."

"No, ma'am," he tells her with quiet firmness. "With respect, you don't see. Nobody sees who weren't there."

Another silence falls. She wants to know more. She wants to hear more about Bob's times with her husband—some detail, some little anecdote, that will help bring him closer. Grace has not been able to tell her much: the subject upsets her. And now, here is Ted's sergeant, unable to make the same journey. He speaks again, over the shadows of the sloping yard. "He was a sort of son to us, Jimmy was. The only son many of us would have." Abruptly, he mops at his face and blows his nose. "I'm sorry," he says. "I'm emotional these days. Over there, I couldn't cry a drop, though the Lord knows we had cause. These days I can't seem to stop."

"I'm so sorry, Bob."

"Don't be. I'm one of the lucky ones."

They cannot go farther, not in this key. They sit in a silence that she realizes is mourning—the mourning of reflection.

The screen door bangs, opens, and two boys come out. The older one she introduces as Will, her brother. He is nineteen now. Since the night Ted brought him home from the river, he has grown into a confident, prepossessing young man, with a spark of lively interest in his gaze. "He's off to university next week," Miriam tells Bob proudly. "And this chap here is my nephew, Charles, my sister's boy." Charles is six; he has Grace's red hair and a nervous blink.

Bob McElroy rouses to the boys, entirely at home with them. He shakes their hands, queries them, watches them go off with a look of satisfaction, though after a few seconds his face empties. She asks him to stay for supper, but he insists he must get back to Toronto. His daughter is taking him and his wife to dinner. Miriam is relieved, for his visit has filled her with a powerful sense of her husband—it is *him* she needs to be with.

She walks Bob to the station. As they stand waiting for his train he cries out, "Miriam—I almost forgot!" He takes an envelope from his jacket pocket and hands it to her. It is yellowed with age, slightly rumpled. On one side, she sees her name in Ted's handwriting, in faded pencil. "He wrote it for you that last day—before we went in. Passchendaele, you know. Gave it to me in case—"

LATER, SHE TAKES her chair on the porch. Behind her, the house is quiet. Down Brockwood's lawn, its shadow has almost reached the street. The first cool of autumn is rising from the river. Somewhere, with a whir of blades, grass is being mowed. She opens the envelope, unfolds its single page, and begins to read.

Acknowledgements

I WOULD LIKE to acknowledge the indispensable support of the following: my editor, Liz Philips, for her keen eye and fruitful suggestions, as well as Thistledown's managing editor, Caroline Walker and her staff; my agent, Hilary McMahon, for her tireless belief in *The River Twice*; Roberta Coulter for her copyediting and comments; Noreen Taylor for her timely gift of Tim Cook's superb histories of Canadian troops in World War I; Roy and Suzette MacSkimming, Marni Jackson, Mark Czarnecki, and Jon Reid, as well as members of my family: Alix Bemrose, Matthew Remski, and as always, my wife and life partner, Cathleen Hoskins.

AUTHOR'S NOTE: THE lines from a soldier's letter in chapter 2 are taken from Volume 2 of D. A. Smith's history of Paris, Ontario, *At the Forks of the Grand*. Several battlefield letters were reproduced there from the archives of the *Star-Transcript*, which originally published them during the war.

JOHN BEMROSE'S FIRST NOVEL, *The Island Walkers*, was a national bestseller, a finalist for the Giller Prize, and longlisted for the Man Booker Prize. He is also a well-known arts journalist who has published reviews and articles in the *Globe and Mail*, the *National Post*, and *Maclean's*. His second novel, *The Last Woman*, was published in 2009. He has also published poetry and written a play, *Mother Moon*, which was produced by the National Arts Centre. Bemrose was born and raised in Paris, Ontario, a place that has inspired the settings for his fiction, including his latest novel, *The River Twice*. He lives in Toronto.